Out of Reach

Out of Reach

Angelina Archer

 Hybiscus 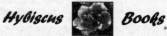 Books

British Library Cataloguing-in-Publication Data. A catalogue record
for this book is available from the British Library.
ISBN 0-9541027-0-3

Printed by Book Press, 4 Maclise Road, London W14 0PR,
United Kingdom.

Angelina Archer, Hybiscus Books, 22 McGregor Road,
London W11 1DE, United Kingdom.

I would like to dedicate this book with love to my Mum and Dad, all my family in the U.S.A. and Guyana. Thank you very much – your support will always be treasured in my heart, and to my late grandfather, Ganesh Balasar, who passed away on the 4th of January 2001. I will always be grateful for the seventeen years I knew you, and may the Lord grant you eternal peace.

Preface.

I'm sure a lot of more experienced authors would say that for certain stories they've written, they've had to diverge themselves from their basic comprehension, especially when writing things they have little or no experience of. This was exactly the case with *Out Of Reach*; most of the subject matter isn't something you can research. It wasn't tortuous, but I won't deny I was stuck in the odd rut. Overall, the words just flowed naturally from my imagination to paper.

Four major influences have made *Out Of Reach*'s concept – my love of satire, my study of Psychology constructing the characters, the interlaced plots, narratives and Gothic darkness of Emily Brontë's *Wuthering Heights*, and a moving letter in a teenage magazine about how a fifteen-year old girl whose crush on a pop star was taking over and destroying her life. Sounds like a rather unlikely formula, but as the old saying goes, you don't achieve greatness by playing by the rules. I'm not so sure about greatness, but I know you don't achieve *originality* by playing by the rules. Verse into prose was one of them, and letting the thoughts and words of the characters speak instead of the actions was another. I realised why *Wuthering Heights* is still such a relevant novel – it is a very intense study of human psychology told with poetic, multi-faceted narratives. This formed the template for my work. I doubt *Out of Reach* will ever have the same depth of *Wuthering Heights*. For me, literature began and ended with that book – it was a real privilege studying that book for my English.

Let me take this chance to warn you about something you will encounter much of in this story – 'language'. I had a tough choice deciding its appropriateness. I believe strong language suits only certain situations, especially violent and confrontational situations, which there is plenty of in this story. Too often, on television and in literature, bad language is used irresponsibly, destroying a more eloquent and refined way of expressing the same thing. In *Out of Reach*, the characters do use a lot of bad language, but they still know how to speak in an inoffensive way.

Plus, a lot of the situations explored may seem mild to some and extreme to others, but the way to read this story is with an open mind – it is written in a way which is open to different interpretations. But don't let the bad language be the determining factor.

At the end of Alana's major narrative, she feels being plagued by all her memories is too much for her volatile state, and attempts suicide. As some background information, I have studied Human Biology, and my mum's a nurse, and has seen people die due to the over-consumption of alcohol. Females tend to absorb alcohol in the bloodstream quicker than males, so the effect it has on Alana is near alcohol poisoning. The fact that she's a habitual heavy drinker backs up the fact that the suicide attempt is not inane, as some people might interpret it.

On to the locale now. I chose Ealing as the main setting, because if I chose a busier area, the outside factors would completely swamp any chance of the characters opening up, and outweigh the purpose of this story. Another reason is Alana's behaviour would be written off as insanity if the setting was in a busier district. The less going on in the outside world, the easier it was to delve into the characters' heads, especially Alana's drunkenness and her intense liking for the television actor Adrian McCraedie. The key places are the University and the shopping mall. Both places bring back bittersweet memories for Alana, Blake and Leila. The University was like a social gathering for the three friends, as well as a place of study. If they couldn't meet at each other's houses, they could always meet there, especially as their tutorials conveniently clashed on the same days. They did well there, especially Alana, because the power of such a tight friendship fuelled success within their triangle. When a chain of terrible events begins to dilute that previously untouched fuel, Alana feels like a scapegoat for the reason behind the split. This is one of the many themes covered in this story – how the power of loyalty and friendship can drive you mentally, physically, emotionally and spiritually to almost a superhuman state.

The female characters are many variations of my character. Alana is the vulnerable, spiritual, sentimental side of me who limits her company to her family and two friends; Katerina is my no-nonsense, objective, positive and harmlessly manipulative side. Leila is my brazen, rebellious, loud-mouthed side of me, who likes to cuss. I'm not man-mad though! She calms down when she's betrothed to flirtatious brunet Trevor Tappet. It's only Christine who bears absolutely no resemblance to me – she is so sickly sweet, your teeth ache! But I do like the way she worries a lot about her older brother's welfare, and sometimes seems smarter than him. I also think it's cool that Blake is close to Christine, where many boys find their little sisters annoying. The template for her is the recent influx of teenage blonde pop stars. Lily, Leila's mum, Eliot and Marlene, Blake's parents, and Tracie, Alana's mum, are all versions of my parents. They play a small, but vital, part in the story. And finally, there's Freda. I wouldn't contemplate what she does to the main characters to my worst enemies. She's like the witch in *Snow White* who feeds Alana the poisoned apple of grief, and wraps poor innocent Blake round her finger as her slave. Blake's characteristics are everything in my ideal guy, really – smart, stylish, charming, cute and funny. He's the 'no-frills' type of guy. You can bring yourself to forgive him for causing so much pain to Alana, because he shows unimaginable, selfless remorse. He's naïve in relationships, and is ruled more by his heart than his head. Being so soft-hearted, he's always hoodwinked by horrible girls. I've noticed many guys are like that today, due to what I think is the intimidating era of excessive female empowerment of today.

All in all, *Out of Reach* shows how the reality of growing up and growing apart can ricochet off certain people, and be like a spear in the heart for others. The innocence of childhood promises doesn't necessarily go swimmingly in adulthood. I felt I owed it to the characters to give them a happy resolution, thanks to an outsider like Katerina. It wouldn't have had the same impact of alleviating tension on the reader as a tragic ending would, because when you read the beginning, you *think* it's going to end in nothing but tears. It's a Shakespeare tragedy in reverse, really. The world would be a happier place if there were more Katerinas around.

This is the result of five months of hard work. Thank you for reading my preface, and I hope you enjoy *Out of Reach*. 'Bye for now!

Angelina Arclen

x xx

Chapter 1.

'Oi, Higgins! Are you sober enough to come to this bleedin' door or wot?' a grouse male Cockney accent growled irately, simultaneously with incessant pounding of his fists against the door. Alana Higgins opened her drowsy eyes against her own will. She wasn't sure how long the knocking went on for, but she knew who it was, so she had to apathetically roll off her bed before he blasted the door down with his booming voice and fists. She grabbed the shaky doorknob and yanked at it violently. A short, rotund man, wearing a holey, discoloured white vest and brown trousers with braces, which seemed surgically attached to him and generally made him a walking health hazard, stood there. His round face was smeared with filth and stubble, and a flat hat covered his bald head. He inhaled once at a cigarette, entered the squalid room and swivelled his head around to examine silently. The wallpaper, which was probably once pink, was peeling at the joints, and stained brown from leaks originating from the above floor. The carpet, which was once cream, was stained with water and mud and was badly eroded – if it spoke, it would bore one to death with stories of previous residents. The ceiling's flaky paintwork was also stained with water. There were two single beds on either side of a bedside cabinet, which was painted in a fading aqua green. They were covered in brown floral sheets and a duvet each, also smelling of a thousand bed sitters who stayed there before Alana. Above the cabinet was a poky window which let in very little light from the view of the main road, framed by dusty dark brown curtains. The sweaty smell of the man mixed with tobacco smoke caused a lump to rise from her throat. *Why the hell can't he see and say what he has to and leave?* He drew again from the cigarette. 'Morning Miss Higgins. I came 'ere to tell ya that you've got a new lodger in your room today. So make 'em feel at home, yeah?' *Here we go again; why does he have to end everything he says with 'yeah'?* Without saying a word, she turned away and sat on the edge of the first bed facing the door and stared emotionlessly at him. 'Why does this person have to

1

stay here? I've been here for nineteen months, and I've never had to share before,' she finally snapped.

'Look, this is a bed sit, young lady. There is no fixed time you get to stay 'ere on your own, yeah?' *Oh shit, here he goes again with 'yeah'.*

'Yeah, well, I don't want to share. I like being on me own.'

'You're gonna share, whether you want or not. If you don't like it, you can lump it – understand?' With that, he abruptly marched to the dry-rotten, camouflage-green door and turned around just before he slammed it. He saw Alana pour a tumbler full from a half-full bottle of vodka, and gush it down her gullet.

'You better have your rent ready by Wednesday.

Perhaps your new lodger will help you dry out.

I don't want no winos in my building, yeah?' he viciously spat out. She let loose a window-shattering shriek, and flung the tumbler to the door, intending to smash in his face, but he slammed it to shield himself. Alana screwed up her face like a scolded child in frustration, curled herself into a ball on the bed, her head on a dusty pillow, and started to sob silently and uncontrollably. 'Adrian, why have you left me like this?' she whispered between falling tears. She eventually lulled herself to sleep by the hypnotic rhythm of her sobs.

Alana sprung upright from lying down on hearing a familiar knock from somewhere. 'Oh, it's that bloody door again,' she muttered, still half-inebriated. She once again rolled off the bed lazily and staggered her legs to the door and her arm to the doorknob. She saw a girl of her height and probably her age of twenty-one, who had square-cut, shoulder-length blonde hair, European features – narrow nose, huge blue eyes only adorned by light brown eye shadow, a pink mouth with a slight pout to it, and porcelain pale skin. She wore a classic-cut, lilac long-sleeved shirt and black loose combat trousers. She had one suitcase in each hand – one black and one brown – which left a tiny gap between their bases and the floor. She lowered them to relieve her sore palms, and extended a hand to Alana. 'Hi, I'm Katerina

Slate. And you are…?' she introduced chirpily in a curious accent. Alana just rolled her eyes, rejecting her offer of acquaintance, and returned to the edge of the bed. 'Not in the talking mood,' she completed sarcastically, shrugging her shoulders. She proceeded to throw one suitcase, then the other on top, on the vacant bed. 'I'm only staying here for few months, till I earn enough money for a flat of my own. I've got to get away from my parents – they're such a pain…' she trailed off seeing Alana staring either at the door or in empty space. She turned away and unzipped the top suitcase half-way, delved her hand in and pulled out a blue cloth bag of toiletries, a clear plastic bag of books, an alarm clock, and a black satin nightshirt. She set them aside on a short stool between her bed and the wall, and hauled the top suitcase under the bed, and the other at the foot of it. On her way to the bathroom with the toiletry bag, Katerina whipped round on hearing the clinking of glass. She widened her eyes observing Alana gush a full tumbler of alcohol in one singular swill. She poured another glass full, and gulped it at a similar speed. Katerina swallowed violently, empathizing how drinking two glasses of vodka in less than a minute must be like swallowing acid. 'Are you an alcoholic?' she managed to utter after her last swallow.

'Mind your bloody business,' Alana snarled back. *I'll take that as a "yes", then.* She gently pulled the door in from the other side, and crept down the five stairs to the bathroom. She was almost overwhelmed by the stomach-turning stench of mould, sweat, excrement…a whole cocktail of health hazards. The shower, which had mould between the tiles and the scum around the drain, had no shower curtain or screen to armour her stomach against facing the nauseating sight head-on. The toilet and sink had scum and hard water in equal measures. It was the things horror story writers thrived on. The mirror above the sink produced a spotty reflection. It was shake-up of the stark reality she was now in – she realised what a luxury her home was compared to this, but as she got older, she could no longer savour it on account of her parents. Returning to her current situation, she grinded her knuckles in her tired eye-sockets, and formed a mental plan on how to use the facilities without catching some disease.

Returning to the room about fifteen minutes later, she saw Alana curled in a foetal position with her back facing the door. Katerina clicked the door with conscious control, and sat on the edge of her bed facing her surly roommate's peaceful expression. She slung the bag over on the stool, and slumped herself on the bed's duvet, facing the ceiling. She reached for the alarm on the bedside cabinet and glanced at its face as she wound the alarm hand to ten past four in the afternoon – the actual time read three o' clock precisely. She originally thought the intense bustling of one of West London's longest roads and the 'neighbours' from every dimension of the building would swamp her chances of sleeping, but with her clasped hands under her shirt on her stomach, she drifted into slumber as rapidly as her eyelids shut...

One skull-shattering electronic bell caused both girls to spasm upright with their palms comforting their foreheads. Katerina bashed her fist against the alarm's button as if it were a punching bag. 'What the frig was that? Why did you have to set that sodding alarm or whatever the hell that was?' Alana snapped more angrily than any other time Katerina had known since she moved in. 'I'm sorry, okay? I was worried I wouldn't wake up in time to study...I'm still tired from travelling here and carrying my own luggage,' she reasoned compassionately. All she received was a frozen stare and a forefinger in her face.

'Don't set it again or I'll smash it on your head in your sleep, okay?' With that remark, she turned over on the bed to face the door. She wept inconspicuously to her roommate and almost herself. Katerina was particularly shaken by that threat, but she wasn't sure if she said that out of hate of her person or her presence in her room, or because of something else. She tried to detract herself from the chill that travelled down the back of her neck by removing her books from the plastic bag on her lap. She proceeded to scribble condensed text from the study materials into a notebook until she could barely see the fine text and the pen in her hand move across the page. She looked at her watch to see the time was seven-thirty – three hours since she began. Stretching her arms above the bedside cabinet to yank the curtains together, a blast from an aggravated cloud of dust nestling in the fabric attacked her face like bees in a beehive. She rubbed her nose, then let loose that hesitant, but violent, sneeze after pushing a switch beside the doorway which illuminated the room from the centre with an orange-yellow haze. She suddenly turned to Alana, preparing to beg for her life for waking a sleeping lion, if needed be. 'Oh,' she exclaimed in diminished fear on seeing that tranquil look on her sleeping face still present. *Bless.* She leaned over her bed for her nightshirt and her toiletry bag again. *Time to brush my teeth, change, unwind and learn these alien surroundings*, she thought as she once again opened and closed the door with quiet caution.

A loud slam cued Alana's eyelids to jerk open from a deep sleep again. She looked towards the door to see Katerina with her back pinned against the door with a grovelling stare in response to her spiteful one. 'Do I have to put up with this kind of noise? Why couldn't they give you your own room for you to make as much noise as you want?' she scowled, looking like an angry mongrel.

'Look, please – I'm sorry, okay? It's the bloody door – the damn hinges are loose. I've been trying to close it carefully all day, but I forgot this time, and I couldn't grab the door before it slammed itself. I didn't mean to wake you.' She tried to sound compassionate in her shaky voice. 'Look, I hardly know you, so why would you think I'd deliberately pick a fight? Anyway, let's face it, we're gonna be dwelling in the same room for a good while yet, so let's have a bit of peace. How about a peace offering of a nice cup of tea? It's the least I can offer.'

'No,' she growled again. She still had a throbbing headache from when she was woken up by the alarm. She sat up, grasped the glass and almost empty vodka bottle beside the bed, and filled the tumbler to the rim, which left the bottle empty, and funnelled it down her gullet, hoping for quicker relief than painkillers. Katerina spotted this and wrinkled her forehead in disgust as she filled the rusty kettle halfway and placed it on the rumbling, rusty metal structure that happened to be the stove. Fifteen minutes later, Katerina strolled delicately with two full mugs of fresh tea from the teapot. She placed her mug on the bedside cabinet, and still holding the other, she leaned before Alana and extended it to her. Alana's face was cupped in her hands, slightly overwhelmed by the pounding against the inside of her skull, as if her brain wanted to do a jailbreak. 'Hey, I've made you some tea. It might make you feel better,' she whispered on seeing her nurse her head. She looked up at her with the softest look she had ever given her, as if the pain had blunted the daggers in her eyes. 'I thought I told you I didn't want tea,' she muttered almost incomprehensibly, her face replaced in the slow comfort of her cupped hands.

'Look girl, just take the tea – it's a peace offering,' she insisted in that characteristically warm tone. Alana forced out a breath which redirected the steam, and finally accepted the mug without making any eye contact. She stared into it for several seconds, then took a sip from it. After a few more sips, she felt an immediate lift, followed by an alertness that she thought was asleep within her. Katerina collected her mug of tea and stood beside Alana. 'Can I sit next to you for a few minutes?' She sighed, her eyes still focused on the tea she was sipping. 'Yeah.' She tried to look her in the eyes from her awkward head angle with a warm smile. 'Are you always this unsociable? 'Cause beneath that grouchiness, I'm sure you're quite nice.' Alana finally twisted her head to make the first eye-to-eye contact with her since she stood before the door. 'Thanks. It's just I don't feel like talking to anyone.'

'Huh, that I don't doubt! You've made that pretty obvious,' she jested sarcastically, causing her to breath out a slight giggle. 'See how nice you look, even when you laugh a little bit?' Alana smiled a little wider than before. 'Okay, first of all, what's your name?'

'Alana Higgins – Al for short.'

'Brilliant. We're making a start. Mine's Katerina Slate, in case you didn't catch it the first time.'

'Strange name.'

'Well, I'm half-English, half-Russian, you see.' She was now enlightened by her appearance and her strange accent. 'My Dad's English, and my Mum's Russian, but I was born and raised here. I still couldn't help myself adopting Mum's accent, because I thought the English one sounded too weird for me when I tried it a few years back.'

'It suits you,' she quietly replied.

'Thanks. So how long have you been here, then?'

'Nineteen months, I think.' Alana reached under her bed, pulled out a bottle of vodka, applied a little effort to twist the cap, and mixed it with the half-full mug of tea and gushed it down her throat, much to Katerina's crumpled brow and upturned nose of disbelief and disgust – she had to induce her jaw to stay up. 'I can't believe you. It took you ten minutes to drink half a cup of tea and it took you ten milliseconds to gush it down your throat when you mixed it with vodka! What are you trying to forget or ease by drinking so much?' Alana cautiously raised her brow. 'What makes you say that?'

'I mean, come on - that's the fifth or sixth drink of that stuff I've seen you down since I moved in. You've probably had more today, so what is it?'

'Do you really want to know? It's one hell of a long story, Kat – do you mind if I call you Kat?'

'No, not at all. But I don't mind hearing it. I've only known you ten minutes, and I already see a person dominated by hurt and sadness, and not hate. You didn't give out the vibes as a bad person when I first saw you, which is why I continued being nice to you even when you were nasty. I'm sure you can't even remember the last time you had a meal – look at you!'

Alana's emaciated figure used to be similar to Katerina's, apart from the sunken, dark and sorrowful brown eyes, lacklustre skin and dark brown hair, which was also shoulder-length and dishevelled. She looked somewhat close to death – her body, mind and heart. The once-fitted faded blue jeans and pale blue v-necked t-shirt hung loosely over her skeletal build. She took a deep breath through lungs which felt half the capacity they used to be. 'Here is partly the reason why I'm like this.' She delved her hand under her pillow, pulled out a piece of paper and passed it to Katerina. It was a slightly faded magazine picture of a lad in a camouflage-green uniform and flat-cap, photographed from the waist up. His face was gently masculine and oval-shaped – he had almond shaped hazel eyes, widened to form a mean stare. The bridge and point of his nose was narrow. He had inverted cheeks that were still bulbous and rosy. His mouth was thin, wide and pastel pink, slightly pouted to form a sullen contortion. His chin was pointed and slightly dimply. His complexion was flawless and ivory-fair apart from a slight tan, and a blond lock of hair hung softly from the cap over his eye. 'Hey, isn't this Adrian McCraedie, the actor from *Green Collar*? I've seen it a couple of times.'

'Yep. I'll find him someday. He's absolutely perfect for me. When I first saw him, I felt something click in my brain, which I'm positive was the missing piece of my life's puzzle being snapped into place.'

'Are you serious?'

'More than serious.'

'But look at what you're doing to yourself – it's suicide!' she shrilled. 'You're torturing yourself for something that'll never happen. It seems millions of girls as I speak are drinking themselves silly because he plagues their minds. Why don't you get on with your life? You'll probably increase your chances meeting a normal guy.'

'Because Adrian, is as normal as normal can be, and he is not like the drunken, football-loving, immature assholes you call 'normal'. If that's what 'normal' is, then I'll carry on searching for Adrian. I used to visit the Internet café down the road almost every time I got off work to try to find out where he lives, but I didn't have much luck, so I gave it up. Surely someone, somewhere must know where he is, but it's who that's the universal mystery.'

'But…' Katerina held her tongue for a few minutes to analyse what she said from her point of view. She nodded her

8

head, even though part of her thought it was imbecilic. 'So what do you work as when you're sober?' Alana breathed out a slight giggle.

'I work as a betting office cashier further up this main road on Mondays, Wednesdays and Fridays. Those are the only days I reserve the drinking till its time to sleep, but I only drink about two glasses at Tuesdays and Thursdays, the in-between days. I earn about one-hundred and twenty a week – fifty-five goes to the rent, thirty or forty goes to the booze, ten goes to some bits and pieces. Like you said, I can't remember the last time I had a decent plateful of food, but the drink takes away my appetite. I…don't have any qualifications apart from five GCSEs and three A levels. I would have had a degree in journalism. My ambition was to write and investigate for papers and magazines. Even in the first assignment, I got a straight A, but everything slowed up and got harder, my grades went down, and in the end, I was so detached from reality, I didn't revise enough, and I failed the exam.' Katerina shook her head in disbelief as Alana squinted to hold back her tears – the product of bringing up the sadness she suppressed with drink.

'Do you still want to talk about this? Because if you don't, I understand – I'll leave it at that.' Alana's eyes, once cold with pent-up sorrow, began to soften at looking at her.

'No, no, I'll talk about it. You might see certain things s stupid and not understand them, but be willing to keep an open mind. I'm really, really sorry for my bad attitude earlier, Kat.' She placed her hand on Alana's shoulder and rubbed it.

'I *am* willing to understand, Al. It's okay, honest. I knew you'd come through sometime.'

'Thanks for persevering. Mmm…' She trailed off into her thoughts for several minutes. 'Let me see…it's such a complicated story, and the events seem such a blur, so forgive my delay.' She cupped her jaw with one hand, and faced her tilted head towards Katerina.

'It's fine. Take your time.'

Chapter 2.

'I have to let you in on a few things before I begin my story. I attended my journalism tutorials on the third floor of the Acton University across over there.' She got up, hiked back a curtain, and pointed diagonally across the road outside the graded blue and orange-laced sunset through the window to a twenty or twenty-five storey, skyscraper-style building of steel girders and glass. It had a concrete porch casting a shadow over the entrance, which bore the its name in bold blue and silver-bordered letters. There was also a small empty courtyard leading from the entrance to the pavement, bordered by a rust-red low fence with a wide gap for a few staff cars to park during the opening hours. Every other building, either offices or blocks of flats, on each side along the second junction of that road was constructed from crumbling red bricks, like the bed sit building, or weathered grey concrete, and looked relatively like ancient ruins. 'Oh! That's where you used to study?' Katerina squeaked in astonishment.

'Yeah. Why are you so surprised?'

'That's where I'm studying too. I go there twice a week for media studies tutorials. I'm working towards a job in television – not broadcasting, but something behind the scenes, you know? It's a correspondence degree course I'm doing, which is why I have all those things on the stool over there.' She pointed to the small pile of vinyl-bound papers she studied earlier.

'Well, I studied a correspondence course in journalism, too. I went for three tutorials a week, because I loved it so much. I did pretty well – I even got a Correspondence Student of the Year certificate in two half years for achieving grade A for every assignment, even the very first one. When did you start? Obviously you must have started after I left, otherwise I would have recognised your face,' she queried on deciding to change direction.

'About a year ago.'

'Well, I took the exam about a month after I moved here, so I did leave before you began. Anyway, on with the story.' Katerina sipped her now tepid tea, and turned her knees towards her.

It the end of a chilly Friday of November 1996 on the third floor of that building. The tutorial, which started at ten, ended at three that afternoon. It was unusually three hours longer than normal, but I didn't find it as tiring as everyone else. However brilliant I found every tutorial and the course, I still felt they missed out on teaching some things, so I always took the lift up to the seventh floor to the main library afterwards. As you probably know, the library takes up two floors with its media – the seventh and eighth floors, which had computer, audio and video libraries. Anyway, I peered out the front window wall, which was on the opposite end of the famous 'row of seven lifts', famous because whenever students sitting examinations took those lifts to get to their exam rooms, they always seemed to pass. Some also think its because seven is a lucky number – I personally think it's a load of rubbish. I wanted to see if my two childhood friends Blake Turpin and Leila Drayton were amongst the weekly student stampede in the courtyard, which was about thirty feet down. They weren't, so I thought I would find them as I looked for journalism books to back up my learning. I wandered amongst the labyrinth of oak bookshelves, picked up three books along the way, and reached the almost clear central area of the floor. It only had four red leather armchairs surrounding an oak coffee table, and enclosing all that was a hexagon of opposing wooden benches incorporated with tables, about twelve benches and six tables. I don't know if anything's changed in there now, but that's how I remember it. After I took the books to the counter behind a gate I entered from the lifts, I still didn't see Leila or Blake wandering around like they should, until I automatically turned my gaze to the magazines and newspapers section towards the back window wall facing the suburbia enclosing my home. I saw a head of shoulder-length russet hair that I'd had ten years' familiarity with. I marched over to her, concerned about the frozen expression on her face. Because we'd known each other for so long, we've learned to sense whenever each other is nearby, a bit like a 'sixth sense' that siblings often have. Her face was in a magazine, so I assumed she was either gawping at the magazine or into outer space. I patted a finger on her shoulder quite hard to get her attention, but no response. I said "hi" quite loudly – no response. She just stood like a statue in front of the tall, wide oak shelf. I thought I needed those electric shock pad thingies they have at hospitals to restart her, but I came up with a less troublesome solution suitable for a library – I grabbed each shoulder and shook her to and fro like a rag doll. She finally twitched around a bit, and turned her head towards me. "Oh, hi Al!" she screeched immaturely and joyfully like a silly little girl.

"What the hell…no, *where* the hell were you?" I yelled, which caused more than one head to turn and nearly tell us to hush up.

"I'm very sorry, Al. I was shocked into oblivion by
the realisation that God hasn't lost his creativity in
making men."

"What?" I shrieked almost aloud. I wondered what she gibberish was coming out with. You see, she tries constantly to sound like a philosopher or something when expressing a thought or an idea, but she doesn't half come out with some rubbish. She continued by explaining "This is what. Is this a gorgeous piece of ass or what?" She shoved the page with the picture in my face, literally. My limbs jerked mildly when I saw it. There was this guy, naked and covered in gold paint, posing seated with one leg stretched out, one pulled upwards and the side of his face rested against his knee, with a relaxed look in his eyes, and his arms around his shin. I was speechless for several second until she pulled it away swiftly. It was obvious what she was staring at, but the one thing that really caught my heart there and then was his piercing brown eyes – honest! But I didn't realise my feelings just yet; you don't know you've got a disease until the symptoms start to show, do you? "Yeah, he's nice. What's his name?" I asked neutrally, a little phased by her over-enthusiasm, which just showed how I felt about him in the beginning.

"Mmm…it's here somewhere."

"I can't believe you! You were so busy ogling him,
you didn't even bother to check out his name!"

"Okay, okay, no need to rub it in. Look, it's at the bottom
here.' She pointed to the bottom-right hand corner of the
picture – it read Adrian McCraedie. It didn't ring over and over in
my head as it does now, though.

"Where's he from? Must be Scotland or Ireland with a
name like that."

"Nope – it's…Staffordshire. He was born and raised
there. He still lives with his parents and big brother.
He's twenty-one years old, he left college last year,
he's five foot ten in height, eleven stone in weight,
has got ten GCSEs – five As and five Bs, which is
un-bloody-believable, and three A levels. Likes music,
partying…generally what most Northern lads like doing." I
silently analysed what I'd just learnt about him.

"So where will we be seeing him then? Is he a model,
actor, singer, what?"

"He's an actor, but he did a stint in modelling last year,
it says here. He's going to star in some new Army drama
serial called *Green Collar*, starting next month just before
Christmas. It says nothing about what the plot is, just the
setting. I hope it's not a brainless as all other Army
dramas."

"Okay, I'll see what that's all about when it's shown.
Can I have the magazine please?"

"You like the guy!"

"Oh, come on – I've only seen a picture and a few vital
stats of the guy, for God's sake – these are just shallow
credentials. The credentials that count for me in a guy
is here and here," I demonstrated, placing my hand on my
forehead and then the left side of my chest. Eventually she gave it
to me, and confessed she bought it because the tiny replica of the
centrefold picture on the cover caught her eye, so I didn't have to
take it to the counter. She said that she'd finished her stay at the
library, because she'd been there for one-and-a-half hours. I
looked at my watch, and it read five o' clock. I decided to
continue the conversation briefly before we both headed for our
homes. As we strolled languidly out of the library to the lifts, we

discussed each other's tutorials – mine always coincided with Leila's nutrition tutorials on the fifth floor and Blake's social studies on the fourth. She explained about the various food experiments she and others performed, and she told me she received a grade B for her last assignment, which was a report of some kind. She also gossiped about the boys at her tutorial – "I'll never date any of them. I mean, there are loads of cute ones, but when I talk to them, they seem stupid and soppy underneath. So as much as you think I haven't had a boyfriend for a while, it's not because my head is stuck in pin-up pictures – it's because the lads are silly, and the ones outside the University just don't want to know. They probably take me for a nerd or something."

"Well, don't worry. The right one always shows up in the most unlikely of places, so keep your chin up, and get on with your life. I haven't dated a guy since I was sixteen, because he was silly too. My brain capacity just didn't match his – the majority of them don't. Maybe we're too smart for mankind!" We just giggled as the lift stalled at the second floor, but no one entered the carriage. I chatted about how Graeme Flegg was shooting daggers from his eyes at me as he and Mr Sutton praised me for my good work on my assignment. Flegg, or Flegg-face as I liked to call him, was very bitterly jealous of my progress, and was always a nuisance to me and the people who admired me, even Leila. I never heard any complaints from Blake, probably because he never had the decency to pick on a boy, especially as he was a good few inches taller than Flegg. That day, he said nothing, but at the corner of my eye as Mr Sutton and I were talking, I felt his spitefulness penetrate me. Mr Sutton was the journalism tutor who had a great talent for making lectures interesting by cracking jokes and generally taking on a whole new approach to such a daunting subject, which was partly why I loved the subject so much. Leila's opinion? "You're only here three times a week, not every day, so sod him – he wants a response from you, preferably an outburst."

"Yeah, but you don't know how many times I've been tempted to say something that will make him pee himself right in front of everyone." She giggled with a hand over her mouth.

"I know, I can see it, but he teases me too with his
bitter sarcasm, but I've never retaliated, because he's
like a virus – they thrive on host cells, that being you,
and what me and every other student who admire you
say about you, but if you don't give him anything to
feed on, he won't pester you. Know what I mean?"
"Yeah I do, but I wish I were a virus – I would use *him*
as a host cell next time I go back in there. Anyway, all
this talk about feeding has left me starving!" We laughed
violently as we exited the lift at the ground floor and whizzed past
the reception area. The receptionist and some guy with her at the
time, must have thought we were crazy watching us almost
collapse with our guffawing. I asked where Blake was after a
short breather; she told me he had gone home early, because he
didn't want to be late for this family meal he was having that
night. We paused from conversing as we strolled out the gate and
towards the bus stop on the other side of the road. Within a few
minutes, a single-deck bus arrived, which was to take her to her
home in Hayes. We hugged each other goodbye until Sunday, as
she promised, and waved at each other as the bus pulled out. I
thought absolutely nothing about Adrian as I marched the zigzag
path of about three streets behind the University, which were
slightly deserted apart from the odd wandering pedestrian and car
passing me by. The bitter autumn breeze burned my nose and
cheeks with near-frozen water vapour. I looked at the downy grey
clouds which threatened the earth with rain, and thought *"For
some reason, gloomy weather gives me more enthusiasm to study
than the sunshine does. Why is that?"* Around fifteen minutes
later, I arrived at my mum's bungalow, which had been ours since
my mum and dad first married in seventy-six, but they divorced
when I was nine, because he was unfaithful. Anyway, I took off
my twig-brown leisure coat and scarf, and my court shoes,
leaving me in dark blue jeans and a red wine roll-neck sweater. I
suspected she wasn't home yet, judging by the silence, which was
quite usual, as her job as a solicitor kept her till around seven,

sometimes eight, in the evening at this little firm in the Hanwell 'town centre' – I call it that, because it's between several shops under the shadow of tall claw-like trees. But I heard a crash of metal from the kitchen. I wandered into the hall to the left from the front door, which had two doors to the left and right. The first on the left was the kitchen. I saw Mum crouching down before the oven, which was one of a set of appliances set in a cuboid in the centre of the room, with a tray in her hands. I knocked against the doorway, she turned to look at me. "Hi baby! I didn't hear you come in," she shrieked in an annoying tone. I hated it when she called me "baby". Why do some mothers do this, even to adult children? I was born on the eleventh of March seventy-seven – that made me nearly twenty, for God's sake. She sometimes did that in front of Blake and Leila, which was embarrassing, though they understood. I kissed her on the cheek as she placed the tray on the worktop. "When did you come home? I thought you were still at work," I asked. She was nearly two hours early.

"Well, business was slow today, so Mr Pratap told me to go home, as the rest of the work was light enough for him to manage on his own." What I didn't know was Mr Pratap and Mum worked together, I mean, *really* worked together, but that's another story.

"Oh. Well, I see you've been busy!"

"Yep. Carrot tea bread, and some fruit pastries over there." She pointed to the nearby tray.

"Brilliant. I thought I recognised that smell. I'll freshen up and we can tuck in."

"Okay. Take your time. They won't be ready for another half-an-hour now." I took a shower and changed, all in all that took about twenty five minutes. In my room, which was dark blue, but was daylight-bright when I switched the ceiling and the bedside lamp on. I slung the rucksack on my double bed, and dumped it out. The items I saw were the bag of borrowed books, my own text books, a notebook with me lecture notes, a can of cola and a bag of crisps I never got round to drinking and eating, and…the magazine I asked Leila for and completely forgot about.

I looked at the cover, reminding myself why I asked for it. Just as I was about to flick to the page with Adrian's picture, Mum yelled for me to come to the table. *I'll sort this rubbish out later.*

At the elliptical table, which was behind the cuboid if you stood at the doorway, Mum presented two mugs of tea and plates with one pastry and two slices of the tea bread. She sat down and after I complimented her baking, we ate silently for a good twenty minutes. I remember seeing six o'clock on the kitchen clock above the doorway just before our conversation started.

"So Al, how was your day?"

"Great as usual. Mr Sutton praised me for my last assignment and, guess what he said – I was a born journalist and could literally walk into a managing editor's job in a paper or magazine. And guess who had to overhear it? Graeme Flegg." She raised her head with a look of obvious concern.

"He didn't harass you again, did he? Because you're always complaining about him."

"No, no, not today. He only pesters me once in a blue moon. He scowls at me most of the time, in a way so that I can see I just want to laugh till I drop when I see that. You don't have to worry about him – I'm not intimidated by little boys. He's got a long way till he grows up, Mum." She laughed at that, almost choking on a mouthful of tea. "So, how was your day, then? That's if there was much of a day." She giggled again.

"Well, the beginning was great, cause I wanted to tell you about this terrific opportunity I've just been offered."

"What's that?"

"The owner of the firm has offered me a chance to co-own it with him. But I have some competition from two other candidates, both younger than me, and obviously with less experience. I want to prove to Mr Pratap that I'm the right one when it comes to experience, skills and initiative. So we all have three months hard slog from next week, except for Christmas and the New Year. Okay?"

"Ooh, getting all high and mighty now, are we?" I jested.

"No. It's just I know I'm right for the job." She sounded as if I'd burst her bubble with that playful jest.

"Yeah, of course you are. I was only kidding.

Congratulations!" She giggled briefly, realising I was just joking. She took the mugs and plates to the sink, situated in the border of the kitchen to my right below a wide window. "So, how are Blake and Leila? I haven't seen them around much lately."

"Well, they're coming round for an afternoon in this

Sunday. They've just been busy with their courses." After a brief silence, I raised myself from the chair, my balance fighting between my full stomach and my back. I strolled over to Mum, who was standing before the sink washing-up, as I stretched my arms to the ceiling. "Oh well, on to my next assignment. Thanks for tea, Mum."

"No problem, hon. I've some documents to type before calling it a night."

"You need any help with that?" I asked, pointing at the sink full of baking trays, dishes and utensils. "No thanks – I'll be okay. Goodnight, Al."

"Goodnight, Mum." I kissed her on the cheek.

In my room, I grabbed the magazine out of the pile of my rucksack contents, and raked the rest to the floor. I lied down on my back against four stacked pillows, and flipped the pages briskly to where Adrian's picture and article was. To my surprise, it covered not one but three pages, including the picture. I skimmed my eyes down the first page, then the second, because I recognised that as what Leila read out to me already. I saw a heading that caught my eyes – 'Mystery Illness':

"Between the ages of fifteen and sixteen, I suffered from a virus that I and no one else had an idea of what it was, or where I caught it. In the summer of 1993, I suddenly started vomiting almost every hour of every day, and eventually lost my appetite and almost four stones in weight – before, I weighed eleven stones; after, I weighed only eight. At my worst, I lied in the hospital bed thinking 'Lying here is killing me. I need to get on my arse if I'm going to recover.' So after some persuasion, they signed

me out, I gathered every little bit of strength I had left
inside me and proceeded to rebuild my wasted body. I
lifted weights of up to twenty-two pounds, did hundreds
of push-ups, sit-ups, etcetera, etcetera. I don't know how
many I did, but it was until my joints ached – it must
have been thousands. I ran on mechanical treadmills and
on natural hills nearby from the boarding school I went to.
How the hell I passed ten GCSEs in that state, I'll never
know. After I fully recovered and did all the exams, my
mates started calling me 'Rocky' after the boxing films,
because of my relentless determination to be more powerful
than the virus. After going through something like that,
you realise how lucky you are to still be here, even though
you worked yourself half to death to stay alive. But I know
nothing this bad will ever happen again."

At first, I refused to believe it. This astonishing regime
seemed beyond human capacity – I mean, even the world's top
athletes would be buggered by that, because that classifies as
semi-suicidal. While I thought about how that could be possible, I
moved on to the next paragraph on the next page – 'On
Romance':

"I'm single at the moment. I used to have several one-night
stands, but they eventually lost their novelty, so now I'm
waiting for the right girl now, whoever and wherever she
may be. When I meet that person, I'll know right way,
and I think she will too, but it still would be nice, though,
to tell her in my own words. If she doesn't feel the same,
I would wait and see if she eventually does, and if she
doesn't altogether, I would be friends with her and wait
for the right one."

My whole being just turned to mush after reading that,
because I couldn't believe that he had those kind of views on
romance and at the same time was lovely-looking. I began to
believe how he got over the illness. After reading it over and over
till I almost sent myself to sleep with it, I was in no fit state to
complete my assignment, so I told myself I'd do it tomorrow
evening, after Leila and Blake had gone home. So I left my room

for the bathroom to change and brush my teeth, then I turned off both lights and went to sleep after knocking three pillows from the pile over to the other side of the bed. I slept without a single dream or thought of Adrian. It still hadn't sunken in yet, even though I read that article repeatedly to believe him.

'If it didn't sink in then, when did it happen?' Katerina intervened during the brief pause. She was strolling carefully over from the 'kitchen' with the same two mugs, refilled to their brims with steaming tea.

When the first programme was shown on the twenty-third of December 1996. Over that whole month, I had developed a subconscious habit of sneaking off at odd moments of the day to look at the picture and the article of Adrian, when I was studying, when I came home from University, when I was usually bursting to have a pee. Even when I was sitting at dinner when Blake and Leila visited, I fibbed about going to the bathroom to look at the mag in my room again. I think it was that night I pulled my head from it, and thought "Why the frig am I doing this? I must be going mad." I realised how irrational it was, but I still didn't realise it was symptom number one of Adrian-itis. All day at Christmas Eve's eve, my Mum and I had been shopping for gifts and food items to be served at Christmas dinner – we spent about two-hundred pounds on everything. We also decorated a real fir tree all in white and silver – it was the prettiest tree we'd decorated in recent memory. White and silver two-toned tinsel, plain white and silver baubles, scattered popcorn and foil bits over the branches and a silver star on the superior branch. For some reason, with every year I became less enthusiastic about Christmas than when I was a kid. Perhaps it's because I recognised the vast commercialism surrounding it these days, which detracts it from its real meaning. I'm not religious, but I did like Blake's, Leila's and my family all coming round for a rare union and practising my tree-decorating art. I really wanted to be resting in my room when the programme started, but judging by the day and what we had to do, I set the video recorder in my room for eight o' clock that evening when I woke up at nine-thirty in the morning. But to my surprise, we finished

everything at seven o' clock, except the Christmas dinner, of
course. Mum and myself slumped out on the living room sofa
after we made a sandwich and a cup of tea for each of us.

"Well, that's that out of the way. Tomorrow is the part
I'm dreading the most," she groaned. "Christmas dinner!"
we synchronised, giggling.

"Yeah, I hate it too. But we can't feed our guests on
crackers and cheese, can we?"

"Hmm…by how I feel right now, that's exactly what I
feel like doing!" We both laughed violently, spluttering
into the tea as we sipped from our mugs. We ate our sandwiches
as we chatted about things completed so far. By the end, it was
seven-thirty. "Well, I'm off to my room to dissolve in front of the
telly, then I'll call it a night. You need any help with anything
else?"

"Nope – all done. I'm going to my room too. Goodnight
Al." We briskly hugged and kissed each other on our
cheeks. "G'night, Mum."

I jumped in and out of the shower (okay, that's a figure of
speech!), into a nightshirt, out of the bathroom and leapt onto my
bed, just happy to be off my feet after what always seemed the
longest day of the year for me. I pressed the power button on the
remote control, pleased to see the commercials were still running.
Before I knew it, the announcer spoke the words, "Good evening.
Now, here is the first episode of a new series, *Green Collar*,
starring Adrian McCraedie. This programme contains strong
language, nudity and some violence." The first twenty minutes
almost sent me to sleep. There was no sign of Adrian, but the
hope of seeing him forced me to stay interested. The plot was
pointless, just like every other Army drama I'd ever seen. Then
the camera pointed outside the entrance to the Army base, which
had criss-cross, barbed-wire high fencing surrounding the whole
field. It focused on the back of this chap by the gates, showing the
guard there a piece of paper. He was granted entry into the base.
Is this Adrian? I thought. He turned around to take one last look
outside the gates. Yep, that's him alright, I breathed. He wore an
open leather bomber jacket, which covered a bold blue polyester

t-shirt that clung to the crevices of his chest and stomach, and black, loose jeans with grey and white trainers. His nape-length blond hair framed his face, the breeze brushed the odd freshly washed lock over his face. His complexion was fair, very fair, especially in the approaching sunset. His huge hazel eyes had a sullen look to them as he rolled them around, but still somehow didn't make him look like a bad boy. About twenty minutes later, he was kitted out in the uniform he wore in the picture I showed you earlier, and was in a whole row of new soldiers, almost grovelling in fear at the thunderous voice of the sergeant. All except Evan Napier, Adrian's character. He and the sergeant had a bust-up, because Evan had the audacity that no-one else in the line of soldiers had to reply stroppily to his commands. As a result, he was commanded to do fifty push-ups on the slushy mud beneath his feet. He still had the brass neck not to accept his punishment, so the sergeant kicked his shin hard and once, so he fell onto his palms, splashing the mud onto his face, hands and uniform. Everyone stood and watched silently, probably thinking he had flung mud in the sergeant's face (excuse the pun!). He performed the push-ups as if he had bionic arms – briskly and tirelessly, with no short cuts. The uniform was short-sleeved, so I relished the sight of his flexing and twitching of his arms as he bobbed his body up and down, and his hair flopping over the sides of his face. Anyway, later in the programme was the scene that shot him to nationwide fame.

'The shower scene, right? I know, because every girl I knew went crazy they told me, "You'll never believe what I saw last night,"' Katerina explained sarcastically, causing Alana to giggle slightly.

'So you never saw it?'

'No, I'm afraid.'

Well, you certainly missed something. At the end of the training session which was close to evening time, the sergeant chased all the soldiers to the shower shack, which was a wooden shed-like structure in the centre – the women on the opposite side from the men. The camera went directly to Adrian's stall, obviously because he was the star of the show. At first, it focused on the side of his face as the powerful stream of water flowed through his hair. Then the camera caught a full-view side shot of him, sorry, let me rephrase that – an *amazing* full-view side shot of him. As he rubbed the soap over his body, the foam and water rushed down his shoulders, trunk, buttocks and robust-looking thighs. My jaw dropped wide enough to engulf the whole house. His right bicep had a kind of a barb-wire like tattoo around it, which I thought looked pretty sexy, even though I wasn't into tattoos much. My eyes were glued through the hour left of the programme.

After that, I switched the telly off. At the same time I heard the video switch off itself from timer recording the programme. I forgot to switch it off, but I thought it wasn't such a lapse of memory, because I could watch it again. I went to sleep almost immediately after *Green Collar* ended, and was dead to the world almost right away. Then I flashbacked to the end of that evening. I watched Adrian slump himself on the bottom tier of a bunk bed on his side, his legs in an almost lotus position, reading a magazine. He was wearing a grey t-shirt, white loose boxer shorts and pale grey socks. He was alone in the room, because they didn't want to put anyone in a room with a difficult soldier. I looked at the clock; it was dead late, especially as I had University the next day, so I rolled off the bed to switch off the video recorder and telly. Everything suddenly shook around me in a mini-earthquake. Before I wondered what the hell was going on, I was vacuumed into this vortex. All my familiar surroundings blacked out. My sight cleared up after a few seconds. I was in this cold, damp, grey-green room with only a little spotlight at the junction of the walls lighting the room, my bare feet receiving a shock standing on a concrete floor. I turned around to see this framework thing – the buzzing confusion of a vision became…a bunk bed with Adrian at the bottom. He looked as alarmed as I was feeling. But after he asked my name, I sat next to him at his request. He introduced himself as his character name. I didn't mind, because I accepted that I was sucked into the telly screen. I wanted to say something, but he pressed his finger against my lips and whispered, "Don't say anything. The sergeant might hear."

He pulled me down onto him and squeezed me against his solid trunk. He looked up at me, smiled that radiant, gorgeous smile at me, and we began a very heated kiss…'

'Okay, stop right there, no more details – I know what's going to happen next!' Katerina shrieked, extending her palm in Alana's face, catapulting the part of her she internalised into her memories to be told, back to reality. She laughed a lot harder than before, collapsing backwards onto the bed after placing the mug on the bedside cabinet, and slapping her hands over her eyes. Katerina followed her. Alana curbed her laughing fit first and sprung back upright.

'I'd love to hear some more of your fantasies – they're better than any romantic novel I've ever read!'

'I could tell you, but I'd never be able to stop laughing!'

'Alright, then. You'd better move on to what happened next.'

'Okay. Would you like more tea?'

'Sure.' Katerina proceeded to her feet, but was pressed on her shoulder back to her seat by Alana.

'No way Kat, you sit down. You've got up twice already. I'll make it to compensate boring you to death with my problems.' She marched over to the stove, swivelled the cold tea in the teapot and poured it down the sink. She dumped two heaped teaspoons of leaves, filled it with cold water and placed it on the stove and stood over the rumbling metal structure as it boiled the tea.

'On the contrary, it's very interesting. You're quite a good story teller for someone who's a bit, you know, tipsy. No offence.'

'No, no, none taken. I am still a bit tipsy, but I've sobered up a bit. In fact I think I'm a better talker when I'm drunk!' They simultaneously chortled away. When Alana brought over the mugs of tea fifteen minutes later, they were still giggling; she almost tilted the hot tea on themselves as she handed one mug to Katerina.

'Okay, I shall continue with my story. Just tell me when you're bored, then we can start again tomorrow or never again.'

'No, this is a good story, honest. I've only known you
for about two hours and I already think you're a fascinating
person.'

'Really? Thanks, Kat,' she shrugged modestly. 'Well, I'll
pick up the story from the New Year, because nothing else apart
from the usual festivities occurred Christmas time.'

'Sure, no problem.'

Chapter 3.

Christmas was okay. Everyone received what they wanted –
Leila got a new stereo from Blake, and Blake got a new leather
jacket from me to replace this shredded synthetic one he had, and
a few other bits and pieces for everyone else. I hardly noticed it
came and went. New Year was even better – we poured several
glasses of champagne, and counted down the last ten seconds of
1996. I can tell you, it was a lot more exciting than Christmas;
perhaps because after so many centuries, the New Year causes
everyone to hold their breaths in anticipation of what their
destinies have in store, and Christmas is now the season of
spending, eating and greed, instead of to be jolly. I remember
Mum asking me what my resolution was a few minutes of being
ushered into 1997. 'To succeed, succeed and succeed some
more!' She breathed out a giggle and said, "My resolution
exactly! Happy New Year, Al," then kissed me on the cheek.
"Happy New Year, Mum." We all clinked our glasses together in
a group toast after exchanging "Happy New Year" greetings and
hearing each other's resolutions. Leila's and Blake's were
somewhat more superficial compared to mine – they both wanted
new beaus! Well, it's still a resolution, isn't it? After playing
board games and having a go at Christine's new portable games
console which she brought over to our place – she was Blake's
strikingly resembling little sister, both had the same features –
oval faces, huge blue topaz eyes, distinct narrow jaw-lines and
pointy noses. The differences were their hair, of course, and their
ages – she had a lovely dyed shade of citrus-blonde, was
shoulder-length, slightly choppy-ended and very sleek; his was a
shade darker, but still quite bright, was scrunched into tufts with
gel and had put black tones in it. She was seventeen, he was
twenty. Actually, you look a lot like her, believe it or not. She
should be about…let's see… he was born in July seventy-six, she
in April eighty, so she must be now nineteen, and he twenty-two.
By two in the morning, everyone was quite smashed, except
myself and Leila. They left through the short hallway leading up
to the front door. From nowhere, Blake grasped one side of my

face and pulled me for a full-on snog. Everyone except Leila
spotted this; she grabbed his sinewy arm weakened by too much
tipple, and pulled him off me and through the door like a
disobedient dog. By that night's close, only Blake's father Eliot
was fit enough to drive everybody home. Leila was still sober, but
she still qualified for a breathalyser test failure. I stood there
dazed for a good few minutes wondering what the frig hit me,
until Mum called me to clear up the plates, glasses and refuse
scattered all round the living room. Then Adrian and that dream
came back into my mind after over a week as I lied on my bed in
my room. Why after all these years of kissing on the cheek would
he want to snog me now? If I wasn't in love with Adrian, I
probably wouldn't have given a shit about it, whether anyone in
the living room saw it happen or not. I would have laughed it off,
even though Leila wasn't laughing when she saw it – I had a
feeling she was going to give him a what-for next time she called
or saw him. He called the next afternoon at around two. Judging
by his muffled voice, he sounded like he had one corker of a
hangover. After I asked if he was okay, there was a silence of
several seconds, until I decided to break the awkwardness it
increased between us.

> "Listen, Blake, about last night…do you know what
> you did?"
> "Yes, Leila told me, and had a right go at me for it this
> morning. She told my dad she'd let me sleep at her
> place, and her mum didn't mind. I'm sorry; I suppose
> I was feeling randy in my drunken state." He sounded very
rueful, either because of what he did or because of his hangover.
> "Well, you'd better not get drunk again, at least not in
> my presence, anyway." I sounded stern enough to pair that
with a stiffened finger through the phone in his face.
> "Yeah, I know. I'm really sorry, okay? Can we all be
> mates again?"
> "Of course, as long as you don't make an ass of yourself
> and me in that way again."
> "I won't. Look, I still have the most awfully pounding
> headache right now, so tomorrow I could come over

yours for a brew and we can talk then, okay? I feel like
an ass already, I don't need to act like one. We've been
friends since we were nine and ten, for God's sake –
why would it take ten years to make a move on you?
If I liked you, I swear, we would have been boyfriend
and girlfriend a long time ago. We're mates, always
have been mates and will be mates, Al," he insisted in an
almost grovelling tone. I couldn't help but agree with that. After
all, drink does funny things to people's heads, right? You know I
know about that. When he came over on his own, we talked about
that subject, and by the end, all was forgiven and we talked and
joked as normal; through that whole evening, I didn't even give a
second thought about symptom number two of Adrian-itis.'

Alana sat down the empty mug on the bedside cabinet,
together with Katerina's, who was now lying on three propped-up
pillows with her arms behind the nape of her neck. 'Feeling
sleepy, bored, that sort of thing?' she queried jokingly, seeing her
eyes half-closed.

'No, not at all, I am listening, you know! This is really
interesting. You're very lucky to have friends like those.
If it were me, I would never stay friends with a bloke for
ten whole years.'

'Really? Why not?'

'Well, because, wouldn't the chemistry take over, like
on that occasion you told me about?'

'No – the drink, not the chemistry, took over him. If
he didn't drink himself stupid on champers, he wouldn't
have snogged me.' She jerked her head to the side to
signify understanding.

'That's true, but wouldn't you say the same about *your*
drinking?' Al gave a stare of approval.

'I drink because it helps ease the pain no one seems to
understand. I'm very conscious that I drink a lot, but
it's not a social thing; it's a personal thing.'

'Okay. Please go on with your story. It's…eleven o'clock
now,' she slurred, concentrating at the alarm clock on the
cabinet. 'I can listen to you till midnight, then we can continue

tomorrow, 'cause I need to go and buy some groceries for this under-stocked place, you know.'

'Sure. Here goes...' she took a deep breath and time travelled through her thoughts.

'I'll fast forward to the end of March, because nothing significant happened between then and the New Year. My twentieth birthday was pretty low-key and balancing my studies and Adrian in my head was easy; I still received grade As and the odd B, but nobody worried, because I bounced back. His popularity, more for his looks than his acting skills, increased with every episode of *Green Collar*. More and more girls - and some guys(!) - were going doo-lally over him. I stood back and laughed at their puerile behaviour, because as much as my liking for him grew, I never looked at him and screamed senselessly. By the end of March, I tried to record every telly appearance, which tallied at twenty at the time, and I kept finding more and more things in common with him – our beliefs, upbringings, hobbies, generally the same line of thinking. I realised then the balance of my priorities was shifting to Adrian out of my power. This was symptom number three of Adrian-itis.

The twenty-eighth was the last Friday of March. On the last Friday of every month, us journalism students are assigned to produce the monthly University newsletter from a few sentences outlining local past, present and future events. This replaced the tutorials on ordinary Fridays. I entered the typing room on my own, which was also on the third floor next to the journalism tutorial room, at ten to ten that morning. It was a room facing the main road – from the doorway I was encountered by a searing sunlight from the window-wall, as I liked to call those windows. The other walls were whitewashed with pastel blue skirting boards. The five rows of five computer terminals left a wide rectangular space enough for another five terminals between where I sat and the window. I had settled in the centre seat in the window-view row, because an outside scene was always a calming influence on me, even though half of it was blocked by the monitor. Twenty-four of the highest scoring journalism students arrived almost simultaneously and took their places. A few minutes after everyone had adjusted themselves to comfort, Mr Sutton marched to face the entire roomful of students in that rectangular space. "Good morning students, and congratulations for dragging yourselves out of bed to come here today. I know you people didn't want to come here on this lovely start to the weekend, but the truth is, neither did I!" Everyone burst out chortling. That's why I and everyone else enjoyed the tutorials. His whole attitude of teaching is very unique and uplifting. He was a guy of about five foot eight in his mid-forties, had a full head of wavy dark brown hair in a "short back and sides" cut. His face was slightly rounded and had a few wrinkles around his grey-green eyes, which was a dead giveaway about his humorous attitude towards life. He wore a white short-sleeved polo shirt and blue jeans, which was a pleasant change from his grey suits. He spoke in a posh Welsh accent, because he hailed from Swansea. 'Okay, let's finish this day as quickly as possible. As you know, we are typing articles of events for our monthly newsletter, and whoever prints the most insightful and informative articles by the time they are read and judged on Monday, will be printed. In a moment, I will be handing out one sheet of blurbs of past, present and future events that have occurred in the West Thirteen area to each of you. Develop them as much as you can in the next four hours, and I shall come round again to collect them, alright?' He wandered over to a paper-piled chair, and handed out the blurbs' sheets, starting from the rear of the room. He then returned to the front of the room. 'Right, you have four hours – you may begin…now,' he slurred, looking at his watch, which according to the wall clock on my left, read five past ten. The room echoed the clacking of keyboard buttons, including mine…

Next thing I knew, it was ten past one in the afternoon. The other students had rampaged to the canteen; I, on the other hand, had an art lecture to attend on the sixth floor. I half-ran through the corridor to the spring-hinged fibreglass doors, which slapped my backside hard when I entered the room. Everyone turned and looked at me curiously. 'Hello, Miss Higgins. Please take your terminal. You're still early,' Mrs Bayer instructed, pacing back and forth in front of a stage with a white cloth-covered navy blue couch. I seated myself on a tall stool before an easel to the left corner of the front row. When Bayer stopped pacing, the low muddled conversation faded to a dead silence. 'Good afternoon, everyone. In today's class, you will be drawing from a live model, who will be sitting or lying on this couch. He should be coming out any moment now.' I heard creaking as this person crept bare feet on the metal steps of the spiral staircase, which led to a veranda and changing rooms. This room had probably the highest ceiling of all, walls on either side of me shielded by steel artwork display boards. The figure emerged apprehensively out of the shadows under the veranda to the spotlights of the main area. It was a lad clutching his black towelling robe up to his neck; either suffering a chill or out of fear of the mainly female students already 'groping' him with their eyes. The guy looked a lot like Adrian…it *was* Adrian, I realised when I looked again – the hair gave it away. I observed him whispering something in Mrs Bayer's ear. After that, she offered aid for him to remove his robe. The girls around me almost fell flat on their backs in giddiness. I heard gasps, near-silent whistles and sighs; I saw jaws drop to the ground, quaky legs, and males grunting in humiliation – some of those girls had forgotten their boyfriends were in the same class, standing helplessly as they went delirious over another bloke. All I did was give a wrinkled smile. I almost yelled aloud, "Come on, this is a flipping art class, not a strip club, so behave yourselves!" but I held it back and listened to Mrs Bayer's instructions and time limit. She went to sit on the bottom step to prevent herself from keeling over herself. I thought, 'Oh no, not you too.' I mean, I certainly liked what I saw, but at least I didn't behave as if I'd never seen a man before. When I turned to focus on the couch, he was sitting in a way which one arm was over the edge, his head was turned to the side, and his legs from his below his bent knees were visible, a sort of 'couch potato' position. The noises of admiration became that of scrawling against paper for two hours.

Time was up. Mrs Bayer collected our drawings while we packed away our materials. A thought came to my mind when I looked behind me and then towards the stage – just imagine if

they were at the front row, instead of *me*; they'd rip him to bloody pieces. Adrian was still seated on the couch, almost struggling to get up, which I thought was stiffness or something. Then I heard him call for Mrs Bayer – she rested our drawings beside the spiral staircase, and stood against this metallic dark blue pole, almost in the light. "Could you pass me robe, please?" he requested in his cosmopolitan Northern accent.
She threw it to him after grabbing it from the second stair. "Thanks."

"So, how did you find your first class, then?" she asked in a deliberately deepened 'received pronunciation' inflection.

"Fine, thanks. Honestly, I thought when I saw those girls' faces, 'Oh God, I'm dead!'"

"Well, you have to expect that. After all, do you know how many girls and women that would kill to have a guy with a body like yours?" His brow wrinkled in confusion. He looked somewhat bewildered about Mrs Bayer's compliment; no surprise, as it was quite a personal one. "Well, back to work. I'll see you later," she seductively intonated, winking as she turned back the staircase. After she brushed past me, I strolled cautiously up to him. He was tying the belt of his robe very tightly – previously, he only used his arms as a belt. "Hi, Adrian – can I ask you something?" I asked in a jolly tone; he raised his eyes to meet mine. "Did Mrs Bayer try to chat you up or something? I couldn't help but notice her body language when she was talking to you." I kept stifling a stubborn giggle as I looked at the "What the hell is going on?"/ "I'm going to pee myself" petrifaction in his face. "Yes. No. Oh, I don't know. I'm not used to middle-aged women chatting me up – I've only just got used to the young ones doing that. The frigging woman thinks she's got it made with me. I don't know how long I can work here now, but I know it's not gonna be for long." I just laughed myself silly. "Look, Mr McCraedie, how about a cup of tea at my place? It's only a few yards away from here, so what d'ya say?" His look of fear softened into one of trust at my jest of addressing him formally. "Sure. Let me get dressed and get the hell out of here. I'll be out in ten, okay?"

"Great. Meet me by the seven lifts?"

"Yep, sure. See ya there."

It was around three-thirty when I looked at the watch. I raised my head to see Adrian marching down the almost peaceful corridor. His hair was similar to how he had it in *Green Collar* – freshly washed, soft strands framing his face. He wore a black transparent shirt, which highlighted that trunk, and black loose jeans. He had a sagging gym bag over his shoulder. Then, my vision turned everything into slow motion – Adrian included. *"God, you have created an angel,"* I maundered. I was snapped back to reality when he asked if I was ready to go. With a yes, we leapt into the first lift that opened its doors.

By ten to four, we were at my house. My mum was still at work at that hour, so it was empty. I invited him to sit on the coral low-backed settee perpendicular to the front door. "Make yourself comfortable while I make the tea, okay?" He nodded as I went into the kitchen. Ten minutes later, I reappeared with two mugs of tea, and handed him one. "Thanks." I sat beside him and took a sip, almost scalding my lips. I was too busy looking at his cherubic face to remember that I'd just made the tea. "So, the reason why I brought you here is because I have this art project to do." I explained further this so-called 'project'. He looked me straight in the face, probably analysing what I'd just asked him to do. I gave him a look that would hopefully convince him that he wasn't in Mrs Bayer's class now, but in my private home. I could see he was still freaked from what happened. He finally accepted, and I instructed him to go behind this screen which covered the patio door at the back of the living room to undress. I got my materials ready from my rucksack as he did so. He emerged about ten minutes later in just black boxer shorts, and I swear I'd never seen such a god-like sight in my whole life. Not an ounce of fat, just all-round, defined muscle – not the chunky body-builder's type, as he had a too narrow build, but that's what made him a sight and a half. Telling him to sit on the floor in front of the sofa was all I could bring myself to say; he posed simply with his knees pulled up to his chest and his cheek rested on his kneecaps. I was done one and a half hours later. When he dressed again behind the screen, he strolled over to where I sat, and looked at the drawing. He was rubbing his hand through his hair, and his shirt wide open allowing every twitch of his trunk visible. He raised his brown eyes to my greens, and nodded silently, but approvingly, with a broad and very cute smile. But he was so blissfully unaware of the ever-growing feelings I struggled to hold in. I was close to breaking point when I stood up, and stared directly into his eyes. "Adrian, you wouldn't believe how speechless I am just looking at you now, but pondering what to say to you makes me even more lost for words, so I'm just going to come out with it – I know you've heard this thousands of times before, but I've never been more serious in my life. I'm crazily in love with you beyond reason, Adrian. I'm sure you feel the same. I saw it in just a few looks you gave me." If you were speechless, you would say corny things like that, too! Naturally, he was freaked out for the second time that day, and I felt guilty for that, so I told him I was taking the mugs to the kitchen to give him a little time to think about it or forget it. But before I went over to get them, he silently grasped my forearm and spun me to crash my front right into the bare part of his torso, slid his hands up each side of my face, aimed for my mouth and gently pulled me into, once again, a very heated snog...

"You've got five minutes, everyone!" I heard Mr Sutton yell, almost causing the whole class's vital organs to leap out of their bodies. I looked at the words at the monitor – it couldn't have totalled more than three-hundred words. I just thought, "Oh shit, what am I going to do now? Everyone has typed about seven thousand words plus, and look Mum, I've stalled." I typed like crazy, my fingers defying wind resistance, until Mr Sutton roared, sorry, *announced* that time was up. I printed out a pitiful number of pages from the printer under the tubular steel desk – one, while everyone printed about fifteen to twenty pages. what did Mr Sutton say? "What the hell is this? You call this your newsletter? This is nothing in terms of a newsletter, Miss Higgins." The whole room had to hear, turn round and snigger at me. "Well, well, what happened to Miss Perfect Student, the one we all know and love? It seems she does have flaws, after all. Where were

you, Higgins? In common students' cuckoo land?" My face
flushed in fury at Graeme's umpteenth slur at me. I usually
ignored him for reasons I explained in the beginning, but today I
was feeling very militant. So I rose from my terminal to march
noisily to his at the centre of the back row. There he stood, bold
as brass, and a good six inches taller than me, but wasn't enough
to dismiss me from attempting what everyone was frightened of –
putting him in his place. I stuck a stiffened forefinger right
between is eyes, and yelled in an animalistic way, "Shut up,
Flegg-face! You don't wanna piss me off – not today, anyway!"
He still had that smug, unnerving expression – threatening him
didn't do a damned thing. "Why? Is it that time of the month
again?" Howls of fake shock could be heard all round at his rather
degrading smear and my look of death.

"Yeah – it's that time of the month when I wish you
     weren't up my ass in the same room!" The whole group of
students rose from their seats and wildly applauded me. Mr
Sutton smelled the risk of a physical assault in the air, so he
tramped over and separated our stances. "The pair of you shut it!
Flegg, Higgins, in my office, one after the other." "But..." I tried
to defend myself. "No buts, from either of you! The rest of you
may all leave." The students slung their rucksacks over their
shoulders and placidly left the room at either one or two at a time.
I overheard their gasps and giggles of amazement at how Alana
Higgins gave Graeme Flegg, a.k.a. Flegg-face, a what-for. "Call
the papers – someone stood up to Flegg-face, the University's
resident pain in the ass!" We left after everyone had cleared the
room, within good distance of each other, of course, to avoid
tearing each other's limbs off.

In Sutton's office, I sat outside on a bench against the wall
separating the two rooms, eavesdropping on his muffled chiding,
and possible downfall, of Flegg-face. The office was one door
down from the typing room and nearer to the lifts. Inside was a
semi-circular desk inverted towards Mr Sutton, which had a
pastel blue surface and was pale pink on the foot board under it -
it made the polished pine floorboards in the spacious rectangular
room look arched. Another window-wall was behind his black

leather reclining chair. I knew this, because I'd been in there several times before for chats, but never for a telling-off. He emerged, still looking untouched by his 'constructive criticism'. "Your turn next, Higgs," he breathed out quietly, in a way so I heard him. I stood defensively from the bench, and shot back the daggers he always shot me with. "Sod off, Flegg, before I knock off that stupid face of yours." I could have scared a lion to death with that tone. I brushed past him before he could express a reaction, dragging my feet against the floor, and entered Mr Sutton's office. I sat in one of the ordinary wooden seats opposite him. A short silence followed. Then he shot me a cold stare reminiscent of my secondary school headmaster. "Okay, question time – what the hell happened to you in the time you should have been typing? I am really, really disappointed in you at the fact that your newsletter won't be published this month. Every month since January last year, when you first came here, you've had it published." He sounded disillusioned at the so-called "super student's" mortal side. Just because someone is good at a subject doesn't make their brain immortal.

"I'm sorry, Mr Sutton. I just kind of drifted away… somewhere into my thoughts."

"If something's bothering you, tell me. I'll try to help. Is it domestic?"

"What? No, of course not," I shrieked, not believing how serious his tone was.

"Well, it must have been something serious if you managed to distract yourself for that amount of time. Five, ten minutes, fine, I would understand, but nearly the whole time? That I don't understand at all." I felt he was going to see right through me with his insistence.

"No honestly. I just didn't get enough sleep last night. I've been so worried about my overall performance ever since I received that D for that assignment last week." I thanked the little voice in my head for supplying me with that good explanation I told him. He looked me in the eyes to assess my reason.

"Well…you're right to be worried, as you haven't

returned to grade A recently. Look, I tell you what…
go to sleep early tonight. It'll help you clear your head
for your next assignment." After finally being satisfied with
my reasoning, we shook hands. I left the office, and eventually
the building, for the final time that week at around two-thirty. I
wandered towards the suburbia behind the University for home.
But I changed direction abruptly and ended up strolling along the
fairly placid main road, gradually speeding up my pace,
skimming past the advertisement board and a row of small shops.
I halted outside a newsagent, and sharply entered. There were
only one or two people in there, apart from the cashier, an Indian
woman in her early forties. I rolled my eyes in a rapid eye
movement-fashion across all the magazines on the group of
shelves. I picked any and every one which had Adrian's picture or
words referring to him on the front page. All in all, I must have
picked eight magazines and a two scrapbooks from the stationary
section, and it must have cost twelve quid. I got some curious
looks from the cashier, I can tell you! Anyway, I went home at
around quarter-to-three. I removed my coat, shoes and rucksack,
and got straight to cutting and plastering the articles, pictures and
etcetera, in the one scrapbook they took up. I did that before I
even ate anything, even though I was starving. Mum wasn't home
yet – even if she wasn't working towards that promotion, she still
wouldn't be home so early. I never hung up any posters on the
wall for obvious reasons, including the one where she would
laugh, so I stuck them in the scrapbook. I shoved the empty
scrapbook under the bed for later pastings, then made a sandwich.
I ate it on the bed, lying on my middle, and my feet in the air,
while reading most of the articles. Most of them seemed to be the
same questions asked and answered differently, but there was one
thing I learned from all of them – he was an angel. He was
intelligent, caring, romantic, enterprising, determined, optimistic,
educated, well-mannered, well-spoken, well-read, spiritual,
sensitive, fun-loving and confident – basically out of this world. I
swear, my emotions moved one inch further towards him with
every new thing I learned about him, and one inch away from
most of my life's priorities. He wasn't just perfect – he was

perfect for *me*, but then I found out every other woman and man thought he was perfect for them! I also read in another article that ever since his overnight fame, he bought a flat in London, because he didn't want his family to experience the pressures of fame meant for him. I thought at the time, "Yes! A sign at last! He's close to home – that'll make it easier to look for him." *Oh come on, Al! Get a grip, don't be stupid* – those thoughts went through my mind. Then I remembered there was a First Year Students' Party on the twelfth of April being set up on the ninth floor for the first-year students (duh!), the abandoned floor which was going to be used for offices afterwards. I had to concentrate on buying a new frock and shoes. "I will go shopping tomorrow with Blake and Leila up the Broadway." I had, had, *had to* try and distract myself from my feelings, however increasingly difficult it was.

Chapter 4.

'Feeling sleepy yet?' Alana had begun to feel a friend's responsibility for Katerina – something she hadn't felt for what seemed years. 'As a matter of fact, yes I am. Can we continue this tomorrow over breakfast or something? It's officially Sunday now, so I've nothing to do except buy a few things for this deprived place.' She slid cautiously under the fusty duvet, wrinkling her nose a little in repulsion to the odour of who knew how many previous residents, and stared at the ceiling for several seconds before turning her head to see Alana crawl under her duvet more subliminally than herself. 'Ah, at last, I'm tucked up!' Katerina released aloud. 'Okay. I need to ask some things about your story before you continue tomorrow.'

'Shoot.'

'What the hell made you think you'd find him just like that, just because he lives in London now?' she demanded, snapping her fingers. Alana inhaled deeply and let her chest fall by itself.

'Because…I guess I thought because the physical distance had reduced, my search span would have reduced via the Internet but the distance here hasn't been reduced at all,' she reasoned almost tearfully, slapping her hand over her sore heart.

'But haven't you thought about it being just a crush, because you have a lot in common with him?'

'Course I have, but if it were a crush, all my priorities would have outweighed my feelings, and my love wouldn't transcend his looks, what he does and what his past was. Even if he was just a street sweeper, I would have still clicked in the same way. That's why I bought all those magazines – so I could find out how he thought, felt and dreamt about simple things. I've never had so much in common with any guy before, except Blake, but he's like the brother I never had. I felt like I knew him forever when I looked into his eyes. He's like a male version of me, and I've always said that

no one understands me other than me, so we would
understand each other really well.'
'I realise that, but have you ever thought what he would
think if he knew you were slowly committing suicide
over him? He'd think you're nuts!'
'You're probably right, but it sends me into a perfect world
with no obstacles, no distance and where everyone finds
true love, including me. When I'm sober again, I feel as
empty as when I first entered. So I drink some more so
I don't leave that world for too long,' she listlessly drew
out, still slightly inebriated. All Katerina could do was sigh
pessimistically.
'But… oh, I give up. Where's your dad in all of this?
You said he was unfaithful.'
He was. Don't know where he is, and I don't care either. He
left when I was nine for some tart he worked with, when my mum
gave up her ambition as the solicitor she now is today to look
after him and me. My mum never really talked about it much, but
she said she found some floozy putting her arms round him at
work, who was sitting before a computer and snogging him
knowing full well he was a family man. My poor mum just ran
home crying. I remember a lot of shouting, waking me from my
sleep in my room that night, and a crash of some sort, probably
crockery. About a month of living together after the incident, she
told him she was divorcing him. Even though I was just a child,
she was dead honest about what was going to happen to my dad,
and didn't try to dress it up. I cried, not because I was missing
him, but because of his betrayal not only to my mum, but to me as
well. He admitted he carried on that affair for the ten years they
were married, before I was even born, for Christ's sake. She
hardly cried, because she was too hurt. It was nearly Christmas
eighty-six when it was finally official. Neither of us have seen or
heard from him ever since.
'I'm really sorry you've had one AWOL parent.'
'It's fine. If I grew up with him, we'd never see eye-to-eye,
so I'm glad he's out of our lives. He brought on the loss of#

his family himself.' Katerina wiped away the oozing salt
water from the corners of her eyes with a fist, feeling her pain as
if it were her own. 'Anyway, it's nearly one, and I'm feeling a bit
sleepy, so I'm calling it a night. Can we continue this tomorrow?'

'You still interested?' she asked, raising an eyebrow. Her
eyes barely shed a bitter or sorrowful tear – they looked immune
to her own pain.

'Sure I am. It's the saddest story I've ever heard, but
I'm too knackered to hear more.'

'I know. Sleep – you're gonna need it, because it's your
first day here.'

'Okay. Look, is it okay to set the alarm now? You won't
smash it on my head in my sleep, will ya?'

'No, of course not. Not now, anyway,' she giggled and
grinned slightly.

'Thanks. Goodnight, Al.'

'Goodnight, Kat.' Alana yanked the duvet over her ears;
Katerina tuned the alarm hand, brushed the blanket over her
shoulders and sobbed silently into a blank dream, feeling herself
wounded by a wounded stranger.

Alana's eyelids jerked wide open once again by that
seemingly incessant electronic bell. She sleepily stumbled over to
Katerina's side and slammed her fist on the button. 'Hello – she's
not here,' she questioned herself, seeing the bed covers neatly
smoothed out. *Well, I know it's ten o' clock, but where the hell is
she? Not that I'm interested, of course.* Grazing her face with her
palms, she returned to the edge of her bed. She opened her sore
eyes to see a post-it note on the bedside cabinet. 'Gone shopping.
Be back at twelve. Might need help with some things. Katerina.'
*Wonder what she's buying that she needs help carrying? Oh well,
I'd better have a drink or two before I get the old Alcoholics
Anonymous lectures again.* She swivelled some water from the
'kitchen' sink tap in a glass, poured it to the rim with vodka from
a bottle secreted under the bed, and gushed it down her throat.
She felt an instant lift from her mind, and yet an instant fall in her
body. She repeated this four or five times, the two further
contradicting themselves from each other. Afterwards, her body

felt so abysmal, and her mind so euphoric, she felt the need to
sleep again. She pulled her legs up the bed once again with her
hands on her stomach, staring at the ceiling, almost spaced out…

The front door slammed again. 'Damn those hinges! Al?
I'm back! Could you give me a hand please?' She snapped her
spine upwards and leapt to her feet. They mutually stared
confusingly for several seconds. 'Good God – did you buy the
whole of Ealing Broadway or what?' she asked as her eyes fell to
the four almost bursting large carrier bags.

'Jesus, Al – why do you look like you've been freaking
     yourself in your sleep?' Her eyes focused on her sweat-
slicked and rosy face. Silence.

'Um…' they simultaneously began. 'You first,' they
restarted equally simultaneously. They both cracked up with hard
laughter.

'I'll begin. I thought the place needs sprucing up, 'cause
     no one else will do it. That ass of a landlord expects us
     to live like pigs for the time we're staying here. You?'
'Actually, I was…as you put it, freaking myself in my
     sleep.' Katerina clenched her stomach to look serious, but
still ended up expelling a lengthy, howling laugh.

'Okay, before we go any further into that, can you give
     me a hand? I've got some other stuff down there,' she
pointed at the door. Still giggling, she opened the door, almost
tumbling down the stairs by tripping on the first step. Katerina
shook her head pessimistically on noticing this. *Probably stoned
again.* Alana dragged up a pull-trolley and a laundry basket.
'What on earth are you going to do with this stuff? This room is
no bigger than a kitchen cupboard, for God's sake.'

'Look, once it's all packed away, you wouldn't even
     notice. Give me a hand if you're up to it later, and
     everything will disappear.' Alana nodded erratically in
agreement. 'Right now, I'm starving. I'll make some breakfast.'
She began unloading one of the bags, which concentrated most of
the groceries – two loaves of bread, croissants, oranges, orange
juice, two boxes of cereal, ultra-high temperature milk, cheese,
natural yoghurt, doughnuts, and a whole medley of other food

items. 'There's a lot to choose from – bread, cereal, croissants, fruit…what would you like?'

'Umm…I'll have…the croissants! I haven't had those for ages. I'm off to the bathroom to clean up.' She darted through the front door, slipping down about five stairs of the ten leading down to the bathroom. *Damn it, I'll never get used to this staircase, but I haven't fallen down the stairs before now.* She leaned against a wall beside the bathroom's doorway while the occupant finished their use of it.

Katerina placed two servings of breakfast on the bedside cabinet – two slices of toast, another plate of three croissants with slices of cheese, and two separate plates of cubed oranges. Two mugs of tea were then set beside the mini-banquet. Alana returned, wearing a long black skirt hanging round her hips, and a blue fitted shirt. Her hair was tied in a high ponytail, which made her bloodshot eyes more obvious. Katerina's reaction of her face was a jerking of nerves in her own face, but continued a neutral expression. 'Here's your breakfast, Al.'

'Lovely. Thanks.' She sat on the edge of the bed, placed the plate of croissants on her lap, and began devouring it in the middle, then its ends. Katerina observed this as she chewed on her toast.

'When was the last time you ate anything, Al? Obviously a long time ago!' She looked up at Katerina with a softened look. 'On Friday I ate toast from the last two slices of the last loaf of bread I had in here,' she informed in a matter-of-fact tone.

'The day before I arrived? Good God,' she whispered.

'Look, if you're going to give me another lecture about my lifestyle, I don't want to hear it,' she defensively warned.

'Hey, I'm not a Samaritan, Al – I just want to know how you ended up here in this state. How you live your life is your choice. You don't have to continue talking about it if you don't want to.' *How come a stranger has never been as compassionate as a Samaritan? Yes, I do want to talk about this.*

'Yes, I do want to talk about this. I've got no one else to talk to.'

'What about your friends, the ones you mentioned?'

'Lost contact. Leila moved somewhere. Don't know where. We had a bust-up about my drinking before the exam. She never knew I moved here. Blake, well…he moved to Dublin in July ninety-seven with a girl me and Leila hated with a passion – Freda Henley. I don't know if he married her or what.' Her heart's constraints seemed to tighten when she thought about him.

'So if it's February now, that means you haven't spoken to them in nineteen months?'

'Yeah.'

'Woah. Um, let's start with what happened with Blake and this Freda person, as the bit with you and Leila seems pretty self-explanatory.'

'Well, good starting point, because we can pick up where we left off, which was the day the three of us went to the Broadway to buy ourselves an outfit each. I think it was the…' She trailed off into her memories again, all on her own again.

Fifth of April – yeah, that's right. The night before, I called Blake and Leila, one after the other, asking them if they would like to join me for shopping the next afternoon. They said yes, as they received news of the First-Year Students' Party too. We unfortunately didn't run into each other the afternoon before when we came back from our tutorials. On that morning, I gorged four bacon sarnies, not because I was hungry, but because I was feeling a bit unstable – believe it or not, there was a time when I scoffed to stabilize myself, but these days I just starve to do the same. I had another Adrian dream that night. I woke up in the middle of the night in a sweat because of its 'blue' nature. But that's another story – on with this one. Mum stupidly gawped as she watched me inhale one sandwich after the other. As I reached out for a fifth from a large serving plate right in the centre of the table, she slapped my hand.

"Al, what's wrong with you? You could go into the

record books with an appetite like yours!"

"I'm fine, Mum. Just famished, that's all."

"Not true. I know something's on your mind when you eat like that."

"Nothing's on my mind, except the shopping trip, of course." She then gave me one of those looks that I always hated – the lie-detecting "You're lying and I know it" looks only a mother's intuition could use to detect what's floating around in a child's unconscious. I eventually took a deep breath and thought, "Well, Al, you'd better think of something good." And I did – not worthy for the Nobel Prize of Excuses, but I said that I didn't get enough sleep last night. She nodded her head in acceptance – the older I got, the more likely she bought what I said, whether it was true or not. "Okay, dear. But remember to tell me what's on your mind if something's up."

"Sure, you know I would." God, I can actually see and hear her laughing her head off if I ever told her what was, and is, really bothering me. She never had any strong likings for anyone in the public eye, so she'll dish out the usual ignorant "Snap out of it, that's so infantile" so-called advice. I raised my head to gaze at the kitchen clock – it read eleven. "Oh damn, look at the time. I'd better be getting ready before they get here." Saved by the clock, I thought with relief.

"Okay. You can take the sandwich if you want."

"Nah. I don't want it now. I'll get indigestion." I placed my hand on her curly, bob-cut, mid-blonde hair, which was usually pinned up in a pleat when at home, but was worn down today. I briskly kissed her on the cheek, and dashed to the bedroom for a set of clothes, and then to the bathroom to adorn myself. Half an hour later, I raced out again, wearing a bottle blue trousers, and a silver Lurex vest. I dumped my house clothes, which consisted of a black fitted t-shirt and trousers which hung at my hips and brushed against my ankles, on this chair between the doorway and the bedside cabinet. In less than five minutes, they would have arrived. I didn't want to keep them waiting. I dug out a long-lined blue jacket, which had one button fastening the front; it feel to my ankles when I slipped it on. I dashed back down the hall, onto the living room sofa. I brought my silver ankle-strap dress shoes, which had a similar-coloured flower motif, and fiddled for a good five minutes with the straps, nearly rolling off the settee in the process. I was disturbed by the doorbell. *Oh shit*, I thought, *please fasten,* as the stubborn buckles wouldn't hold in the strap. Oh God. "Mum, could you get the door please? I'm still strapping these rotten shoes!" I growled impatiently. "Well, it was your idea to buy them."

"I know, OKAY?" I angrily answered back, which just caused a giggle from Mum, which hinted she knew she would get on my wit by saying that. She opened the door, and greeted Leila and Blake with a kiss each. Blake stretched his head over Mum's shoulder to see me still struggling with my shoe. "Hi Al!" he grinned his cheeky little grin and waved at me. He probably wanted to laugh at my face, because I felt, and obviously looked, flushed and aggravated. "You look a little annoyed. You okay?" Leila asked out of concern, also stretching her head. I just threw myself with my arms against the back of the sofa with a sigh. "I can't fasten my shoe, guys. HELP!" I screamed. "Oh dear. Here, let me help," Blake offered in that naturally smooth tone. He kneeled down, looked at the holes in the strap, and looked at me in a look which I interpreted as a look of mockery. Because I was too busy looking at him, I forgot how long it took for him to do up my shoe, but he actually did it. "There."

"Thanks, Blake."

"God, you're behaving like you don't have any other pairs of shoes," Mum interrupted.

"I do, but when I go out with these two here, I like to go all out." The pair of them smiled simultaneously at each other over what I said.

"Even if the pair of shoes is a pain to fasten?" They giggled like clucking chickens, turning to me.

"Come on you two, let's go. I'd rather not answer that." They all burst out into loud laughter, knowing she was right, and I didn't want to admit it. I kissed Mum on the cheek again as we said we would see her at around three that afternoon. It was a beautifully sunny Saturday mid-morning, only slightly tarnished

with a bitter breeze, but not enough to put Blake off raising the
roof off his convertible pale blue Beetle. So we hopped in over
the doors, and we waved at Mum as he started the engine and
turned in the opposite direction of the University down a fairly
hectic, and yet still, Uxbridge Road. The drive would've only
taken ten minutes if it wasn't for the bloody parking, but it took
an hour, which pissed us both off; everywhere looked like a
sardine tin of parked cars. Blake was constantly cursing under his
breath and his driving became more aggressive, even as we told
him to calm down, but you should have heard the language that
came out of that boy's mouth when he aimed for a spot a few
paces away from the mall, and someone else beat him to it! But
we found this tiny little space in one of the small suburban streets
behind the shopping mall, away from the parking attendants on
the main road, but it was a good quarter-of-a-mile walk. Myself
and Leila looped around each of Blake's arms, and proudly
strutted back up to the main road. We loved the expressions on
people's faces which literally screamed, "He's got *two*
girlfriends?!" In fact, we rose that subject during the walk up to
the mall, and had a good laugh about it, which left Blake
squirming, probably feeling like the inferior gender whenever we
discussed that. Ten minutes later, we took the final turn which
lead us nearer to the mall's entrance. It was a tall Victorian
building jazzed up with glass panels and mod cons at the bottom
floors. The most striking feature of this particular mall we went
to, which I always thought was really cute, was the clock outside
– it had an ordinary-looking clock face with Roman numerals, but
it had a Big Ben-type jingle every hour, chimed by two town crier
figurines, one wearing green and one wearing red, on either side
of it holding bell-chiming rods which struck the bells in front of
them. It was right on top on the building, incorporated in the old-
fashioned part of the building.

    'Yeah, I know – I've go there regularly, 'cause I'm from
       Hanwell,' Katerina interrupted, anxious for the story to
carry on.

Oh! Well, we stood beside the frame of the wide entrance, which was outside a record shop window, and playfully began to argue about which shop to go to first.

"There's no way were going in with you – we know what
    a fussy shopper you are!" Leila mocked, as she stood
beside me facing Blake.

"What's that supposed to mean?" Blake queried in pretend offence.

"It took two hours to pick one pair of trousers the last
    time we went shopping – if you want to pick something,
    do it yourself. At least we can go home while it takes
    you till the place closes to choose something!"

"Thanks Al, you're an awful lot of help, you," he
sarcastically replied, crossing his arms.

"Okay, back to the heart of the matter – where are you
    going, Blake?" Leila changed the subject to keep the peace.
No matter how much we squeezed ourselves out of the crowds, mad rushes of people still kept obliviously brushing or crashing into us, and it wasn't even Monday.

"I'm going to that shop over there. I haven't been in
    there before, so I'll try that out. You?"

"We're going up the first floor, but we won't be in
    any particular shop, so you'd better check all of them
    out if there's any chance of finishing before us."

"Okay, marathon women – I'm here if you finish before
    me. But don't blame me if I come out looking like an
    old man or a penguin!" We both cracked up laughing at
that; he always had his own sense of style – he never followed the fashions or looked like everyone else, so he wanted to do the same for the party. That day, he wore the leather coat I gave him for Christmas over a straight-cut silver short-sleeved shirt and navy blue combat trousers – one-hundred per cent Blake – simple, yet stylish. He sort of influenced us girls on choosing our individual sense of style by not being a sheep to fashion, so both of us had a very precise idea of what we wanted.

"Okay, point taken. We'll see you later." Leila grabbed my arm and gently dragged me under the tinted, divided glass window walls above the sign and entrance, to the escalator to the first floor. We waved at each other as we rose higher off the ground floor. I sometimes wonder why the hell we went to that mall, because I would have still had my best mates in the world with me.

Two hours later, we had finished; we had a couple of cups of cappuccinos each at this Continental-style café further up on the same side of road. We sat round one of the outdoor tables to savour the mild sunshine; at first, we were overwhelmed by the pungent ciggie and coffee smells, but we got used to it after a few minutes. All of us took a sip, and looked at each other's bags under our chairs.

"Okay, let's see what the marathon women have bought!" Blake jested.

"Ho, ho – that's funny. It's…wait for it – my dress!" I slung the bag on my lap, and yanked out a long pale blue evening dress weaved with metallic strands. "Forty-five quid." He stroked the silky material between his thumb and forefinger.

"Mmm…not bad. In fact, it's beautiful. How 'bout you, Lill?"

"I bought…this." It was a knee length pale pink satin frock when she threw it open. "It cost forty quid – obviously because it has less material." We giggled at that.

"This is lovely, too. You'll look like the Marilyn Monroe and the Jane Russell of the party!" Our laughter grew louder when he said that.

"Don't tell me I have to dye my hair blonde now!" I groaned in faux dread, stroking my hair protectively.

"Nah, you can be a brunette Marilyn instead!" he replied sassily.

"Okay, thanks, I will. So, what did you buy that took you such a short time in there?" Leila was still sniggering, spluttering into her cup.

"Well, I bought…this shiny blue shirt, black trousers and this grey jacket. I had some help from an assistant, who stood back and amused herself with the fact that I didn't see anything to my tastes there."

"Explain how she helped you choose. She sounds like
an amazing woman!" Leila playfully requested.

"Oh shut up, you," he defended, punching her shoulder. I
giggled at her impertinence. "Well, I was in the little place I
pointed to just under the escalators, and firstly I sifted through the
selection of trousers. Nothing I saw suited my style or age group.
'Everyone's going to be in black suits – I've got to be me,' I
thought to myself. I went further into the shop, and looked at the
jackets and the shirts. Nothing again. I looked at the ties. Nothing.
I reiterated my search for the next half-an-hour, but was still
dismayed that I saw nothing. I was about to walk out and join you
girls when this girl, who was standing by the till watching me the
whole time and giggling. 'Can I help you?' she asked, still
giggling. She had straight, pleated coffee-coloured hair, dark oval
brown eyes, and slightly mixed skin with a small mole on her left
cheek, and was wearing a red shirt and black trousers. She looked
around nineteen or twenty, and around five-foot-five. 'What's so
funny?'

'You've been here an hour, looked over the same stuff
twice, and you still haven't seen anything!' Her giggling
became a fully-fledged laugh, which I thought was cute. She had
what I thought was either an Irish or Scottish accent.

'Can I help it if you don't have a range of suits for the
younger generation?'

'Believe me, so many people have come and gone here
today, so you're not on your own. Besides, I'm from that
generation, too, you know!'

'I know. I'm sorry. Can you help, please?'

'What's the occasion?'

'A party at my University. I want to be unique, not a
penguin! I'm me in everyday life, and I want to be the
same at the party.' She continued that lovely little giggle
again. 'Okay. Let me measure you up, and I'll bring a choice of
outfits.' She led me into this room behind the cash register, and
began wrapping her tape measure round my shoulders, my upper
arms, chest, waist and thighs. She seemed to linger longest round

my thighs. I wasn't sure inconspicuously running hands along them was part of measuring, but she didn't think I noticed."

"Are you saying she liked your thighs?"

"Possibly by the way she 'measured' them." We began laughing our heads off again, kicking underneath the table, possessed by unbearable humour. "What? Loads of men would like that. Anyway, she brought me back out, and scribbled them down in a notebook. 'Right. You wait here…what's your name?'

'Blake Turpin. Yours?'

'Freda. Freda Henley.'

'Take a seat, Blake, and I'll bring some things fit for your uniqueness,' she joked cheekily with a 'come-hither' kind of look. I just gave a squinted smile to myself, 'cause she thought her method for chatting me up was subtle. I just wanted to see what she was going to do next. Five minutes later, she came back with three trousers, jackets and shirts. I only had to look at this suit to know it suited me. But the shirt was from one suit and the jacket and trousers was from another, but she said they allow 'cross-breeding'. I spent about fifty quid on the entire outfit. Before she gave me the receipt, I noticed her writing something on the back. She finally handed it to me. I thanked her and said 'bye. I looked at the back…and it was her phone number!" Blake showed us the receipt, and gave it to Leila for both us girls to look at.

"Boy, that was certainly subtle!" Leila sarcastically joked, stuffing the receipt back in his shirt pocket.

"Yeah, it was, wasn't it? She probably wouldn't give me a second thought if she never measured my thighs!" We cracked up chortling before we'd even recovered from our last bout.

"True, but go on, give her a call. You can invite her to the party if you like, as your date." God, if only *I* knew. I would go back and warn myself, and him.

"Sure, good idea." We took our last sip each, then Blake asked for the bill. "It's two-thirty. We'd better be getting back."

"Well, all our shopping here is done, so let's go." With that, we did that arm-in-arm strut back to the car, and within five minutes, I was home again. They joined me and Mum for a quick cuppa after a welcome-back greeting. We showed her what we bought at the mall; she whooped in excitement at everything. We even told her what happened to Blake at the mall, bringing up a blush to his cheeks, at which she never stopped chuckling. By quarter-past-three, they were ready to leave. We kissed them goodbye, and they said they'll call later and tomorrow evening. Mum and I waved at them through the window beside the front door as they drove out of our road. God, if only *I* knew.'

Chapter 5.

'Want anything else to eat?' Katerina asked, noticing her hand on her now protuberant stomach.

'Nah. I'm full, thanks.' She piled up two pillows against the bed head, and leaned back against them, feeling quite leisurely. Katerina placed the mugs and plates in the dark scum-slicked sink. 'So, when you met this Freda, did you dislike her right away, or as you got to know her?'

'As I got to know her. I shall fast forward a week to the night of the party, because that will explain my answer.'

'Sure. Let me get myself comfortable, and you can restart.' She also leaned against two piled pillows, and placed her arms behind her back. 'Go on.'

Saturday the twelfth of April, six-thirty that evening. Us two girls decided to get ready at Leila's place in her bedroom – sort of a just girls' thing. I upped my hair into a looped bun almost on top of my head, and pulled a few strands to cover the nape of my neck and cheeks. I helped Leila pin up the sides and underneath her ringlets together on top of her head, leaving half its length loose. We were already in our frocks, and we'd assumed to be each other's hairdressers, so it was just our make-up now. A blot of foundation here, dust of blusher there, powder noses, a couple brushes of mascara, a smearing of eye shadow, a dab of lipstick – voilà! I told Leila Blake was right about one thing – we looked like we were going to be the Marilyn and Jane of the party. I had pearly olive green eye shadow, which brought out my green eyes, and a dusky pink lipstick. Leila had a violet and deep blue eye shadow; her brown eyes and tanned skin didn't make the colour bruise her eyes, and a deep violet lipstick for a touch of quirkiness. "Well, I think we look pretty damn good, don't you?" I gloated, both of us admiring ourselves in the wide, full length mirror.

"Yeah, definitely. Hey, you don't think Flegg-face will try to chat us up now, d'ya?"

"If he does, he can go to hell! I wouldn't mind Adrian

McCraedie chatting me up, though."

"Me neither. You think he believes in threesomes?" she
cheekily asked, wiggling her eyebrows.

"Lill, you can be one sleazy bitch sometimes!" I jested
hoarsely, punching her shoulder and pretending to be offended. I
knew she was just kidding. 'Lill' was the alias I regularly
addressed her with.

"I like being a sleazy bitch sometimes!" We both laughed
wildly, and playfully scuffled like football players often do, and
did a high-five. I was sure he got offers like that every day. I
didn't feel so possessed by him then, and that was another reason
why I think I'm right for him – I would never force him to make
an unreasonable choice between me and fame because of a few
randy fans. We composed ourselves on hearing the click of the
door. It was the auburn head of Leila's mum, Lily. "You girls
ready?"

"Yeah. We'll just sit on the bed for a while and wait
    for Blake's call." She replied calmly.

"Okay. You look terrific, girls – you'll knock 'em dead."

"We know, and that's what we intend to do!" she
ostentatiously bragged in a posh accent. "Shut up, you!" I
punched her shoulder, causing both of us to giggle.

"Okay girls, enough showing off. I'll see you downstairs."

"Sure," we synchronised joyfully. We eventually got the
call from Blake, saying he was on his way. Over my dress I wore
that same long-line jacket I wore shopping the week before, and
Leila wore a matching pale pink shirt over hers. We sat on the
edge of her double bed, reminiscing about the year gone by. Her
room was about the same size as mine, but was in a magnolia
colour, the wardrobe was double the size of mine before the bed's
foot, and had sliding mirror doors. She had a white set of drawers
with a telly on it, and a larger window on one side of the bed –
gorgeous. Mind you, houses are slightly larger in Hayes than in
Ealing. Before we realised it, it was seven thirty, half an hour
since we finished primping. We raced down ten curved stairs,
cued by a hoot of a horn from the driveway; I reached the bottom
first. "Hi everyone!" Blake shrieked, obviously in high spirits.

"Hi girls!" We ran up to him and kissed him simultaneously on each cheek.

"Hi, Blake! Everything fine?" I asked.

"Brilliant. I'm really happy, 'cause it's been ages since we've been to a good knees-up!" He had a scary screeching pitch to his normal velvety voice. But he looked like a true Prince Charming that night in that suit – in his own unique way.

"Us too. Is this the lovely lady you met in the men's shop?" Leila queried with a warm smile.

"Yup. Say hi to Freda Henley, everyone. Freda, these are my childhood friends Leila Drayton and Alana Higgins." We all exchanged hellos and handshakes, including Lily. She wore a figure-hugging dark brown, boat-necked velvet dress with long sleeves, and wore her mid brown hair down with two diamante pins on one side of her scalp. Blake was right – she looked like a mix of Indian, Irish and something else – probably Latin, who knew? I did think she was pretty to start with, but that was soon to change. The whole time, she gave us girls a weird stare every time she tightened her grip on Blake's arm, like she was worried we'll steal him away for a threesome or something! We had a pretty uncomfortable chat as Blake drove us to the University, still subliminally treating us like her rivals. Never did I think there was something so sinister about her. During most of the twenty-minute, two-and-a-bit mile drive down the third junction of the M4 motorway, I took comfort in the red and orange-mingled violet sunset adorned by a wispy crescent moon, which was in full view from the raised roof.

We could hear the pulsating music before the lift had even arrived at the ninth floor. It sounded it was in full swing only a few short minutes after it began. We were shaking our shoulders to the beat before the doors even opened to warm ourselves up for the evening. The whole of the floor, almost rocking from the beat and everyone's moving feet (hey, that rhymes!), looked like an authentic discothèque, with its dizzy coloured lighting, and a hired disc jockey stand a good distance opposite the lifts; it was hard to believe this floor was soon to be a field planted with desks, chairs and computers. That night, I wasn't to let Freda's

curious possession over Blake stop me from having a good time.
After all, he was a grown man and could see if something's
wrong on his own. A couple of minutes after arriving, we greeted
the tutors, including Mr Sutton, who stood beside his wife with a
beer, then I grabbed Leila's hands and began throwing ourselves
around like mad things to a fast song. God, it was fun. I can't
remember the last time I actually shouted into someone's ear
because the music was too loud. But after a pause, a crap tune
came on – it was one of those annoying novelty records, so I
yelled in Leila's ear, "Let's get a drink," to distract ourselves
from it. She nodded, and I dragged her to this custom-made bar.
"Two Martinis, please." Blake had stopped dancing with Freda,
and came up to us on his own as she went to the ladies room.
"Enjoying the night so far?"

"Yeah, it's better than I thought so far. They should have
a party here every week!" Leila and Blake mouthed a
laugh. "So how's it going with your date, then?"

"Brilliant so far. We only talked in the car and on the
phone, but we will some more when we get a table.
Wanna join us?" We looked at each other, hesitating due to
the discomfort she was causing. But we didn't want to dampen
his euphoria by a too-honest opinion of her so soon.

"Yeah, alright then." He led the way to a table next to the
window wall facing the crazy weekend roads, and collected our
drinks for us. We drank and bantered till Freda rejoined us. Blake
received several kisses on his cheeks and looks of lust; we got
scowls and fake smiles. Leila and I both spotted this. She was
deliberately making out with him in front of us, and Blake, God
bless him, misinterpreted it as a loving gesture.

"Excuse us, we need to go to the ladies." I said on our
behalf.

"Of course. I'm sure Blake here wouldn't mind waiting
for you." I distinctly recognised that bitchy tone she
addressed us with all evening in her Irish accent, the one implying
we never left him alone. In the empty bathroom, we adjusted our
make-up before a mirror over the sinks.

"Good God, Al – who the fuck does she think she is,

talking to us like her love rivals!" She gasped, dabbing a
powder puff on her face.

"I know. She's behaving like she owns him, and she's
only known him a week. Un-bloody-believable."

"And he's not noticing that tone of voice she uses on
us – has looking at his thighs affected her *that* much?"

"You're not funny, Lill," I replied in a disillusioned tone.

"I know, I know, sorry. What're we gonna do?"

"*Stop it, somehow* - but not tonight. Let's just have fun." I
nodded as we picked up our handbags and returned to the dance
floor. We danced to the pumping beat, which was just as
powerful as when it started. Somehow, I saw every lad staring
from the corners of their eyes, including Flegg-face. Leila spotted
this, too. I told her I don't go for jackasses – she almost laughed
herself into fainting. We rejoined Blake, ignored Freda and
continued drinking, dancing and knocking everyone dead with
glamour no one was used to seeing us in. By eleven o'clock, the
DJ spun the final ballad. I politely insisted to Freda if I could cut
in the dance. "Have him yourself!" she snapped with a
characteristically nasty look, then stroppily stormed off with
some bloke, a student I wasn't familiar with. He really looked
pissed at that, and identified with my shocked expression. "Oops
– have I done anything wrong?" I asked in fake concern,
shrugging as I took his hand.

"No, not at all. I don't think she expected a cut-in from
you."

"Well, I am entitled to dance with a friend, aren't I?"

"Of course, m'lady," he suavely accepted, causing me to
giggle. With one arm round me and the other gently squeezing
my hand, we swayed slowly in time for the next five minutes or
so, feeling a bit like Cinderella and the Prince Charming I spoke
of. We studied each other's smiles, feeling my knees give in
slightly at the loveliest cheeky grin I'd ever seen him exercise. It
was then I summed up that he had a powerful charisma, a soft
heart and was idealistic, and if Freda had her way with him, he
would get hurt. By eleven-thirty, everyone left after applauding
the DJ. Almost reaching the doors of the lifts, Freda yanked my

arm off his from behind to provoke me with that 'love rival'
bullshit again.

"Hey, that was a little rude!" I sarcastically retaliated.

"What is?" she answered back innocently.

"We only intertwined our arms."

"Oh, well, that's the strangest sign of *friendship* I've
ever seen!" Before I repelled her verbal poison, Blake
snapped, "Hey you, now that's enough! I told you we are
childhood friends – *friends*, okay?! What's wrong with linking
arms?" Leila and I nodded in agreement.

"You may have been childhood friends, but look at
them – they're both women, now, aren't they?" I was
fuming almost to explosion, but I reminded myself not to stoop to
her level. *Oh God, here we go,* I shivered when I noticed Leila's
screwed-up face.

"You shut *up*, Freda! No friend of ours will go out
with someone of your ignorance! We've been mates
for ten years, for Christ's sake – if you can't live with
it, sod off!" Leila loudly hissed as if we were alone in the
whole floor, pointing a finger in her face. At that moment, Blake
just watched Leila silently and wide-eyed. But I still think she
overreacted there by stooping to the level I was trying to avoid.
The cleaners spun their heads around, and stopped sweeping to
watch the 'soap opera' going on.

"Blake can make up his own mind, can't you, Blake?"
Silence and a blank stare. "Blake? You're not gonna sit back and
let them talk to me like that?" she squealed in mercy.

"Freda, this is our first date. If there's any chance
whatsoever of a second one, you're going to have to
learn to appreciate the fact that these girls are my
friends – not lovers, not girlfriends, not wives, my best
friends, understood? There was no need to be so
unpleasant to them." Silence again. They stared at each
other. I just threw my hands up at the pointless suspense.

"Oh, I've had enough of this crap. Blake, you're on
your own. I'm going home. Leila, you can sleep over
mine till these two get it together, and you can ring

your parents. You coming or what?"
"Definitely. It's raining outside, but I've got a brolly
in me bag. Let's go. Goodnight Blake." With no reply, we
strolled into the lift we'd missed so many times watching Blake's
and Freda's drama. Huddling and shrieking under the brolly, we
scampered home with great difficulty due to our high-heeled
shoes on the soaked pavement, in which every inhabitant seemed
to have dissolved into the ground. What would have been a
flawless evening through and through was screwed up by our lad-
friend's 'date' – nothing more than a jealous, over-possessive,
pathetic whore with no frigging personality, as we found out.

'Excuse me, Al, but can I go to the toilet? I won't be a
minute.'
'Huh? Oh, yeah, sure. I can decide where to start off
next meanwhile.' Katerina flew herself off the bed and
dashed furiously through the front door, her thumping footsteps
sounding like she tumbled down the stairs. Alana snorted a giggle
to herself.

About five minutes later, she returned and jumped onto the
bed equally furiously. Alana sniggered again. 'Lord, no wonder
you're desperate – I can't remember the last time you went to the
loo.'

'Well, I went this morning – I'd rather hold it in all day
than go into that slop-house!' They both cracked up
into echoing laughter.
'But you don't have much choice here. You have a point,
though, but you get used to it.'
'Yeah, I suppose. Okay, you can start your story again.
One question, though – how did this Freda make Blake
equally unhappy as she did to you and Leila? I mean,
what did she do to Blake and you girls?'
'Some examples, you mean?'
'Yeah.'
'Well, there was this time in…'
Seventh of May, about three weeks later. They continued to
date funnily enough, despite that false start at the party. It was a
Wednesday, as I recall. At ten-to-eight, I took the usual stroll to

the University for my tutorial. While I waited for the lift doors to open, Blake and Leila concurrently halted on either side of me, and Blake commented that I looked nice – I was wearing a vibrant pink boat-necked sweatshirt, and a long black satin skirt. I wished I could say the same about him – he always shaved his face, but not that day. Once out of the lift, we briefly talked about his latest date with Freda. He sounded half-dreaming when he described his day-date of lunch and a stroll along the Thames. All he got was a fake bloody apology for her behaviour, and he fell for it. I felt like being physically sick at his blindness, and I sensed Leila seconded that sentiment. But then his stubbly face relaxed from his elation to almost tears as we wandered through the corridors. "Are you okay?" Before he answered me, a bell alerted. "Hey Blake, you missed your floor." He raised his head in the realisation that he'd followed us to the third floor, and ran a hand through his tousled hair. "Oh shit! Girls, I have to go. We can talk later in the canteen, okay?" He dashed back into the lift, leaving us worried like hell about why his face lengthened like that. "My God, Al, you think he's okay?" Leila gasped.

"I dunno. I suppose we'll find out after the tutorials. I'll see you later, Leila." I was frowning a little. *Could it be that bitch again?*

"Yeah, see ya." Throughout the three-hour tutorial, I tried my utmost to stay alert; even Mr Sutton flashed a glance of concern at me during the lecture, because I looked far-off. I'm sure he thought that because of the way I was acting recently, I was going through some personal anguish that prevented me from performing at my normal best. I *was* listening and taking things down, though. On the way out from the lecture room at midday, he grasped my arm before I acted on rushing to the canteen to find Blake. I turned to face him. "Miss Higgins, are you okay? These past couple of weeks, you've been so spaced out, it's worrying me. Are you sure nothing's bothering you?" *Only my friend, but not so much Adrian these days*, I wanted to say, but I held my tongue and put my brain through a marathon for the right answer. "Yeah, of course. It's just that our neighbours are doing some building work that's keeping me from concentration or getting a decent night's sleep, that's all."

"Oh. Well…" he accepted my answer, thank God, so he trailed off for a few seconds. "Buy some earplugs, and let's get the old Alana Higgins back, please. I don't want you to fail your exam," he grovelled. He obviously missed marking As on my assignments, especially as the exam was in ten weeks time.

"Okay, I will. Try not to worry. I swear, on the Bible if I had one, I will try and get through this one," I tried to comfort him, patting his back – he honestly had a father's concern and upset in his tone. He let me off, and I raced down the corridor, shoving past everyone, into the lift, my stomach turning in dreadful anticipation, out of the lift on the first floor. I came to a dead stop at the doorway ending the stretch of bright, wide hallway. I roamed my eyes around the spacious canteen, completely full with chattering students from most of the floors, apart from this table far back near the window wall facing the road to the suburbs, which had a solitary person amongst the two benches, sipping from a cup. It was Blake, his head turned, gazing at the odd car turning off Uxbridge Road. He looked close to tears, so much so, I could feel his pain and tears just by standing there looking at him. I was snapped back to reality by the hard brush of someone's shoulder. "Oh hi, Higgs. Come back from your own little planet, yet?" I instantly knew it was Flegg-face before I even turned round. but I wanted to see his ugly mug anyway.

"Flegg, I'm warning you – shove off. I'm not in the mood for your crap," I warned fiercely, my finger in his face again.

"Why ever not? You were before," he replied, as brassy as ever.

"Oh, fuck off." I just pushed past him, and marched desperately to that lonely little corner where Blake sat. My hand on his shoulder alerted him out of his thoughts.

"Hi Blake. Can I join you?"

"Sure." He sounded really glum, more than I can remember. I sat opposite him, and bent my head to face him. He looked like he was crying when he looked up at me. So I asked: "Were you crying, Blake?"

"No. Yeah." He sounded ashamed to be weeping by his uncertain answer.

"Look, there's nothing wrong for a guy to be crying.
It's better than going to the pub and drinking yourself
stupid to drown your sorrows." He took a deep breath, and wiped his knuckle under each eye.

"Oh God, Al! What have I done to be treated like this
by her?" He groaned in desperation. Yep, that answered all my questions. "Oh Blake, I knew it was Freda. It was written all over your face. What happened?" He inhaled deeply again.

"Right. When we were coming back from the Thames,
we got into my car, and drove down Oxford Street. She
wanted to shop for a few items for her flat, so I turned
off and parked at a corner street, and we both went into
a grocery shop. We both walked around together, laughing
and picking up things along the way, then she told me to
wait by the door while she paid for the stuff. I politely
asked if she needed any help with the half-a-basket of
groceries, but she refused. My jaw dropped when I saw
her smile and laugh flirtatiously with the cashier, a tall,
dark-haired chap of about six foot, who clearly saw me
with her and the look I was giving him when he looked
at me. I was so upset, I could barely bring myself to utter
a few words during the hour drive back to Hayes. All I
could say was 'Goodnight,' and speed off before she even
went through the door. What on earth did I do wrong, Al?"
His tears started flowing again, obviously the memory clawed his throat as he spoke. I pulled a tissue from the pocket of my denim jacket, and brushed it under his eyes with one hand as I held his with the other.

"Come on now, enough of that. Don't cry over her. She
doesn't deserve you – I mean, look how miserable she's
making you. What's the point of caring for someone
who's gonna make you cry like this?"

"But that's just it. The weird thing about all this is, I still care for her, even though she hurts me with her jealousy. Why?" I couldn't believe what I was hearing from his shaky, sorrowful voice, but I accepted he was too upset to think straight. *"Just try and be compassionate"* was my priority thought at that moment.

"I don't know. But she's jealous because she doesn't trust you, Blake – how can you date a woman that can't even put a little trust in you?"

"I really, really wish I could tell her we should call it off, but I can't. It's almost like I *want* her to hurt me the way she does. It's so difficult to explain. God, I sound like a real wimp, don't I?" We both exhaled a giggle.

"Just a bit. Look, go home and get some rest, then you can decide what you want to do about your relationship, okay?" He nodded, and downed the final contents of his cup. "Do you have any idea what motivated her to flirt with the guy? For example…did you mention me or Leila or both of us? Anything that could have set her off again?" He widened his eyes at me, almost like I'd slapped his face.

"Oh my God, that's it!"

"What?"

"I mentioned on the way to the grocery shop in Oxford Street that I was planning to call you two that night. Remember when you called when I was too upset to call, and you asked why the hell I didn't call? That must have been it." Right then, it hit me; that Saturday, it was ten o' clock, and he was supposed to ring at eight after he dropped Freda home. I called to ask why he didn't call, but he was quite apprehensive, like something was bothering him. I thought it was probably an assignment, like he excused during the call. So for four days, he tried to carry on as normal till he couldn't keep it in anymore. *That's why he stumbled in looking so haggard this morning, and that's why he tried to lighten the moment by describing his date as wonderful, then his face fell and the glint in his blue eyes dulled.*

"Blake, I have never held you back from your happiness, but what I'm about to tell you now is for your own

good – drop this girl, and do it soon before I see you
with this face again." Silence.

"I'll try. Right now, I'm in no mood to decide. I just
want to go home, and lock myself away from my
parents and sister for a good long while." I patted his
shoulder.

"Sure. But I *will* ring later to see how you are."

"Okay." He half-smiled, his crying almost over; I was
relieved to discover my doubts about Freda were now founded by
her treatment of my best mate – she really was a cow. That
evening, after a casual chat with Mum, I called Leila in my room,
explained what was up, and I described the plan I had to split
them up. With her help, I could put it into order.

'What plan was it, specifically?' Katerina asked very
eagerly.

'Well, I'll explain it in the next episode, as it's difficult
to sum it up in one sentence.'

'Sure. Carry on.'

Saturday the seventeenth of May, one and a half weeks
later. He, Christine and their parents planned to take a week's
break in Scotland, not only for relaxation, but also for Blake to
have some peace to revise and to reflect, away from especially
Freda. Three days before they were due to leave, we explained the
plan to Christine on a visit when she was on her own in the house
in her scatty bedroom. She didn't like Freda either, because as his
sister, she was the inside source on the effects she had on him
emotionally. We were sitting on the carpet in lotus positions,
myself and Leila facing her, each of us sipping tea and stuffing
down fairy cakes.

"So, what do you think? Are you in or not?" I demanded.

"Al, like you I would cut off both my hands to ensure
Blake's happiness; he's my blood, and I hate seeing
that cow take over him like that. He can't even think
straight, which is probably why he actually still likes
her and believes her apologies. Yes – I *am* with you

on this," she agreed aggressively in that cute, wispy little
voice of hers, with a spark of determination in her blue eyes, as
much as I thought the beginning was somewhat cheesy.

"Great. We need to find a way to get you to stay home,
like pretend you have studies or pull a sickie or
something," Leila enthusiastically suggested.

"I'll…I know! Al, give me some of your old assignment
papers, and I'll pile them up, and I'll briefly pass them
under Mum and Dad's eyes to say I've been given extra
work before the exam, so I can stay here and help you.
How's that?"

"They don't look at your work with a magnifying glass?"
She giggled girlishly, twisting a lock of her hair round her finger.

"No. In fact, I can't remember the last time they looked
at the question papers, 'cause I use e-mail to help me
with problem questions."

"Brilliant. Well, remember what we told you, and we'll
see you in a few days," I concluded as we rose to our feet
and each of us pecked her on the cheek.

"Sure. Thanks for involving me. I shan't let you down.
'Bye girls."

"Bye, Chris." We saw ourselves out, and dashed, hand-in-
hand and shrieking, to the bus stop just before the end of the
suburban street alongside a speeding bus back to Acton. She
briefly reported on the situation a few hours after Blake and his
parents left on the three-thirty four train to Glasgow after taking a
cab to Euston station. He asked to leave slightly earlier so that he
could say 'bye to me and Leila, who was at my house at the time.
We hugged, and stood outside the doorway waving as the taxi
pulled out. This is the conversation we had, as I recall:

"What's to report, Chris?" I asked, with Leila standing
beside me in my room.

"Well, Freda wasn't exactly very happy when Blake
didn't call her back, but I told her about the 'argument'
between him and his parents, and about him walking
out to God knows where. She was almost in tears. I told
her to try ringing you to find out if you know anything

about what's going on, so be prepared." A brief silence.
"All that's great, but…how the hell could Blake not ring
her before he left? Is he fed up with her finally?" I was
optimistic about not executing the plan if that had happened.
"No. I insisted to Blake that I would ring her on his
behalf, and that he should just have a good time. He
doesn't truly know how I feel about the bitch – yet." *So
much for that*, I thought, disappointed.
"Well done, Chris – you should be in the secret service,
you know! You're good at this."
"Hey, take it easy – it hasn't even started yet!"
"Okay. I'll report after Freda has rung. See you later."
"Okay, bye." Me and Leila punched our fists in the air, and
hugged while leaping all over the place, screaming like
teenyboppers. But then the phone rang again, interrupting our
little triumph. We cautiously picked up the receiver. "Hello?"
"Al? Hi, it's Freda." *Oh shit*, I thought. I mouthed her name
to Leila, who mouthed an "Oh fuck" exclamation.
"Hi. What's up?"
"Have you heard what happened with Blake?"
"Yeah, it's awful. It's come as a shock to us too. I always
thought he had the perfect family, you know."
"What happened?" A long silence followed as I memorized
what to say.
"Look, I know we haven't on the best of terms these
past few weeks, but I'm worried about Blake as much
as you. Please, tell me, what happened, and is there a
chance of finding him?" She pleaded. I took a deep breath.
"Okay. He argued about, oh I dunno, probably you.
They probably think it's private, which isn't fair, because
we've talked about most things over the past ten years.
I haven't a clue where he's gone, or if we'll ever see
him again. The University will obviously be meaningless
if he wants to get away from his family."
"Does he have any other family in this country or any
other?"
"No, I'm afraid." He had aunts and uncles in Scotland,

which was the real reason why he left for a week. She seemed to buy what I said, but I was frightened about what she would break her silence with. "Look, enmity is the last thing we need now. We have something in common – the man we love is missing. How about burying the hatchet and coming for a drink down the pub? There's a terrific pub near Shepherd's Bush. Wanna join me Leila and myself?"

"Well, that's a very welcome offer, but I'm worried about your friend."

"Who, Leila? Don't worry about her. Her mouth just seems to run away with her sometimes. She is embarrassing to me sometimes, too." A that point, I got punched on the shoulder by Leila.

"Sure. See you at six." I reported this back to Christine, who couldn't come because she was under eighteen. Leila changed into my white trousers and pearly-green shift dress, and I changed into a watery blue wrap skirt and a purple Chinese-style top. We met her at the pub and time she specified, sitting in the corner on her own. It wasn't so smoky and crowded that day for some reason. We ordered one half-pint of beer each, but for the umpteenth time since my eighteenth birthday, our ages were questioned. Luckily, our age cards dispelled the stout landlady's doubts, and served us the beer. We chatted like old friends about her background – she was twenty, she was born, raised and lived in Dublin. Her sister was treated superiorly over her, which made her feel really pissed off, until she got a rented flat here in London when she turned nineteen the year before. I forced Leila to apologise for that night at the party, both of us not meaning it. She forced back tears, probably upset about not having anything to control now. But something else was weird about her behaviour – she was nice to us, and was horrible to us when she's with Blake, meaning she was only possessive over Blake when we were around or mentioned by him. Weird or what? I mean, did she ever think how fucked up that really was? That was the artificiality of her, which I'm sure Leila detected too. She was like that for the rest of the week.

'Let me guess – the moment Blake came back, the pair

of you were done for?' Katerina assumed with slight
sarcasm.

'Well...yeah, good guess, Kat.'

'Well, it was obvious!' They giggled through their noses.

Anyway, it was great having her suck up to us, but that
didn't last, sadly. I think she was nice to us because she was
emotionally vulnerable at time, or because she knew she had no
choice but to be nice to us if there was any chance of getting
Blake back. Next Saturday the twenty-fourth of May, he was due
to return from Scotland, hopefully relaxed and focused for the
exam in five weeks. Freda was by my house again, in my room,
eating some cakes my mum had baked. She seemed to take a
liking to her, not knowing the whole story. Leila wasn't there that
day. I excused myself to go to the bathroom. I heard the phone
ringing from outside the bathroom door. *Oh great – it had to be
while I was in the bathroom*, I thought. Then I heard it stop.
Nothing after that- no talking, nothing. Five minutes later, I
rushed out of the bathroom, and back to my room to attend to
Freda. "Who was that, then?" I asked.

"Who was that? Who was that she asked!" she squealed
scornfully, standing hard on her feet. *Uh oh*, I thought, realising
who it was. It was Blake ringing me to announce they'd returned,
but ended up talking to Freda instead. That's when the beans were
spilt.

"This whole damn thing was a charade, the whole time!
This whole friendship façade! By hell, Al, I've seen
some bare-faced cows in my time, but this really takes
the biscuit!"

"Hey, who are you calling a cow? You made him cry
and we made him smile again! You are so God damned
jealous, you're hurting his feelings!" I screamed in
retaliation.

"Well, he seems pretty happy with me so far. That's
the advantage I have over you – I can touch him in
a way he wouldn't let you dare try." I was at boiling point
there, I can tell you.

"I may be just his friend, but trust me, if I were in his

shoes, I'd rather have a friend who made me happy
than a girlfriend that made me miserable, like you!"
"Well, let's see what he has to say about this, then!
I can bet you he'll never talk to you again for controlling
his life!"
"Yeah? He doesn't know what's good for him anymore,
because you've taken away his free will to choose what's
right! We're the only ones who knows what's best for
him! After ten years, it's difficult *not* to know these
things!"
"That's it, I'm telling Blake about this! If you say I'm
domineering, that makes you no better than me!" *Don't
bring me down with your ship,* I thought.

"Go right ahead! I'm not stopping you!" She stomped out
before she acted on the urge to wallop me. *Shit, what a bitch!* I
thought to myself, still infuriated. Naturally, I wanted her out of
my sight for talking to me like that, but never, for one second,
think what twisted tale she was going to tell Blake. I might, *just
might*, have saved our friendship and got rid of her in one fell
swoop, but at that point, my mind was probably as fuddled as
Blake's. I collapsed on my back across the bed, feeling dizzy by
the blood risen to my skin. Mum barged in, obviously startled by
the commotion. "What the Jesus was going on up here, Al?" I
took a deep breath to eliminate the angry adrenalin rush in me.
"Mum, I've got some explaining to do."

Chapter 6.

I sat her down and explained everything. Naturally, because Blake was like a son to her, she was shocked at her attitude towards him. "Blimey, Al, how could he be so stupid as to let this girl twist his mind like that?" she gasped.

"I don't know, Mum. Ever since that University party,
   he's brainwashed into thinking her intentions are honest.
   I'm worried that if this carries on, she'll turn him against
   me and Leila." True fear echoed in my voice. She detected
and comforted this by squeezing my hand.

Around six o' clock that evening, my Mum and I sat at the kitchen table eating dinner, as we did when she came home early. There was no tutorial that day, so we discussed her progress at the firm, trying to lighten the mood. We heard a violent, incessant doorbell ring. I insisted to answer it. I quickened my march as the ringing aggressed. Yanking the door open I saw Blake, his face flushed cross, which startled me. "Hi Blake. Why were you bashing the doorbell for?" I quietly demanded curiously.

"Don't come all innocent on me, Alana! That was a
   downright childish, pathetic and cruel prank you
   pulled to split me and Freda. Don't you have a life
   of your own so you can stop trying to ruin others?" He
hissed, pointing his finger in my face. His tone shocked me into a short silence – I couldn't remember the last time he called me Alana, indicating clear annoyance which frightened me.

"Hey, now, Blake, don't you *dare* accuse me of anything!
   If anyone's doing the ruining, it's that girlfriend of yours!
   What did she tell you exactly?" I growled in return in his
irate tone and finger-in-face.

"Maybe if you didn't keep throwing slurs at her, she
   wouldn't be so nasty to you!"

"Yeah, yeah! Just answer my damn question!"

"She said you told her that I'd fallen out with my family
   and had moved out, but you didn't know where, and
   that you had jealousy issues and tried to split us up."

"Well, surprise, surprise – she's actually telling the truth,

apart from one thing – why the hell would I be jealous
about you, when I wouldn't date you if you were the
last man on earth?"

"Thanks very much! I've got one thing too – who the
fuck do you think you are to interfere? We are happy,
me and Freda.' He sounded as if he was trying to convince
himself that.

"Oh really? Then explain to me why you were bawling
your eyes out only a few weeks ago because of the way
she was treating you? Who made an effort to cheer you
up when she was somewhere not caring a shit how she
made you feel? We did! Me and Leila."

"I didn't understand her as much as I do now. She doesn't
mean to be jealous, but she does that because she worries
about me, and to insist I'm not spending enough time with
her."

"Wrong answer, Blake! She doesn't trust you, and she sees
you as her personal service, not a boyfriend. A real woman
would *ask* for more attention, not get it by flirting with
every man in sight and slagging us off! I can't fucking
believe this is you talking such bullshit!" My pitch
heightened as more bitterness poured out.

"That's her way, Alana – get used to it! You're the one
talking bullshit, not me, and you wanna know why?"

"Why?" I yelled a level higher, my brow crinkled in fury
and my hands thrown from my sides.

"You're jealous because I have someone who cares for
me and you don't! You're stuck in the past. As children,
we used to spend all our time together, and now you
can't come to terms with the fact that we've grown up
and have lives of our own." My mouth dropped open on
hearing this. He didn't hit me, but this was as good as. I was
arguing with Freda, not Blake, because never, from the depths of
his soul, would he say such blatantly nasty things.

"Now that's crap and you know it! I may not have a guy
in my life at the moment, but at least I'm not making it
miserable by someone who won't trust me! You're

saying I'm immature for pulling that stunt, but you're
even *more* immature than me if you're implying that's
true!"

"Right, well, you obviously not accepting our relationship,
so fuck this! We're finished!"

"What?" I shrieked.

"You heard! I'm not talking to you again until you grow
up, like what the rest of us have done. I'll get some friends
who'll accept Freda for who she is, like I have."

"Fine! It's your life!" I yelled, then slammed the door in his
face. Mum rushed to the door with her jaw open. "Good God, Al
– what the hell was that all about?" she gasped; after all, it was
difficult even for Glasgow not to hear our exchange of
obscenities. My hardened, angry face softened into a sorrowful
one, and eventually, melted into tears which gushed heavier every
second. "Oh baby, what went wrong?" she whispered, pulling me
gently into a hug. "Oh God, Mum! My best friend of ten years
doesn't want anything to do with me anymore. This is my worst
nightmare come true. I had high hopes that the plan would make
her leave Blake alone, but it backfired, and I've ended up losing
Blake instead. What am I going to do?" I sighed between sobs, I
hadn't cried in front of her for ages, but it wasn't much of a
remedy. She prolonged the consoling cradle till I stopped crying,
but no one knew my soul's eyes were still tearful. I dreaded the
tutorial the next day, not only due to seeing Blake, but also
because it would be like trying to run with two badly wounded
legs. An hour later, I rang Mr Sutton's personal number to cancel
– he believed me saying I was ill, even though an inflection of
suspicion lurked in there, probably because I only cancelled once
before, and I went *even* when I was sick. But he believed me,
even if he had to force himself. I insisted to Mum that I wanted to
stay in my room all day the next day to recuperate alone. Leila
rang me about two hours after the incident, saying she too was
cursed up by Blake on her doorstep. She quoted almost the whole
argument, which consisted of four letter words worse than what
he told me – he probably got angrier during the interval between
my house and hers. "Freda's a right bitch, but Blake is a complete

ass to put up with it," was her opinion on the matter. When I asked what Christine thought of the whole sorry situation when I rang her to ask if she could report anything else, she said Freda was playing with Blake's free will like a harp of dominance. I was surrounded by so many angles, I couldn't judge and conclude whose fault it was myself. In my room the next day, all day I thought a good sleep would quell all the confusion, but in actual fact, they had accumulated to be unbearable before I'd considered it. After a morning and an afternoon trying to sleep, I spent the entire evening listing every circumstance between Blake and Freda to my knowledge on a page I tore out from my notebook on my desk. I wrote with black ink:

Situations involving Blake and Freda, and who I should blame.

1. The party ----- Argument. Freda's fault. Too domineering. Or maybe it could be Blake's fault for being so blind? After all, he knew damn well that to the untrained eye we looked like his girlfriends. Why did he just stand there like an idiot instead of standing up for her?
2. His date ----- Indiscretion committed by Freda. Flirted with cashier because he mentioned Leila and I. What's her fucking problem? Can't accept two girls as boy's friends? Bitch. Made him cry, probably all night. Why can't he leave her?
3. Blake and Freda's mouthing off at us ----- Because we plotted to split the two of them up. Freda treated us like the enemies. *Us!* Blake was foolish enough to believe that cow, and to do the same to us when we tried to do him good. Said nasty things to both of us. I can't believe he could be so weak-willed.

VERDICT: Undecided. Both their fault – Blake for being so lily-livered, and Freda for her distrust, dominance and maliciousness.

I chucked myself on the bed at around eight o' clock, feeling dissatisfied and disappointed that I couldn't blame one person for what happened. That's probably why I started blaming myself. I really felt Blake had ripped out the piece of my heart that responded to him for ten years. I felt so alone, even though I still had Leila and Christine. I watched *Green Collar* on the telly, which I hadn't watched for weeks, surprisingly. I hadn't even bought any magazines or newspapers with articles of him in it for weeks either. But after thirty minutes of seeing Adrian again brought a current of relief and repressed feelings back up again, that sense of belonging whenever I looked at him. It was like being reunited with a first love or something. Unfortunately, I hadn't set the video recorder, so I finally lulled my eyes to close by replaying the episode of him in my mind. Once I switched the telly off, I was assured that my future was that guy on the screen, and pacified into a floaty dream with us cradling each other till the morning in my bed, the first I'd had in over two months. I was shocked awake by the phone. I groaned, rolling off the bed to my desk, the slit of sunlight blinding me, causing my toe to clonk painfully on its leg. I picked up the receiver after five rings, squinting to ignore the pain as it numbed itself. Nothing made sense after I said hello, but I recognised the shrill voice as Christine's, which was an alarm clock in itself. This was what she broke to me:

"Al, I hate to tell you this, but Blake found out I was a 'mole' in our plan."

"Say what?" I shrieked disbelievingly, now snapped to full awareness.

"Yeah. He found the assignment papers you lent me when he was tidying up my room when I was at school, then when I got home, we had one hell of a row, effing and blinding at me almost like a drunkard, and now he won't talk to me at all. Obviously Mum and Dad heard, 'cause they were both home, they expressed their views about Freda, and now…" she paused after half-sobbing, half-whimpering.

"He won't talk to them either?"

"Yeah. How did you guess?"

"It's obvious. Freda has detached Blake from one of the most important things in his life – his family."

"I know. You know, my own brother, well, *our* brother,

has turned into a right asshole," she said bluntly, now
sounding angry. "I was lucky he didn't hit me." She paused again
after a deep breath.

"Yep, you don't have to tell me that. He's treating us
like his enemies after all these years, and his own
blood too? Jesus Christ," I groaned.

"I know. There's nothing we can do now. We can just
hope and pray to God he snaps out of it soon. I know
it sounds harsh, but he won't listen to any of us – we
have to face facts." I took a deep, apathetic drawl, forcing
myself to accept the correctness of what she said.

"Yeah, you're right. The old Blake will come back soon," I
said listlessly. Over the weeks up till late June, I restarted
collecting bits and pieces of Adrian from papers and magazines,
and looking at the once forgotten scrapbook at almost every little
chance I got. It filled the void Blake left, who didn't even call or
drop by once, and scowled at me and Leila at the University, and
I felt that pining for him again.

'Lord, that must have been the pits for you,' Katerina
commented empathetically.

'It was, Kat. But Adrian helped me to get through it. I don't
miss him so much now.'

'But if you took away Adrian, would you miss Blake
more than you do now?' Silence as Alana stilted her eyes
upwards in thought for a minute or so. 'Oh, never mind that. So
what happened next? Your drinking problem – that's it, right?'

'Well, not quite. I'll begin a week before the exam in
late June, which was nearly five weeks after our argument.'

'Okay. Well, before you begin, how about a cup of tea?'

'Sure.' Katerina turned her head back to the sleeping area
from the 'kitchen' to look at Alana, whose appearance was
somewhat…fatigued, like she'd been down a hundred miles of
bad road. Her eyes filled up with pity again, but then decided to
leave the sorry feeling to her new friend. She returned her
concentration to balancing the metal teapot on the stove. She
looked at the clock above the doorway – it read quarter-to-two in
the afternoon.

Chapter 7.

'Thanks, Kat,' Alana whispered as she accepted the warm mug. Katerina nodded. She rested the mug on the bedside cabinet before lobbing herself on her back on the bed, rolled onto her side and propped her head with a hand, and taking a sip. 'Right, let's start again. You wanted to talk about before your exam?'

'Yep. One week before the twenty-seventh of June, which was the date of my exam. Here goes…'

Adrian-itis further infested me. My assignment results went further down the pan – from As I got Ds and sometimes Es, which was disgraceful, I know – mainly because I was suppressing memories and sightings of Blake with feelings for Adrian; in other words, my heart overtook my head – so maybe you are right, Adrian stopped me from missing Blake so much. Anyway, during those five weeks, I made a fruitless attempt at finding him through clues in articles, detective work, the library, directory enquiries, and so on, but that was before I thought of the Internet Café idea, and was earning the money to pay for it. I couldn't understand why he was living in London and I still couldn't find him, but then I thought this is a big city, so my search wouldn't be as narrow as it would if it were somewhere outside London. I don't bother with it nowadays – it's just overrated nonsense. I tried to revise as well as I could in that last week, but my brain felt so shallow, I didn't even know what day it was half the time; it was a slap in the face when I discovered it was only seven days to the day my ambition depended on, but every day of that week alone was more detrimental to me than the past weeks. I'll take you through day-by-day:

Friday: my skull felt like it was going to split the moment I awoke, mainly because only a wink could describe the amount of sleep I had, at ten to eight that morning. I just threw on a fitted white t-shirt and beige loose jeans, my hair into a high ponytail, and smeared some black eye shadow and pink lipstick. At the breakfast table, while Mum was preparing herself for work in the bathroom, I took a couple of painkillers. I was tempted to take an extra one, judging by the excruciating pain, but I knew it

wouldn't be just the pain I'd be killing. At around eight-thirty,
Mum breezed past me, kissed me on the cheek. Before I knew,
the door vacuumed shut from the outside. She was supposed to be
there at nine, as usual.

At the University, once I reached my floor, the tablets still
hadn't kicked in yet – I honestly didn't know how I'd make it
through the morning. I bumped into Leila in the hallway when
she on the way to the science tutorial room, which was on the
same floor. "Hi Al. My God, you okay? You look terrible," she
gasped, almost unable to speak as she patted my shoulder and
guided me to a corner out of the chaotic rush of students. She
knew I always took as much pride in my appearance as Blake and
herself.

"I've felt terrible for the past month and half, Lill.
Blake looks at us like we don't exist. How do you
think that makes me feel?" I groaned with a palm on my
forehead.

"I know, I know. But it's like Chris said, we can only
wait till he sees sense for himself."

"I've had to force myself through each day, including
this one. That stubborn asshole that used to be my
friend has reduced me to this. Sometimes, I wonder
why the hell I still come here," I groaned, throwing my
hands up despairingly.

"Now, come on, don't bloody well say such a thing!
It'll be all over next week, so try and cheer up. Has
Mr Sutton questioned you?"

"No, not recently. I don't think he cares anymore. Or
maybe he's still worried, but doesn't wasn't to ask,
because I keep giving him the same answer."

"Well, that's good enough. How about a night in tonight
at my place?"

"I'll think about it. If I don't feel any better by this
evening, I won't bother."

"Oh please, Al, don't leave me with that long face stuck
in my head for the rest of the day," she pleaded girlishly,
pairing stomping her foot with folded arms. Before I could

answer, the bell rang with a shrill that quaked my head. Leila saw
this.

"Damn that bell. Okay, I'm off. See you after class,
and hang in there."

Throughout the lecture, I tried to keep listening and writing
things down. From what I gathered, it seemed Mr Sutton was
giving me stares indecipherable other than concern and
disappointment, but he just carried on pacing and talking. It also
seemed that whether I wanted to pass or not was my choice. I
thought "Thank God" when he announced it was over, which was
around midday. As I guessed, he didn't confront me on how I
looked or anything else, so I dashed into the lifts and out of the
building before anyone saw me, and waited for Leila to follow. I
stood at the bus stop for ten minutes, shaded by the fierce noon
sunrays, but not the bitter, contradictory autumn breeze. I saw her
stride across the road, her hair violently slicked back by the
breeze and her impulsive dash to the bus stop, till she saw me
standing there. "Al! What are you doing here?" she shrieked.

"I had to get out of that University before he saw me.
I've…umm, decided to join you after all. I'm not doing
anything tonight. Sod him – if he wants that woman to
control him, good luck to him." Of course, I was only
lying to make myself feel shallowly better.

"Who, Blake?" I nodded. She said 'Who, Blake?' Who else
would I be talking about? That's how much she cared about the
whole incident. Either she thought I was too soppy about the
whole thing, which couldn't be helped, couldn't care less, or just
succeeded where I failed – blocking it out. But I was too upset to
raise the issue with her. "Yeah, I agree. Thanks for choosing to
join me! We can order pizza, buy some booze and a couple of
videos. Here's the bus – I guarantee it'll make us feel a whole lot
better, okay?" We stepped into the folded open doors, paid the
driver and wobbled our way to the back seats of the partially
empty bus. We popped into this local hypermarket a few paces
away on the main road from her suburban home, and bought two
bottles of vodka and some other bits and pieces, the adjacent
video rental shop for two videos, then her home at around four. I

greeted Lily, who sat on a white leather sofa watching the telly. I saw her making a grovelling facial expression. The living room she sat in was a wide space to the right from the front door, platformed with polished artificial wood flooring, and surrounded by two walls on the inside with a large curtained window incorporated into each. Opposite was another wide space with an all-white kitchen – white cupboards, white tiles between the gaps, a fridge fitted into the smallest side of the three-sided rectangle, and a small window over the sink facing the garden, shielded by a white lace net curtain. We excused ourselves to go up the stairs, which started next to one of the kitchen walls. "Whew – thank God she didn't ask about what was in the bag." she gasped as we strolled up the stairs with our stuff.

"Yeah, but I'm sure she will tomorrow morning."

"You've got to promise me something."

"What's that?"

"Whoever goes out first must take these bottles for chucking out."

"Deal." We did a high five to salute that.

"Right, well, I'll phone the pizza place." She dashed over to the phone on her bedside cabinet, while I sat with my legs stretched out on the aqua carpet and poured ourselves two glasses of vodka. I turned round to glance at the clock above the doorway – it read four thirty. After she returned from the phone, she sat beside me in a similar posture, and received the glass I handed to her. "Right, what shall we toast to?"

"Mmm…let's see…ah, that's it! The exam!" I squeakily decided.

"Okay. Good luck to our exams, Al. Cheers." We clinked our glasses together as I returned the gesture. Before we finished the first glass of the undiluted stuff, she heard the doorbell. She dashed down the stairs, and returned ten minutes later with a flat box with our pizza. We squealed as I opened the box, and she slotted one video into her video recorder and turned on the telly opposite her bed. We spent the rest of the evening stuffing, drinking, watching movies and giggling like kids again. Well, maybe except for the booze, of course.

About three hours later, everything became a fragmented, buzzing confusion. I looked at the empty vodka bottle, increasing my appetite for more. I felt like a vegetable, but loved the warm, fuzzy feeling it gave me –the distinct tipsiness tipsy people raved on about. I completely forgot Leila was in the room whenever she ceased talking, even if it was just a few seconds. I saw her struggle to heave herself to a seated position. "I'm opening…the…other…bottle…now. You…want some?" she stuttered, partially sleepy, just as I felt, too. "Yeah, why not?" I was so inebriated, I felt asleep without meaning to. We were sitting on the floor, so I must have dropped off right there, and Leila wasn't far behind. The last thing I remember about that evening is Leila calling my name, which gradually quietened to total silence, then I found myself strolling along some deserted shore somewhere, and my hand being clasped by someone. I heard this male voice calling my name next to me, as well as clashing water. I looked to the sky – it was a clear night with a full moon as a spotlight on the entire area, adorned by a couple of wispy clouds – then I turned my head to him. It was Adrian, still with that relaxed, boy-next-door adorableness I described earlier, wearing a loose grey silk shirt, and black crinkled karate outfit-style trousers of some delicate material, probably silk too. "Yes?" I finally answered gently.

"What were you thinking about?"

"Oh, I was still thinking about Blake, and what he said."

"Look, I know you're still upset about losing him, but
you can't keep dwelling on this and blaming yourself.
As an adult, it's his choice to make or break his life
however he wants to. I can't bring him back to you no
more than you can yourself, but I can try and make you
happy again. I love you, Al. The reason doesn't matter;
I know I do." I literally floated in that mild voice and accent of his, while staring at him, trying to absorb what he just said. With that, he slid my arms round my waist, squeezed me against his trunk, and grasped the nape of my neck for an impassioned snog. He then broke off and gazed into my eyes as if his life had begun and ended at the same time. We aimlessly

strode a little towards the edge of the placid waves, then he grasped my shoulders, pushed me down with him into a crouch, then on top of him between his legs. We began that snog again, the waves washing over our feet, each wave gradually coating higher over us as we began unbuttoning our shirts…

The next memory after that was finding myself lying on the floor, facing Leila, who looked half-dead lying on her back at right angles from me on the floor, with an ashen colour all over her skin. I frowned as I thought about that dream and what set it apart from the others. The whole floor was scattered with pizza bits, glasses, and the empty and full bottle of vodka – she never got round to drinking the other one. I stood up, my head began throbbing more angrily than when I was lying down, but I concentrated on the pleasant part of it. "Leila? Lill? Wake up, it's morning. It's…nine-o-nine in the morning," I slurred, trying to focus my blurry vision on the clock. She murmured some gibberish, which she sometimes does when she's awake, turned to face me, and blinked her eyes open. "Morning, Al," she strained. "I've…got the most awful headache. I…I can't move…the stuff! Get rid of it before Mum comes in here!" she suddenly yelled, disturbing the levelling process in my head. "Shut up, Lill! She's gonna hear us!" She accepted my offer of help, then I pushed her shoulders from behind to a seated position. "Oh God, I'm gonna be sick…take me to the bathroom, now!" she groaned and then yelled, her throat distinctly jerking. I yanked her to her feet by her armpits, and with her arm round my shoulder, dragged her quickly out of her room to a perpendicular door, and kicked it open. I pushed her onto her knees with her face down the toilet bowl. She began convulsing and heaving the stale booze out her stomach seconds later. The sound, and smell, of it wanted to make me do the same, so I told her to come back to the room when she'd finished cleaning herself up. Half an hour later, she stumbled from the bathroom wearing a violet bathrobe, wet hair slicked back, still looking washed out (Course she'd look washed out – she just came out of the shower! Ha ha! Ahem…) The night before, she wore a vivid pink tank top, and blue jeans, both stained from the food and drink. "How you feeling?"

"Rotten," she whispered, running a comb through her hair. I giggled. I had made two cups of black coffee from a kettle and supplies in a small cupboard above her desk. I felt a bit guilty for not stopping her from drinking that much, but I didn't realise getting drunk was so pleasurable. "Here, drink this. And here are two painkillers. This should do the trick." She accepted the mug and tablets, and she desperately chucked them down her throat, recoiling from the mug as it burned her lip. Luckily, I found out her parents had gone to work, and decided not to disturb us. I stayed until about eleven in the morning, then I caught the bus back home, my head not lightening with the deep breaths of the fresh morning air I was taking during the walk. On the middle seat of the bus, I wondered why the hell *I* wasn't sick, even though we drank half a bottle of vodka each, and both of us woke on the floor with splitting headaches? When I reached home, I turned the key to a lonely house, which was usual at nearly midday, so I just slumped my limp, hung-over self on my bed and flicked through the scrapbook from under the mattress, dwelling on the wonderful multi-dimensional sensation of that drunken dream. *When I was drunk,* not *when I was sober,* I rethought.

Later on Saturday: I lied in my bed for the remainder of the morning and all afternoon, in complete solitude and peace as if the house weren't shared at all. Still feeling a bit smashed, I was still comparing the sober dreams of Adrian and when from when I was stoned. I could've sworn that someone, or something, transported me to that beach, wherever it was, and extradited me back to Leila's room. And towards the end – I don't know if I brought it on myself in my sleep or what, but I could've sworn I felt that shudder normally associated with lovemaking – not that I'd know about the real thing, of course. That had to be the main difference. So at around three that afternoon, I changed from my pyjamas to a pair of navy blue combat trousers and a black, v-neck, fitted t-shirt, took a twenty-pound note from my box of pocket money Mum gave me, which I hardly used, and dashed out the front door. The weather was really damp and morbid; it drizzled a little, which mixed every impurity in the air and on the ground into slushy puddles all over the place. The steely grey skies swamped the slightest chance of sunshine seeping through. Nice day, I thought sarcastically. I headed to Ealing Broadway. I halted and turned into the shop I was looking for with eyes narrowed to shield the rain. I went up to the cashier as I pulled out the note. "A bottle of that vodka, please," I requested to the middle aged, dark skinned Indian guy. He handed it to me, I paid him, and he didn't ask about my age. I was really pleased, because I was eighteen at the time, even though I looked younger; kids of twelve get away with it without being asked once, and here I was, the legal age, and I kept being questioned when I bought things intended for adult use. Ridiculous, huh? I sprinted back home, pulling the hood of my leisure coat over my head, and holding the bottle tightly. When I reached outside my door again, and twisted the key in the front door, I prayed that Mum wasn't home yet. Her home times were so erratic at that time, because her work load varied. There was still silence in the house, just as I left it – she hadn't returned home, thank God. So I took off my coat and shoes, rushed into the kitchen for a glass from a little ornament cupboard with a glass door perpendicular to the supplies' cupboards behind the cuboid. I dashed across the hall from the kitchen door to my room, and slumped myself on the bed. I desperately twisted the bottle cap, dumped a whole glass full of the stuff, and gushed it down my throat. I ended up spluttering out half of it back into the glass, because of its sheer bitterness, but when I engulfed a mouthful again, I decided to swivel it around in my mouth to dilute it a bit. It actually worked in dulling the taste a bit, but not the power it had over my head. The last thing I remembered doing was shoving the glass and the vodka under the bed. All of reality and time faded away as I felt sleepier. My last thought was, "It may be bitter, but it's liquid sugar when I think of you, Adrian," then I fell asleep, and as I predicted, I dreamed of him…

I was in my own kitchen, chopping vegetables on the worktop with a bored expression – I didn't like cooking that much, and neither did Mum. I think I must have been preparing supper, because it was five o' clock in the afternoon. I was expecting someone home, but it wasn't Mum – the dream was about actually having that whole house to myself and my husband or something. I heard the front door click, and a male voice calling my name as he closed it. I excused the task I was doing to stand in front of the doorway, brushing the vinyl black apron I was wearing. Adrian finally faced me after he removed his black fabric mackintosh coat, grey jacket and shoes, and squeezed me into his embrace and kissed me on the cheek. "Hi, Mrs McCraedie." My face always sparked when he called me that.

"Hi, Adrian. How's your day?"

"Oh, awful. Right now, I wish I didn't have to go to
work tomorrow." He stood with his rump against the worktop, running a hand through that lovely head of soft hair, as I returned to chopping. "Cooking dinner?" he queried curiously, gazing on what I was chopping. I gawped at him yanking the noose-like tie half-open, and releasing the top buttons of his shirt till it almost reached the middle of his chest. I slammed down the knife pessimistically in a disguised response to that. "Yeah, and getting pretty sick of it, too."

"Aww…" he pulled me possessively into his arms, and began tenderly and circularly rubbing my top of my back, with the other arm round my waist; he felt the same surge of pleasure that bolted through me. He slightly inched away from me, so that our eyes met for what still seemed like the first time. Then he eagerly grasped each side of my face, and a *very* passionate kiss ensued, tongues and all. We deliberately stumbled backwards till I almost bruised my bum on the edge of the sink. We awkwardly shifted along there, still snogging, till my lumbar region was a little sore. Still petting all over our bodies, he suddenly stopped as my hands were on the curve of his chest, about to unbutton his shirt, and pushed me down into a crouch with him along the side of the washing machine, so I sat with my stocking-coated legs bent and wide open to encase his hips. He then unfastened the front of a dowdy, floral housewife's dress I was wearing under the apron, revealing the not so dowdy undies I was wearing – it was an aqua blue lacy bra, but I don't know what I wore on my other half. His heavy breathing and anticipation made me more fervent for him. I then reached my hands down for the fastening of his trousers, and unbuttoned and unzipped it. "Oh, Al..."

"Al?" Adrian's impassioned heavy breathing suddenly became a familiar, whispery voice. I languidly opened my eyes against my own will. I saw Mum hovering over me with a plate in one hand and a mug in the other. "Al, you're awake! I've made some tea and a ham sandwich for you." A bit drunkenly startled, I jolted myself to recline my back against the bed head, and received the plate on my lap as she rested the mug on the bedside cabinet. "When did you get back?" I asked croakily, rubbing my eyes.

"Only half-an-hour ago. How come you fell asleep in your clothes? Where did you go?" *Oops, I thought*, gazing at my slightly crinkled clothes. "Oh, umm...I just went for a walk towards Broadway – not completely there, but almost. I just wanted to clear my head a bit. I...guess I was a bit knackered after that." My voice was still a bit slurred. I rambled blasphemously about Blake again, which I think scared her a bit. She then told me to stop blaming myself, because she knew Freda didn't respect me and Leila, and yet he still dated her. After ten years of defending him in arguments, I was still convinced it was Freda's fault. But I didn't care anymore. I spent the rest of that day in my room, as Mum went to type out her documents and make phone calls. I slept without a dream after that.

Monday: Got up at usual time of ten to eight. Freshened up. Mum wasn't there. Ate breakfast on my own for the umpteenth time in a good month or so. Went to University for the tutorial. Not out of duty as before, but just going through the motions. Bumped into Leila. Blake looked at me like something stuck to the bottom of his shoe again. Mr Sutton still giving me those funny looks throughout the tutorial, those "What am I doing wrong?" looks. At noon, I went to the canteen. Sat at the same table as Leila. Discussed each other's tutorials, without so much as a mention of Blake, or a sighting for that matter. She showed me this funny wire model of, oh I don't know, probably a genetic one – I can't really recall. I burst out laughing at its crudity, and Leila sternly looked at me in faux offence, then joined in my chortling. I instinctively looked behind me. About five seats

away, a rather good-looking guy I didn't recognise flashed us a
really broad, inviting smile, and gave a slight wave. "Hey, Al,
that guy over there is looking at you!" she howled quietly,
holding my hand and winking assuredly. "No he's not – he's
looking at you!" I protested playfully, nearly blushing.

"What makes you say that?"

"He waved when you turned your head."

"Nonsense. He eyed you up when you were laughing."

"Well, I've got an infallible method for finding out."

"What's that?" She warily twisted her head round the whole
room.

"Al, I'm off to the ladies. I'll see you in a mo," she
announced loudly enough for him, but not the whole room, to
hear. "God, you are so embarrassing sometimes."

"Just go with me here, okay?" she whispered near my ear.
She strutted through the tables and chairs, leaving me
uncomfortably on my own. I fidgeted with the coffee cup handle
for several seconds. Until I saw him tilt his head before mine to
make eye contact. "Hello," he said almost jokily, flashing that
warm smile again. "Hi." He sat opposite me, still smiling. "I'm
Ryan, Ryan Creed. You?" *Direct – I like that*, I thought to myself.
"Alana Higgins. You new here?"

"No. I've been studying Statistical Maths here for the
    past seven months. How about you?"

"I'm preparing to take my Journalism exam next week.
    How come I've never seen you before?"

"Dunno. Probably some force above said we should
    meet today." I twitched up my eyebrow at this guy's James
Bond-style smoothness that charmed a smile from me. "Who's
your friend?"

"Who just left? That's Leila Drayton. She studies
    Nutrition, and her exam is on the same day as me.
    We've been friends for ten years, now. She's like a
    crazy sister to me!"

"Wow. I wish I had friendship as long as that."

"Well…" I trailed off at his flattery.

"I hope I'm not too forward, but do you think we could

go and see a movie or something tomorrow?" *Ooh, so it really was me he was looking at. Well, what's to lose? This guy has Adrian's sort of charm, so...*

"Well, I'm not doing anything except my assignment, so why not?" His very dark eyes practically lit up when I accepted. "Well, okay, then. My forwardness often puts girls off, so I'm really pleased. Shall we swap phone numbers?"

"Yeah. Wait, I've got a paper and a pen in my coat. I prefer directness – I hate hanging on a string."

"Well said, too." I tugged out the pen, tore the paper in half, wrote each other's numbers down and swapped the scraps. "Cheers, Ryan. I'll see you at about...seven?"

"Yeah, seven's fine. I'll see you then. Call me."

"Sure. 'Bye." He upped from the chair, grabbed his duffel bag from his previous seat, and proceeded to the doorway. He looked over his shoulder to wave again. I returned the gesture. Before I decided to turn my head back to my own business, Leila returned from the ladies (or from doorway eavesdropping!) to return to her seat next to me. "See? What did I tell you?!" she squealed, grabbing my face and kissing my cheek repeatedly in a hyped-up way. "Alright – that's enough! He only asked me to a movie, for God sakes," I said in a low-key manner, pushing her away.

"But it's the first date you've had in years!"

"Yeah, but I hardly know a thing about him, apart from the fact he studies Maths here."

"Oh well, you were always the modest sort. But congrats anyway."

"Thanks." I spent the rest of the day thinking how much Ryan resembled Adrian in terms of confidence, directness and charisma. He was cute, too – cropped dark curly hair, mixed race skin, about five-nine in height and medium build. He wore a jade green shirt and black loose jeans, which also reminded me of Adrian due to its simplicity. Mum was dead pleased with my new 'beau' when I described him, and looked forward to meeting him soon. I spent the evening working on the last ever assignment with an enthusiasm I hadn't felt for ages. He also had an advantage over Adrian – he was having positive effect on me. I watched *Green Collar* at eight, looked at him on the screen and thought, "I'll get over you, Adrian – somehow."

Tuesday: That afternoon, I wandered around Shepherd's Bush market like a stranger, oblivious of the whizzing shades of dark and light skins, feeling bubbly about the date, only overshadowed a little by the exam. I called Ryan to confirm our date – that night at seven. I gazed amongst the stalls, looking for an outfit, and exited the other end so I could pass the job centre on the spidery network of roads. I was eighteen, for God's sake, and I was still scrounging off Mum. Well, it was caused by my course, which I needed not worry about then, and Mum's home law – as long as she works, no child of hers works under her domicile. That law classifies a young adult as myself working as child labour or something. I was, and still am, grateful for all she'd given me as I grew, but adult independence turns that into scrounging. I dashed through the market to the other main road, equally crazy, for the bus stop at around four.

I kipped till six, when my preparations swung right into action – dash in shower, dash out, best undies (for my ego boost – I'm not that kind of girl, okay?!), new outfit of a purple crocheted cardie (decent enough not to need a vest underneath) and a blue-pink hologram-type pencil skirt. The franticness slowed down as I slicked my hair into a high ponytail and dabbed pastel pinks on my lips, cheeks and eyes. *Oh no, I look like a blancmange*, I thought, so I wiped off the eye shadow, and smeared a blue-green instead. *There, I look human, thank God.* I rushed out to the living room and stood in the middle. "Ta-da!" I shrieked, calling Mum to lean against the hallway frame. "My, my Al – you look sixteen again, and great." She strolled over and kissed me on the cheek, recoiling, studied my appearance and sighed in pride. "I'll make us a cuppa while your prince arrives." I breathed out a modest chuckle. "Well, I wouldn't call myself a Cinderella."

"You look like one, though."

"Thanks." She headed back to the kitchen as I backed my bum onto the sofa and crossed my legs. As seven approached, I began twiddling and yanking the rings on my four left digits, and nibbling at my bottom lip. Mum had finished cooking, surprising me with the fact that she remembered how to cook, and plonked herself next to me, exhausted but content. My breathing became irregular and heavy. "God, where is he? For Christ's sake, where is he?!" I begged hysterically, Mum observing me almost pulling my fingers from their sockets. "Alright, alright, calm down. Stop beating yourself up and lie down. That's what I'm going to do, so rest here till you hear the door," she shrilled reassuringly, stroking one shoulder blade. I replied with a deep breath and, "Alright, then." With that, she smirked amusement, and left for her bedroom. I slung my legs up, and rested my head on the squashy cushion in a way not to ruffle my hair…

Next thing I remembered was my shoulder being shaken by a firm hand. I turned my head to see it was Mum. I was startled to my feet before her, and asked, "Is it seven-thirty yet?" Her eyes softened with disappointment into my pink and sore eyes. "It's ten-thirty, dear. Oh God, I'm so sorry." Was I disorientated, dreaming or really standing? I didn't really know. "Wha…what do you mean?" I muttered. She inhaled deeply. "You've…been stood up. It seems this Ryan fella isn't all he's cracked up to be."

"Well, I didn't really raise my hopes…" I drifted off, trying to lighten the humiliating moment. Then I accepted defeat. "This was a chance to start over, for God's sake – to know a nice guy to end the University, but…it ended before it even began, didn't it? It seems I dressed up for bloody nothing." I exploded, which ended with a whine, almost to tears. "Come here." She encouraged a cradling embrace to prevent me from fully crying. It worked, but I was too tired and upset to cry anyway. With a compassionate look, and clasping each side of my face, she whispered, "Get an early night, Al. You can deal with him tomorrow, okay?" I nodded, and brushed past her and the hallway. "Al?"

"Yes, Mum?"

"You know, I've never met this guy, but he's a complete bloody idiot. What guy in their right conscience would stand up a beautiful, intelligent girl like you?" I modestly smiled and rolled my eyes.

"Thanks. Goodnight, Mum."

"Night, dear." I stumbled into my room, and changed into a nightshirt immediately. Under my duvet, staring at the opposing wall, I sipped the last drop of the fourth glass of vodka, needing to dream again. At around twelve, I crashed into an instant sleep.

Chapter 8.

'Did you confront Ryan successfully?' Katerina queried with a raised eyebrow, trying to avoid the topic of her drinking again.

'Well, yeah, but I still felt humiliated and stupid. I mean, wouldn't you feel the same if you hadn't had a date in four years, and then when it happens, you get stood up?' Silence as she pondered, then finally answered with a nod.

'Course I would. But why did he smooth-talk you into a date in the first place?'

'Good question. Maybe I looked like an easy target to a smooth-talk or something. Anyway, nothing particularly interesting happened on Wednesday, unless you count going to the University and wallowing, so here goes with Thursday and Friday of that horrid week…' Alana preceded with a deep breath.

Thursday: Lord, what a wonderful dream I had that night, I maundered as I fluttered my eyelids at the ceiling, feeling flustered. I'd invited my friend Adrian to my house, which was isolated as usual. Stuffing our faces with pizza, we watched three film tapes from my collection in the living room. The front of the sofa propped our backs up. A few hours later, I switched off the telly, and managed to talk him into staying for a while longer. I spotted my make-up bag on the tea table between us and the telly before I returned to my seat. I inconspicuously insisted that we played a game. He accepted, which cued me to grab the bag. "Let's see what you'll look like with make-up on."

"Huh?" he shrieked, springing forward.

"It's okay, I'm not turning you into a ponce or anything!"

"I hope not! I get accused of it already in my job." I wrinkled my mouth to stop bursting out laughing, and instructed him to sit back and close his eyes. I delved my hand in for a crimson lipstick. "Here goes your makeover, Ade."

"Don't I get to make you over, too?"

"Not yet, pal. You just sit back and enjoy," I growled in a silly, and rather pitiful, Southern accent. I began by tracing round his mouth, then circling his cheeks, nose and forehead, till he looked as if he had clown-itis! I giggled stupidly, which shrank his face to a cross look. In a flash, he clenched my shoulders and rammed me to where he sat, swapping places. He pinned my arm above my head, forcing me to give in when he grabbed the lipstick. I pushed my tongue out at him in pretend disappointment. "Right, time's up – time for your makeover." My giggling fit loosened into a fledged explosion of laughter as he began copying the same facial paths on me, while using his other hand to pin my arm up. "Keep still." I suddenly sparked off a playful scuffle on the floor to regain power over the lipstick, still laughing our heads off. He won by straddling me, both our bellies cramping up from the laughter. He collapsed on me as a result, till our nose tips made contact. The chortling faded into a mutually desirous stare, which ended at a snog with equal desire and exploration that eventually spread to our roaming hands, resting at the bases of our spines. He retreated with a look of rue on his crimson-smeared face. I didn't feel the look on his face, so I kneed him gently over to his back, and sat across him. With an evil little grin that he failed to interpret, I snatched the lipstick from his fist. "It's okay, Ade. We didn't do anything wrong, and I can prove it." I lifted off his pale blue clinging polo shirt, my eye automatically rolling down that chest and that stomach, and began drawing in the grooves of his segmented muscles. I involuntarily moaned in approval at this sight, which finally enlightened him of my feelings. He giggled at the tickling, even more so when I leaned to peck along the drawn areas. Well, you know what normally happens when chemistry takes over, don't you?! I focused my blurry vision on the alarm clock – it read midday or something. Once again, I woke with an agonising headache, but also a wonderful buzz from that dream, the same reason as before.

That day, I was determined for a justification of how he had the conscience to stand any girl up, let alone me. Mum discussed her disappointment for me and wished me well for my confrontation over breakfast. I took this to heart, however much I was dreading it. In my room, I dialled his number unhesitatingly, and waited for about four rings. "Hello?"

"Hi, is this Ryan?"

"Yeah?"

"This is your date speaking," I replied almost sinisterly.

"Oh," he answered somewhat guiltily.

"You know, I don't know what your problem is, but
      if you had cold feet, or if you did this because of some
      sick joke or a bet, did you ever think to let me know?" I
stuck a stiffened forefinger at the mouthpiece.

"Look, I'm sorry, okay?"

"Sorry? *Sorry?* That's all you can say? What a bloody
      pitiful prat you are! Why?"

"Umm…"

"What? Come clean, Ryan!" I snapped.

"A little birdie has changed my mind about dating a drunk."
he said in an insulting growl.

"A drunk? What the…what are you talking about?"

"You heard!" Who the frig wanted to spite me with
something that was overblown and was none of anybody's
business? So I asked just that.

"Okay. And who, might I ask, is this little birdie who
      filled your head with this crap?"

"I don't rat on my sources. You, a future journalist,
      should know that."

"If you don't tell me, I'll rat *you*!"

"And I don't *rat*!"

"The only rat here is you, pal. Now tell me before I rip
      your vital organs out in public tomorrow!" I hoped my
increasingly threatening voice would crumble his defences. I was
right.

"Alright, alright, it's Leila! Satisfied?" A dead silence
followed.

"You really have some bloody nerve accusing her of such
      a thing!"

"If you want proof, ask yourself."

"Right. I will."

"I don't need to convince some drunk…"

"*Fuck off*, Ryan! And good riddance!" I screamed. With that, I smashed the receiver down. *Bloody terrific. Now I'm going to be remembered as the fabulous student who fell on her bum because of booze.* I prayed that Leila didn't have anything to do with it, because if I ditched her over it, the fab three, as we were known to our families, would become from the fab two the fab none. Without further ado, I dialled her number, and innocently asked her to come over to mine to discuss a personal matter. She accepted, and said the quickest she could be over was an hour, because of the erratic bus service. At around two, Mum answered the unmistakable double knock, and allowed her access to knock on my room's door. I looked up to see her peer through my room's door.

"Hi, there, Lill. Come in and shut the door…" I trailed off in a sweet tone, then I roared, "…and tell me what the hell is going on?! What part did you play in thwarting my date with Ryan yesterday?" She whipped her head to me in surprise.

"Huh?"

"Last night he stood me up, and when I confronted him about it, he said it's because I was a drunk. And who told him? He said it was you! So shed some light on this matter, now!"

"What?! The little…why?!" she growled with a crumpled brow.

"You tell me!" I yelled back.

"The bastard! Can't you see he's winding you up? Who told him to bring me into it?" That last sentence slipped from her mouth through my ears, but I retrieved and revised it. *Oh God, it's worse than I thought.*

"What do you mean, 'Who told him to bring me into it?' Are you saying…oh my God – why, Leila? *Why?*" I pleaded squeakily. She gawked her eyes at me in surprise.

"I…I…"

"No Is, Lill! Out with it! What do you have that suggests I'm a drunk?" I roared.

"Right, let's see…how about…the bottle of vodka and

the glass under your bed?" She pretended to speak ponderingly.

"What the hell were you doing in my room yesterday?"

"Oh, just looking for my purse I left here on Friday… looked all over your room for it…and I happened to bump into your booze stash."

"And here's you pretending you had nothing to do with it!"

"Look, why do you do that?" she sympathetically questioned.

"None of your business! I don't have to tell you everything!"

"Oh, so it's none of my business? Your health and well-being is none of my business. Just great, that is!" she crossed her arms in a strop and tore away her eye contact.

"You wrecked my date!"

"It was for his own good. Men go off drinking women, so this had to be aborted before it happened naturally."

"I am *not* a drinking woman! *I* should have been in charge of where and when to tell him! Since when have you put others' good before my own?" I raised my voice again.

"You're so damn self-centred, you're pretty much the same."

"What's that supposed to mean?"

"At least after Blake refused to talk to us, I moved on. You're still dwelling on old times."

"I can't fucking believe our friendship meant that little to you! You know, this condemnation echoes Freda – she treated us like shit, and now he's gone, you're doing the same to him and now me, and that's not the you I remember!" With that, she struck me right across my cheek, the sting rushing blood to the surface.

"Well, it's me now! Don't you dare compare me with that bitch! You don't want to get used to it, so let's call it quits now!"

"Fine. I don't bloody well need this!"

"Neither do I!" I was violently shoved into reality and tears by two aggressive door slams. *Oh God, I thought the worst happened was Blake leaving. I suppose I deserve it.* Lill and I plotted to split him and Freda up, and now she tried to split Ryan and me up before we even began. If he can get someone so resilient against such plots, why can't I? Could it be the fact that she's still affected by the whole thing, but is too damn stubborn to admit it, so takes it out on me? *Who bloody well knows.* I collapsed backwards onto the bed, my hands slapped over my eyes to contain my sobs, but it still could be heard through the half-jarred door, as Mum entering proved. I delved my head into a pillow to procrastinate even facing her. "Al, are you alright?"

"What does it look like? How would *you* feel if *your* best mate just gave you the boot? She sabotaged my date with Ryan."

"What the hell…?" I finally accepted that there was music to be faced, and I had to face it, so I raised myself to the edge of the bed. "Yes, it's true. Why, I don't know," I lied. "I've lost one childhood friend; now I've lost the other. No big deal, I mean, we're grown-ups now – these things are inevitable, right?" I shrugged.

"Wrong, Al. They had no right to treat you like this after ten years of loyalty. Come here." She sat beside me, and enveloped her arms round me for at least ten minutes. "You want me to talk to them?"

"What's that going to do? They're past listening to anybody, especially Blake. But thanks anyway. Oh God, what a great way to start a new life." She abruptly pulled me away and stared at me with a sorrowful look, as if I said something that clicked.

"Oh no, Al. Your exam is tomorrow. What are you going to do?" she gasped. I shrugged my shoulders in forced hope.

"I'll get by, somehow." After more brave faces and sobbing, I was finally alone – in the room and in life. Nothing really had any relevance anymore – the exam, ambition, nothing, because for ten whole years we supported and pushed each other through primary and secondary school, college, and University. What use was all that if they weren't there for my new life?

'No wonder you're so aimless – no offence, mind,' Katerina commented sympathetically with careful revision.

'No, no, none taken. You're right – I am aimless, and
I don't know if my aim will ever return. Those people
were my heart; a person cannot live without a heart.'
'I know, I know, but have you ever thought of looking
for them?'
'Where? Blake's in Dublin with that Freda bitch, and
Leila – where's she? Plus, have you considered the
fact they won't talk to me again?'
'True. It's unbelievable how something so perfect could
turn so bad.'
'You haven't heard the worst part yet. Let's move on to
exam day.'
'Sure. Take your time. I'm still interested.'

Friday: *Help me*, I uttered through a gulp as I wavered my eyelids open. My revision was very shallow over the weeks I should have been doing that. In the bathroom, I looked up and stared at my sorry reflection in the mirror above the sink. *Is that really me?* I thought dismally. My eyes were pink with dark circles round them, my face had shrunk to almost a faded strip, and my dishevelled hair looked lacklustre and bristly. I must have lost at least half a stone in weight, because stepping out of a long, warm shower, my limbs and trunk appeared to be losing flesh even as I looked in the full-length mirror. It seemed the first time in weeks since I'd studied myself in the mirror, and it wasn't a pretty sight.

It was about quarter to eight when I left the empty house again. I knew she wanted the promotion, but *why*? We had a nice house, with good furnishings – it made me wonder what else she wanted in life, because I certainly didn't want more than what I already had. It made her so oblivious to my sorrow, she could only give superficial comfort – I had no siblings to confide in, so I felt very alone. Blake and Leila were my siblings, as far as I was concerned; it was almost like they both died within weeks of each other. *Please help me, God*, I choked out again, entering the building minutes later. It was one of the most important days of my life, and I had nothing or no one to push me. I looked at every corner as I entered the lifts – everyone sitting an exam that day had someone patting their shoulders. *That should have been me, Leila and Blake,* I thought, almost breaking down. The journalism floor hallways were pretty deserted; they must have taken their seats already. Five minutes before the exam, I quickly dashed to the bathrooms perpendicular to the lifts, locked myself in a stall, grabbed a juice bottle which I'd filled with vodka, and gushed about half of it down. I felt a buzz which made me alerter than before. Deep breath, then rushed out to the exam room. I entered unintentionally loudly, turning heads. Mr Sutton was nowhere to be seen, just his petite Chinese assistant, Mrs Wang. I hurriedly took my place in the centre seat, and ignored Flegg-face in the front row, and trying to be collected in the atmosphere of uneasiness, despite Mrs Wang's efforts. "You have three hours to complete the exam papers before you. You may not talk to any other candidates, and you may raise your hand if you need extra answer sheets." She instructed in her perfect 'Received Pronunciation' accent. She glanced at her watch as she stood in front of her desk facing us. "Your time begins…now." Everyone round me had flicked the first page over and started scribbling; I apprehensively picked up my pen after a good five minutes of staring into outer space, wondering how I'd make it on my own. *How?* I resumed from my inner panic attack, and sluggishly filled in the lines of the paper. Twenty lengthy questions in three hours. *God, help me.*

After completing the exam paper, I suddenly felt suffocated by the walls of the University. I dashed out of there before anyone saw me, hyper-breathing like an asthmatic. Anyone who did see me whiz past them must have thought I was mad – if I saw myself doing that, I would've thought the same thing. I was finally out on the main road, but I was still gasping, almost near passing out. I perched on the bench in the courtyard, shut my eyes and inhaled till my lungs almost burst, held it in, and exhaled. Better, but why did my breath turn to gasps, I hear you ask It wasn't the exam, 'cause I didn't give a shit about that anymore. Blake and Leila? Maybe. Ten to fifteen minutes later, I proceeded to the Broadway. I didn't so much as roll my eyes at the shop windows or anyone breezing past me; I needed my own world. I opened the door to the still desolate house at about three-thirty. I glumly thought that I may need to apply for ownership of the house off Mum, because she was hardly ever in it. Feeling no appetite, I dragged my weight to my belly onto my bed, my face snuggled into a pillow trying to smother out my outburst of sobs…

Next thing I knew, there was pattering against the front door. *Great, maybe she mistook her home keys for a door at work,* I thought in sleepy sarcasm. I lazily rolled off, brushed my crumpled grey fitted t-shirt and yanked straight my dark blue jeans, and half-heartedly dashed to peer through the frosted glass panels. *Oh, it's not Mum* – a lofty silhouette stood motionless there. I opened the door cautiously, and…

"Blake!" I shrieked. "My God, what a surprise. I…" I faded off.

"What?" he responded in a blunt tone.

"I'm…just surprised to see you. Umm…come on in." His hands were delved into the pockets of a black nylon three-quarter length trench coat – not the leather one. He wore a navy blue shirt outside black combat trousers. *Cute. Looking deadly serious, but cute anyway.* "I've…come her to tell you something. I'm not staying."

"Oh, well, that's…fine. You want a cup of tea?"

"No thanks, I had one before I left."

"Oh. Good…" An awkward silence between us ensued as we both stared at the wall, twiddling our thumbs. We finally uttered each other's names simultaneously, causing us to breathe out a giggle. Was he here to make up with me? What the hell was going on?

"Umm…so, how is, ah, Freda?"

"She's very well. Her exam was last week. You?"

"I've…done my exam today. It was hell." He giggled again.

"My hell is on the thirtieth." I slit-smiled away from him.

"What's she doing?"

"Maths."

"Oh." *Right, enough with the suspense,* I thought. *Why is he here? I know for a fact...oh, what do I know?*

"So, uh...what was it you wanted to tell me? It must
be important, otherwise you would've told me over
the phone."

"I didn't feel this was something to break over the phone."

"What?" I took a deep breath in anticipation for the good or bad news. *Oh no, it's bad news; I know that tone.*

"Me and Freda...well, after my exam, we're..." He inhaled, almost like he was choking back a lump in his throat. "We're moving to a flat in Dublin." Silence.

"*What?* Look Blake, this is no time for bad jokes.
Why did you come here?" I slurred in fake disinterest.

"I'm serious, Al. We're getting a flat in Dublin with
our savings, and we're living together." *Oh no, this is the end*, I thought. The cloudiness I suddenly felt was ready to strike him as thunder.

"Okay, so this is what you came here to tell me? You
know, I can't bloody well understand you – we fall out
and you avoid every opportunity to even look at me,
and when you do talk to me, it's to say you're leaving
the country? Christ, what is this?"

"I felt even though I'm still angry at you, I needed to say
goodbye."

"*Goodbye?* If you're still mad at me, why the hell didn't
you just up sticks with her and leave?"

"'Her' has a name, you know." He growled out of nowhere.
"You've only known *her* nearly three months, for Christ's
sake."

"I love her, Al. Why can't you just be happy for us, even
pretend?" he reasoned in a calmer tone.

"Because I know you don't love her at all. You can't make
decisions affecting your life with someone you've known
for three months."

"Yes, I can. I believe in my heart I'm doing the right

thing – this is the girl I want to commit to, but not
marriage yet, though."

"Well, thank God for that. Your heart says all that, but
have you listened to *up there* is saying, Blake?" I verbally
defended, almost drilling my forefinger through the centre of his
forehead. "Okay. Let's say, for argument's sake, you want to
move in with Freda. Why can't you get a flat in London, eh?
What's wrong with that? You can still see myself and Leila, if
you want to. You know, compromise," I said in a pleading gasp,
desperate to drive home my advice. Silence as he inhaled
pessimistically. From his crumpled face, it was clear he wasn't
happy.

"We need to get away. Away from your influence, my
family's influence, both equally negative to this
relationship. I believe this will work as long as we're
away from everything." I couldn't believe the coolness in
which he trashed such a long friendship.

"Oh God, what has this girl filled you head with?" I
groaned, throwing my hands up. "*She* is the negative influence
here, Blake. She's the one belittling us so she can have you all to
herself. We're like her love rivals. It shouldn't be like that."

"Oh, really?"

"Yes, really. Does ten years of friendship mean *anything*
to you? I mean, what's more important to you? Staying
here, or living in Dublin with someone who hates our
guts simply because we're girls?" Silence.

"I'd choose the second option. At the end of the day, it's
not your friends who love you in a way other than
friendship love. That kind of love spans only a certain
limit. After that, it's nothing."

"Nothing? *Nothing?* Have you lost your bloody senses?
So, we're nothing now, right? Haven't you heard the
saying, 'Partners come and go, but friends are forever?'
Have you forgotten how she made you cry? If she makes
you cry again in Dublin, whose shoulders are you going
to cry on?" Silence again.

"She's not going to do that again. I know her better than

I did in the beginning."

"Lord, what a dilemma! You know, if it was someone
we liked, we would have wished you the best, but this
girl...she's doing weird stuff with your head."

"You hardly know Freda, Al. Not only that, I've got
news for you – we are not children." You should have seen
the blood inflame my pallid cheeks.

"Yeah, well, you don't have to tell me twice! I may
not know her, but I know *you*. Fine if you don't want
to listen to me after all these years, but if you think so
little of our friendship, all those years of supporting,
helping and guiding each other, you have permission to
get the hell out of this house, and my life, you got that?!" I
yelled, my fuming anger completely evident in my face.

"Right, I will! I've had enough of this patronising!" He
rose from the sofa, and stomped to the doorway, twisting to
spitefully stare in my eyes with that wrinkled brow.
"Fine! Good! Have a nice life with your bitch!"

"I will!" He violently tugged the door shut with a shotgun
bang. *Oh well, that's that down the toilet.* Both Blake and Leila
were so nasty to me – *why?* If this is what adulthood brings, why
the frig do we grow up? Was I the only sane one in this asylum of
adulthood? Anyway, after that verbal punch-up, I wondered
what's the point of common sense and intuition if it couldn't save
my best friend from making a big mistake? I cried and cried,
more than I could ever remember crying, with my face back in the
pillow, swamping all hopes of anyone hearing or helping me – I'd
cracked up on my own little island of grief.

Chapter 9.

Between four and seven, while Mum was away, I stared hypnotically at the telly screen with Adrian in *Green Collar*. The last thing I remembered was his character in the sergeant's office; at that point I must have dropped off, because I didn't need a mirror to know my eyes were all puffy and tired from blubbering.

'What a horrible day that must've been.'

'Uh – the worst,' Alana groaned in disillusionment. 'You know, if childhood promises for the future apply only to childhood situations, what's the point in them? They were just fragile, innocent promises.'

'I know. A lot of things about you make sense now. You drink because you dream of Adrian. You like Adrian because he's the only thing you can rely on in your life. Your liking for him grew when Blake and Leila fell out with you; you fell out with Leila because she sabotaged your date with Ryan, and Blake because you and Leila attempted to sabotage his and Freda's relationship. You and Leila did that because Freda is a bitch, and he was too stupid to see, and that all started at the shopping mall. Right?'

'You've certainly impressed me by recapping all that!' Katerina let out an echoing laugh.

'See, I was listening! Course I was listening – I'm your roommate, and I need to know why you chuck that junk down your throat,' she explained frankly as she rolled to sit at the edge of the bed, and lean towards Alana, who was in a similar position.

'Now you know. Anyway, it's not finished yet. I made a last-ditch attempt at doing what I do best – sabotaging – losing Blake forever.'

'Carry on.'

Monday, the thirtieth of June – three days after my exam from hell. For the first time since I began the University, I arrived there at around eleven-thirty. Not for a tutorial, of course, but to see Blake, 'cause his Social Studies exam was today. Up the

floors I went in the empty, musty and dark lift carriage, my pulse
echoing those door slams of Blake and Leila. On the fourth floor,
where he studied, I drifted about the corridors, very alike to my
floor, during which I crashed into a man whose voice I recognised
when he said sorry. "Mr Sutton!"

"Why, hello, Miss Higgins. What on earth are you
doing here? Not out of your old habit yet? If not,
you're two and a half hours late!" he jested in a fake threat.
I giggled half-heartedly, because it's not easy to be in a jocular
mood when you're at your wits' end. I was a little confused about
what he was doing on that floor, but that wasn't the point.

"Very funny! Well, actually, I'm here to see Blake. Have
you seen him?"

"Yes. He arrived here a couple of minutes late for the
exam at ten past nine, looking pretty haggard."

"Oh God," I groaned with a nauseous expression.

"Why? What's wrong?"

"We had a disagreement. Umm…maybe it's best I
explained everything. Can we go in your office, please?
I don't want anyone else to hear this." His face shrunk from
elation to concern. Back at his office at the third floor, I explained
the argument between him and me, and his leaving with Freda
tomorrow.

"Is he mad? Okay, he has a right to make his own
decisions – he's twenty years old, but not out of haste
like that, especially as he's hurting you. Come on, that's
wrong, wrong, wrong." He insistently opined.

"That's what I said. I can accept the fact they want to
be together, despite the fact I hate her guts, but couldn't he
get a flat here in London if they want to live together? For
Christ sake, London is a big place. But he's fooling himself
to please her."

"True. Just try your best, okay? He'll find out for himself
sooner or later, but try and make use of the remaining
situation." *Now, why didn't I tell him sooner? That's
brilliant advice.* After shaking his hand and accepting his well-
wishes for my exam result (groan), I returned to the fourth floor,

and sat on a bench outside the lecture room, which again doubled up as the exam room, and anxiously delved my elbows into my lap and cupped my chin with my palms. Honestly, it felt the longest ten minutes of my life. Exam over in ten minutes…nine minutes…eight…and so on, glancing at my watch. Still knackered, my eyelids were shutting down against my will, till I felt a rush of cold air awakening the hairs on my arms. I saw that all too familiar pandemonium of students on the cue of the proctor. I felt like an old woman whisked back to a scene from my University days. Everyone looked unfamiliar, unfamiliar and unfamiliar still...then I automatically grasped a hand before I even looked up at the face. Yep, it was Blake. I leapt from the bench, and faced him to block off his path. "Blake, Blake, we need to talk..." He tore his eyes away with a grim look to his feet.

"There's nothing more to say, Al. Myself and Freda are packing our bags for tomorrow's flight." I almost sunk my grip into his sinewy arms as he stood limply.

"Oh please God, no! Look, Dublin is nearly a thousand miles away! Why?" I shrieked. "You can get a flat here, so at least you'll have us if things go wrong."

"That's all that matters to you, isn't it? *If things go wrong.* You'll be cracking open the champagne when that happens, won't you? Well you can save your sermons – I'm going anyway."

"Can't you see? I saw your face when you announced you were leaving – you weren't happy, and you're still going to be unhappy if you move there. If the relationship was worth a shit, you wouldn't need to move away!"

"How the hell can a relationship bloom when we're surrounded by bigots left, right and centre? Like I said, plead till the cows come home, we are going tomorrow at ten. Out of my way!" He tried to push past me, but I still blocked him, my stare hardening to a threatening one.

"You listen to me, Blake Turpin – you leave my sight, kiss our friendship goodbye – for good! I don't want to hear or see you ever again, you hear me, pal?" I thought two could play at that game, even if it made me feel worse.

"Whatever. Out of my way!" He finally shoved me to one side, but my mind was all over the place. I could've gone after him, but as my tears welled up again, I thought I was trying to retrieve something that wasn't mine anymore. "It's over. It's all over. *Why did I let him go?*" I whimpered as I stood helplessly watching Blake stab our friendship to death by letting those lift doors close. I felt a hand behind me. I whipped round, and saw Mr Sutton. "Mr Sutton, I failed. He's gone. He chose an appalling woman over me and Leila. How could he? *How could he*, the stupid bastard!" I groaned, my voice guttural from crying. He pulled me into a hug. Not feeling any better, I rethought I *might* have one last chance, and I dashed out of the lift for the umpteenth time that day. I came across him in the car park, stepping into the car that transported us all over the place since he learned to drive in ninety-four. I bashed my fist against the driver seat window. "Blake, you have one last chance to listen to me! I love you – you're the big brother I never had, and I need you around me. Do you know how many things we've done for each other over the years? Remember how many times you stood up for me, especially when I felt like pulling a sickie? When Flegg almost ruined my reputation by saying I rigged the tutor to get good marks, when we stood up for each other when boyfriends and girlfriends came and went, and God knows how many more things? A girl needs a big brother around, no matter how old she is. Remember all those promises to live, achieve and die together when we were ten and eleven? Why should that change now? I would die if I didn't have you around, Blake. Come on, come to your senses, please!" I could've dropped to my knees in imploration at that point. He wound down the window, and looked me in the eyes with a very harsh stare.

"Because we're not children anymore, Al. Everyone has to go their own way someday, and I have to go mine.

Goodbye, Al." I couldn't believe he could sound so bloody cold. Standing there dazed as the charging of the engine before soon turned to motion, I gawped in a wide-eyed stare as the Beetle buzzed out of the driveway down Uxbridge Road towards his foolhardy destiny. The welling of my eyes already there

107

quickly flooded my cheeks and nose tip. I staggered homewards, trying to prevent a scene gathering round me from the loud sobbing sounds I made. Honest to God, my system was on the brink – one more shock was all it took to snip off the last thread it hung from. *How could he be so bloody cold?* I felt like strangling that bitch, but I also wanted to strangle *him* – whose fault was it? Her for her manipulativeness and spitefulness, or him for his gullibility and for acting like an asshole? *Who?* Maybe it's both, I dunno. A year on, I'm still too upset to decide. I finally reached my doorstep at around twelve-thirty, and pushed the key in with my shaky hand. Just me and that lonely house again. Or so I thought. I could distinctly hear muffled noises from the hallway, something between giggling and…something else. *Ooh, look who decided to come home for lunch,* I thought mockingly. I swept away my tears to a thin film with my knuckle, and fixed my face to the best of my abilities when you don't have a mirror. More chortling, only slightly resonant than before. *Someone's finding something funny on the telly,* I thought. I tiptoed down the corridor. I jarred the already unlocked door to gain a view of what was going on, 'cause the closer I got, the more I could here not just Mum's, but someone else's, giggles and groans. In whose company was she in? And why were the curtains closed? The view was limited to stirring silhouettes, so I flicked the light switch on, and…

"Mum?" I whispered. I looked again, and just as I guessed, I saw two figures…in bed?! "Oh my God…!" I shrieked as I saw her in her underwear and some bloke, both in bed, half-naked and flustered from head to foot, springing upright from an embrace.

"Al!" She said in a reflected shriek. Like I said, my system couldn't take anymore shocks, but it looked like it had to withstand a final one. I was angry through betrayal and upset through everything else that transpired, the perfect formula for speechlessness, so I slung my eyes away from her and the door in, dashed to the bathroom and slammed the door before she caught up with me. I ignored her hammering fists on the door as I slumped on the cold aqua tiles, clutching my cramping stomach. My hands moved up to bury my face as I started crying violently

enough to think I'd flood the bathroom. "Al! Al! Open this door
now! I can explain! Please!" *Yeah, that's what they all say – 'I
can explain.' My dad probably said the same thing to you. Don't
make promises you can't keep*, I thought dolefully. I glanced at
the small puddle my tears were making between my knees,
wishing I could shrink myself so it would be the size of an ocean
to jump in. "Sod off, and leave me alone!" I screamed
breathlessly through my sobs.

"No!"

"Whatever, but I'm not coming out!" She continued the fist-
banging, probably till her knuckles wore down, and I continued
bawling with my hands clasped over the back of my neck.

"Yes you are, so come out of there now!"

"Make me!"

"Right, I'm kicking this door down! One, two..." It was
apparent that there was no stopping her, so I pessimistically
heaved myself to my feet, marched up and wrenched the door
handle open. Before me she stood on her own, wrapped in a pink
towelling robe, with an angry frown and crossed arms. We locked
bitter stares for several seconds until...

"How could you, Mother? Who's your 'colleague' in
the bedroom? And why the hell didn't you tell me?"

"Look...firstly, he's Navin Pratap – my... boss,
and secondly, I didn't tell you because I didn't get
round to it."

"*Mr Pratap?* Oh God, this is ridiculous, this is! You
didn't get round to telling me, but you got round to
bedding him!"

"Watch your mouth, girl!"

"No I won't, Mother! I've had several of the worst days
of my own life, and what a wonderful way to end it!"

"What the hell are you talking about?"

"Well, let's see...I've lost Leila and Blake as best friends,
*Blake is packing his bags for the ten o' clock flight to
Dublin tomorrow with Freda*, and basically, I'm fighting
a losing battle with coping on my own." I stressed the
centre of the sentence. She gasped with her hands over her mouth.

"Oh my God – he's gone?"

"Yeah, and this is all I need to top it off. Right, back to my question – what's going on?" She inhaled deeply in ponderation.

"Well, we've been dating since I took part in the promotion, and I think I'm falling in love with him. He's a nice guy once you get to know him, I promise you…"

"Mmph…funny, that's what Blake said about Freda, and I can't believe you hid this from me, your own daughter! And since last November, too? What the hell's wrong with you?"

"I knew you wouldn't take too well to this, which is why I didn't tell you…"

"Hey, it's not the fact that I don't want you to anyone, honest – it's the fact that I came home and found you in bed with him that's bothering me!" We paused when I saw him crawl up behind her to view the commotion. "What the hell's going on, Tracie?" he yelled in a throaty, watered-down Indian accent. The guy looked in his mid-forties, re-dressed in a blue shirt and dark grey trousers, a full head of black hair with a few grey streaks, slim build and quite youthful physically for his age. "My daughter, Alana Higgins. Al, this is Navin," she replied in a distressed tone. I pulled my hand from his handshake offer, which gave a mixed reaction on his face. "You can go back in – this concerns my Mum and me," I ordered with a frowned brow.

"But…"

"Stay out of this, okay?" I snapped with my finger in his face.

"Al, don't talk to him like that!" she insisted, which I thought would be paired with a slap.

"Why not? He's interfering."

"It's okay, I've got the message." With that, he returned to the bedroom, and shut the door.

"You know, I know what your problem is."

"What?"

"For you, your dad's shadow still lives here."

"Don't you dare bring him into this! I couldn't care

less about him, and you know it! That shows how
much you know about my thoughts, but of course,
you're hardly at home, so obviously I'm asking too
much!"

"Yeah, well, I still have the right to make my own
decisions."

"And I as long as I live under your roof, I still have an
opinion about them, okay? That's not independence –
that's secrecy, and you don't keep secrets from your
own daughter, especially if it affects me too!"

"If you feel second best, you've done that yourself!
You would feel first best if you accept that I have the
right to date who I want."

"The owner of the firm, and a promotion lurking around?
What does that tell you?" Her hand recoiled into a stinging
whack across my cheek for the first time in my life. I widened my
eyes at her in shock as I rubbed the struck area, seeing an anger in
her eyes I'd never seen before, which scared me. "How dare you
speak to me like that! If you can't respect my decisions about my
life, and if you can't drop that attitude of yours, you can get out
now!" she snarled.

"Right – I will!" I bolted to my room, slammed the door and
twisted the key hanging from the lock. I hauled a brown medium-
sized suitcase from under the bed, and chucked it on the surface.
One by one, I hauled and folded as many items as possible from
my wardrobe furiously to leave it empty, snapping a few cheap
plastic hangers in the process. Once a small tower jutted from the
suitcase, I plonked my bum on it and zipped it up beneath me. As
I changed into a white fitted t-shirt and blue jeans, I was
obviously absolutely blazing angry for many reasons – because
Mum had been moonlighting as more than Mr Pratap's employee,
I didn't really know if she slept with him out of love or of the
promotion. I was left to nurse my own wounds when Blake and
Leila fell out with me, and most of all, as a child, she taught me
never to resolve arguments with violence – so, what the hell did
she just do then? In my opinion, people who do that are complete
bloody hypocrites. Anyway, thank goodness I was old enough to

make it on my own. I was troubled from my thoughts by a
desperate knock on the door.

"Al, please, for the love of God, open this door now!"
That's the corniest thing I've ever heard you say, I shrugged to
myself as I proceeded packing my smaller belongings in the gaps
– make-up, jewellery, and other bits and bobs, including my
Adrian scrapbook. "Oh go away, Mother! I don't want to hear it!"

"Look, people do weird things in the heat of the moment –
I didn't mean to hit you."

"What, all those teachings against violence went out the
window in the heat of the moment? Pathetic."

"Okay, I was wrong, and I'm sorry, but can't we work
this out somehow? You're my daughter, and I love you."

"I'm your daughter only when it suits *you*. When I was
small, I was your daughter, but now I'm only your daughter
part-time." Silence. I began filling a large handbag with
some more stuff from my dressing table, drawers and bedside
cabinet. I halted when I heard her inhale and exhale deeply.

"True. I confess, I haven't been the best mother to you in
your most difficult times, which I stupidly ignored thinking
you could cope, but please, can we talk and figure
something out? I don't want you to leave. Where will
you go?"

"Anywhere but here."

"Please, no, Al!" she shrilled.

"Yes! The time I open this door will be the time I'm
leaving. I'll use my savings to figure out something.
Nothing you say will get me to stay." Silence again, which
was slightly more reassuring. I dragged the suitcase and handbag
to the door, and unlocked it when I freed my hands. I saw Mum
stood there, staring blankly and limply at me as I hoisted my
luggage again and proceeded to the front door. She suddenly
caught up and leapt before me to block my path. "Don't go, Al! I
said I was sorry, didn't I?"

"No, Mum. You're sucking up because you don't want
me to leave. Right?"

"Look, I'm running out of ways to make you stay so we

can work this out. Please!" Her voice was punctuated by desperate wheezes.

"That's because you've run out already. 'Bye, Mum." It was almost as if her breathing stopped dead when I said those words. I grabbed my coat off the stand and placed it on top of the suitcase, and deliberately heaved the door loudly without looking back, mimicking the slam I was all too familiar with hearing every morning. I stood on the top step admiring the sky tinged with an orangey-brown haze, scattered with a few spear-shaped grey clouds. It was almost five. Time to find a place to stay before it's dark, I thought as I strolled along the regularly deserted street to Uxbridge Road, full of rush-hour bustling by pedestrians and vehicles. The first place I went when I was pissed off was Leila's or Blake's. I almost hopped onto a bus to Hayes once I crossed the road to the stop, the habit still imprinted in my brain. I'm on my own now, I'm on my own now, I kept repeating to myself. A bed and breakfast place a few paces towards the Broadway I read about then sprung to mind.

By about seven o' clock, I had gone and returned from the Broadway to withdraw enough money from my savings to check into the B&B. The room was very basic, but very nice – obviously because it was thirty quid. It had a sink opposite a double bed, two seats perpendicular against the walls, between which was a tiny telly on an oak stand. The wallpaper had a brownish wavy-stripe pattern, and so did the carpet, which looked freshly vacuumed. I instantly felt the childhood weight lift off me – everything was quiet now. The bathroom was adjacent to my room, which also was very basic – a sink, toilet, shower and towel rail all in circled in the cramped aqua green cubicle. A chilly drought wafted over me from the wide-open window over the toilet, giving me goose bumps. It had a pleasant smell of air freshener, and everything looked polished especially for me. By eight, I had freshened up, changed into a red nightshirt and slumped myself on the bed in front of the telly just like old times – it really did feel like years, even though it was just hours – but without the constant heaviness hanging over my head. While I waited for *Green Collar*, I scoured through the ads section of a local paper I bought while at the Broadway. I had to find somewhere I could call my own – at least for a while. "Good evening, and welcome. Now, here is episode forty-one of *Green Collar*." *Forty-one already? Good God.* So for the remaining hour, I hypnotised myself with his movements on the screen, reminding myself how it felt to dream of Adrian. Nothing in my heart and mind had changed there, but everything in my life had turned upside down literally overnight. He was the only thing worth going on for. So after the episode, I felt sleepy, and decided to take a couple of swigs from the vodka bottle I stuffed in my handbag. Last thing I remembered was switching off one bedside lamp, leaving a soft amber glow in the room, and then that dream of me and Adrian at the beach at midnight recurred, feeling the heightened sensation of his lips really kissing me, his hands really caressing me, and our lovemaking on that clumpy sand. I awoke feeling flushed at about eight o' clock in the morning. *Hey, this isn't so bad at all – I should've done it ages ago*, I thought, delighted at not feeling abnormal not waking in my bed at home.

About five days later, I took my leave – all in all, the hotel stay cost one-hundred and fifty quid out of the four hundred I withdrew. In that time span, I had finally found a place through the paper, rang them up from the B&B's phone downstairs and booked a viewing of my future abode. It was the sixth of July last year, a Friday. I booked a taxi from the hotel, which carried me the distance equivalent to the stroll from my old home to the University, back to Acton with my heavy luggage – the driver probably gave me a look implying I was a lazy sod taking advantage of my privileges as a woman. Anyway, in the building, my hopes fell as my nose was caught in one of the first repulsions I would have to withstand in this place as the owner, Mr Peel (I still don't know his first name, and didn't want to either, judging by the state of him, too – a black short-sleeved shirt faded and holey, green, stained combat jogging bottoms and filthy trainers that probably made up half the pong of him) introduced me to my room – a description would be the exact state as it is now. The word 'gruesome' took on a whole new meaning when I first saw it. I wanted to tell him, 'No way, mister – maybe yes if you clean

this shit-hole first,' but I held it back when those scenes of me,
Leila, Blake and Mum replayed like a rewound video in my head,
and I thought 'Anything to get out of there.' So obviously, I
accepted it, and moved in that morning after paying him the fifty-
five pounds rent. After that first day, I barely noticed the
difference between this room and my room at the house, because
almost every moment of every day, I was wrapped up in a
drowsy, drunken fantasy of Adrian, which would have been
quenched if there was the slightest glimmer of hope that I would
find him, but knowing that I wouldn't really sucked – my heart
took it badly, but my mind slowly absorbed it. The drink worked
wonders at keeping that disappointment from dominating me; it
started with about a quarter bottle. Later, half, then one whole
bottle after about a week or so, but I still wanted more to prolong
it, but at the same time, I couldn't use up all my savings. I
completely lost my appetite for food and life, but I had to earn a
living, somehow. So that day, as I used my last twenty-pound
note to buy more vodka, I bought another local paper to see what
jobs were on offer – a week later, I accepted a job as a betting
shop assistant, which I accepted, as I only needed instructions
about the punters and the cash register. So in order not to go to
work drunk, I organised a pattern for my drinking – only a glass
or two on days before working days, which were Monday,
Wednesday and Friday, from ten till three – thirty-six quid. It was
a clean and respectable place, which I've still got no complaints
about. Peel found out about my drinking when he found me
asleep on the floor that December, which I still haven't managed
to scrub the remainders off me yet. So, that's the story of how I
ended up here and as a drunk. Sad, eh?

'It's bloody tragic, a studious girl like you in this state.
But tell me something,' Katerina groaned in alarm,
which lowered to a tone of curiosity.
'Shoot.'
'Okay, so, you, Blake and Leila don't talk to each other
any more; but does Blake and Leila still talk to each
other?'
'Not a clue. I'm sure they do, 'cause they're both victims

of the same thing – me. I wouldn't be surprised if she
moved to Dublin with Freda. I dunno…'
'Stop blaming yourself for the break-up of your friendship.
All the things you did shows what a loyal friend you were,
who always wanted the best for both of them.'
'I suppose…'
'And your Mum had no right not to tell you such a thing –
she was the only parent you had to confide in, yet she
didn't return that? Come on, that's out of order.'
'Yeah,' Alana forced out hopelessly. Katerina's face fell to
one of compassion as she stretched a hand to cup her shoulder.
'Come on, cheer up. You want a cup of tea? It's on me –
as a proper offer of friendship. Tough if they don't want
to be your friends anymore – I'm your friend.' She finally
smiled from her expression of doom. *Wow – if she could make me
smile for the first time in weeks, this could really be something*,
she thought optimistically, looking into her eyes.
'Thanks, Kat. Sure I'll have a cuppa.' With that, she
grasped Katerina's handshake vigorously. 'After that, I'll call it a
night. I can't believe I've been telling this story for nine frigging
hours! Look at the time!' Alana shrilled in fake surprise as she
glimpsed at the wall clock, which read thirteen past nine in the
evening, an evening which fell round both of them without
either's knowledge. Hearing Katerina bumping her toes on
something and cursing excruciatingly, she leapt to her cramped
feet to yank the curtains and flick the switch on.
'Cor, that's better – do you always make tea with no lights?'
Alana giggled.
'Sorry. I don't – in fact, before you came, I didn't even
switch on the lights, 'cause I was asleep most of the time.'
She proceeded to fill the kettle and placed it gently on the pre-
heated stove. She whipped her head round to look at her lying on
her back on the bed with her arms behind her head, meeting her
eyes from staring at the ceiling, considering the figure of a tragic
transition from childhood to adulthood lying there. 'Oh.'
Half and hour later, after seeing Katerina off to bed, she
dashed to the bathroom with a bursting bladder, also to freshen up

and change into her nightshirt. Under the duvet, she maundered for several minutes over the picture of Adrian she kept under her pillow, kissed the pad of her forefinger and placed it on his lips. 'Goodnight, Adrian, wherever you are,' she whispered.

Chapter 10.

Katerina made some last-minute adjustments to her appearance, then glanced at the wall-clock. Creeping to the doorway, almost tugging the front door to a silent click, she took one last glance at a fast asleep Alana, with her limbs splayed out beneath the duvet; she almost sobbed as she recollected the story she told. *This is so horrible...* she trailed off sorrowfully in her thoughts as she finally closed the door. She muscled it aside to clench back her tears and focused on the short journey she was embarking on.

Well, first tutorial of the week finished. Not bad, not bad, she sighed contentedly as she fumbled with the contents of her rucksack bang in the middle of a sudden outbreak of whizzing students around her, some actually slamming blindly into her shoulders. 'Hey, watch it, you lot!' she screamed fruitlessly at the cluster they formed by the lifts. She waited for them to clear off before strolling to the lift and pushing the down button. She gently twisted her knuckle in her eye socket. *God, I'm knackered. Can't wait till I take a kip. Oh, wait! Just a second! I completely forgot – I was supposed to figure out a way to help Alana...I know how!* She snapped her fingers as she stood alone in the shaky carriage, which landed at the ground floor seconds later. Her immediate action was dashing to the notice board, perpendicular to the revolving doors and about a hundred paces away from the reception desk, and rapidly scanned her eyes over the bits of paper pinned to the steel-framed cork structure about as tall as her and ten times as wide, till they halted at a heading: "NAMES OF DEPARTMENT LECTURERS". A whole load of crack-jaw names covered the first half of the yellow paper, misters this and misters that, until..."Mr Glenn Sutton, Journalism Lectures and Tutorials, 4th floor." *Ah-ha!* She then scurried over to the receptionist area, and screeched to a halt her words as she waited for a fair-faced girl, probably in her mid-twenties, with boyish brunette hair and brown eyes, wearing an orange shirt, to say a final few words to end her phone call. 'Can I help you?' she finally uttered in a girlie accent. 'Yes...is it

possible to have a few words with the Journalism tutor, Glenn
Sutton, please?'

'Are you a student of his?'

'Well, no, but my friend is – *was* – and would like to
contact him again.'

'Okaaay…can I have you and your friend's names
please?'

'Sure. My name is Katerina Slate, and my unavailable
friend is Alana Higgins.'

'Oh my God, you know her?' she gasped with her fingertips
over her mouth.

'Yeah, course I do. Not very long, but I feel like I've
known her for years,' she bashfully giggled while smiling
proudly.

'She was one of our best ever students. What happened
to her?'

'Oh, it's a long story…' Katerina sighed as she observed
swift fingers investigating her name on the computer keyboard.

'You're from Media, right?'

'Yup.'

'Okay, I'll give him a bell. Bear with me for a few
moments, please.' She dialled a number, while Katerina
leaned against the edge of the desk, leisurely gazing at the
scattered folders and papers all over the desk, which was
shadowed by a semi-circular orange-beige concrete hood with
small spotlights, creating her own little shell to work in. Then she
was snapped back into looking back at the receptionist a minute
or two later.

'He's on his way down here. You can wait here if you
like, or you can sit over there,' she said with a welcoming
smile.

'I'll wait here, thanks.' The receptionist attended another
enquirer while she rolled her eyes around the entire ground floor
– the row of seven lifts, the high whitewashed ceiling, a row of
oak doors with glass panels which lead to God knows where, and
eventually to the polished, and slightly marred, pale wooden
floorboards. She was almost boring herself, not with the

surroundings, but with the ten or so times she'd been looking at the same thing, until she saw a man, matching Alana's description, in a grey suit, a burgundy tie and silver shirt, marched out of the lifts and towards her. She stood in a proper posture to introduce herself to him. 'Hello – are you Katerina?'

'Yeah, I am.'

'I'm Glenn Sutton.' He held out his hand for her to shake with enthusiasm. 'I believe you know my old student, Alana Higgins?'

'Yes – she's my new roommate. Look, umm…do you think we could go to your office to discuss this? 'Cause what I have to say will probably be a little alarming to you, but I'm telling you this because you're the only one who can help in this matter.' With a crumpled brow of curiosity, he led her back to the lifts to the fourth floor.

'…So that's the story, sad to say. Losing her two friends has left her severely disturbed. You know, that story really shook me. It's such a tragic story, Shakespeare has nothing on this girl.' She was waving insistent gestures with her hands as she leaned her elbows on the edge of the desk. He sighed through a slit smile.

'I've been teaching here for fifteen years, and I've never heard anything so awful happen to a top student. I remember her crying in front of me when she couldn't get through to Blake. I hugged her, she went after him one last time, and that was the last I saw of her.'

'But I want to reverse this. She will still have the choice of whether to start again or forget it, but she can't do that if she's sitting there, drowning herself in drink.'

'True. So, what can I do?'

'Well, do you keep files of previous students?'

'Of course. We have an archive that dates back at least twelve years.'

'Okay. Well, I was thinking…maybe you could gain access of Leila Drayton's and Blake Turpin's files, which should have their parents' addresses and phone numbers.' He replied with a rapidly widening gawp.

'Are you mad? I could lose my job for giving out that
   kind of information to other students!'
'Do you want to help her or not?'
'Of course, but…oh, okay, then.' Katerina's face lit up with
hope. 'Hopefully, I should get it together by Wednesday or
Friday, alright? But I'm not promising anything.'
'That's good enough for me. Thank you very much for
   your cooperation, Mr Sutton.'
'No problem. And thanks for informing me about
   Miss Higgins.'
'Sure. I'll see you around.'
'Okay.' She rose from her chair as he switched on his
computer screen, but alerted her before she left the office.
'Sorry, but I forgot to ask your address.' *Oh no, he's gonna
visit her. She'll kill me,* she thought frantically. Then…
'Umm…alright, but you've got to promise you won't
   see her without a good reason. This is top secret, okay?'
'Deal.' She accepted his fountain pen, and scribbled down
the address of the bed sit. After shaking his hand again, she
rushed out the door, through and out the lifts, and eventually the
building. The sudden burst of energy came about partly because
she was desperate to take a nap, and partly because she was
bursting with enthusiasm about completing the first part of her
plan.
'Oh, hi Al,' Katerina muttered sleepily, rolling onto her side
to face the front door as Alana snapped it shut. 'Well, that's
another couple of quid earned,' she drearily groaned as she kicked
her high square-heeled shoes and tossed her handbag against the
oven door. 'Sorry if I woke you.'
'Umm…no problem. What time is it?' She said, rising to a
seated position.
'Five o' clock,' Alana said as she slung herself on her back
on her bed.
'Oh damn, I'd better get ready for work myself. Sorry
   'bout this – we can talk later.'
'Sure. How was the tutorial?' *Wonderful – for you more
than me*, she thought to herself. 'It was very good, actually.'

'Funny, you should be asking *me* that,' she said in a deepened tone of resent. Katerina hopped about the room, wrenching on her indigo jeans, black v-neck top, and her court shoes on. She raised her head in confusion, almost lost for words.

'I know. I'm sorry. Look, can't you retake the course or something?' she suggested in desperation.
'With what? I don't really have the brain, the impetus or the money to do such a thing.'
'I suppose. Oh well, I'm going. We can talk later, okay? And remember, no drinking,' she warned sternly, with a finger pointed to her. Alana giggled with a hand cupped round her mouth.
'Sure thing, boss!' she obliged in a strained Southern accent. They both cracked up laughing simultaneously, Alana's palms slapped over her eyes, and Katerina threw her spine back, almost collapsing on her rear on the floor. 'Oh God, what a crap accent! Don't do that again, otherwise you'll kill me!' she managed to squeeze out of her violent laughing fit.
'That's what I intended to do!'
'Okay! Well, I'm off. There's a good fifteen minute bus trip up there, as you know.'
'Sure. See you later.' She slipped on a denim trench-coat, and knotted the belt. Alana scrutinized her footsteps and every move till she heard the door click. She suddenly leapt up, reached her hand under the bed for the cold, heavy surface of a glass bottle. 'No drinking while you're here, Kat,' she mumbled as she tipped the rim directly into her mouth, tasting nothing as the alcohol stream unconsciously gushed and burned her throat...

Ten-thirty; not bad, Katerina thought to herself as she glanced at her watch before shoving the key into the eye-level lock. *Ooh, it's dark in here. The silly girl slept and forgot I live here.* She clicked the light on, its sharpness almost blinding her eyes, which focused in surprise at Alana's stillness of her neatly positioned body under the duvet. She focused down on a violet sweater and black jeans piled on the floor beside the bed as she patted her shoulder. 'Al, I'm home. Wake up,' she gently coerced.

No response. So she turned her on her back from her side to gaze at her pallid face, which prompted not even a twitch from her. *Oh God, what the hell is going on?* 'Come on, girl, wake up, will ya? Please!' she pleaded, now slapping both cheeks furiously. She paused, and sniffed something around her mouth… something very familiar. *Oh shit, no! Not the drink again, please!* On a whim, she fumbled her hand under the framework, finding a dry bottle. 'Oh my God!' Her fingertips began to tremble over her mouth. She stormed through the half-locked front door, her wobbly legs almost failing her on the way down the stairs. She hammered on a dark, dry-rotten door at right angles to the front door, her breath and heart sprinting through fear, dread and horror. At last, a click. 'Wot's wi' you, huh?' Mr Peel responded rapidly, slobbering himself along the doorway.

'Please, you've gotta help me, please! Alana has passed out or something, and I need to call an ambulance! She's not waking up!' she gabbled through sobs, almost dropping on her knees.

'I always knew this would happen…' Automatically, she grasped him threateningly through the holey straps of his vest till their noses almost touched, causing his eyes to widen at her gritted teeth.

'Listen here, pal, if you don't call 999, *you* will be responsible for the death of my friend, and I'll be out of here, even if I have to live on the streets – you hear me?' she screamed with a whine of panic. He had little choice but to sigh in an acceptance of defeat.

'Okay.' He finally hopped to the phone in his room on her grip's release.

She whizzed back to her room, almost tripping on a couple stairs, and silently wept and prayed as she stroked Alana's hair throughout the almost eternal eight-minute wait, her tears splashing against her lifeless face. *Stay with me, please…*

'Miss Slate? Wake up, please.' A whisper became a murmur, then a soft, and deep woman's voice, paired with a cupped palm on her shoulder. Then it all came back to her – she was escorted to the hospital in the ambulance, clutching Alana's

hand for dear life. Katerina's blurry vision was slightly swamped
by harsh white lighting, but eventually cleared to form a picture
of a short, round-faced Afro-Caribbean woman in a white shirt-
dress, finally interpreted as a uniform, and bouffant wavy melanin
hair. 'Miss Slate? Hi, I'm the sister here. I have news about your
friend.' She leapt to her feet before her, at full attention and
staring in anticipation. 'What? What is it? Is she okay?' she
breathlessly implored. 'Yes, she's going to be fine. She over-did
it with the alcohol a bit, so she had to have the excess alcohol
pumped out of her stomach.'

'How long will she be here, Sister?'

'About four or five days.' Her eyes rolled to her feet in
slight disappointment, still heavily breathing. While collecting
herself, she ran a hand through her hair. 'Does she have any
family that we can get in touch with?'

'Umm…no. She just has her Mum, but she's on bad
terms with her, so I don't think it would be a good
idea to contact her.'

'Okay, fair enough,' she nodded.

'Umm…can I see her, please?'

'Sure, but only five minutes. She's conscious, but only
barely.'

'Okay, thanks very much.' She shook her hand, and was led
to an intensive care room. The door to the pale blue and white
room, with a white glossy floor, a small window hidden by blue
curtains, and then there was Alana, lying there in balance between
inertness and consciousness on a bed that looked too small even
for her thin frame, with tubes attached to her wrists and up her
nostrils, almost like a human drainage system. Her face now had
a sickly blue tinge to it, but was as anguished as she remembered
it, and as peaceful. *I told you, I told you, I told you…* she
repeated, feeling partly self-resentful, sitting beside her; a short
outburst bringing little relief preceded enough composure to look
at her sorrow-bruised and still face again. Katerina squinted the
tears down her cheeks, while caressing her dull, smooth hair.
'Why, Al? Why? You're only twenty-one, you've got the world
at your feet, whether you believe it or not. I know it's Blake and

Leila who are responsible for causing this to you, but it seems to me that the very people who caused your pain could also be your cure. I *will* find them for you, Al. Something tells me there's still something there. I can't find Adrian, 'cause he's just not something meant to be, but I will find them as soon as I can, I promise you.' A lump rose from her throat as she whispered her vow, almost costing her that laboured poise. She leaned over to peck her forehead, and roughly brushed away a droplet under her eye with a knuckle. 'Miss Slate? Time's up.' A deep breath preceded a stroll in almost complete stupor to the main corridor, which had nurses, doctors, and patients' families and friends as anxious as she was, rushing around her beyond her senses. She turned a deadpan gaze to the sister, patting her shoulder. 'Oh God,' she barely gasped. She guided her to the seating area outside Alana's room, and held Katerina's hand long after she returned her to the prickly wooden bench.

'Don't worry. Would you like to tell me what happened?'

'Well, I came home from work at around ten-thirty,' she paused as she rolled her eyes away from hers to the clock. 'Good God, it's twelve-thirty; fancy that, it's two hours I've been here,' she shrilled, deviated from her last, incomplete, sentence. 'Look, if you don't want to talk about it now, we can discuss it later…'

'No, no…look, I'm sorry. I came home from work at ten-thirty. I work at a bingo club a few miles away. I saw her lying in bed once I switched the light in the room on. I had a pang that something was wrong, because obviously, she normally switched on the lights at that time. But seeing her asleep made me think "Oh well, maybe she didn't notice." So I tried to wake her up – no response. So I turned her over to face me, and the more shocking part was seeing her face. I'd never seen it so, so…waxy before. My head started doing circles, wondering what the hell was going on. After a few seconds, my hyper-breathing levelled itself, now reacting properly to the emergency. Then I smelt something like alcohol around her mouth. I'd seen her down copious amounts of alcohol before, and store a

spare bottle under the bed, so I looked there, and saw
it – completely empty. I told her not to drink, but she
didn't listen, the stupid girl. I called the ambulance,
then ten minutes later, we were here. I fell asleep
waiting for news.' The sister widened her eyes, narrowed
them and nodded.

'So she drinks regularly, then?'

'Yeah, about one or two bottles a day. I thought she'd
eased up, but I guess her depression got the better of
her. I can't stand the sight of her incinerating her
insides like this, but what can I do?' she sighed in dismay.
The sister nodded again in understanding.

'Look, I know it's too early to decide about overall
welfare, but maybe you should think about referring
her to a specialist…'

'No way! I mean, no offence to them, but that's exactly
what she's trying to avoid. I'll deal with her myself.
I have a plan. I'll use the therapist thing as a last resort.
But thanks anyway.'

'Okay. Well, you might as well go home now. We got
rid of the excess alcohol in her stomach before it reached
her bloodstream and poisoned her. Now what's left in her
blood will rid itself safely.'

'Terrific. Thank you very much, you've been a great help.'

'No problem. 'Bye bye.'

'Bye.'

Katerina fleetly trotted along the main road lit by amber
street lights, white headlights of vehicles and blues of emergency
vehicles. She turned her head to the faint silhouettes of a multi-
arched railway bridge someway across a field opposite the
hospital, the mild breeze warmed her nostrils pleasantly. Only her
own footsteps and the odd car could be heard. Her limbs still
numb with empathetic grief intensified as she sought the logic
behind what Alana did to herself. She approached a bus stop, and
waited for a night bus, no longer feeling safe as the only citizen
on the entire pavement. The bus took about ten minutes to arrive
and take her back the fifteen minute drive to Ealing. On the few

paces to the bed sit, her words sprung to mind: '*Funny, you should be asking me that,*' and '*I don't have the brains nor the motivation...*' sprung to mind. After twisting the key, she almost ran into the patchy shadow of Mr Peel in his usual putrid appearance. 'Umm…is Higgins okay?' Katerina bolted an unforgiving stare directly in his eyes. 'Look Peel, I'm happy to pay rent here till I get my own flat, but you have no right to ask about Alana's well-being; you wouldn't have rung the ambulance if I didn't threaten you to stop using her alcoholism as an excuse to treat her like shit, you understand me? Now let me through.' She butted past him, stomped up the stairs, leaving him standing there at a loss for words.

She barely dragged herself out of the bathroom back to her room in a grey cotton nightshirt, ruffling her damp hair as dry as she could with a towel. As she dragged a comb through, she twisted her head and recoiled in near shock at the time. *Yikes! Quarter past two…a good lie-in tomorrow, that's for sure, after I see Al…*She then flung the towel on the chair, and then her weary self on the duvet before nestling under it. *God, I'm so tired…small price to pay for making sure she's alright, though…*She immediately dozed after silently praying for no nightmares about Alana to destroy the ease she took so long to find in herself…

Chapter 11.

Katerina walked brisker and brisker, almost screeching across the road leading her to the University's courtyard, then a burst of speed and a dead halt lead her to the entrance. Only managing to breathe out small puffs, she blinked back stars as she collapsed her upright stance against the door frame and slapped a palm over her breastbone. *Good God, that was only fifty yards or so. I've really got to get back to the gym.* She then switched her gears to stroll to the lifts. She twisted her head round only to see that the ground floor wasn't its usual bustling self, either because it was five minutes to nine, or because half of the students and staff went off sick. *Huh?* she thought as her patient wait for the lift doors to open ended with an equally deserted carriage. *Oh well, I'm certainly not complaining, just surprised…eight fifty seven; on with the learning…*she thought as she narrowed her eyes to focus on her watch's face in the dim light.

The tutorial wound up at its usual time of midday, in time for lunch. But she had business other that her studies to do. *Gotta see Mr Sutton. I'd better go and find out what's going on now.* She tried to keep up with the pace of the rushing cluster of students simultaneously signed off with her. She tried to hop into one of the seven lifts before infestation took place, but couldn't. So she was forced to breathe in muddled sweaty smells from them. *Oh God…*she thought as she drawled in a breath and held it in, labouring to keep herself conscious. She brought her eyes from the ceiling to a shocked expression on a redhead below everyone else as she turned around to face a boy whose height opposed the girl's, and stood well above the crowd. 'Hey, you kicked my leg!' she shrieked.

'Did not!' he sniped back with folded arms.

'Did, you little bastard!'

'Who are you calling a bastard, shorty?'

'Right, you asked for it!' She lunged at him from her corner, almost toppling everyone over like dominoes, eliciting a few cries of shock.

'Oi! Shut up you two, will ya? Can't you see we're in

a crowded lift? Save your scrap till outside. This lift
is cramped enough without you two at it!' Katerina
interrupted in annoyance.

'He started it!'

'Did not, bitch!'

'Shut up!' she snipped fruitlessly.

'Keep out of this, blondie.'

'No! Everyone nearly crushed each other to death,
and you're telling me to keep out of it. Stupid asshole!' The
surrounding students let out a few quiet cheers of approval at her
protest. 'Oh look, the doors are open. Now you can kill each other
if you want,' she continued sarcastically. The contents of each
carriage dispersed. In the one Katerina was in, they evicted
themselves almost as if they wanted to get out of the building
before things got ugly. Katerina marched out, pretending he was
too angry to remember to confront her, but was proven wrong as
her path was blocked by the boy. 'Hey, look, I tell you
what…forget shorty over there. How about you and me wrestle
about on the floor instead?' he suavely invited, curling his finger
at her to signal this. Katerina just rolled her eyes at the guy,
whom she had seen wandering outside the Media Studies room,
but didn't know his name. The girl he had been picking on
glanced at each of their facial expressions in petrifaction.

'Look pal, I may not be as tall as you, but at least my
mentality isn't as stunted as yours. So bugger off!' She
yelled with a forefinger shoved in his face aiming at his forehead,
then stomped off towards the reception area. The girl fell forward
into a crazy fit of laughter at his wrinkled brow of defeat and
humiliation. He hunched his shoulders and paced to the main
exit. She stood on the same spot, clutching her stomach and
squinting her eyes to prevent them from being laughed out of
their sockets. Katerina leaned against the counter as she watched
the same girl from the other day complete scribbling something
down on paper. She finally raised her head at her. 'Hello, Kat.
What can I do for you today?' she joyfully chirped with a
welcoming smile, clasping her fingers on the desk.

'Hi, ma'am. I was wondering if you could tell me

where I could find Glenn Sutton please? We were to
continue our chat about Alana today.' What she was going
to say to the receptionist crossed her mind during the tutorial, but
within seconds, she thought: *The simplest is usually the best.*

'Sure, just one second. I'm not sure if he's still
tutoring, or if he's in the canteen.' She then picked up the
phone and pushed some buttons. Once again, she glanced around
the whole floor, her eyes resting on the girl she 'rescued' dashing
towards her, adjusting the strap of her rucksack on her shoulder.
She halted with an over-enthusiastic grin on her round fair face,
while panting like a dog. 'Thanks a lot, Kat. That pain in the ass
has been harassing me for the four months I've been here, mostly
because I'm only five-one and he's six-one,' she squealed
between the short breaths. Katerina was rather surprised she knew
her name, because she never saw her before. 'Hey, no problem.'

'Anyway, gotta go. Thanks again.' She shook her hand
almost like a vibration.

'No problem. Tell me if he harasses you again.'

'Oh, well, judging by the look on his face just now,
I think it'll be a while. Anyway, 'bye.' She dashed towards
the revolving doors, and disappeared instantly.

'Okay, Kat?' She whipped her head round to the
receptionist's voice. 'He's in the canteen. I rang his mobile,
which would usually be off if he was tutoring.'

'Brilliant. Thanks very much,' she replied with a smile
transmitting new-found eagerness.

'You're welcome.' She then dashed back into the centre lift,
her last glance falling on the digital clock over the doorway. It
read twenty past twelve.

Using Alana's description of the University for bearings,
Katerina scanned her eyes around the hallway of the first floor,
inhaling the alluring smells, hearing muddled conversations and
clinking and banging sounds of dishes, cutlery, pots and pans.
*Damn, they have some nice-smelling food here. Maybe I'll try
something here for once...* Standing under the doorway, gazed
around again for Mr Sutton amongst the staff and students, seated
against and before the doorway in about four rows of seven, with

a narrow clearing in the centre. The canteen area was perpendicular from the doorway, not instantly noticeable standing there. It was a shady hollow in the pastel pink wall with a serving area and a sense of urgency instilled in the white-jacketed staff. All except one eater was too engrossed to notice her presence; that person, furthest from the door alone in the darkest corner, raised a hand to signal an invitation. She replied with a raised brow. She rushed over, swerving her feet to avoid slamming into the chairs, and urgently plonked herself on the edge of the bench. 'Hi, nice to see you again, Mr Sutton,' she said, shaking his extended hand. 'Well, what's to report?'

'I've…umm…' he stuttered, trying to lower his voice and twisting his head in awareness.

'Well, spit it out!' she resonated impatiently.

'Hush! keep your voice down!' he grated out, flapping his hands. She slapped a palm over her mouth.

'Oops, sorry.'

'I've told you once, and I'll tell you again – this really contravenes the confidentiality rule we have here, and if anyone found out, I'll be looking at the Labour Exchange pages.'

'I know all that. Now please, tell me what have you found out?'

'Well, Leila's and Blake's previous addresses were in Hayes, and I think her parents still live there, you could try that number,' he finally explained, sliding a folded piece of paper across the table to her. She hurriedly shoved it in her dark denim jacket's breast pocket. 'And?'

'And Blake's parents' address, which again, I think is still their address, is on that paper as well. You can ring them, introduce yourself as a friend of Alana's, then explain what happened to her to them and why she needs them.' She lowered her head to hide her rueful eyes, breathed in deeply and swallowed compulsively. 'What's the matter, Kat?'

'Umm…there was something I wanted to tell you about Al. She… she tried to top herself with the drink on

Monday.'

'She *what*?' he shrieked.

'Yup. I came home from work at around ten at night,
tried to wake her up when I saw the curtains weren't
closed, and she didn't wake up, no matter how much I
shook her. I dashed downstairs to alert Mr Peel, the
owner of that bed sit, and he saw how shaken up I was,
and yet I still had to threaten him to call an ambulance.
At the hospital, they said she almost had alcohol poisoning
and had to have her stomach pumped. She was still
unconscious when I visited her yesterday.'

'Holy… why didn't you tell me before? Is she okay?'

'Yeah. She's fine and coming back on Friday. I called
the betting shop as Al, where she works part-time, and
told them she'll be returning next week, due to sickness.
I needed to get the addresses urgently, to stop this damage
she's doing to herself. If this goes on, there's a good
chance I'll come home from work one night and find her
dead.'

'True. Anyway, thanks for telling me. Go for it. I now
know it's for a good cause.'

'I know that, too. Thank you very much for doing this.
It really means a lot to me.'

'Let me know how you get on, okay?'

'I will. Thanks again,' she raised herself from the bench,
and slung the rucksack on her shoulder. 'Hey, aren't you having
something to eat?'

'Umm…is the food good here? It's just I've heard funny
stories about canteen food,' she jested, unable to suppress
her ever-loudening stomach simply by placing a hand over it. He
smiled in humour.

'Well, you can dismiss those funny stories when you're
eating in this canteen – the food is great! Just go to the
counter, and see for yourself.'

'Sure.' She ambled to the counter without her bag. About
five minutes later, she returned with a steaming cup of tea and a
square portion of lasagne loaded with dripping cheese, which

reminded her of home cooking. *Oh no, don't mention home, girl...*she chided herself as she returned to her seat. Immediately after adjusting her rear on the solid bench, she shoved a forkful of food in her mouth and chewed scrupulously. 'Hey, this really is great.'

'See? I told you so.' They both breathed out a slight laugh. She began eating more assuredly as he finished a pasta salad in some sort of tomato sauce. 'So, explain to me the full story about you and Alana. I've not got much to do today, so take your time.' She inhaled deeply again, both prepared to synchronize themselves with the mixture of simultaneous echoing discussions. 'Here goes...'

'Mmm...Blake...Blake...get off me, please...don't
touch me...why don't you go back to your bitch?' Alana maundered, which increased to a pitiful yell as she writhed on the padded surface, feeling two or three things popping out of both her fretting arms. 'Wake up, Al. Wake up.' She tried blinking her gritty eyelids apart, welded together by unconsciousness. Eventually, a woman, a slim, dark woman in a pale blue nurse's uniform, probably West Indian, her waist pinched in by a midnight blue belt, leaning over her. 'Back off, Freda! Back off, now! I'll kill you, you fucking bitch!' she screamed ear-shatteringly, flailing her arms about again still lying down, whipping over the steel drip holder beside the bed. The woman recoiled to avoid her assault, her face stretched to one of alarm, and crouched to pick the pole up. With all her effort, she clasped her wrists to either side of the bed as she still ground her teeth for freedom.

'Al, calm down, calm down! I'm not Freda, I'm a nurse;
I'm nurse Stevens. I'm here to help you, okay?!' She shrilled. Alana blinked again, and finally realised her mistake simply by her comparatively clean accent. She slumped back against the pillow-cushioned bed head, and sobbed almost to herself in her palms.

'What's wrong? Are you okay?' Alana removed her face from her palms and stared blankly at the nurse, who was rubbing the back of her neck.

'She took away my best friend, nurse. She took him away from me…' she trailed off as she broke down again in her hands. The nurse outstretched her arm to re-insert a tube through it, then circled to the other side of the bed.

'Here, bring your other arm. What happened? Who took him away from you? This Freda person?' She nodded remorsefully.

'She…she's Blake's horrible girlfriend…separated us after ten years…can't get over it…don't know where he is…you look like her…' she gasped between cries.

'Oh God, I'm sorry I remind you of her. Look…'

'No, it's okay. Has a Kat Slate been in here?' she asked, finally pulled together, brushing away her tears with a knuckle.

'Umm…actually, yes she has. Yesterday, it was. She was talking to the sister. She came in here. She even declined therapy for you.'

'I've only overdone it with the booze, so why are they treating me like I'm a mental patient?'

'Well, because they want to find out why you did that, psychologically speaking. But Miss Slate insisted for therapy to only be a last resort – yes, that was her exact quote.' Alana tried to utter something, but was overwhelmed by a thoughtfulness she hadn't seen since her friendship with Leila and Blake while their territory was unspoilt.

'Umm…I'm absolutely touched, nurse.'

'She seems a good friend.' Alana stretched her discoloured, chapped lips into a grin.

'Funny thing is, I've only known her for…what day is it today?'

'Wednesday the third of March ninety-nine.'

'Well, that means I've known her for only four days.'

'That's great.'

'Anyway, I'm sorry about earlier.'

'It's okay. I've seen worse. Would you like some food?

134

Your stomach has stabilized, so you should be able to
hold in something.' She sniggered.

'Sure.' Nurse Stevens raised herself to her feet, and headed
to the pine doorway. 'So, what's the best meal you have here?'

'I'd recommend some bangers and mash for someone
in your state.'

'Umm…okay, I'll have that then.'

'Coming up!' She finally dashed out into the main ward.
Alana felt goose bumps ripple her skin from the fresh blast of air
from the air conditioning. She felt her blood had become the
drink, barely alive without it, and also felt sleepy from the brief
coma. The nerves in her fingers trembled since the nightmare,
though the memory of it was already pithy after such a short time.
All she remembered was Blake trying to squeeze her whole body
to death or something with his, not with his hands round her
throat. Her eyelids' flutters decreased, and eventually stopped by
sleepiness. *I'll wake up again when she brings the food…*

Ho-hum, I'm finally home, Katerina yawned as she stepped
into the black room. Once she found the light switch, all its
mysteriousness became a scene ever so familiar – tossed-up
duvets and clothes piled on the floor, and a sink full with dishes
and cups. She flung her jacket and rucksack on the bed, and
herself on her back with her arms behind her head, studying the
ceiling, blinking her eyelids compulsively to keep her exhausted
self awake as she inverted into her recent memory to retrieve
something. *Another insignificant but productive day at work to
pay the rent…*The night before, she had just returned from seeing
Alana's near-dead body, shaken just like when she found her in
bed. Drunkenness never startled her, but the state it left her in,
did. she had curled herself on the bed in an almost catatonic state
– no tears, no laughter, no movement, just staring through the air.
She amazed herself simply by showing up at the University that
morning. Her twitching eyes halted wide open, then with a reflex
action she shot her arm to her side, and fumbled for the jacket.
She found the piece of paper Mr Sutton gave her, and studied it
for several seconds. *Mmm…let's see…Eliot and Marlene*

Turpin...Blake's parents...Lily Drayton...Leila's mum...I'll ring tomorrow. At ten-thirty, it's too bloody late now. With that, she hauled herself off the bed, grasped the grey nightshirt and a toiletry bag from the chair, and rushed to the bathroom in a gust of wind, causing an almighty bang. *Whoops...*

Chapter 12.

"Yippee! No work today, no work today!" Katerina sang loudly, almost laughing at herself at that involuntary outburst. She wiggled along to iterative electric beats on the radio as she scraped the margarine against the toast. A sudden waft of humid morning breeze ruffled her already tousled hair from behind her ears, which she tucked back. Giggling to herself stupidly, she sat crossed-legged on the edge of the bed and took the first nibble of her toast, shimmying her shoulders in her own little imaginary disco. Humming with her mouth full, she grabbed the piece of paper from the bedside cabinet, and studied it once more. Poking the last morsel of grease-sodden toast in her mouth, she stretched her arm to toss the plate in the sink, grabbed her toiletry bag and clothes from the day before, and sprinted re-energized to the bathroom…

She squeezed her bottom through the gap of the half-open, graffiti-embellished glass door of the phone booth next to the bus stop a few yards from the bed sit, finally shielded from the wind that frustratingly threw off her carefully combed hair into a hay stack. For a second or two she hugged the jacket's collar round her neck, caught her breath and looked up at the glumly-coloured skies. *Damn, I should've brought my brolly.* She delved her hand into her hip pocket for two one-pound coins, and the other hand in her jacket pocket for the paper. She then pushed the numeral buttons. *Okay, Al, all for you…*she thought, shivering nervously as she waited for a voice. 'Hello?' a lady replied after five rings.

'Hi…umm, is this Marlene Turpin?'

'Uh-huh. Who's speaking?'

'Well, you don't know me, but my name is Kat Slate, and, uh, I'm a friend of Alana Higgins. I believe you know her?'

'Yeah, well, I used to, because she was my son's best friend. Why are you calling me?'

'Well, I've two reasons. First is Alana is in serious trouble. She's my roommate, and she was really hostile to me to start off with, but she began telling me the whole story about her friendship with your son and stuff.'

'Oh. Carry on.'

'Umm…the second, and most shocking reason is, that
she's become an alcoholic, and nearly drank herself to
death. She's currently stable in Ealing Hospital now.'

'What?!'

'Yup. Anyway, she wants him and Leila Drayton back,
but doesn't know where they are, so she asked me to
call you,' she lied in an instant as confidently as if it was
rehearsed.

'Umm, sure. I know he's in Dublin, but…hang on, I
think he wrote something down before he left – not for
us, because he rowed with us as well over his girlfriend,
Freda.'

'Okay. I've got a pen here, so read it out and I'll write it
down.' During the pause, she fumbled in her other jacket
pocket. 'Hello?'

'Yeah?'

'I have his address and number here in his diary…' Katerina
scribbled urgently on the paper, almost breaking the nib as
Marlene dictated them to her. 'Okay. Thanks again, Mrs Turpin,
you've been a wonderful help.'

'No problem. Thanks for telling me this. You want me
to ring him?'

'No, not a good idea. He's not talking to you, so he'd
probably slam the phone down once he knows it's you,
and if he did talk to you, he'd probably think you're lying.'
Silence for several seconds.

'Yeah. You're absolutely right. Thanks. Good luck…
Kat, was it?'

'Yeah. I'll let you know how I do.'

'Okay. Bye.'

'Bye.' She placed the receiver down. *Yes!* She punched
upwards, feeling victorious. Glancing at her watch, it read nine-
thirty. *Shit, it looks like bloody midnight*, she thought, downcast.
*Okay, on to step two…*About five minutes after a similar
introduction, questions and answers with Lily Drayton, and
received a similar answer. *Double yes!* she screamed in her mind

after replacing the receiver, repeating her air-punch. She then shoved her hand in her hip pocket again. *Have got more pound coins…?Yes I do! God, this is a pain. I've got to get a mobile soon…*she heard a ruthless rattling sound which she could not mistake for reception problems. *Oh shit – rain and no umbrella. Just wonderful – and typical…*

'Hi, honey, I'm home!' yelled a pre-pubic voice from the brilliant white, Victorian front door.

'Oh God, do you know how puerile that sounds?' a male voice gnarled in annoyance from the kitchen. Stopping his task, his ears were occupied zooming in on the loudening paces. Then a pair of arms encircled his waist, and her lips pecked his stubbly cheek.

'Ah, well, it's because it is puerile that I like annoying you with it!' she snobbishly answered through her nose.

'Oh, I see!' He turned to face her, giggling slightly at the height difference between them – she was only up to his shoulder. She wore a long, red wine jumper and wide-legged, dark blue jeans. After his invisible mockery, and admiration, he squeezed her into an embrace, eliciting a groan from both of them. 'Welcome home, Lill.'

'Thank you, Tre, even though I've just been to buy some breakfast things.'

'I've only been up half an hour. It's difficult to sleep without you.'

'Aww, bless. Here's the bag of goodies; let's fix breakfast together.' She lifted out of a carrier bag a loaf of bread, two one-pint bottles of milk, raspberry jam, croissants, a brick of butter, and a bag of coffee granules.

'Good.' As she rolled her sleeves up, she glanced at her watch – it read quarter to ten.

'Well, I thought we might as well celebrate having no work today.'

'Can you think of any other ways to celebrate such an occasion?'

'A clue is in that little bag over there,' she pointed with a suggestive smirk. Tre eagerly marched to the elliptical bronzed pine table diagonally from the worktop where she stood splitting open the croissants. His hand felt a rough material, inspiring him to lift it out. It was a red lacy bra and briefs set, interweaved with gold. 'Yup, I think I have a pretty good idea.' Both chuckled as he lowered it back into the jade bag. He marched back over to help her place the croissants onto the grilling rack. After she turned the dial to the appropriate temperature, they returned to each other's arms, squeezing not only themselves, but also a straightened grin on both their faces as she ran a hand up his fair, shapely cheekbone to his raven hair that stood in lengthy spikes. She then placed her weight on the tips of her toes to rub both of their narrow noses together, still grinning and giggling like childhood sweethearts. Then the bell of the phone between the kitchen doorframe and the fridge made both their nerves leap. 'I'll get it. God, I've got to adjust the volume on that thing.'

'Yeah, well, it's hard to hear when clattering in the
    kitchen takes place, if you know what I mean.' He paired that with an evocative glint in his eye. She just rolled her eyes in amusement, and focused her ear to the receiver. 'Hello?'

'Hi, is this Leila Drayton?'

'Yeeeesss?' she slurred in curiosity. She didn't know anyone with a foreign accent of some sort.

'Hi, um, you won't know me, but my name is Kat Slate.'
'Who?'

'Kat Slate, and I believe I know your friend, Alana
    Higgins?' Her heart felt it was about to drop to the floor like a loosened pendulum; her attention was now undivided to this 'informant'.

'Umm…whoa…umm…how do you know her?'

'She's my roommate at a bed sit room.'

'I see, but what happened? She lived at her Mum's.'

'Yeah, but she said she had a row with her over a man
    Al found her in bed with.'

'Oh my God. But what's this got to do with me?' She queried, just wanting to return to her everyday life there in the present time. Katerina just raised her brow in incredulity at what she thought was concern in the beginning.

'Oh boy, Alana would certainly be charmed if she was here.' Katerina took a deep breath to renew her patience. 'She's depressed, Leila. She failed her degree – and she's now an alcoholic – only working in a betting shop to pay for the rent and the booze. All in all, she's just a shell; no heart, no spirit, no conscience. I expected just an itty-bit of feeling from you.'

'Look Kat, or whatever your name is, it's the alcoholism that split us up. I found out about the vodka bottles under the bed, and we had a blazing row. I'm in no position to dry her out – if she wants to do that, she'll do it herself!' she snapped, weaving a shaky hand through her hair. Katerina inhaled deeply once again, and ran a hand through her own hair anxiously.

'I can't believe after nearly twelve years you don't care! Can't you see, it is because she has no reason to give it up that she ended up in hospital to have her stomach pumped!'

'She…what?!'

'Oh, didn't I tell you? She's in hospital after trying to commit suicide with vodka. Can you fucking believe it? I didn't ask her, because when I visited her yesterday, she was still unconscious. Why? Because she's been feeling sorry for herself for the last eight months due to you and Blake. And what's your answer to all this? Emigrate to Cardiff or wherever the hell you are! You and I can bring her back to life again. So either you grow up and put the past behind you, or there's gonna be a second suicide attempt, and neither of us will be able to rescue her.' A dead silence followed while Katerina breathed deeply again for the third time in about three minutes after squealing imploringly through a single breathe.

'Umm…look,' Leila began in a quiet tone, which signalled a probable defeat. 'Where are you now?'

'I'm in Uxbridge Road, just outside the University.

The bed sit is about fifty yards away from this phone
booth.'
'Okay. Umm…I'll give Blake a ring…'
'That's not a good idea. I'll tell him myself. I have his
number.'
'One thing…'
'What?'
'Where did you get my number? From Al?'
'No, through Glenn Sutton, who gave me both your
parents' and Blake's parents' numbers. Al knows
nothing about this.'
'Oh. Well, good luck with Blake, as you may find him
a little more difficult to come through. You know why?'
'Yeah. Al told me a few days ago. Hey, don't hang up
yet. What are you going to do?'
'I'll take the train from here to Southall. When you ring
back, I'll tell you my plans to travel on Saturday. Can
you be contacted?'
'Not really.'
'Okay, look, I'm sorry for my apathy earlier; I admit,
I could have reacted better. Tell me when you come
to an understanding with Blake.'
'Sure. Anyway, I'll call later to tell you. 'Bye bye.'
'G' bye, Kat.'
'Okay, okay, I'll remember that. G' bye.' With that, she
replaced the receiver, slumped her back against the fridge door,
almost sliding to the beige-tiled floor, and her face close to
breaking down as she stared into space. Tre was about to open the
grill door with a tea towel when he spotted this. He reached a
thickset arm, covered with a white short sleeve, round her
shoulder for support. 'What's wrong, honey?' She turned to face
him, noticing his crumpled brow of concern. 'Tre, I know this is
all double Dutch to you, but it's all my fault that my best friend's
in hospital. *I'm* killing my best friend, Tre; someone who isn't my
enemy, but my sister,' she groaned out between sobs. 'What are
you talking about? *Who* are you talking about?' As he pulled her
in for a comforting hug, he ripped two kitchen towels from the

dispenser, and dabbed under her eyes and nose. 'Come on, what is it?' he continued to softly coerce.

'It's one hell of a long story, Tre. Switch off the cooker, and let's go to the living room.' He swiftly pushed a switch, and led her out the doorway to the rose-coloured living room, adorned by wall plants, an electric chandelier from a circular panel on the high whitewashed ceiling, their bare feet sinking into the mauve carpet. With one arm still around her, he led her past the circular glass table, and sat her down onto the cream, square-backed couch. Then he sat facing her with a hand on her knee…

Combing his eyes through each photograph on each of the pages, from when they were ten years old upwards, they fell as they reached the last picture they took together. He wondered why that three-quarters full story of their lives couldn't continue. *Maybe I should just forget this strife and get our friendship back on track. But Freda won't have it, and I love Freda to bits. It's too much to sacrifice…* He stopped flipping the pages at the last one, which was a portrait of Alana, facing sideways, with a navy blue velvet cloth draped off her shoulders. She was eighteen; March 1995 was inscribed in gold at the bottom right of the photo. Staring into the brown eyes of that picture, he felt like he was shut away in a deep, dark cave in solitude where he was right then. *God, I wish I could reach into this picture…* He flung the album under the bed, and on his stomach, rested his cheek on the backs of his hands, his arms folded in on the surface of the bed…

He wavered his eyes open again, completely in a haze at how long he'd been asleep. His next sensation was a tube or something poking him in the side. He found himself lying face down on the fluffy, white duvet, his feet opposite the head. Raising his read, he focused on the sliding window door, realising it was not closed the way he left it. The wind was extremely bitter, almost freezing the skin on his face. Rolling over onto his back, he saw a narrow figure, dressed in a black sweater, black jeans and a black balaclava. He just stared till he felt something tubular poking into his waist. 'Oh shit…who are you?' he groaned, his eyes gaping as he trembled with his limbs motionless. No speech, the person hauled him by his underarms to sit up against the bed head, then straddled him. 'Oh shit...' he strained again. But his nerves levelled a little at the realisation that it was probably an off cut of a scaffolding tube, not a gun. He frowned in confusion. Then the silent captor slid a hand under the mask, and shook the brown hair which clung to the scalp. 'Oh my God! Alana?' he shrieked. She pressed a black satin-gloved finger to his lips. 'Hush! Where's the bitch? Some girlfriend she is, leaving you all alone here,' she rasped in a sexual tone, which emitted a laugh from him. 'You're a cheeky sod, Al! I've missed you. Can't we put this argument behind us, please? It's been on my conscience, leaving you in the lurch like that. Will you forgive me?' he pouted out like a little boy.

'Umm...probably. As for your putting-behind business, maybe I could put these...' she said softly as she raised her hands to his view. 'On *your* behind instead. Would you like that, huh?' He widened his attentive focus into her eyes as she slid her hands under his bottom. 'Oh go on then!' he gritted out, his body losing patience with her teasing. He rolled both of them over to cover her, and restrained her wrists above her head. He studied her figure through the polo-necked jumper, noticing her chest had burgeoned to probably twice the size it was, and looked up with an approving smile at her. She then peered down the hanging collar of his shirt to examine his toned, hairless torso, looked up to his eyes and smirked bashfully and invitingly at the same time, which strangely turned him on. He then attempted to muffle her giggling fit by leaning over to seal his mouth over hers...

'Blake? Blake? Wakey-wakey, I'm back!' He fluttered his eyes open again, only to see Freda kissing his cheek. He found himself exactly where he was lying before the 'break-in'. *It's just a dream; just a sodding dream...of Al? What was I thinking?* he squinted in frustration, then in shock. 'So, taking a kip, eh?' she squealed eagerly as she clinked her shoe heels across the polished floors to sit beside him, and slung the bag across the room near the window door. 'So, uh, how was your night-duty, then?' he uttered shakily.

'Huh, not all that. Think you could make a cup of tea?' she grumpily ordered, as she lied on the edge of the bed with her arms behind her head.

'Sure.' He unenthusiastically rolled off the bed to his feet, and went through the left doorway to the short aqua hall, leading either to the kitchen on his left, or the living room perpendicular to that entrance. As he flicked the switch to proceed boiling the kettle, he was startled by the phone ringing. 'I'll get it,' he whimpered.

'No, no, I'll get it. You just continue making the tea.' She rolled to her side, and reached for the receiver. 'Hello?'

'Hi. Uh, could I speak to Blake Turpin, please?' Freda frowned in confusion. She didn't allow him to work, so he couldn't get to know anyone there.

'Who is this?'

'Well, my name is Kat Slate. I know Blake's old friend, Alana Higgins. Can I speak to him please?'

'No, you can't. He's not in. G' bye.' she abruptly growled before slamming the receiver down. Moments later, Blake sauntered in, precariously balancing one cup of hot tea in each hand. 'Who was that?'

'Oh, just a wrong number. Okay, now let's talk…'

'That fucking bitch! I swear, if she was in the same room as me, I'd be carted off to Strangeways for murder by now! Bitch!' Katerina screamed beyond her lung capacity, ramming her foot almost through the glass panels. No one was around, so the last thing on her mind was feeling self-conscious about airing her frustration. She halted, clenched her fists and eyelids, and restricted her wheezing. *Come on, Kat, calm down. Right, let's try again…* with that, she pressed the redial button, and bashed her back against a panel, still outraged.

'It's me again. Could I speak to Blake please? Come on, and don't say I didn't ask nicely. I know he's there, Freda, so put him on the bloody line!'

'Hey, how did you know my name?'

'Never mind that! Just put him on!' Silence. Freda, dumbfounded, accepted defeat at this mystery caller. *He couldn't be...he only goes out with me...* 'Blake, come to the phone. It's for you,' she quietly called to bring him back into the bedroom from checking the post in the living room. 'Who is it?'

'Some girl – don't know who. I thought you might know,' she said in a teasing intonation, hoping to sense a change in his expression.

'Huh?' he squeaked in confusion, taking the receiver from Freda, who had that very same look on her face. 'Hello?'

'Blake Turpin, my name's Kat Slate – listen to me and listen good – I know your old friend Al Higgins, and I rang you because she needs you.'

'What? How do you know her?'

'She's my roommate in the local bed sit.'

'Bed sit? Wha...what's this got to do with me, anyway? We were friends a long time ago. It's ancient history, whatever your name is. Why open up old wounds?'

'Oh, so that's how you see your own best friend? As a wound? That really is charming.'

'Look, you don't know what really happened, so stay out of this!'

'Oh yes I do know what happened! You fell out because of Freda, right?' Silence on both ends. 'I can't hear yoooou?' she howled sarcastically.

'Yeah. Well, I don't need any lecture about my personal life from some one whom I don't know one shit about, okay?' Silence again.

'You know she's in hospital? Did you know that?' she returned, half-serious, half-humorous.

'What?'

'Yeah. Lying there, recovering from having her stomach pumped. Probably just came round after three days.'

'What happened? She's been there since Monday?'

'Yeah, for your information. Tried to top herself with alcohol. Now will you show some concern?'

'God, how could she be so stupid as to juice herself

like that?' Katerina dropped her jaw, then scrunched up her mouth.

'What, you think it was a booze-up? No way, mister!
She's depressed, all because you couldn't care less
about the state you left her in! Neither you nor Leila!'
'You rang…'
'And you know what else? Try picturing having a row with
your best friend, feeling you have no one in the world and
feeling drink and memories are the only way to get by, and
going through each day feeling sorry for yourself. You just
imagine that. It's not a pretty picture, but it's reality, Blake.
So are you going to stop acting like an asshole and come
and see her, or will I have to go to Dublin and drag you
here myself? I have your address, you know!' His mouth
fell open, wondering what on earth hit him just now, but no sound
came out.

'You know what? It's your call. You're an adult, or at
least I think you are, so decide your God-damned self.
Good morning,' she hissed, then hung up before he could
reply. 'Well, what the hell is going on, damn it?' Freda screamed,
wide-eyed at Blake.

'It's about Al. She's in hospital.'

'So? It's not your problem anymore.' Blake's eyes gaped at
her coldness.

'You know, you can be so bloody callous sometimes.'
'Why? It's the truth, isn't it?'
'Yeah, but you wouldn't say that if it were me in that
hospital bed, would you?'
'Since when did you care?'
'Now, apparently. Please, can I see her?'
'No!'
'Please!'
'No, no, no! She was nasty to you, she was nasty to me.
If you love me, you're not going anywhere. But if you
buy that plane ticket, that door will become a wall, you got
that?' she yelled militantly, pointing a finger in his face. With the
cup in her hand, she threw herself upright off the bed, and

stomped angrily to the kitchen. He sighed as he collapsed on his back onto a pile of pillows. *Why do I put up with this?*

'Well, that's that. Set me back nearly a hour and six quid, but at least it was a shelter from the rain,' she resolutely told herself, rolling her eyes upwards at the refreshed sparkle of the warming sun with a satisfied smile. 'Oi! Other people have to use this phone too, you know! Get out of there!' boomed an Anglo Afro-Caribbean voice. She whipped round in alarm at a tall, dark chunky man with a black baseball cap, a black vest and white jeans which bunched up round his ankles.

'Alright, alright, keep your shirt on! I'm coming out!' she yelled, handing over the handle of the door to him. 'Thank you.'

Wow, what a change of weather, she thought as she set herself on the cold and slightly damp plastic bench on her own as she waited for the bus. *What time is it now? Ah yes, nearly eleven. Time to see Al...have I got enough change...?* She rummaged through her purse for a five-pound note. *Uh-huh, I certainly do...bus driver will be pissed, though. Hope that asshole Blake will come round. She needs him...* her thoughts were cut short on hearing the bus pull up. 'Ealing Hospital, please.'

Chapter 13.

Katerina strolled coolly down the brightly-lit corridor of the Intensive Care Unit, passing doorways which alternated between dark and alight ones. Her shoulders were brushed by frantic nurses and doctors, and families and friends pacing in paranoid; she tried her best to keep her strides as limited as possible to calm the ringing in her ears caused by her shoe heels clinking against the white floors. Noticing the only still white-uniformed nurse there, standing outside what was probably the twentieth doorway, fiddling with something. She marched over and patted her shoulder. She was likely to be a staff nurse, because Katerina remembered someone telling her what the coloured uniforms meant. 'Err, excuse me, could you tell me where an Alana Higgins is please? I'm a friend of hers.' At first, the nurse gave a curious look, then an entrusting smile. 'You wouldn't happen to be Kat Slate, would you?'

'Why, yes, I am. Are you the nurse looking after her?'

'Yup. I'm Nurse Stevens,' she introduced warmly, extending her hand to Katerina, which she accepted. 'Look, I'm not family, but I'm the nearest person to her at the moment.'

'That's okay.'

'How is she, nurse?'

'She's now very conscious, although she did thrash about when she came about yesterday. She screamed obscenities at me and was very delirious. She must have been having a bad dream. But she was asking after you as well. She'll be ready to go home tomorrow,' she replied plainly, but ending proudly. Katerina widened her eyes in surprise. 'Really?'

'Yup. She apologised though. But she's perfectly in the green.'

'Thank you very much, nurse. Can I see her?'

'Sure. Follow me. It's door twenty-eight.' She tried to keep up the swift-walking nurse's pace further down that apparently never-ending corridor, and kept looking up at the signs above the door. 'It's here. I'll be back in fifteen minutes.'

'Cheers.' After watching the nurse practically bouncing herself as she walked back down the corridor, she peered through the doorway, and smiled in relief at seeing her sitting up with her head down joyfully in a magazine. 'Hey, boozy!' Alana shot up to attention.

'Kat! What a lovely surprise!' She dashed over to the bed and hugged her in eagerness at seeing her that would only exist if they'd known each other for years, and eagerness at not seeing her without circles round her eyes, or her hair greasy and dishevelled; she still looked undernourished beneath the blue nightgown, but not as painfully thin as when they first met. Katerina broke the embrace to look at her directly in the face. 'Good God, are you really the same person? Or have you met some tasty doctor or something?' Alana let out a belly laugh, which secretly startled Katerina, as she hadn't heard such an honest laugh before. 'Huh! Dream on! Have you actually seen the doctors here? They're either too old, or the young ones look like they're from the Glastonbury festival or something!' They both laughed so hard, they saw stars beneath their eyelids when they stopped. 'I see! Well, how are they treating you here?'

'Terrific. Have you met Nurse Stevens? She's been lovely.'

'Yeah. She took me here. I heard you'd been a bad girl when you woke up, right?' Alana snorted.

'Um, yeah. Um, I...had a dream or something about Blake wanting to kill me here in this bed. Not by strangling me with his hands, but by squashing me with his whole body. I was murmuring, "Blake, get off me, go back to your bitch," or something like that, but when I saw Nurse Stevens shaking me, I thought she was Freda, and I screamed at her. Till she told me her name and listened to her non-Irish accent, I thought it was her, because of her skin colour for starters, but she calmed me down eventually.'

'Weird dream. Why would Blake of all people want to kill you? From what you told me, he adores you. Has Freda got

to you so much, you're hallucinating about her?'
'Yeah. I hate her for what she's done, and will never,
ever forgive her. As for Blake, we did say some
horrible things to each other towards the end – I
wouldn't be surprised if he does want to kill me.
Freda is a cunning, crafty cow, so I wouldn't be
surprised if that happened. Anyway, what have
you been up to?' *Have a good guess*, she thought cheekily.
'Oh, not much, just going to University, work, the same
as usual. I had to keep going as normal, to stop myself
from feeling upset about you, and I called your workplace
and adopted your voice to say you were having the rest
of the week off.'
'Thanks a lot for doing that.' Katerina suddenly adopted
a serious glare at her.
'I need to ask you something – did you try to do away
with yourself, Al?' she asked sternly. Silence, then a deep
breath, instilling anticipation in both of them.
'Yes, I did, Kat. When I remembered all the events
telling my story, everything came back to remind me
I'd lost everything with no chance of retrieval,' she sighed,
frowning and turning her head away in shame.
'Maybe, but pack in the self-blame – it doesn't suit you.'
'I'm trying to. You know, I can't thank you enough for
caring. I mean, we've known each other for less than a
week, and it's like I've known you for years. You are
right; sod them, let them go wherever and do whatever
they want.'
'Hey, I'm not saying throw away eleven years of your
life – I'm saying get on with it again. Give up the booze
and the self-pity, first and foremost. Then start your
degree again – I know you have limited money, but
can't you pay in instalments? Surely Sutton would
have some pity on you. From what you told me, it
seems he had great respect for you. Thirdly, get
moving again. The world is waiting for you, girl!' Alana
compassionately looked at Katerina, the thought of what she had

done to deserve such a good friend crossing her mind. 'You
know, that's is what I like about you – you're such an optimist.
How the hell do you do it?'

    'Simple! My motto has always been, "If there's a way
    in, you can be pretty damned sure there's a way out
    of it." There's no such thing as a bottomless pit. If
    you adopt that one formula for life, you can achieve
    anything.'

    'Lovely. I'll try that when I get out of here.'

    'Well, you better start subliminally absorbing it now!
    Forget all the bad times, stand tall and have some
    respect for yourself.'

    'Okay then. Thanks a whole lot for that. You know,
    I feel better already.'

    'Good. Oh, I nearly forgot,' she extended a hand
downwards for a plastic bag, and placed it on the bed. 'I did a bit
of shopping in Ealing. I bought a punnet of strawberries, a bunch
of grapes, a little tub of moisturising cream, and a deodorant
stick. I know how horrid you must feel lying there. Oh, and look
what I bought for myself.' She removed a rectangular box, and
placed it on Alana's lap. 'A mobile phone? These cost a bomb to
keep! Are you mad?'

    'No they don't! Plus, I'm fed up of asking that asshole
    Peel every time I have to make a call. Did you know I
    had to practically beg him to ring the ambulance, even
    though he could see quite clearly I was panicking? I told
    him that if you died, it would have been his fault. So
    these things are worth it in the long run, especially in a
    place like that bed sit.'

    'Are you serious? He actually was that heartless to not
    see you were distressed?'

    'Yup. Anyway, as for him finding out, he's not going
    to find out as long as I keep it on silent.'

    'Hmm, true. Good thinking, especially as the nearest
    phone box away from there is about fifty bloody yards
    away.'

    'Exactly, so this is an investment. It doesn't need to

have fancy features, as I won't be using it very often.
I'm not a compulsive telephoner, as I've no one to
phone.' They giggled again as Katerina set the bag beside
the bed.

'I realise that – now! Can I have the strawberries?' She
handed her the plastic container from the bag. She picked the
largest one from the top and shoved the whole fruit in her mouth,
chewing with difficulty. 'You greedy pig! You have teeth for a
reason, you know!'

'I realise, but I haven't had strawberries for ages.
Plus the food here is gross, apart from the mashed
potatoes.'

'Oh, I see. Can I have one?' Alana picked one from the
container and passed it to her, holding the stalk between her
thumb and forefinger. 'Thanks.' Katerina slurped it noisily,
causing Alana to roll her eyes.

'God, listen to you! You're no better than me!'
'Well, I haven't eaten for four hours. I'm trying to reduce.'
'How contradictory. I need feeding up, and you need
slimming down, but you're scoffing again.'
'It's fruit, Al!'
'Yeah, I suppose…'
'Well, I'm glad to hear you're back on track. Remember,
a bottle of vodka is an inanimate object – it can't resolve
your sorrows, but a friend on the other hand, like me, can
at least try to put things in perspective for one's own
solutions, if not solve it completely.'
'Let me tell you something, I don't want to be in this
bed again, or worse, a body bag. Not a nice thought,
I can tell you, but being my old self again, *is* a nice
thought.'
'So?'
'I'll fill in a form at the University on Monday. But I'll
rest this weekend. Maybe we can go shopping together
for a change for my birthday next Thursday.'
'What about this Adrian business?'
'I'll try my best to give him up. I don't know when I'll

find the guy of my life, whoever he is, but I will wait
for him. After all, it's likely I'll click in the same way
as with him, right?'
'Maybe, but it's certainly better waiting ten years for
someone real than drinking away those years wishing
for something that won't come true.'

'You're right!' The giggled as Alana kept handing her more
strawberries while stuffing every other strawberry in her mouth.
They were alerted by someone clearing their throat by the
doorway. 'Umm, Miss Slate? Fifteen minutes is up.'

'Okay, I'll be out in a mo. Al, great to see you're back
on track, enjoy the goodies, and I'll be back tomorrow
to pick you up.'
'Thanks, Kat. I don't know what time…hey, nurse
Stevens! What time am I due to leave? My mate
here is picking me up.'
'Uh, about midday to one o' clock. You can come
about then.'
'Okay. University would be finished by then, so that's
fine.'
'Shit, I forgot about that. Okay, see you tomorrow then.'

Kat stood up, straightened her jeans, and threw her arms round
her again, which Alana returned the gesture. 'Have a nice day,
Al.'

'You too. Bye.' Kat flapped her hand at her as she left
the doorway, as lead out by the nurse.
'Cor blimey, she looks so much happier from when I
last saw her. What medicine did you give her, nurse?!' she
shrieked, still surprised at her newfound exultation. The nurse
giggled. 'Anyway, thanks for looking after her.'

'No problem at all. See you tomorrow.'

'Okay. 'Bye.' Katerina continued stomping down the
corridor, trying to speed up the long walk ahead, as the nurse
entered a doorway about four or five doors away from Alana's.
*Yes! She'll drop down with a heart attack when – and if – she
sees Leila and Blake again, but it'll certainly make her world*

*revolve again. Blake will change his mind – it'll be on his
conscience if he doesn't.*

Blake sprung himself upright from his bed, struck by the
feeling in his skull like a burst fissure in volcanic ground, and a
prickly pain on the left side of his chest, and his cheek felt rigid.
He noticed the lights were still out, and limited to a little glimmer
of moonlight, its glowing sphere visible through the net curtains.
He twisted his head, noticing Freda was still asleep with her limbs
splayed out to almost the whole span of the bed. Strange, low
grunting noises screwed up his eardrums as he sat propped up by
his arms for several minutes. He wiped the perspiration from his
forehead, not sure why it was there, as several surges of night
breeze blew the curtains aside and upwards in a flow. He rolled
off the bed, wearing only black boxer shorts, and grasped the
dressing gown from the floor. Halted his creep to the doorway to
the hall, he turned back, and felt no spark whatsoever that people
in long-term couples feel when they look at their partners,
whether asleep or awake, with just a glance or lying in bed with
them.

In the icy kitchen, he twisted a half-full glass of milk,
literally hypnotising himself with it, as he pondered the universal
answer to that one question: why was he staying with her? His
memory whisked him back a few hours before...

'Hey Blake? How about we went out tonight or what?' she
questioned as if it was an order. He lied, wrapped in a white
towelling robe, with his back propped up against the bed head, his
fingers clasped on his stomach, and a sorrowful look on his face.
He was still haunted by his dream earlier on, and she was the last
person he wanted to have an argument with.

'Nah, I don't feel like it tonight,' he groaned
unenthusiastically.

'Well *I* do. So are you going to get your lazy ass up or
do I have to drag you?' His eyes widened at her slave-
driving attitude.

'Lazy ass? You know how much housework I've
done today? Washing, cleaning, ironing, hoovering,

wiping and God knows what else, and you're calling
me a lazy ass?' He protested insistently, pointing a
forefinger at her.

'What did you say?!'

'Don't call me a lazy ass! I'm tired, so forgive me
for feeling a bit pissed off at your orders!' he retorted in an
impertinent tone, folding his arms. Freda gasped, then frowned
her forehead, infuriated at him.

'Right, that's it!' Freda lunged, but his arms successfully
shoved away her raining assaults. But she grabbed him by the
neck hem of his black dressing gown, and yanked his weight onto
the back of his head. 'I'm going to teach you a lesson for
answering back at me, Blake!' she snarled through her teeth. 'Get
off me, Freda!' he screamed, as she unlaced the belt. She recoiled
her hand, and slapped the back of it across his cheek with such
power and heat. He screamed terrifyingly again, everything
whizzing round in a horrifying vortex, with Freda's irately
gnarled face trapped in it with him. 'Shut the fuck up!' she hissed,
backhanding him again and again, feeling a thick ring on her
finger bruising the skin; one cheek, then the other. The blood
rushed to the surface, eventually turning bluish-purple. Still
whimpering, she attempted again to silence him by sinking and
dragging her claw-like nails across the same cheek she injured,
the slurp of instantly seeping blood clearly audible, a deathly
shriek rattling through the room. 'Noooooo!!! Please, get off
me!!!' The tips of her toes pinned his feet down as she lied on top
of him, and she wrapped his hands against the poles of the bed
head with a belt from her blue jeans. *Please, please, stop this
now! Stop, stop, stop! What have I done to you to deserve this?!
Please don't kill me!* He squinted his eyes in prayer, hoping God
would show some mercy, even if she didn't. His intense pain was
evident from the pleading sobs, sweating fits of panic, and tears
mixing with blood. It became so unbearable, the last thing he
remembered was his boxers being pulled down. Then everything
blackened out...

Rubbing a palm on his face, rough from stubble and dried
blood, he hissed at its pain. Blake tried to relive, scrutinize and

fill in gaps of those events in his head, trying to believe they actually happened. Then every scene, every transpiration in his mind unexpectedly snapped into place. *She raped me...she could've killed me. Al, I need you now...I need you...* He kept chanting in a pitiful voice over and over in his dazed head, tears steaming down his face, stinging the wounds as they plinked into the milk. He stared at the spots of blood on the centre of his palm in remorse at himself. *Maybe I'm just a jackass. Why couldn't I fight her back? Oh shit, I can't take this anymore...Al, you were right all along...she's nothing but trouble...look what's she's done to us, and me...she's been violent before, but not nearly this bad...she's never wounded me, never...raped me before, only slapped me...got to get the hell out of here...before she kills me. God, I'm going to be sick...* He kicked the chair aside, sprinted into the bathroom, and held it back long enough to shut the door quietly. He hurled violently into the toilet bowl, more and more as the images of her words and that face of pure evil and brutality reappeared and rammed themselves home in his head. After about ten minutes, still not feeling any sense of relief, he swivelled a few mouthfuls of water in his mouth to rid the bitterness. 'I can't take this anymore,' he groaned through his sore throat, raising his head into focus of the mirror, studying the abominable red, blue, purple and skin-coloured combinations, the three narrow, mealy blood canals in his left cheek and globs of fresh perspiration washed over the old, and water dribbling from his stubbly chin. *Look at my face...like a great big monster scraped half the flash out of it...* After splashing some of the water on his face, the expression on his face suddenly changed. His eyes widened in surprise, and his jaw fell slightly after seeing what he thought was Alana's face for a spilt second in his own reflection. Like her portrait, the one that caused him to moon over her momentarily. Then something clicked... *That's it! That's it! That's why I had that dream! That's why that girl rang, telling me where she was! That's why she was the first name I called for just now...oh shit, why didn't I realise this sooner? For ten, nearly eleven years, that's who I've loved all along – Alana Higgins. Yesterday's events were a sign. There is a God somewhere... She probably* *hates me, not that I can blame her, but I've got to make it up to her somehow...it's her, it's her, it's been her all along...*New tears, this time of relief and happiness, rolled down his cheeks into the crease of his smiling mouth, but Freda's belligerence still hovered over him like a shadow of approaching death. He knew he needed to run, but he now knew where he'd be safe and happy; somewhere right before his eyes he never saw before. He grabbed a couple of plasters from the cabinet beside the mirror, and precariously squeezed the scabby edges together, flinching slightly, and stuck them across all the scrapes. He smiled at himself as he walked away. Dropping to his knees on the chilly blue tiles beside the toilet, he meditated on a short trip of thought. *Right, I think I've got some money in the suitcase, and my bank account card, too. Suitcase is in the closet. I'll sneak out to the travel agent tomorrow, and I'm getting the first plane out of here tomorrow night or the next day. God, what a horrible, horrible mistake I've made, and look what I've lost for me to discover it...*

'Please, think about it, love. This girl could be someone trying to wind you up,' Tre pleaded as he stood by the bed watching Leila place one t-shirt after the other in a small grey suitcase.
'Look, not many people knew Alana – just me, Blake, her Mum, and Mr Sutton at University. She hung around a very small community, if you know what I mean.'
'Yeah, I know, but what if it was a psycho ex-student who knew her there who hated her guts about getting high grades, and wants to get their own back on you?'
'Oh, come on, don't be ridiculous. The only person who pestered her there was this guy called Graeme Flegg, but he pestered me too. Besides, that's impossible, so stop being paranoid.'
'I'm not. It's just...London is like two-hundred miles away...'
'And I used to live there, Tre. So take it easy, and let me handle this.' Silence as he turned away, and Leila zipped up her levelly-packed case with ease.

'No, no, no. I'm not convinced. I'm going with you,' he
insisted. Leila shot her head up in wide-eyed disbelief from what
she was doing.

'What? No! Someone has to look after this place.'

'I don't care. I'll get my dad to look after it. How long
are we staying there?'

'Oh shit, Tre, have you lost your mind? Umm, about a
week or so…'

'No. As a matter of fact, I'm quite sane. Come on, Lill,
I'll never be at ease as long as you're over there and
I'm here.'

'I'll be phoning every day – twice a day, even, so stop
behaving so crazy!' Silence. Then he inched up towards
her, his hands sliding round her waist, and kissed her forehead.
They smiled at each other as he studied her facial features with
full admiration of them. She returned that to his brown eyes, as
she twiddled her fingers through his spiky hair. 'Look, you were
my responsibility since we met. This is a complete stranger
you're going to meet, probably some maniac, and I'd never
forgive myself if something happened to you. If you were going
to see your friend directly, fine, but it's not, is it? I love you, and
don't want anything to happen to you.' She smiled, slightly
blushing at his genuine concern. *God, what have done to deserve
such a gem of a guy?* she thought with a sigh. 'I know, love.
You're the best thing that ever happened to me. But it won't be
forever. A week, then I'll…oh, for God's sake, get packing,
otherwise we'll miss the three o' clock train! You have
about…three hours – two to pack, and hour to get to the station
and wait,' she said, glancing at the wall clock above the doorway
at right angles to the bed and closet. He laughed slightly, pecking
her on the lips. She laughed her head backwards as he crazily
dashed, spun and leapt like a school kid for one suitcase, the same
size as Leila's, under the bed against the lilac wall in the centre of
the room, and began excitedly hurling hangers of shirts and
trousers out of the closet opposite the foot of the bed, and shoving
them in carelessly, much to Leila's humour. She rested beside her
suitcase on the edge of the bed, watching her boyfriend act like a

man possessed. 'Hey, hey! Calm down, and pack properly, silly!' she giggled, as she watched him almost yank the zip off the seams. She smiled in wonder at him. *Jesus, he's mental, but to be honest, I wouldn't want him any other way...*

'Oh Blake? That's the mail. Could you get that please?' Blake was in the kitchen, turning a couple of fried eggs over. 'Okay, okay, hang on. I'm cooking here!'

'So? You can leave the cooking for a second, can't you?' He marched out the kitchen, to see Freda still cosy under the duvet, with the chilly sea breeze blowing at both of them.

'Yeah, well, don't moan at me if it's burnt!' he stroppily snapped back. Freda just stuck her tongue out at him in response. *I could get mad, but it's not going to be my problem anymore soon...* Standing by the curtained, frosted glass door, perpendicular to the burgundy couch in the centre of the room, he crouched down to the pile of envelopes on the floor. *Newspaper, electricity, phone...ticket! Yes! Yes! Yes! I'm outta here!* Yesterday, he snuck out at eight-thirty in the morning, and sprinted to the local town centre's travel agent, an hour before Freda was due home. Rubbing his palms, he was held up for a brief time, before the keeper finally opened the doors. He then booked his emergency flight out of Dublin to Heathrow for Saturday. He paid for it with the cash he pinched from his suitcase. He was promised the ticket via mail the next day, and here it was, like a precious jewel in his hands. *Oh shit, the breakfast...!* He wanted to dance in joy, but instead he hastily shoved the envelope under his shirt, and handed the rest of the mail to Freda, still too wonderfully comfortable in bed. 'Oh God, nothing but bloody bills. Go and serve the breakfast, Blake.'

'Yes, mistress,' he scornfully obliged.

'Don't start me off, Blake,' she retorted with a scowl. Untouched, he returned to switch off the frying pan stove, and scooped the eggs onto two plates with a spatula, not giving a damn whether they were wholly on the plate or slopping off the edge. With a pot of tea, a couple of teacups and two plates of eggs, baked beans and toast, he delivered it to the bedside cabinet.

'Thanks. Look, I'm sorry about earlier on,' she said in a tone that sounded halfway to being compassionate.

'Are you?' he asked bluntly, refusing to raise his eyes to her as he poured the tea and stirred in the sugar and milk already in the cups.

'Course I am. Come and sit down,' she enticed while lying on her side, stroking his short dark blond spikes. He still had his head facing opposite hers 'Look, this you should know by now, I get cross when I'm pissed off, and I get pissed off when nothing goes my way, okay?' *Oh, so you admit it*, he thought in faux shock. 'Yeah.'

'But when I'm in my right mind, I don't really mean it. Honest, so cheer up and give me a smile.' *You can be summed up in one word: schizoid. Oh well, I won't be here for much longer, so you can stop that pretentious, fake-ass act that you care about me, and I might as well show my best side for now*...He finally turned to her with his characteristic broad grin, thinking that if she can be two-faced, so can he. 'That's better. Now will you eat with me?'

'Sure I will, but I need to go first.'

'Okay.' He trotted to the bathroom, and immediately slammed the door to illustrate urgency. He urgently placed his entire weight on the toilet seat lid as if it was a chair, jerked the letter out from the waistband of his khaki trousers and ripped it open. *Yes! It's the ticket and the itinerary. Right, let's see...Saturday, sixth of March at eight-thirty AM...good, that means I can sneak out while she's asleep...flight time one hour, arrival time nine-thirty – of course, unless Ireland is slowly drifting away from England...umm, weight limit thirty-five kilos...fine also, just my clothes, books and some other stuff...and the receipt. And I have my passport. Perfect. I hope Al isn't seeing anyone*...He stuffed the papers back into the envelope and back into the waistband, and breathed deeply to cool his flustered cheeks of anticipation to return to the bedroom to eat breakfast.

At around five that evening, Freda was out buying a few groceries before she hopped off to work, which was around nine for nine-thirty. Staring at the television as scenes whirred past his

steely eyes unconsciously, he was completely lost in a state of
nothingness. Then the phone shocked him out of it. He slumped
to his feet and over to the cabinet behind the couch. 'Hello?'

'Hi, it's me, Katerina Slate again. From yesterday?'

'Oh, hello. Look, I'm sorry about Freda yesterday. How
is she? Is she going to be alright?'

'Sure. She was given a good bill of health and was
checked out this afternoon. I picked her up after my
University tutorial. She's actually asleep at the moment.

So don't disturb her.' He smiled at the thought of her with
her eyelids shut peacefully as he recalled the time he first saw her
in bed asleep when she was thirteen. He was checking her in her
room during a sleepover, remembering being charmed by how
cherubic and at peace she looked, never giving a second thought
to it till now. 'When I saw her yesterday, she was a very happy
person, quite unlike the Alana I knew when I first moved here,
and she was the same when I came to pick her up this afternoon,
joking about the doctors and nurses and everything else, and
having me in stitches, if you know what I mean!' He snickered at
her half-funny joke.

'Thank God for that. Look, I'm coming over there
tomorrow morning,' he finally blurted. Silence.
'What?'

'I've…used some money I stashed away to buy a
plane ticket yesterday. I'll be leaving here at eight-thirty
tomorrow morning to be there at around nine-thirty at
Heathrow.' Katerina was dumbfounded for several seconds.
'Umm…wow, umm…what's…brought on this change
of character?'

'I decided to stop being an asshole. No, seriously…
I want you to understand that I can't believe that I'm
telling a complete stranger this, but it's on Alana's
behalf.'

'Why? What happened? Is it something to do with
Freda?' He inhaled deeply, squeezing his eyelids together
to gather up courage to say what bothered him.

'Last night, we had a fight…'

'And?'

'And…' he gasped, a tear falling down his cheek, which he wiped away with a knuckle. 'She beat me up, and scratched my face real deep, and…she…she…'

'What?' Katerina begged for the reason of his sudden loss in composure on hearing him break down.

'She raped me, Kat. She raped me…' Katerina inhaled sharply, with a hand over her mouth, unable to fathom what he'd just admitted. 'How…oh shit. How the hell…?'

'Well, how do you think, huh? She's gone shopping now; God knows when she'll be back, but after this call, I'm going to shove my clothes and stuff into my suitcase, and I'm getting the hell out of here in the morning before I'm dead,' he whimpered out while sniffing.

'Jesus, Blake, I…I'm so sorry. You're absolutely right,' she apologized, trying her best to not sound fake. 'I mean, let's face it. I've been her slave here for nearly two years now, and I can't take it anymore. I've started protesting against her slavery, which narks her off. She did that because she wanted to go out and I didn't, but I think it's because you called to tell me about Al. Anyway, I'll explain tomorrow. Listen, don't tell Al I'm coming, and please come to the airport. Did Al tell you what I look like, or showed any photos?'

'Umm, no photos but she described you. She said you have blond hair in spikes with black bits in them, and a distinctive dress style.'

'Well, yeah, but I don't have the black bits anymore – it's still blond and spiky, but it's sort of a dark blond now – my natural colour. I like simple, un-tacky clothes, me.'

'What will you be wearing and where will you be?'

'I'll be wearing a black satin shirt and a khaki trousers. You can wait by one of the information booths. I'll be arriving at nine-thirty, but should be until about ten till I come through. It's Terminal One, flight 423 from

Dublin, okay?'

'Sure. And just in case you need to contact me, this is
my new mobile phone number. I didn't give it to you
before because I only bought it yesterday. It's…' Blake
quickly scribbled it down on the notepad next to the phone,
ripped out the page immediately and shoved it carelessly in his
trouser pocket. 'Thanks a lot, Kat. What do you look like? Just in
case I need to look for you.'

'I have shoulder-length, straight bright blonde hair. I have
sort of European features, because I'm half-Russian, and
I have blue eyes. I'll be wearing a pink mid-sleeved shirt
with a blue denim jacket, and black combat trousers.'

'So that's why you have that funny accent.'

'You know, you're the second person to say I have a
funny accent.'

'Who's the first?'

'Al, of course!' Both of them chortled loudly. 'Anyway,
take care of yourself. But hey, what if she tries looking for you?'

'I'll jump that hurdle when I reach it.'

'Fair enough, but shouldn't you call the police if she…
you know…'

'No way! They'd say it's my fault. They always side
with the woman in rape. Plus I just want to forget it
once I board that plane. When I reach there, I want to
tell Alana something important about us.'

'What is it?'

'Shh – top secret! It's something good to me, but I'm
not so sure if it's so good for her.'

'Oh, I see. Well, when we talk again, then you can tell me.'

'Okay. I finally meet you tomorrow then?'

'Yes, brilliant. I'm proud of you, Blake. See ya!'

'Bye Kat, and thank you. Hang on! Did you contact
Leila Drayton, our other friend?'

'Yeah. She too was apprehensive, but she said she's
taking the three o' clock train from Cardiff. I phoned
her before she left, because I'm going to meet her at
Southall in an hour. The buses take so damned long,

I'll be leaving as soon as I finish talking to you.'
'Okay, terrific.'
'Have a nice afternoon. Bye!'
'Bye!' He hung up, relieved to turn around and not see
Freda back yet. *Right, nearly half-past five. Time to chuck a few
things in the case. I'll stuff the case back in the closet where it
was to keep suspicion down...*he bolted for the closet, which was
in the hall between the bathroom and the living room doorways,
and hauled out the huge black case, filled with an enthusiasm of
his realisation of love and freedom, and started flinging the
weighty hangers into the slightly musty, discoloured hollow.

Chapter 14.

'And where the hell have you been?' Katerina leapt at the threat of Alana's tone as she clicked the door shut. Her fearful glare met Alana's hardened gaze at her. She crept her bare toes towards the sink, where she broke off scrubbing it, and continued the gaze with the washcloth piddling water into a well in the carpet fibres.

'Umm, I went for a walk. I got a bit fed up with the assignment, so I went for a long walk in Southall. And I bought some Indian sweets from Southall. Look!' she squeaked in a simulated enthusiasm to lighten her up. No response. Katerina's face fell to an unemotional one. *Okay, time to be smart here*, she thought. 'Look, Al, I know it's eight o' clock, but the bus from Southall was slow, as usual, and I needed to get away from that frigging assignment. Please!' Alana finally loosened her eyelids in belief of what she said, recalling her own experiences with her University course. 'Okay, then. I just got worried. Daylight is very limited these days, even though it's spring. There are a lot of weirdos about, you know.'

'I know, I know, I'm sorry, okay?' she grovelled, throwing down her hands. Alana at last smiled and slapped her shoulder blade, both exhaling a laugh. 'It's okay. Just don't scare me like that again, okay?' she shrilled, pointed her finger to the tip of her nose.

'Okay, okay. So, what have you been up to? Shouldn't you be resting?'

'Well, I was cleaning the sink with the scouring powder you bought, 'cause it was a bit scummy, and was going to make a sandwich after that. Got fed up lying down. Why did you buy sweets?' She grinned innocently as she tried to milk her brain for some sort of idea.

'It's been a week since we first met, right? So, I decided we should celebrate after all we've been through.'

'A day early?'

'Well, yeah, because…look, just take the sweets, okay?'

'Alright, alright, I'm not complaining. Put them down

over there, and we'll scoff 'em. Would you like a
sandwich too?'

'Yeah, sure. A tomato and cheese one?'

'Yeah. Have a seat. It's on its way over.' She nodded, and
flung herself on top of her bed, which was surprisingly still-made.
Very nice – she's going all domestic now! Then on a whim she
sprung upright again. Not caring if Alana turned to her in
curiosity, she dropped to her knees facing her bed, and ducked her
head under the curtain of the beige valance sheet. *No bottles?* she
swithered with a frown. She returned hastily on her back on her
bed, and smoothed her hair. 'Hey, in case you were wondering, I
got rid of all my booze.'

'What?'

'Yup – poured every bottle down this sink here, and
disposed of the bottles at the recycling centre up the road.'

'Umm…wow…umm…congratulations, Al! This
is…this…you've done the impossible here!'

'Kat, you've gotta know something – that was the
hardest thing I've ever had to do, but it made me
feel great that I could actually do it, you know,
as a spur of the moment thing.'

'Well done. So no more sneaking out to the off-license?
I mean, you *are* officially dried out?'

'Hell yes!' Both of them breathed out a room-rattling laugh,
both clenching their stomach muscles to prevent their insides
from flying out. 'You wanna know something? During that
hospital stay, I've really mulled over this; it's not Adrian, Leila or
Blake that's driven me to drink – I did that myself. I let myself
slip into a groove of self-pity. It took all the willpower I had, and
the willpower I didn't, just to chuck that stuff down the drain. Of
course, I thought about cutting down, but one glass would never
supply my dreams, and would turn into ten drinks. The only way
was to quit altogether. Oh, and guess what? I chucked all my
Adrian scrapbooks and pictures away, too! As far as I'm
concerned, the less hold he has on me, the more I can pursue my
journalism dream again, see?' Katerina rose from the bed, her
brain frozen and dazed by this new fact, and wandered over to

where Alana stood. She halted from slicing rounds from a tomato, and both held their gawks for several seconds. 'Al, I'm absolutely proud of you,' Katerina finally managed to whisper. Then they extended their arms and clenched and cradled each other, both belly-laughing again over each other's shoulders. Facing each other again, with both of their eyes welling up with all the anger, relief, happiness and sadness that had occurred over the past six days. 'God, look at us. We've turned into two soppy gits, haven't we?!' Alana groaned through a sniff. 'Oh well, congratulations, as I've said before. We could have a beer if it was safe to leave it round the room while you're drying out, and if it wasn't so late on a Friday night!'

'True. I couldn't trust myself! Let's have a cup of coffee instead.'

'Sure.' Katerina volunteered herself to help by filling up the kettle. She stared inside the kettle, and wondered if her eyesight was fooling her at its cleansed, descaled element and walls. 'Have you descaled the kettle, Al?'

'Yup. I bought some tablets about half an hour after you left. Looks nice, doesn't it? I've done quite a lot while you were you gone.'

'So I noticed!' Both sniggered. Alana ran a hand through her hair, and tugged down her brown, torso-hugging suede-like shirt. 'Okay, the sandwiches are ready, so get some tissues, and the coffee, and let's tuck in!' In one hand, she held a large plate with two piles of three white-bread sandwiches, and two saucers in the other, and strode towards her bed's surface, where she decided they should have their feast, then slung the bag with the sweets off her wrist to the edge of the bed, almost hitting the floor. About five minutes later, Katerina cautiously tiptoed to sit beside Alana, and set the two mugs, held together by a curled forefinger round the handles, on the cabinet, and chucked the scrunched-up kitchen towels just past the plates. 'Okay, my coffee has one sugar, yours has two, to fatten you up a bit!'

'Oh thanks!' she sarcastically intonated. 'Anyway, that's something else I need to do – fatten up.' Katerina chuckled before chomping the sandwich almost in half. Both ate silently and ravenously for around forty minutes. *Lord, have I got a lot to be grateful for that hospital stay. Okay, she nearly killed herself, but look what it's done for her – absolutely un-bloody-believable…*

'Great dinner. Great coffee. And great sweets, too. Thanks.'

'No problem. Food tastes great when you haven't had a proper meal for some time.'

'And when you've had shitty hospital food, too!'

'Oh yeah. I forgot about that.' Both girls snorted, their mouths still chewing the last morsel of the Indian sweets. Alana was the first to swallow hard. 'Right, who goes to the bathroom first?'

'You can go. I'll do the washing up. It's only fair since you made dinner.' She shrugged in acceptance, and grabbed her blue cotton nightshirt hanging off the back of the chair, and her toiletry bag from the surface of it, which looked as it were rotting a little day by day.

'Hey, where's the black satin one?'

'Oh, I took it to the launderette next to the off-licence, along with some other stuff.'

'Okay.' Alana then inaudibly snapped the door shut. Katerina then piled up the plate, saucers and mugs, leaned them against her chest with the mug rim brushing her chin, and lowered them gently into the sink. She grabbed the empty sweet box and dumped it into the white pedal bin. *A pedal bin? Where the hell…? Lord, she* has *been busy, hasn't she?!* she wrinkled a grin to herself. She then picked up the scouring pad, loaded it with washing-up liquid foam, and proceeded scrubbing the mugs. *I can't believe I'm living with the same person…*

'See. what did I tell you?!'

'Well, I was right to be wary, wasn't I? That girl could've been anyone, and somebody had to put up a fight for you if she was someone dodgy.'

'Yeah, but I didn't see you putting up a fight when you saw she had blonde hair and blue eyes, right?' Tre widened his eyes at Leila as she skimmed back and forth round his seat on the bed with hangers and items of clothing from her suitcase. The room looked slightly cluttered with its two pine wardrobes on either corner, but had a glow created by the peach wallpaper, and small framed pictures on each side of the double bed characterized that wall. The glow was enhanced by the frosted buttercup-style shades of the ceiling lights, central to a rotating fan wafting chilly air above both of them.

'Look, she *was* beautiful…'

'Oi!'

'Alright, she was cute, but so are you – in fact, even
    better.' She stopped for breath facing him, irritatingly
folded her arms and stared meanly into his eyes as he looked up
in some regret at what the effects of what he said were going to
be.

'You're just saying that 'cause you're feeling guilty!
    She introduces herself, and what do you say? "Oh,
    my name is Trevor, but you can call me Tre, sweetheart!"
    And you kiss the back of her hand on top of that! You're
    unbelievable, do you know that?'

'It's normal to ogle, Lill – you ogle men in magazines
    all the time!'

'Yes, but they don't talk back to me – it's indirect ogling,
    so don't give me that!' He finally sighed in defeat as she
rested beside him. She petted her shoulder, trying to relive her of
her quiet sulk.

'Okay, okay, I'm sorry. It won't happen again. I get
    carried away sometimes. I don't fancy her; I only
    merely admired her. I fancy you and you alone, you
    got that? So come on, pack in that face and forgive
    me.' He stroked a finger along her cheekbone. She finally
responded by twisting her head to him, still tilted down. Half-
grinning, she reached a hand and pinched his cheek painfully as
his punishment. 'You're a cheeky sod, you know that?'
she giggled.

'I like pissing you off a bit sometimes. If you didn't
    love me, you wouldn't have got mad.' Her smile fully
fledged into a laughter.

'True. Well, it's only fair that I piss you off too, only

differently from your method.' Both sniggered again.

'What is your method, then?'

'Well, I could do this…' she then faced him and leaned over, slid her hands round his waist, her fingers eventually trailed down and closed painfully around his bottom, causing him to jerk slightly off the bed in surprise.

'Hey!' Tre's eyes, from a gawp of shock, narrowed into and evil little glint. Leila flinched slightly on interpreting what he was up to. 'Oh, so that's your method?'

'Oh no…'

'Oh yeah…I'm gonna get you, Lill!' Giggling aloud, she escaped by crawling to the other edge of the bed, but was swamped when his grasp closed round both ankles, and hauled her onto her back. She was now pinned down under him, her arms above her head, still tittering at that glint in his eyes and smile. With one hand restricting her wrists, he used his other hand to gently grate against her sides, tickling her. Twitching about, she laughed uncontrollably against her will. He suddenly stopped, then brought his mouth down to seal hers – honestly, lovingly, ardently. She still sniggered when he broke off to gaze into her softened eyes. 'We're okay, aren't we?'

'Yeah, sure we are – providing you stop that.'

'What, this?' He resumed his teasing of her ribcage again, loudening her laughing and weakening the defence she had to him. *God, he's…mental, but I…wouldn't want…him any other way…*she thought contentedly between panting breaths.

Okay, that's everything, Blake thought with a deep breath from a puff of cool morning air, from which was hopefully to be his morning of promise. Peering through the window on his toes, the dawn had only barely broken from its confines of night. *Good – it's dark enough to sneak out without waking her up…*It was six-thirty when he turned towards the clock on the wall opposite the bathtub. He had dressed in the clothes he was to be identified by this Katerina person. His hair was ruffled with a little gel with his fingers. Satisfied with his appearance, he crouched down onto the cold tiles, its bitterness shooting through his kneecaps, and jostled his electric shaver in a small sports bag, which he had to replace with a quieter, and less effective, solution – a lady shaver and soap and water. He then followed that with his aftershave lotion, underwear, a shirt and pair of trousers, in the event of his suitcase being lost, and that finalised his packing. His suitcase was waiting under their bed, ready for collection as quietly as possible. He zipped up the bag quietly, as the bathroom door's glass panel provided little soundproofing, and slung it on his shoulder. Tiptoeing to the bedroom again in fear of the slightly squeaky floorboards. Freda tumbled over to her stomach, causing a jump inside and a violent gulp. *Oh shit, please don't wake up, please...* He kneeled before the bed, and ducked his hands underneath, trying to limit the shuffling the suitcase made. With one almighty lift, although it thankfully wasn't heavy enough for one, he crept through the hall again to the living room, lowering it before the front door. He then unloaded the bag beside it. *Phew, that's everything, I guess. Au revoir.* With that, he scrupulously slipped on his shoes and leather coat, smiling as he reminisced the circumstances of Alana's gift for a split second. With the sports bag on his shoulder and the suitcase in his hand, he slid his keys under the inside doormat and controlled the door with his heel. He inhaled a lungful of sea air in relief of not waking her up, almost like he held his breath from the moment he awoke. He barely slept that night. To make Freda tired enough not to be awoken, he used his body and repressed his love for Alana for the last time, with any luck. He proceeded to walk briskly towards the main road along the seaside avenue, elapsing several other terraced houses as he pounded his feet up the steep, desolate pavement, the sky still a steely grey, even though it was ten to seven. Even the hardly-visible sea waves beyond the low fence opposite the terraces looked as still as everything else. Finally reaching the main road, he looked down from where he began, thinking if he'd just climbed up an urban Mount Everest or something, then he looked at both ends of the main road – completely deserted. *Oh great, how the hell am I supposed to get a cab now? Ah-ha! I'll use a payphone to call a cab from the card I have in my pocket!* Spotting a phone booth about thirty or so paces from where he stood, he hauled his luggage the short distance, and lowered his bag. Before he even got a chance to pick up the receiver, he saw a little shadow from the distance, the first car he'd seen since he arrived there. It turned out to be a cab. *Yes! At last!* He leapt out almost to the middle of its path, which left it no choice but to halt. 'Hi, um, could you take me to the airport as soon as possible, please?'

'Sure. Hang on, I'll help with your luggage, Sir,' the young, flat-capped and narrow-faced man accepted in a husky Irish accent.

'Okay, thanks.' He rose to his feet and rushed over to phone booth. Within a couple of minutes, he had bungled the suitcase in the boot, and Blake kept the sports bag beside him on the back seat. 'So, where are you off to, then?'

'I'm returning to London.'

'From a holiday here?'

'No, I lived here with a girl, but we split up, so I'm going home.'

'Sorry to hear that.'

'It's okay – I'm not.' The driver sniggered a little. 'So where in London are you going?'

'In Ealing, which is not far away from Southall.'

'Oh – Little India? I've heard a lot about it on the news.' Blake smiled.

'When is your flight?'

'Well, I'm supposed to check in at nine-thirty, and the plane leaves at ten-thirty.'

'Well, you're well within the time, 'cause there won't be any heavy traffic till about ten.'

'Okay.' The rest of the journey passed uneventfully and silently, as he stared through the blurry, and gradually lighting, alternating greens and urban districts, surer and surer about his future as each mile was left behind him. *You know, I do want to marry her someday...*

Right, who could this Blake character be...? Katerina wondered, bearing in mind the description of himself, as her view of the arrivals lounge increased from the rising of the escalator.

The entire lounge, bubbled with an international stew of people from corner to corner. To her right was the arrivals platform, with streams of passengers joining this stew, and one long string of information booths and desks to her left. All that was left now was to decide on the nearest booth to wait by. She elbowed her way through some people at an awkward standstill, and stood beside a cube-shaped information booth right next to the path of the escalator. She checked the time on her watch – it read five to eleven, just enough time to get a coffee from the coffee shop she happened to observe amongst all of those bureaux de change and information booths. Under five minutes later, she returned to her standing place, taking a sip from the paper cup. *I can't believe it – two and a half quid for a half-full paper cup of tepid half-coffee, half-milk, and one and a half quid for a cube of walnut cake the size of a die. If it wasn't for the fact that I snuck out early without any breakfast just to catch a five pound cab trip here, I wouldn't even bother.* She continued nibbling discontentedly at the cake and sipping through the coffee lid. She waited, and waited, and waited, only to realise that it was only eleven-fifteen when she looked at her watch again. Because it seemed everyone else except this Blake person had got off the flight from Dublin, exited the platform and reunited with their friends and families, and his baggage was still in the hall, according to one of the flight information screens on the wall above the arrivals platform. *Damn, this guy is slow!* she screamed in annoyance in her mind, anxiously running a shaky hand through her hair as people banged against her as if they were blind while she stood by the booth, listening to her message being played for what was probably the fiftieth time amongst some other call-outs. *How much further in this frigging corner can I shrink just to stop these assholes running into me?* One final person slammed his bag into her, finally inducing her to express something to him. 'For Christ's sake, can't you look where the fuck you're going?' she hissed finally.

'Sorry, sorry, I…' he finally made face contact with her, something the other bumblers didn't do. His look softened from apologetic to one of curiosity, as he studied her facial features –

blonde hair, blue eyes, foreign looking. 'Hey! Um, are you a Kat Slate by any chance?' Katerina had a chance during this gaze to study his height, which must have been six feet as he towered over her, his dusky blonde hair and brown eyes, and the clothes he described.

'Why, yes! So you must be Blake, then?'

'Yeah. Nice to finally meet you.' She accepted his extended hand to shake.

'Likewise. Sorry for the language. It's just that I've been waiting here for the past forty minutes and everyone has been running into me and I didn't say anything. I even nearly dropped my coffee.'

'Sorry to hear that. So, how is Alana?'

'Fine, at least, I think so.'

'What do you mean, you think? I've risked a hell of a lot to come back here, possibly my own life, and the last thing I need is unsound information, understand?' he snapped.

'Hey, hey, calm down. Of course I'm sure. It's just that since she came back from hospital, she's stopped feeling sorry for herself, and has decided to get on with it, much to my disbelief.'

'That's great! Is she getting that journalist job, then?'

'Can't. She failed her degree exam, because she was upset about you.'

'Oh God! I didn't know. I swear, I'll never live myself down.'

'Too late for that. Anyway, where are you staying?'

'Well, me and my family don't talk anymore, so that's the last place I'd want to stay, so I might stay...'

'Oh, I know! I'll ask the cab to drop you off at the bed and breakfast Leila and her boyfriend are staying.'

'Oh my goodness – she has a boyfriend?'

'Yeah, a real flirt, you know. Tried charming the pants off me right in front of the poor girl. His name's Trevor – Tre for short. We went for Indian sweets and a stroll along Uxbridge Road as an introductory course to

Southall.' He tittered briefly. 'I'm not surprised. You know, you could pass as my little sister Christine, except for your accent. She had guys chatting her up all the time.'

'Oh! Well, Al said so, actually. Thanks!' she shrilled appreciatively, stroking the back of her head.

'Anyway, that's wonderful. She's never been lucky with blokes, so it's good she's found one. Let's walk.' Katerina flung her back upright from leaning against the banister next to the booth, and stood on the escalator as it escorted them down. A silence to think to himself came out of nowhere. She observed this, noticing he didn't respond when she looked at him. 'What're you thinking about?'

'Well, you know that thing I wanted to tell Al?'

'Yeah?'

'It was the fact that…oh nothing.'

'No, go on.'

'No, I'd rather not say.'

'Oh, I give up.' He half-smiled as they leapt off the last step below the lounge, and dragged the baggage trolley carrying his suitcase off it, and down the soft carpet of the brightly-lit, tribally designed corridor to the exit leading to the misty, gusty outdoors. *God, I've missed this place*…he breathed in relief of being only a few miles, rather than a thousand, from Alana. 'Anyway, what did you mean you've risked a hell of a lot, possibly your own life, to get here?'

'That's what I wanted to explain. Let's get a cab first.'

Chapter 15.

So, here I was at Dublin Airport's taxi drop-off point, finally relieved from that woman's twenty-four seven persecution, and the instinct to always be submissive to her was finally extinguished with it. I got out of the cab, paid the driver, who helped place my suitcase on a trolley, containing the only possessions I carried with me when I came here, and headed for the departures lounge. It was downright crowded wherever I looked. I saw a couple of yards in front of me several queues, all parallel to one another, corresponding to which plane of flight they were boarding – as you know, AI 423 was my own, so I scanned my eyes across each sign above each queue for the number. It was towards my far right under the dimmer light. I frowned a little in disappointment when I saw the length of it – must have been about thirty or forty people, while the other more fortunate travellers had about only fifteen or twenty people in front of them. I just wanted to check-in and check-out as soon as possible, if you know what I mean. So I studied my ticket details once more, then my passport details and photo – *well, others have had worse than mine*, I thought when I saw myself with my old hair colour before I changed it back to its natural colour like it is now, and my face without those ugly scars that are going to mar my face for God knows how long. Then suddenly, I was dragged from my own little world of hopefulness when I felt an asphyxiating hand grip round my upper arm, nails and all, and hauled me out of the queue, to the many I bumped aside's annoyance. I then came face to face with the person…"What the fuck..? Freda! What are you doing here?" I hissed. Right in front of everyone, she charged her arm up and gave one slap that could've flung my head off my shoulders. It was right across this barely-healed scar. I felt it bleed through the plasters when I tried to comfort it with my palm, but I didn't see any blood on my hand. At first, I didn't know what hit me, apart from her hand, but a few seconds later, my eyes widened and I switched into a very defensive mode. "How dare you sneak out like that, you little bastard, you! You're coming home with me right now!"

"No way! For what? To tie me back on your leash?
To take orders like an enslaved stray mongrel? No
way, lady! Oh hell, look who I'm calling a lady! I
can't believe I've been so stupid to think you were
worth giving up everything for – my friends, family,
everyone was right for saying you're poison!" I protested in
one or two full breaths, shoving my finger in her face. The queue
was getting shorter and shorter to about five or four people, and
she still didn't find her tongue to say something; she did nothing
but just gawp at me, because I'd just shown a side of me she'd
never seen before – the non-conformist side. Our little interaction
turned a few heads around our area in the lounge.

"Sir, are you on this flight?" the girl at the check-in desk
alerted me in a posh accent, on seeing me standing in the path of
the now empty queue.

"Yes, I am. One moment please," I signalled to her, then
faced Freda again, with a grovelling expression on her face.

"Blake, please, we can work this out, somehow. Come
home with me. I'm a very highly-strung woman – you
should know that by now. I get jealous very easily, but
that's because I love you. Any woman in my position
would be jealous if they're with a gorgeous guy like
you. Look, I promise to let you sit back and relax a bit
more. I didn't know if you could be trusted, 'cause I've
been double-crossed before, but apart from this incident,
you're the trustworthiest person I've ever met, so I will
loosen the leash on you a bit, okay? Do we have a deal
or not?' I looked at her with deadpan eyes, deciding who to
choose – Alana or Freda, the same choice I had to make two years
before.

"Sir, you must check in now, or you'll miss the flight."

"I'll be over in a minute, okay?" I once again returned to
that butter-won't-melt look of hers that hooked me every time
before then. I only had one thing to say to her:

"Forget it, Freda! If you had any respect for me at all,
you would never be jealous of me. And how the hell
do you know any woman would feel like that? Taking

178

over a couple of lousy chores wouldn't save this relationship. And as for the fact you've been double-crossed, you don't enslave men to take revenge, okay? And what about Al? If you were loosening the leash, would you have let me see her in hospital?'

'That girl has a serious problem of letting go. Oh come on, Blake – she treated you and me like shit, so why should you want to know?'

'Because now I realise she had a point. Yep, I thought as much. Sorry, but I'm boarding that plane, and I'm going back to my people. Good riddance, Freda.' With that, I twisted the trolley round, and without even taking a last glance at her, I shoved it to the desk and finally checked in, and had my sports bag and suitcase weighed. After I went through the barrier, I looked back, and she was finally gone. I took a deep breath of relief, for the umpteenth time. *It's over. It's all over. And I did it all by myself.* I was quite proud of myself, because I knew other men suffer that from their women, but are too cowardly to leave. I also knew how women must feel when they suffer this from their men, but I just wanted to board the plane and get my life back on track. But until I make up with my people again, it's going to be difficult to forget it ever happened. I said some horrible, horrible things to them in my pig-headedness, but I swear, I will win them back with my last breath.

'That's absolutely lovely, Blake,' Katerina finally commented whisperingly. 'You're a brave guy, you know. Not many men could stand up to women like her, because they put principles before their own lives.'

'True. Well, I'm free, and I can do what I want. It's nothing but my way now. *My* way!' he said, reinforcing his rejoicing by pounding a fist against his chest once.

'Great. And what do you plan to do now?'

'My family. And friends, and my girl.' Silence as Katerina grinned stupidly at him. 'Well, come on, who is she?' Blake just bowed his head away from her, determined to keep silent. Then Katerina raised her brow and clapped her hands in sudden realisation. 'Ah ha! I think I know who she is! Ha ha! It's Alana,

isn't it?' He raised his eyes to meet her gaze again, sighing with
the knowledge of his bashfulness hiding nothing. 'Damn, all that
for nothing! Yes, it *is* Al. God, I can't believe it's been almost
twelve years. I've always been fond of her, but I didn't realise
how fond till after Freda…you know. I was nursing this wound
on my face…' He pointed to the scratches. She trailed her
forefinger along them, trying to study them, and wrinkled her
nose a little in disgust.

'Jesus, Blake, this looks really bad, you know. That
bitch is a frigging lunatic, you know!' Katerina gasped.
'It was bad, but they'll heal though. Anyway, I was
really upset, and begged for Al in my mind as I sat
in the kitchen. Then I thought of your call and put
two and two together – Alana was the one for me.
Then I thought of my ideal girlfriend, friend, wife and
mother of my future children, and all I could think of
was not a singer or actress or sports star, not a teacher
at school or college university, not someone off the
street, but beautiful Alana.' Katerina giggled, thinking how
melodramatic he sounded, but also sighed at his sincerity.

'What's wrong with Leila? Sorry if it sounds weird…'
'No, no, it's a reasonable question. Leila…I can't see
any further a relationship with her apart from another
little sister. With Al, I can see something beyond the
friendship I grew to appreciate.'

'I understand. Well, it's going to take a hell of a lot to
regain her trust. It's only now she's begun to forget
the past, so you have to understand if she's still mad
at you. The same applies with your family.'

'I know. I can't thank you enough for tracking me and
Leila down. I could've carried on the way I was till
she killed me.'

'No problemo! Hey, driver, could you stop outside this
hotel coming up please?' she instructed, tapping the taxi
driver on the shoulder.

'Sure.' He diverted smoothly off the main road into Hanger
Lane. The whole view except for the sky blacked out by a growth

of dark green hedges above a brick fence dirty with moss sprouts.
They hopped out of either side of the taxi, and studied the
singular row of red brick houses, the windows and doors framed
by white swirls. They approached the chequered pathway to the
house with the 'Guest House' sign above the door. 'This is the
B&B where Leila and Trevor are staying. But they said they're
going shopping at the Broadway today, so I don't think they're in
now.' Blake trembled slightly at the creepy nature of the
exteriors. But then he thought it couldn't be worse than living
with Freda.

    'Oh well, never mind. I'll check in here for a couple
of days, and meet up with them when they come back.'
Katerina nodded, marched up to the doorstep and pressed the
doorbell button, which was the only one there. The door opened,
introducing a middle-aged man with dark cropped curly hair,
wearing a blue shirt and white jeans. 'Can I help you?' he queried
in an indistinctive, but clear, accent. She turned to Blake, and
poked him on the arm. 'Yes, um, could I have a single room
please?'

    'Certainly, come in.'

    'Okay, one second. Kat, I need to ask you something,' he
asked with pleading eyes.

    'What, what is it?' He breathed deeply, and felt that bashful
spell flush through him again. Katerina remained quiet in
anticipation.

    'Is Al seeing anyone?' She let out a crackly laugh, throwing
her head back.

    'Blake, of course not. Think about it – if she's smashed
twenty-four seven, how the hell can she see anything
except a bottle of booze?' He chortled through what was
probably the widest grin he'd ever smiled.

    'I suppose. Okay, thanks. I'll ring you later from your
mobile phone.'

    'Okay, 'bye.' With that, Blake hauled his suitcase through
the gap the door left, with his sports bag on his shoulder. A gush
of wind brought it to life, and it slammed itself. Katerina smiled
to herself. *Well, that's step two complete – I've got both Blake*

and Leila right where I want them. She hopped back in the taxi, thinking numbers ticking on the meter. 'Okay – to Ealing University, please.'

Katerina tiptoed through the room's door at around one o' clock. She was well aware that she seemed to be doing a lot of creeping these days, but prepared herself to lie her way through each time she was caught out by Alana. *Eh?* She revolved her head round the room, even studied the bed for any human lumps underneath the duvet, but nothing. The room was completely empty. *What's this? Have I been perspiring for nothing?* So she exhaled a breath she didn't realise she was holding in, slumped on the edge of the bed and tossed her shoes beside the door frame, still wearing her jacket. Deciding to make a cup of tea, she raised herself up, caught with the kettle tap water that filled it about halfway, and returned it to the stove. She then twisted a dial to the appropriate heat, and dumped a teabag in her mug. Her nerves leapt as high as the volume the door slammed. Quickly whipping her head round, her eyes widened at who it was. 'Alana?'

'Okay, happy wanderer, where the hell have you been all morning?' she snarled, more in annoyance than in anger. *Right, time to come up with something good.* 'Umm…'

'Come on, spit it out!'

'I went for a walk down Southall. I had trouble sleeping, because of that same assignment, and it really bugged me. The last walk I took yesterday didn't solve anything, and whenever I walked on my own for a long distance, the solution to any problem always seems to pop up out of nowhere. But not this time, so at about nine, I went for another walk. I'm sorry, okay?' A long silence followed.

'Look, all you had to do was wake me up and ask for my help.'

'Yeah, but you looked so peaceful, I didn't want to disturb you. Plus you need rest after that hospital stay, especially as you're going back to work on Monday, so…'

'Thanks. Well, I'll help. You making tea?' Alana queried, pointing in the direction of the stove.

'Yeah, it's coming up.'

'Well, make two teas, and I'll see what I can do. Don't know much about Media Studies, but I'll try and make do with common sense.'

'Thank you. Where the hell were you anyway?'

'I was in the lav. You must have come in as soon as I left.'

'Okay. Sit down, and I'll bring the tea.'

'Thanks.' Alana grabbed the pile of papers, folders and books on the bedside cabinet, leaving the lamp to perch on its edge, and transferred it her own bed beside her as she sat in the exact spot as Katerina before she entered. Around five minutes later, she returned with the two mugs, gripping a plate of about six tiers of buttered bread with her little finger under one mug, and sat them down on Alana's cabinet as she aided Katerina with the plate. 'Just feeling a bit peckish.'

'So am I, thanks. So, let's begin,' Alana said positively, briskly rubbing her palms together.

'With pleasure – and dread,' Katerina groaned as she came face to face with her 'eyesore'. Both snorted as simultaneously as they bit into a section of bread each, and flicked a page of a book, a notebook and flipped open a cardboard folder.

'Cor blimey, how the hell can you love shopping here, Lill?' Tre gasped, feeling blood flushing his face in annoyance, as he trailed behind her into the dark eeriness of Hanger Lane with a shopping bag in each hand. 'The place was swarming with people walking fast and blind, or completely stupid, or both!' Leila chuckled under her breath.

'Oh come on, Tre – it wasn't that bad. Besides, this is London. It's like this all the time.'

'I realise, you did bring me here before you know, but how do you put up with that load of shit day-in, day-out, huh?'

'Because I was born into it, but we're out of it now, so

stop whingeing!' He gulped in a breath to instil some peace in himself.

'Oh, alright, then,' he accepted in a stroppy tone, sighing. A brief silence followed.

'Cardiff is a city too, isn't it?'

'Sure, but at least people don't run blindly into one another like here – they consider each other, and have more of a sense of direction than this lot here.'

'I realise, but that's like two-hundred miles away from here. It's a different world here – a commuter's world.'

'I suppose…' he shrugged.

'Anyway, cheer up. We're almost back at base now, aren't we?'

'I know.' He pecked Leila on the cheek just as they were approaching the familiar red door of their hotel. 'Here, hold this for a second,' she requested, handing him one of her two shopping bags, after trying unsuccessfully to push the doorbell with a bag hanging from four fingers. She tried again with her free hand, sounding like a buzzing insect from outside. The door finally opened, introducing the owner. 'Ah, Miss Drayton, Mr Tappet, welcome back.'

'Thank you.' They crossed the doorstep, into the warm, slightly dark but welcoming corridor, to their right was the entrance into the living room, which was a pale blue wash all round, with a chandelier-type light on the ceiling, which seemed to make the room smaller than it was, a small television in one corner, an ornament cabinet in the opposite corner, and a two-seat couch diagonal to the television, and a few country pictures on the wall. The man's wife was sitting on the sofa, talking to a young man with tufty hair, wearing a silver shirt and black combat trousers, obviously a guest, handing her a ten and twenty-pound notes bunched together. At first, Leila didn't trust her instincts as to why he looked familiar. But she looked again, basically staring at him; he was still blissfully unaware of her. 'Hey! Are you on this planet, Lill?' She whisked her head round to face Tre, standing behind her, with three of the bags of shopping.

'Oh, I'm sorry! Here, can you take this bag and put it
up in our room, please?'

'Why me?'

'Oh, just do it and stop whining!' she snapped, shoving the
bag into his stomach.

'What is your problem, girl?' She was too enraptured by the
flaxen-haired guy to be even aware of what he said, but Tre was
inquisitive now, so he looked over her shoulder. She stumbled up
to the lad, interrupting them from their conversation. 'Umm,
excuse me, but…uh, what's your name?' she managed to utter.
He just stared back at her for several seconds, equally as
enraptured. 'Oh my God.'

'Oh my God! It's…Blake?!' she shrieked.

'Leila?! Good God in heaven…I don't believe it!' he
muttered, taking a pace back to examine her long denim-dress
coated form. Both widened their eyes and laughed in disbelief.
They then threw their arms round each other and squeezed tightly,
still laughing with a tear or two falling from each their eyes when
they met again. 'Um, excuse me, but what the hell is going on?'
Tre asked, obviously still disturbed by her behaviour. Blake
gawked in curiosity at her, then at him. 'Oh, I'm sorry, Tre. I was
looking at him, because I thought my eyes weren't fooling me.
This is Blake Turpin, my childhood friend, the one I was telling
you about. Blake, this is Trevor Tappet, my boyfriend.' Tre
exhaled in relief, while Blake warmly smiled at him and extended
his hand to him. 'Nice to meet you. So, you're the one who's
finally got through to Leila, ay?' Tre giggled bashfully. Leila
wrapped her arms round his waist from the side again in
enthusiastic disbelief.

'I missed you, bro! I can't believe it! Last time I saw
him, he was cursing his ass off!' she shrilled again,
releasing him and punching his shoulder.

'Why?' Tre asked curiously.

'Because of his stupid girlfriend, Freda Henley – no
offence!' she teased deliberately, hoping for a peeved
response.

'No, none taken. Well, I'm here to see both you and

185

Al again.'

'What happened to your hair?' He rubbed a hand through it vigorously, laughing.

'Got bored with it, so I changed it back to natural.'

'Well, we're here for Al. A girl called Katerina rang my number, telling me what happened to her, and here we are.'

'Me too. I had to come after hearing that.'

'What? Freda let you come here? Where is she, anyway? Still in Dublin? Jesus, what happened to your face?' He felt his heart sink again, but also amused by her gabbling string of questions. 'That's actually what I wanted to tell you. Both of you can come up to my room, have a cup of tea and we'll talk,' he offered with in a bleak tone. She nodded in recognition of that tone.

'Sounds more serious than I thought. Okay. Come on, Tre.'

'Umm, I'll put the shopping up in our room first. I'll bring the grocery bag to...what room is it, mate?'

'Room eight.'

'Okay. Be back in a mo.' He dashed up the stairs, and disappeared within seconds. 'Well, that's great. That's the first *"Surprise Surprise"*-style reunion we've ever had at this hotel! Congratulations, you two.' Both smiled and shook the man's hand, with his wife peeking out the corridor doorway from the couch, smiling.

'Thanks. Good afternoon, sir.'

'Good afternoon.' Blake followed Leila up the single flight of stairs, stomping to grip their feet on the carpet, shadowed by the brown floral wallpaper and dim lighting. At the top of the stairs, they cast their eyes round the short, country-style corridor of about six doors opposite each other. 'That's my room,' he pointed to the very end of the corridor to his left. Leila then turned her head to see Tre exiting the door directly opposite Blake's, holding one of the shopping bags. 'Hi. I've put the stuff away. So where's your room, Blake?'

'Over here. Come in.' He lead the way and twisted the key from his trouser pocket, signalled them to enter before him, then shut the door quietly.

'...so, that's when happened, Lill. I snuck out when she was at work to buy the ticket with money I had in my suitcase. I have about two and a half thousand in the bank account Mum opened for me when I checked it yesterday, but I don't want to touch that. You, Al, Christine, Mum and Dad were right all along. When you, Al and Chris tried to split us up, I thought you were horrible people, even more so when my family agreed with them, but now I wish you'd succeeded. It's so strange feeling like the one who makes common sense in a world of madness, but in the end, *you* turn out to be the mad one.' They all sat facing each other in lotus positions, forming a triangle on the double bed, and took occasional nibbles from a large bag of peanuts, and sips from their mugs of tea.

'I'm...speechless – completely lost for words. I'm not going to say you're a wimp, 'cause it's not about that. I've never heard anything like that before, but it's a horrific thought to think a woman could be so brutal,' Tre managed to express, his head numbed by the graphic description of Blake's girlfriend's brutality.

'Well, we're heading into a new century, so I think anything's possible.'

'Yeah, but that's no excuse, though. But we warned you, and you spouted hell and damnations at me and Al, so...'

'It's all my fault, Lill. I still can't forgive myself for what I've done, especially to Al, 'cause she's suffered the most out of all of us. When Freda's endless flirting made me cry, you and Al always tried to tell me to break it off with her, but I just...couldn't, even though she was hurting me. Then I told her I didn't want anything to do with her because I thought she was interfering... I feel responsible for this horrid chain reaction of events.

At one point, I said to myself I loved Al so much, that
I'd give her the entire Universe if I could. I've never
shown it, but that's still true, and I want to prove it to
her,' he said as his voice broke down again, trying to catch
his tears with a knuckle before they stung his wounds. Leila and
Tre were both left with gaping mouths, stunned by the sincerity of
those words, which were new to Leila. Then, something clicked
in her brain about the ring the words gave. 'Blake, are you trying
to tell me something?'

'What do you mean?'

'Are you trying to say…you love Al?' His head shot up
after poking a peanut into his mouth. 'Is it *that* obvious? You're
the second person after Kat to say that.' Both giggled as they
chewed on a handful of nuts each.

'It most certainly is! That's great – I always knew you
had an attachment to Al more than me, even when we
were small.'

'Really?' Tre said in surprise.

'Yeah. Whenever he had a problem that he felt
uncomfortable talking to his parents or sister about,
Al was first as his confidante and I was second. I didn't
mind though, cause she's a better agony aunt than me.' Tre
sniggered, almost spitting out his mouthful of peanuts.

'Well, try pouring your feelings out in a poem or
something,' he mumbled as he chewed.

'I'm not the world's best poet, but…'

'You don't have to be. Just scribble down what you
feel you've done, and how you feel about her, etcetera,
and with any luck, your friend'll come though.'

'Okay, but I have a lot to make up for, and it's going to
take more than a poem to do that.'

'I understand. You're forgiven, but don't ever do
something like this again, ever!' she growled, slapping his
temple, then drilling a forefinger into his forehead once he
retracted it from her swipe. 'Look what it took for you to make
you see that Freda for the bitch she was! Two years of shocking
abuse and domination, and you have a scar on your face for God

knows how long. It's just a bloody relief that you got out before
she killed you,' Leila firmly warned, pointing a forefinger at his
wounds. Tre nodded quietly.

'Ow, that hurt, damn it! Look, as long as I have Al, it
won't. You know, if things work out between us – don't
tell her this, please, neither of you, when you meet her –
I might ask her to…marry me.' Leila and Tre's jaws
dropped open at this new knowledge of his intentions. All these
revelations were like a ton of rubble toppled on her. The silence
lasted several minutes.

'I…I…good God. You love her *that* much?' she gasped out
with a giggle, still with her mouth and eyes gaping open.

'Yes, I definitely do. She's the one person I admire
more than you, my parents and sister. I've laughed and
cried with her more than anyone else,' he proudly said,
raising his chest in defiance of any doubts she and Tre may have
had.

'Aww, that's…absolutely beautiful. But how come it
took you to blow it till you realised it?'

'I was scared, especially as we were friends for so
many years. My feelings didn't float to the surface
till Thursday. I thought about it on the plane, and that's
the only reason I thought of. Anyway, I know what her
favourite jewels are – garnet and blue topaz stones – so
I'll know what type of ring to buy.' Leila and Tre's breaths
howled in inhalation.

'Hey, hey, slow down! With what, exactly?'

'With my savings, of course. I never worked over there,
'cause she didn't trust me enough to get a job. We lived
off her earnings.' She shook her head incredulously, then
retracted her head from his gaze, throwing her hands up.

'Blimey, Blake – how could you be so stupid?'

'I don't know. I'm kicking myself in the ass as I speak,' he
groaned, dropping his face hopelessly into cupped palms. Leila
reached her arm and patted the top of his spine.

'Never mind, it's all over now. I'll help you as much as
I can, together with Kat. After all, she brought us all

together again, so we can't forget her. We'll chat our
way into a plan sometime. If she's staying at a bed sit,
she obviously works, so we'll have to find that out
from Kat.'

'I was supposed to ring her number later today, so I'll
ask her then. She should be a private detective, 'cause
she's done a brilliant job at it. I'll stay here and find a
job while I'm waiting for things to happen. I took nine-
hundred pounds to Dublin – nearly two-hundred for the
ticket, about thirty for the taxi fare, and thirty for here.
So I'll have enough to buy groceries and the ring.'

'Blake, steady on!' Leila shrieked, punching his shoulder.

'Look, keeping the ring near me till the time comes will
be the only thing that will keep me going, okay? I'm
buying it on Monday.'

'Alright. Well, it's fantastic to be with you again, and
I'm glad you told me this.'

'Yeah, and it's nice to meet you, too. At first, I thought
Lill had a ex-boyfriend knocking about!' Tre jested,
intonating it as seriously as he could.

'Tre!' she protested, almost shoving him off the bed. He
elicited a roaring laugh at his sentiment.

'Not bloody likely! Mind you, it happens all the time!'
Blake intervened sassily. His face fell from the smile to his
reaction. 'Well, I'm sorry to hear what happened to you, and I
hope you get over it soon.'

'I will, Tre. You'll see.' He smiled, and rolled his legs off
the bed to an upright position, with some difficulty as his joints
creaked. Leila had the same trouble as she stood on the opposite
end of the bed. She flung her knees up, one after the other, on
walking towards Tre, to relieve the stiffness. 'Anyway, me and
Tre will be taking an afternoon kip. I'll see you at about…three or
four, okay? We're a bit exhausted from shopping, you know?'

'Okay. I'll sleep too. Maybe we can watch a bit of telly
later on and stuff some of the other things you bought,
just like old times?'

'Sure! See you later.' Leila wrapped her arms round his neck, delving the side of his face into the side of her warm neck. She let go of his hand with an eager smile. He waved them off as they disappeared behind the closing door. He released himself from his lotus position to lie down on his back against the pile of pillows, just to stare at the ceiling, and smile and lull himself into a visualisation of the thought of the day he'll say the words to Alana that would completely enliven his spirit again: *Al, will you marry me?*

Chapter 16.

'See? What did I tell ya, huh?' Leila jubilantly yelled in a fake Cockney accent immediately after Tre quietly snapped shut the door, leaping up and down, punching her fists in the air like a football supporter.

'Well, I'm not the one who grew up with him, am I?' He insisted slightly stroppily, chucking his hands in the air. Leila flashed a controlled smirk at him as she went to parallel the corners of the pink satin-covered duvet against the bed, rumpled from that morning. He followed in helping her by jerking and patting the opposite sides even. 'Anyway, your friend seems like a nice guy, but why is he thinking about marrying a girl who he doesn't know will accept or not?'

'Well, I'm really happy that he's found his soul mate after what he's been through, but you are right. Still, no matter how much I have to convince myself sometimes, he's not stupid, and if he says he loves Al, then I believe him. He's a man who's tormented himself to realise the truth, so he wouldn't fool himself again.'

'I guess, but what if he's still reeling with grief after what happened, you know, like something patients have on doctors... you know what I mean?'

'Yeah. I never thought of that, but either way, I'll support him always.' He couldn't help but extend his mouth in his broadest grin, and admire her hazel eyes that always widened when her full attention was focused on him, and deviated and returned from his grey-green ones every few seconds or so.

'Lovely. No wonder I love you so much.'

'Why?' she asked in a sweetly innocent tone, resting beside him on the edge of the bed, and intertwining her fingers in his grasp.

'You accept people for the life they choose, and the person they are, and that's why they've kept you for a friend for so many years.'

'That's my whole philosophy of friendship – Blake's

and Al's too. But sadly, a stupid lapse in that rule by
both of us, almost killed poor Al. So I'm not going to
be hypocritical about it.'
'I know, but if you didn't care, we wouldn't be here to
make amends now, would we?' She turned away from him
to ponder those words for a few seconds.
'Yeah, I suppose so…' She raised herself form her seated
position, only to have her hand gently tugged upon by Tre to
return her next to him. 'Please stay here for a bit more,' he
insisted softly, returning a loving look to her.
'Oh, alright, then.'
'What does this Al person look like? You've talked so
much about her, and I still haven't seen any pictures.'
'Oh, I'm sorry. Well, I have a photo in my purse. Hang
on…' She stretched a hand over to the clean natural pine
bedside cabinet, where her brown leather wallet was placed. She
flipped the top flap up to reveal a group photo of about eight
people in a background of a blue marble pattern, resembling a
family portrait. She then pointed to a smiling girl in front with
shoulder-length dark brown hair with squared ends curled
inwards, wearing a dark blue classic-cut shirt, and a black floral
mesh material pencil skirt, seated on a stool next to herself and
Blake, while the others stood behind them.
'That's Al?'
'Yup, when she was eighteen. She should be about…
twenty-two next week actually – her birthday is on
the eleventh of March – the coming Thursday, actually.'
'Talk about good timing! She looks like a nice girl, though.'
'She's the best. We're quite similar in traits, and we're
both the same ages, but my birthday is on the twenty-ninth
of October as you know. Blake's is on the tenth of July,
so Blake'll be twenty-three soon.'
'Who are these other people?'
'This couple here are Blake's parents, Eliot and Marlene.'
She poked at a lady with a platinum blonde, slightly grey bobbed
hair, wearing a pastel blue trouser suit, and a slightly rotund man
with receding dark blond hair, wearing a traditional grey suit and

black tie, both standing with great poise. She then moved her
finger to a tall, skinny woman in a plain black evening dress in
the centre of the group. 'This, as you know, is my mum, Lily, and
this lady with blonde curly hair and blue beady dress here is Al's
mum, Tracie. Both our mums are divorced. Blake is the only one
with two parents, and the only one with a little sibling other than
us, who's this girl that looks like that Katerina – her name's
Christine, which we got on well with too.'

'Nice people. His sister certainly looks nice…' he smirked,
staring admirably at her broad smile, subconsciously trailing
down and along the v-neck of her vibrant pink cardigan.

'Trevor!' she shrieked in annoyance.

'Alright, alright, I'm just winding you up again.'

'You have a thing for blondes, right?' she returned in
forceful sarcasm, at which he could only snicker at loudly with a
snort.

'No, I have a thing for the auburn lady sitting next to me
now.' He cheekily replied, lengthily pecking her on the cheek.

'Awww…'

'You know what's funny?'

'What?'

'Blake and his dad are the only men in this picture!' he
chirped, prodding at Eliot's figure with closed eyes.

'Because it's only Blake's dad who knows what the
word longevity means,' she sighed with slight sadness,
which was all too easily detectable even if she tried to hide it in
her face and tone. Then something rang in his head, something
cued by her sadness about her dad, and rhymed with the word
"longevity".

'Look, Leila, I need to talk to you about something…' he
said in a deliberately earnest, nervy tone.

'Sounds serious. I'll put this away, and we'll talk.'

'Sure.' She crouched to shove the purse in her black leather
handbag just under the tiny square window, shielded with delicate
white lace net curtains offering little safeguarding to the grey-blue
of the threatening night and view of the dustbins down below the
concreted back yard and the short, rotting wooden fence splitting

that house from the nearby one, and trod on the fluffy aqua-coloured carpet back to sit beside Tre. She glanced at the alarm clock, which read quarter-to-two, then observed him twiddling his fingers with his eyes raised to the sunlight white ceiling and sphere light in the centre. She joined his muse subject, then returned to study his cheek, wondering if he'll ever notice she's sitting next to him again. 'Well, Tre, what was it you wanted to talk to me about?' His head fell to hers at her anxious tone. Still fiddling with a ring on his middle finger, and diving his gaze away for a split second, he finally found his words in his mind. 'Okay, here goes…'

On the pavement under the breezy shadows of rustling trees just a few hundred yards short of the Broadway, Blake slotted a pound coin into the bank of the telephone, removed the piece of paper Katerina gave him from his three-quarter length black nylon coat, placed it on the counter and dialled the number on it. The whizzing, incessant road noises had to be blocked off with a finger in his ear, just to hear the dial tone with the other. 'Hello?' the familiar accent answered after about two rings.

'Hi, Kat? This is Blake.'

'Oh hi, Blake! How's everything?'

'Brilliant, brilliant! Me and Leila reunited, and I met her bloke, we caught up a little, and now they're taking a kip, 'cause they were a little harassed during shopping at the Broadway. How's Al?'

'I knew you were going to ask that!' she mocked playfully, with a slightly scornful laugh. 'She's taking a kip, and I'm out walking in Acton Park to unwind myself for a kip too. I'm really knackered from the airport, checking you into the B&B, excusing myself to Al, etcetera and etcetera!' He giggled quietly, and relished the thought once again of Alana's sleeping state. 'Why aren't you walking in Ealing Common opposite me now?'

'I was born and raised in Hanwell, so knowing every grass there can get slightly boring!' He chuckled slightly. 'I see! Look, Kat, can I ask a few questions about Al's life now? I didn't get round to it before.'

'Sure – she's your friend as well as mine.'

'Well, I know she failed her degree, and she can't go
to journalism, so what does she do?'

'She's a betting shop cashier on Monday, Wednesday
and Friday mornings from nine to four. It's about a
hundred yards from the bingo club I work at from four
till ten on the same days. My media studies tutorials
are on those same days, from nine to twelve, then I go
home, eat, wash and rest for work.'

'So you don't see each other till late on those days?'

'Right.'

'Is she drinking again?'

'Not to my knowledge, but she wouldn't look so
healthy within a week if she was. She's put on a little
weight, 'cause she's eating regular meals, and the bags
under her eyes have disappeared, and her skin and eyes
sparkle like never before since I've known her, which is
only a week today.'

'Wow. I'm…amazed. Thanks for caring about her. Not
many people would do that for someone within a week.'

'I know, but it was unbearable seeing her like that. Plus
it's like there's a kinship between us. When I met her,
she spoke as if I was a parasite feeding on her sorry
lifestyle, but I felt it was the best conversation I'd ever
had. So I'm not doing this out of pity.'

'I realise. After all, it's too much work if you pitied her.'

'Certainly. Anything else you want to know?'

'Umm…not really.'

'Okay. So when will I be seeing you again?'

'Well, you could come over to my hotel room if you
want. Me, Leila and Tre are having a little get-together
in front of the telly with some food.'

'No, sorry – I can't. If I stay out here anymore, Al will
get suspicious. In fact, she's getting suspicious already,
and asking questions. I have to come up with excuses
almost every time I pop out.'

'Oh. Okay. Look, Leila mentioned something about

the reunion, and… oh shit, the money's running out.

Hang on, please.' He desperately rummaged through his dark blue cord jeans' hip pocket for another pound coin, seeing the flashing display impatient to cut him off. He managed to insert it before it did so, though. 'Yes, sorry about that.'

'So, what did Leila say?'

'She said we should talk our way into some sort of plan
   whenever you have time off.'

'Well, when Al is at work on Monday, I'll meet you all
   at Ealing Common on that bench near the main road?'

'Okay. So you won't be too tired?'

'Not if I go to sleep early today and tomorrow, so we'll
   meet at around…one-thirty or so? 'Cause I need to get
   back to the bed sit to eat something.'

'Sure. We owe you one, Kat.'

'Yeah, but don't feel too obliged to owe something,
   okay?'

'I won't. If Al does accept to marry me, you can either
   be a bridesmaid, or a maid of honour – your choice.'

'Hey, take it easy! Making wedding plans already, and
   you haven't even asked her yet? God, talk about jumping
   the gun here!' she gasped in faux shock.

'It's just an offer for everything you've done.'

'A drink at the pub someday would do just as well!'

'Okay, done. See you Monday.'

'Bye, Blake.' He hung up the receiver, noticing there was only five pence left on the display before it disappeared. He smiled contentedly to himself, before re-approaching the guest house in the opposite direction. But he whipped round when a post office sign caught his eye. *Mmm…that gives me an idea, you know…* With that thought, he spun round towards the first door of the Broadway itself into the post office.

'Again, where the heck have you been?' Katerina was immediately greeted with the second she shut the front door. She held up two carrier bags, one of which emitted a pungent smell of vinegar and oil, filling the whole room. 'I've brought some fish

and chips and a couple Cokes, that's all,' she replied naively.
Alana scowled from over the kitchen sink, where she refrained
from washing an apple. 'For nearly an hour?' she shrieked
incredulously.

'Look, I had to wait for a new batch of fish and chips
to fry – that must have taken about twenty minutes of
loitering in that shop, then it must have taken about
twenty minutes walk each way. I tried to come back
earlier, but I couldn't, okay? Plus I didn't want to
hang around in here and disturb you. You could've
threatened to smash my alarm clock over my head, like
you did last week!' After several seconds of pondering her
pleading tone, Alana giggled with a bowed head and accepted the
bags from Kat's grasp.

'It's alright. Thanks for the sentiment, though. It's just
that you seem to be out a lot these days.' Katerina gulped in
a breath of pessimism.

'Al, you see these books here?' she began with a groan,
pointing at the pile of study materials on the bed. 'This whole
fucking course is pissing me off! I don't know how the hell I'm
going to finish it when I'm stuck right in the middle of it!' she
screamed, sweeping them off the bed aggressively, which emitted
a loud thump against the carpet. She then hurled herself onto her
stomach on the cleared bed, and let out a hard, distressed sob into
the pillow. All Alana could do was watch wide-eyed in shock and
concern. Eventually, she placed the bags on the worktop, rested
herself beside her and stroked her back. 'Oh God, oh God, oh
God, how am I going to get myself out of this? Why can't I just
pack it all in?' she blubbed out clutching the pillow even tighter.
Alana continued stroking her back, hoping to calm her outburst.

'Hey, what happened, Kat? You can tell me – what is it?'
she whispered. She raised her head revealing puffy skin pooling
her red and blue eyes with a half-grin.

'Do you really want to know?'

'Sure. I mean, it's wasn't long ago I was in the same state
as you with my course, in case you forgot.' She breathed
out a giggle, which fell as quickly as it appeared, and then she

reached her arm to the bedside cabinet for a piece of paper, independent to the pile of stuff on the floor, and tossed it in Alana's lap. 'This is the problem. God, this really sucks! If this world was free enough, I would have ditched that stuff out of the window a long time ago!' Alana narrowed her eye to study the paper carefully. 'You got a grade C in your last assignment?'

'Yeah. I've had As and Bs before now, and now I'm only expecting things to get worse now!' she woefully groaned.

'I know what you mean. Look, don't let it get you down. Sneaking out to avoid it isn't going to help anything. I'll try and help through common sense, 'cause I'm not familiar at all with Media, but I'll help if you just ask, okay? So stop blubbering, and let's tuck into the fish and chips before they get cold, okay?' She reluctantly raised upright into a seated position, and grinned at Al. 'You want help?' she offered in a voice gritty from crying.

'No, no, it's okay. Just sit there and I'll bring the plates over with a couple of cans of cola.' With that she turned around to face the 'kitchen', and unwrapped the plastic and paper from the meal. Katerina snatched a tissue from the box on the cabinet, and roughly dabbed under her eyes and nose. *Sheesh – cod acting, but thank God that worked,* she thought, exhaling deeply in relief as she looked through the letter C overwritten on her assignment report.

Blake lied on his back on the bed, his hands clasped on his stomach, which still had a niggling throb beneath the skin from Freda's assaults. He smoothed a palm over his cheek, pleased that the pain had gone and the three wounds had already begun to close up. To obstruct any more horrid thoughts resurfacing, he trod back to his unconscious. His dream about Alana…

He and her were simply wandering together along some windy shore, sometime in the approaching evening, judging by the increasing number of stars amongst the millions of blue, orange and yellow hues, blurred together by misty clouds. The shallow waves of water only just missed their feet. He wanted to think of that heavenly place as somewhere in the Caribbean – preferably Tobago. The two of them and nobody else were holding hands, chatting and laughing just like old times. Then, he observed a large boulder of rock towards the end of the stretch of beach, directly under a tilting coconut tree and the smell of lemongrass and the cleansing sea air, the odd tropical bird call and the clicking of crickets from behind those tall blades of grass. They suddenly stopped talking, then he gently pushed her shoulders, so she sat down on the rock. He took a deep breath, his eyes absorbing her brown hair wavering in the wind, widened green eyes rolled up at him, and the silhouette of her body beneath the long lilac sundress. 'Al, I need to ask you something.'

'What is it? It sounds serious.'

'I've never been so serious in all my life, Al.' He inhaled again without even realising it, ruffled his hair with a trembling hand, then crouched down beside her and took one hand and stroked it like a glass sculpture.

'Here we are in this exotic wilderness. There's no one around, so no outside influences can force us against our natures, except nature itself. This freedom from inhibition has allowed me to seek my soul for the answer to all my happiness, and to end the uncertainty and horror I've been through. It's been right in front of me almost forever, but fear cast its spell on me, making me blind and a puppet to actions out of my character. But it's not just being here that's dispelled all that – it's being here with you, holding these hands, looking into those eyes and completely forgetting this jewel of the Caribbean.' He then rolled his legs so he still crouched before her, but on one knee, and reached a hand into the pocket of his white silk trousers. It was a small velvet cube. He flicked it open, revealing a gold band incorporated with alternate garnet and blue topaz stones. Alana's jaw was wide open, her eyes welling up till the figure of him was a blur, and her cheeks coloured by a rising flush of shock.

'Alana Higgins, will you marry me?'

'Oh my God...' she gasped with her fingers over her mouth. One of her hands eventually took the box from his grasp, just to study it as well as she could through her teary eyes. 'Blake, we've been friends for almost eleven years now, and... I really can't believe, or would ever believe, that out of every guy I know, you would be the one to propose to me. But I also can't see any other guy asking me such a question, so yes is the answer – I will marry you,' she finally breathed out through a throat choking back tears. He smiled beamingly, extended her left hand and slipped the ring on...

'Blake? Blake? Come on! Wake up and answer this door, dozy!' He was jumped back to his hotel room by Leila's incessant yelling and pounding against the door. 'Oh shit! Sorry, Lill! I'm opening the door now,' he shouted back, rolling off the bed in a nervy state, almost missing his feet. He straightened his silver shirt, and finally opened the door to see Leila and Tre standing there, holding hands. 'What the frig happened to you? Were you drunk or something?' she squealed, almost causing him to laugh at how seriously concerned she sounded. 'No, I was...dreaming, I think. Come in, and anyway, you can talk I must say!'

'What do you mean?' Tre queried innocently as he and Leila sat on the edge of the bed with one carrier bag each.

'You're two hours late! It's six o' clock, you know.'

'Sorry, Blake, it just...' she turned to Tre and flashed a flirty smile to him, and clasped his fingers tighter. 'well, me and Tre, we have an announcement to make.'

'What? You've discovered clocks?' Both of them giggled.

'No, better! Me and Tre, well...Tre asked me to marry him and I said yes.' Blake widened his eyes, and felt an involuntary tremor shake through him slightly.

'Congratulations, you two! Whew, talk about déjà vu.'

'What do you mean?'

'Just when I was thinking of proposing to Al, you suddenly tell me you're marrying Tre.'

'Good God – so that's what you were dreaming of!
Well, we could have a double wedding, you never know!'

'This calls for a celebration, and I'm not just talking about Cokes and beers here – how about some champers instead?'

'Yeah, brilliant! But…who'll get it?' Tre shot his hand up like a pupil in a schoolroom.

'I will! I've got twenty quid in my pocket, and I saw an off-licence not far from here, so I will. See you in a bit!' He pecked her on the cheek, and quickly dashed out, both Blake and Leila sniggering at the immediacy of both door slams. 'Good Lord, it seems you accepting his proposal has made him all silly! What exactly happened in there? I bet you made good use of the bedsprings in there!' She replied with a playful punch to his shoulder.

'That's none of your bloody business! Lord, my head is still spinning like mad,' she squeaked, pressing her palms to her temples. 'One minute I was introducing the three of us and our parents in a photo in my wallet, then he stumbled his way into asking me to marry him!'

'Whoa! Talk about spontaneity!'

'I know! Listen, I need to ask you something about your feelings for Al.'

'Yes?'

'Tre mentioned something that made me think – are you sure it's not a crush you have on Al, because you're still a bit… disturbed from what Freda did to you?'

'What?' he exclaimed in an almost appalled tone.

'Hey, I'm not doubting you love her, and neither is Tre, but…are you sure it won't wane once this Freda thing is out of your head?' He sighed at his need to explain.

'I'm positive – she's the one. You don't take something like what I'm feeling lightly. Every girl has been and gone, and she's always been there, advising me, warning me, and pushing me like my guardian angel beside me. I've always known there was something special about her, but I didn't realise it until Freda beat me – that's when I'd realised "Oh God, I've really fucked up here." So I know for sure she is my future, Lill. It's not a crush.'

'That's…lovely, Blake. Well, I'm right behind you, as I've always been, and thanks for clearing that up for me. It's just she's still like the sister I've never had,

and I still want her to be happy, even though I'm on
bad terms with her at the moment.'
'She will, don't worry. So, mind if I ask some questions
about Tre?'
'No, absolutely not. Fire away!'
'Tell me some basics about your future husband.'
'Well, his full name is Trevor Tappet, he's twenty-three
and comes from Cardiff – born and raised. His parents
are Jenny and Carl. Nice people – in fact, they remind
me a lot of your parents. He lived at home till we decided
to move in our own flat last November. He's a newspaper
photographer, and through that we met. He was assigned
to take photos of the Ealing area, and he was taking
pictures outside the University the day I finished my
Nutrition exam – the second of July ninety-seven. He was
snapping, I came out with a few other students, he saw me,
I saw him, and that was it – we clicked, if you know what
I mean!' He smiled uncontrollably at her hyped-up
enthusiasm behind her unintentional pun.
'What happened after that?'
'He stopped me, we introduced, and almost right away,
asked me on a date. I said, as a pre-date thing, we walked
to the pub up at Shepherd's Bush. For about two hours we
chatted, found loads in common, and swapped numbers!'
'What did your Mum think of moving in with him?'
'Two words to sum it up – not happy. I mean, she liked
him as a person, but when I announced last June that we
were going to live together, she was happy. But the
entered the word "Cardiff", and all hell broke loose.
We rowed in pretty much the same way you and your
parents rowed about you and Freda living together –
why can't you get a place here in London, blah, blah,
blah… I hated seeing him only every month, which was
partly the reason I did it. It ended in a slap, then I packed
my bags and hauled myself to a guest house for a day while
I called Tre to tell him what went wrong and when I was
coming over. And that was it.'

'I'm sure she had your best intentions in mind. I mean,
I know my parents did when I did exactly the same thing.'
'I know. But I wouldn't up sticks with anyone all of a
sudden, especially to Cardiff, plus I'd been dating him
eleven months, not eleven days, so surely she expected
better from me.'
'You've hardly been out of London in you life without
us or your mum, so it's understandable she's scared for
you. Well, that's what we're here for – to be on good
terms with everyone again, so don't worry. So now you
live in Cardiff with him, what do you do there?'
'I work as a dietician at the town centre's slimming club.
I've found a job that'll put my degree to good use. I advise
which foods certain people should eat, such as pregnant
women, diabetics, the really obese, and so on.'
'Sounds interesting!'
'It's fantastic. I've always wanted to do something like
that. Everything in my life has snapped into place – well,
nearly everything, anyway.' He patted her shoulder.
'It will, don't worry. The missing part will complete my
life as well as yours.'
'I know. So you'll be deserting us again when you go
back to Cardiff?
That is, *if* you're going back to Cardiff?'
'Hell no! Of course we're going back to Cardiff, but
we've decided to visit every weekend, and feel free to
visit us too.'
'Sure, but I hate this visiting lark – can't you get somewhere
in London?'
'Look, Blake – I've laid my foundations in Cardiff now.
Tre hates London – you should've seen the state of him
after one shopping trip today! He even complained about
it over that drink in the pub when we met! Plus, it's my
idea of paradise in this country, actually. I mean, look at
this place – it's overcrowded, the pads cost a bomb, and
a thousand other things – it's turning into hell on earth!'
'Well, as long as you're happy with Tre and living in

Cardiff, I can't really complain. You've accepted that I
love Al, so it's only fair that I accept your decisions.
Plus, Tre seems a nice guy – a bit on the laddish side,
but quite charming and obviously loves you, so there
you go.' Her eyes softened to one of relief, and cupped a
hand on his shoulder, covered by the same black shirt he travelled
with. 'Thank you, Blake. I owe you one.'

'Like what?'

'Let's all get married together. We'll put off our wedding
date till you come to an agreement with Al, so we really
can have a double wedding! Deal?' She extended her hand
to him, which he clasped with a slap and shake.

'Deal! It's only fair that we marry together after all
we've done together as kids, right? Plus, it'll seal a
truce between us after saying such horrid things to
each other, okay?'

'Okay – done!' she squealed, pointing at him with a
definitive smirk and a wink. Then their conversation was
interrupted by the unlocking of the door. 'Oh look! The
champagne delivery boy is here!' she hooted, pointing at Tre
entering the room, struggling to smile through his shivers,
handing the bottle and the tower of plastic cups to Leila, quickly
shedding his coat onto a chair beside the television stand. 'Cor
blimey, it's bloody freezing out there!'

'Mmm, looks expensive.'

'It cost sixteen quid that, and the cups cost one-ninety
nine,' he explained slightly sarcastically as he sat next to
Leila on the bed.

'Terrific – you've got good taste. Blake, will you do
the honours, as you're stronger than us?!' He sniggered
bashfully, then took the bottle and pushed upwards on the cork
with his thumbs. *Pop!* The cork fell to the floor. A kind of vapour
floated vertically out of the opening. 'Woo! At least it's not
spraying everywhere! Bring the cups please!' Leila passed one
cup at a time, filling each to the top. Then they raised them in the
air simultaneously, as each thought of something to toast to.

'Right, what shall we toast to?' Blake asked, not wanting to interrupt if they thought of something better.

'To my future husband here, and your future wife –

hopefully! – and to the future itself! Cheers!' Leila proudly declared. Both men smiled and nodded and clinked their cups together, not having the same effect as glasses, but were glad it was a special toast nonetheless. 'Cheers!'

Chapter 17.

'Come on, Al, get the hell out of there! It's eight-thirty!'
Katerina bellowed, pounding her fists against the hollow-
sounding bathroom door. 'Alright, alright, I've just come out of
the shower – I'll be out in two minutes, okay?' Alana protested
from the other side.

'Hey, keep it down, will ya?' a gruff voice indistinct of
gender came from behind the wall of the staircase. 'Oh shut up!
It's morning, you should be getting your lazy self up too!'

'Thanks a lot!' the person snapped back. Katerina just rolled
her eyes and focused them onto the door when she heard it
unlatch. Alana emerged in a grey criss-cross neckline top and
blue jeans flaring out at her ankles. 'About bloody time! I don't
want to be late for University, you know.'

'Hey, I remembered – I've been there before. I don't
want to be late for work either.' Katerina sighed in
acceptance.

'Okay. I'll be out in fifteen minutes. Thanks for breakfast,
Al.'

'No problem. See ya.' With that, she clicked the door
closed. Alana made her way back up the stairs to her room, which
seemed to look humbler every time she left it and returned. She
perched on the edge of the bed, and cupped her chin with her
palm. *What the hell am I going to tell them at the betting shop –
oh, by the way, I tried to commit suicide with vodka? God, that's
a sure ticket to lose my job – Leila was right. No man likes a
drunk, and the people there are mostly men anyway. I'll think of
something, thanks to Kat...* She then leaned herself back against
the two piled pillows with her arms behind her head, and began a
conversation with her conscience. *Speaking of Leila – perish this
thought I'm having after the way they treated me – but I wonder
how they're doing now? I don't care, really – Blake's with his
bitch in Dublin, and Leila's probably cutting up frogs and rats,
figuratively speaking, but as far as I'm concerned, they can go to
hell...*

'Hey, have you fallen asleep or something?' A squeal from the front door twitched her head towards the voice. She saw Katerina chucking her nightshirt over the chair in a direct hit, then the towel. 'N-no, of course not.' She buttoned up her turquoise shirt over her black combat trousers. 'Well, get your shoes on – it's time to go!' Alana idly rolled off the bed, reached for her square-toed, chunky-heeled shoes by the doorway, the fact obvious that she'd forgotten she had shoes until that point when she had to brush the dust off them. 'You…got everything?'

'Yep, it's all in here,' Katerina said assuredly, patting her slightly sagging black rucksack on her bed. Alana nodded and slipped the brown leisure coat that had been hanging on the wall hooks for God knows how long, and slung her black leather satchel on her shoulder. 'All done!'

'Great. You go down. I'll meet up with you in a moment.' Alana's slumping footsteps down the two creaky staircases were interrupted by a tap on her shoulder. 'Oi, Higgins, I've goh a lettah and a parcel here for ya.'

'Oh, good morning, Mr Peel,' she began in fake enthusiasm. 'Can I have them, please?' In a couple of seconds, he returned from his dishevelled den with a white, tall, rectangular box with a pale pink ribbon across it, and a pastel blue envelope. With the box under her arm, she studied the envelope – it was addressed to Alana. *Who the hell knows I live here?* Before she planned opening the flap, she was patted on the shoulder. 'Hi, Al. Blimey, what's that?'

'It's a letter and a parcel. Peel gave it to me just now.'

'Oh. Well, let's look at it outside, huh?'

'Sure.' Katerina received the parcel as they left the doorway into the cloudless, delicate blue dawn laced with wine spear clouds. Once on the almost deserted pavement, Katerina unlaced the ribbon and lifted the lid on the box. She gasped at its contents. There were about eight or ten red chrysanthemum flowers, coloured yellow under each petal. 'Good God,' both howled in a gasp. 'they're…they're beautiful. Who're they from? Who knows you live here?' Alana was still fumbling with the envelope, till she eventually pulled out a plain white horizontal card. 'I have no idea, but someone knows that these are my favourite flowers. I haven't received any mail for months. Let's see what it says on this card.' She skimmed her eyes over it, unaware Katerina was casting a shadow leaning over her shoulder. She sucked in a breath at the verse inside it. Then she scrutinized each word, written in beautifully slanted cursive calligraphy:

"Everyone has to go their own way someday –
I went mine, but I was terribly misguided;
My eyes were blinded by my awe at your beauty.
I'm a total fool not to take the obvious way,
But I'm also a fool in love with you.
Now I know my path is to the Universe
And back through the one-way street to your heart
To lay every moon, star, planet, and my heart, at your feet.
Whether you accept or not,
My spirit is now awakened from its sleep of denial
By this new realisation –
I love you beyond distance, space and time."

Love,
Your Secret Admirer.

'Good Lord. Kat, this is…wonderful. I'm absolutely gob-smacked.' Both girls had a hand to their mouths, taken aback by the poem.
'Well, this guy certainly has a way with words, I can tell you that! Anyone you know?'
'That's just it – even at work, I don't know anyone as much as no one knows me. I don't have a social circle there – I just provide a service to earn a bit of dough. But it sounds like it's from an old flame, even though I've only had two… well, one. I'd hardly count that Ryan as one.' A giggle from Katerina preceded a silence as they began a slow stroll along the pavement, bunching themselves together. 'Well, let's get thinking!' Then she glanced at the watch

– it read ten to nine, and slapped her forehead. 'Oh shit, look at the time! Can I put the flowers in the room till you get back?'

'Sure. Let me keep the card in my bag. If I get a spare moment, I'll study it.' Silence again as she leaned the box against her chest, and went her way to the short, vertical-bar gate, red with rust and paint. She then suddenly turned back to her, standing in the centre of the pavement, shrugging her arms up.

'Hey, you think its Peel?' Alana gaped her eyes at her, slightly fazed.

'Oh come on, don't be stupid! The guy can't even sign his own name!' she retorted, throwing up her hands. Katerina smiled and shook her head in humour, then vanished behind the self-closing, window-panelled brown door.

'I suppose. Keep thinking!' Her feet still glued in place, Alana was at a loss for thoughts and words from knowing someone, somewhere likes her. *Could it be someone from University? Could it be someone from work? Could it just be some psycho...? I can't think of anyone this good with words...*

'Okay, time to dash! See you later.'

'See ya, Kat.' They parted with reluctance to their corresponding paths, regularly turning back.

'Hey, any ideas yet?' Katerina called from the kerb.

'So soon?'

'Sorry – just anxious, that's all.'

'Come on – he's my admirer, not yours!'

'How do you know it's a he?' she blew a raspberry in mock at her tasteless joke.

'Alright, alright. See you later.'

'Okay, 'bye.' Kat then split from Al by sprinting across the deadened main road. From the fresh smell reminiscent of the park or a little forest, it was evident that either they hadn't woken up yet, or the workers were on strike. Before she knew it, the revolving doors were right in front of her, almost walking into them. Inside the ground floor was warm to the point of being almost stuffy, and it was busier from how she remembered it. 'Good morning, Kat,' called the receptionist.

'Oh, good morning, ma'am.' She pressed a button with her thumb to switch off her phone, and replaced it in the plastic case attached to her trouser waistband. 'Oh shit! Just what I was trying to avoid!' she snarled through her teeth as she was tossed around by a tornado of people to all seven lifts. She had to resort to being last in the lifts, only just about squeezing herself and her rucksack behind the doors...

'Are you sure it's here, Blake?' Leila queried as she and Tre sat together with their fingers intertwined under the wide-openness of the cloud-free skies behind the distant, bunched-up oak trees, listening to the buzz of the moderate traffic behind them. Blake cast an annoyed glance to her impatience.

'Look, this what she said, and I quote – "meet me at the little bench at Ealing Common, but I may not be on time, because I have some things to do first."' The field was empty, so they had nothing but their conversations and chirps of blackbirds and pigeons to entertain them.

'Well, she's not on time, so she's doing something! You think she's leading us on?' she asked, almost whining in panic.

'Oh come on, Lill! You know, you say some really stupid things out of paranoia sometimes.' She lowered her head away from both men towards her knees.

'Only a thought.'

'Well, it was a lousy one! Besides, I can go to that call box behind us and demand some answers if we stay here too late.' He pointed at a triangular call box situated at the bend in the main pavement. She smirked and shrugged in acceptance, then looked at her watch – it read ten to two.

'I suppose...'

'Not only that; she brought us all here, right in the middle of west fourteen, then she leaves us in the lurch like this? I'll go and beat my head against a wall now!' Leila and Tre roared out into mad laughter, throwing their heads till they almost snapped off. Leila then shoved a palm at him, intending for his face, still chuckling.

'Alright, alright, I got the point!'

'Hey! Pipe down, you two!' Tre intervened bravely.

'I'm sorry – it's just your fiancée really talks some crap sometimes!'

'You've known her longer than me, so no comment!' Leila tried squeezing her palm against her mouth to stop chortling in vain. It eventually deadened out, and the three twisted their heads round the panoramic, freshly-groomed lawn, which could envelope the bench they were sitting on about a thousand times. The odd roller-skater passed by on the footpath far perpendicularly from them, so were practically on their own there. The opposite side of the field had some lane with a car or two passing per minute. 'This is a nice park, Blake. I can't believe I'm still in London.' Blake and Leila breathed out a slight laugh.

'This was where myself, Lill and Al picnicked from when we were ten upwards, but we gave up when we started University, which was only a few weeks between each other.' Leila sighed, rolling her eyes skywards. 'Growing up can be such a terrible thing.'

'Can't we all go for a picnic – assuming this thing with Al is solved soon? You know, go time-travelling!' Tre suggested eagerly in an offbeat way.

'Could do… yeah, why not?' Blake agreed with a smile. Leila snuggled up to Tre's shoulder again as a reward for that suggestion. 'Well, I quite like it here. If I had to wait on a bench in Ealing Broadway, I'd go mad!'

'I know what you mean, but it's a good shopping place.'

'Uh-huh…'

'No, seriously! Oh, look over there!' He trailed off, then pointed towards a running girl on the pavement parallel to the main road heading towards them, struggling to keep her rucksack on her shoulder as she sprinted, and her blonde hair flicked back by the breeze. 'Phew, that's a relief!' Leila exhaled lazily.

'See? What did I tell you?' Katerina halted and butted the three of them aside with her hip for the end piece of the bench.

'Sorry, everyone. I had a whole heap of things to do before coming here.'

'Like what?' Leila asked in a deadpan tone.

'First, I was stopped by Glenn Sutton in the University as I was leaving, asking me how Alana was – I told him she is now a completely reinvented woman, just in time for her birthday, and asked him for an application form for a refresher course in journalism for her. I also had to pick up the laundry, and get something to eat, and buy some bread, milk and stuff, and buy a vase from the odds-and-ends shop. I had to do those things to stop Alana asking questions when she gets back.'

'That's terrific! Will she fill in the form?' Blake questioned keenly.

'Sure. She's finally realised that she can't work in that betting shop forever.'

'At last!' Leila sighed in elation, causing a breath-laugh from Blake.

'A vase?' Tre confusedly questioned, raising his eyebrows.

'Yeah. Al got a bunch of chrysanthemums from a secret admirer – God knows who, but it's someone who knows his English!' Blake, Leila and Tre sniggered.

'Has someone been stalking her? I can't think of anyone, except us, who knows she has a thing for chrysanthemums,' Leila asked, intending to sound mocking.

'Well, a poem was sent with the flowers. Al still has it in her bag, but it was a lovely poem.'

'Wow. So she's okay then?' Blake queried in surprise.

'Yeah. She's at work at the mo. She's a very happy person, would you believe it.'

'That's all good, but could it all change when she's reunited with these two here?' Tre asked, leaning forward to face her.

'All will be revealed tomorrow. So you mentioned something about meeting up at the mall tomorrow?'

'Yeah. She used to love going there with us, so that's why I thought of that,' Leila answered.

'Sure.' Silence for a few seconds. 'Umm, guys…there's something I need to tell you…something I didn't mention about Al's drinking problem.' With only the mention of the last two words, Leila, Blake and Tre all turned towards her noiselessly, eyes bulging and jaws dropped open. Katerina cowered slightly in the presence of those staring eyes of disbelief – *whoops, I've blown it now…* 'Kat, how could you not tell us something about the drinking problem that almost killed her? What is it, anyway?' Leila shrieked in demand.

'Well…' she began, frightened of the bomb she was about to drop would detach them from the only link to Alana they had – her. She inhaled deeply. *Got to get this right…* 'She's drinking to live in her dreams of Adrian, but the true root of it is you two, especially Blake.'

'Me? How?' he asked, perking up an eyebrow in curiosity.

'Well, I'm no shrink, but it seems losing you has had the greatest effect on her as you know. If she fell out with Leila first and had you, it wouldn't have hurt so much. Secondly, haven't you noticed how much you look like a darker blond, shorter-haired version of him?'

'Huh? Um… yeah, I suppose so…' he stuttered incredulously.

'You do. Oh, and she also said the more she drank, the more her dreams seemed real. And what saucy dreams they were, too – she described a couple to me.'

'So this Adrian acted as a substitute Blake to her?' Tre intruded in the name of logic.

'Yeah. Good summary, Tre,' she praised, aiming a forefinger at him. They all turned their attention to Blake, whose gaze was fixated away from them in space, trying to absorb the shock of his answer in this new information.

'So, if those dreams you say are… you know, x-rated, and he was a substitute me, then… there must be a chance that… she… she…' his words fell short of his voice at that point.

'She what?' Leila encouraged.

'She… feels the same about me as I do for her?' he gasped out, with a hand slapped over his chest, then over his mouth. Tre smiled with Leila, then she rubbed his shoulder in a congratulatory manner. 'I certainly think so, too! I think the saucy dreams were meant for Blake in the first place.'

'But it won't make things any easier. Her hurt has buried her feelings so deep, it'll take more than an excavator to dig them out!' Katerina jested. Blake half-laughed, then his face fell to a sigh. 'I know.' His head was whirring round and round in disbelief.

'So this crush of hers has been good as well as bad to her?' Tre summarized once again.

'You could say that, but she doesn't know that yet, just like she doesn't know you've been good as well as bad to her.'

'She's still my sister, and I love her to bits. I'll try my best to make it up to her, and I know Blake here especially feels the same.'

'I certainly do!' he howled comically, smiling.

'So you're not mad at me for retaining info, then?'

'Course not. You've told us now. Besides, we would've probably told you to sod off!' All four of them elicited a lukewarm laugh.

'True, true! Anyway, on with the plan…' Leila shrugged with a smile in acceptance and due to the fact that she'd been won over by Katerina's eagerness to help her roommate. For the next forty or so minutes, they discussed who should meet up with who first, whether or not gifts should be involved, where the meeting place should be in terms of any of Alana's favourites, and the most important of all – if sorry will ever be enough.

'Al, I'm home!' Katerina trilled as she shut the door deliberately noisily, and slung her handbag to the ground and her shoes off her feet. *Phwoar…these shoes pong a bit…*she recoiled with a wrinkled nose, without having to stick her nose into the shoes. Then she saw the duvet on Alana's bed bunching up to reveal a head of tousled hair. Katerina sighed in relief. 'Phew, you're awake.'

'Look, Kat, you can trust me now not to do something like that again,' she insisted in a voice scratchy and quiet with sleep. Katerina sat on the edge of her bed, next to the curve of her waist. 'You okay? How was work?'

'Fine. Nothing much to write home about when you're working amongst a bunch of old buffers!' Both girls chuckled, then a brief pause.

'So, I never asked you this, but what exactly do you do there?'

'Oh, didn't I tell you? I help operate the electronic board that generates the numbers.'

'I see. How long have you worked there?'

'About a year. To sum it up, well…I don't like talking about this, but my family thought like a Hindu family when it came to me – it was either their way or no way at all. About two weeks ago, I came home from University and found them talking, eating and drinking tea with this boy – he must have been about eighteen or nineteen, dark cropped hair, brown eyes, smartly dressed, looked like a University student like me. They asked me to sit down as they had an announcement to make, so I sat between my Mum and Dad on the couch opposite him, and asked what the hell was going on. They had such a hopeful expression on their faces, so soap-opera-ish, I could have vomited. Then they introduced him to me – forgotten his name now – but I shook his hand still sitting. Then they waffled their way into telling me they were going to arrange a marriage between me and this guy, whom I'd only met about sixty seconds ago. I was so frigging angry, I could have set the entire house and street alight with my argument. Our guest was a bit bemused at what he just saw, and so was my Mum – I think she was angry at my decision as much as he was, but at least she looked somewhat remorseful, and didn't lash out at me. So I grabbed my handbag by the doorway, and stormed out. That day, I got a newspaper to check out any local flats or bed sits around while I sat on that bench in Ealing Common – I rang this one, saying there was a room available, but there was a likelihood that I had to share. The next week, I carried on going to University while I packed to leave. During that time, it was always my Mum who came up to my room to check if I was okay, and offered to straighten things out. But I refused, and said how I was set on the decision that I wanted to move out and find myself. She couldn't accept it for the whole week, until the Friday morning I was due to leave. She hugged me and said, "I know I haven't been supportive of all your decisions, but I'll support you all the way with this one, and if you need any help paying for University, just tell me okay?" I was so touched, because all the time, I thought Mum and Dad were like-minded individuals, and that proved that my Dad was more stubborn than Mum. I nodded, hugged her, and waved as I left the doorway for the last time. My Dad was still asleep, so he didn't see me leave. I'm still mad with him, but I also feel I've been a little insensitive to him.'

'That's total bullshit, Kat! They were controlling your life, so you had every right to get mad, especially as they almost forced you to marry someone you didn't even know. I'd pity you even more if you had a sibling to put up with that too. If your dad was too small-minded to accept your plans, then you were right to move out to prove him wrong.'

'I suppose...' she tailed off unenthusiastically.

'No supposing! You *were* right!' Alana insisted, punching her shoulder.

'Well, I just thought I'd tell you why I'm here. No reason, just it's only fair that I tell you my story, since you told me yours.'

'I know. It's okay. I could see why you didn't want to talk about it.'

'Yeah, but I feel better telling you anyway.' She then took a deep breath, and leapt to her feet. 'Oh well, enough with that. How about a cup of tea?'

'Sure.' Katerina then hopped over to the 'kitchen', and placed the kettle on the stove. Alana then heaved herself up

against the pillowed headboard, and hugged her own shoulders.
'God, it's bloody cold!'

'Hang on, I'll shut the window after I put the kettle on.'
Katerina then marched over to the window between her bed and
Alana's, reached for the frame on her toes and tugged the slight
gap down. 'Okay, it's closed. So, how was your day?'

'Oh, not bad. Nobody came to mind when it came to
   that poem, though,' Alana said, glancing for a spilt second
on the vase on the kitchen worktop next to the cooker. 'Thanks
for getting a vase, though.'

'Oh God, I forgot about that. No problem.'

'I studied it line by line on the bus – nothing, but something
   does seem familiar, though.' Katerina widened her eyes,
and shuffled her way back to sit next to her again. 'Really?
What?!' she shrieked in eagerness, shifting up and down like a
hyperactive dog.

'Hey, hey, steady! Could you bring my handbag over there,
please?' She rose up and leaned a short distance for the handbag,
then placed it in her lap. Alana then rummaged her hand into it,
and pulled out the envelope. Katerina then tossed the bag back
next to the door, and watched as she unfolded the card, her
eagerness still consistent.

'Okay, Kat. This first line here is strangely familiar, but
   the rest of it isn't.'

'Why is it strangely familiar?'

'Because this "Everyone has to go their own way someday"
   line was exactly the last thing Blake said to me before he
   left with Freda, when I was literally on my knees begging
   for him to stay.'

'You what?'

'Yep.'

'Are you saying this is Blake?'

'No; he wouldn't write something like this. Plus, he's my
   friend, and he probably doesn't want to see my face again,
   let alone declare love. Plus, he's got Freda, as much as I
   hate it.' *Oh no he hasn't,* she felt like telling Alana. But she
curbed the urge somehow.

'I know, but maybe, if it *is* him, things have gone wrong,
    and he wants to make things up with you?' Alana suddenly
cracked up laughing so hard, she almost dropped the card to the
floor with her head tilted up to the ceiling. 'Hey, what's so
funny?'

'By saying he loves me all of a sudden? Don't be silly!
    He snogged me once, but he was drunk, and he apologised
    the next day. Nothing will ever happen between him and
    me.'

'Okay, okay, I'm sorry, but don't laugh at me.'

'I didn't mean to.' Katerina then got up to check on the
kettle. About five minutes later, she returned with two mugs of
piping-hot tea, and handed a mug to Alana. She nodded in thanks.
'So, you think you'll get anymore of these things?' Katerina
asked, holding up the card.

'I'll wait and see.'

'Anyway, would you like to go to the Broadway on
    Wednesday – look around, perhaps get a new outfit or
    something?'

'Yeah, why not? I've asked for Wednesday off.'

'So have I, and I've cancelled a tutorial. You wish for
    anything special for your birthday?'

'Mmm…not really… oh, I know! A Discman – I wanted
    one of those for ages.' Katerina returned a compassionate
glare.

'Well, we'll see what they have there.' Alana nodded away
in acceptance. *Right, time to ask about this as casually as
possible…*

'You know you mentioned Blake? Well, I want to ask
    something about you, Blake and Leila.'

'Sure – what is it?' she asked, frowning in curiosity as she
took another sip from the mug.

'Do you hate them, and would you take them back if
    you met up with them tomorrow?' Alana just stared blankly
at her for a minute or two.

'Whoa, what a question. I've asked myself that, actually.
    I'm…they've hurt me so much, and it really got to me.

I can't forgive what they did, and I'm not sure if I'll ever
forgive them, but I still don't hate them – I can't hate
them, believe it or not.'
'Oh.'
'Does that answer your question?'
'Yeah, it does, thanks.' Neither of them spoke a word
during the time they took to drink their tea. Both supped the last
drop at the base of the mugs, and Katerina took them to the
kitchen sink. 'Thanks for the tea, Kat.'
'No problem. Look, I'm sorry if I caused discomfort
in asking that.'
'No, no, it's okay. It's a good question after everything
I've said about them during my story.'
'I guess so. Anyway, you can go to sleep. I'm going
to freshen up now then I'm going to sleep,' Katerina
announced as she picked up her black satin nightshirt from the
pile of laundry she observed Alana had neatly piled onto the
chair. On the way out of their room, she took a final glance at
Alana, her back turned against the door, and the tips of her hair
spiked out form the duvet over her head. She smirked self-
satisfied to herself as she shut the door.

Chapter 18.

'Hey Al, are you okay? You seem to be in a world of your own,' Katerina alerted Alana in curiosity. Fifteen out of their twenty-minute stroll was spent with Katerina rambling away about her studies, yet it never even touched Alana's ears, let alone entered them. She occasionally slipped in and out of the memory of Katerina being next to her, wondering who or what has turned her into temporarily into a vegetable. Realising there was nothing more to hypnotise herself, she suddenly whipped round to face her. 'Ah, so you *are* still with us,' she declared sarcastically. Alana just returned an expressionless face to her. Katerina cocked her head sideways, desperate for a reaction. 'Hey Al, are you okay?'

'Yeah.'

'Oh, so you do have a voice!' She just sniffed a giggle. 'What're you thinking about?'

'Um, I didn't show you this earlier, but I'd better now.'

'What? What is it?' she asked worriedly. Alana then stopped the two of them near a spiral-topped church a few hundred yards from the shopping precincts by a hand round her forearm, and bade her to sit down on an oak bench under the chilly shade of a few trees. She desperately hurled her satchel onto her lap, rammed a hand inside, and yanked out an envelope.

'Have you found out something about that poem?'

'Before I had a chance to find out about the first one, I got another one while you were waiting for me outside the bed sit.'

'You're joking! Let me see,' Katerina shrilled with a frown, snatching the envelope from her. She removed a similar looking card from the last, and lifted it open to see another verse, written obviously by the same pen in the same script, by the same person:

"I bat my gritty eyelids open
I look ahead from my bed; something's not right.
I certainly don't remember
Leaving that window open last night.

Before I inspect, black gloved hands wrestle my defences
And aggressive grunts and breaths warm my ear.
The intruder, not so much as a verb, dominates my
frozen frame
As I perspire, tremble and shed the odd tear.
Maybe I'm still asleep, dreaming out of paranoia,
Or maybe it's all a terrifying joke – that's right, it's a joke,
Otherwise why would you pop that mask over your head?
Your long hair springs through back-flowing fingers, I
nearly choke –
It can't be, it just can't be – it *is* you!
Straddling my legs, arousing me like no one or ever before,
The woman I was thinking about just now.
You still sweetly silent, I can't take your teasing eyes
anymore –
I flip us over; now *I* have *you* where I want you;
Underneath me to work my imagination overtime
Of ripping the black clothes from your clad frame.
I feel you demanding for me, though giggling adorably in
shyness.
In my dreams, you've burgled the house of my ritual
nightmare,
Here for our night passions to be wild and untamed."

Love,
Your Secret Admirer.

'Holy…who is this guy? Some pervert who likes bondage?'
Katerina shrieked incredulously. Alana dropped her head as her
eyes welled up; she spotted this, and hugged an arm round her
shoulders in comfort.
    'I don't know, Kat. I really don't know. I don't know if
    I can ever step out of the bed sit after today. Even today,
    when I first read that, I had doubts about coming out with
    you.'
'Hey, hey, come on, don't be like that,' Katerina gasped.

'I can't help it. I can't get the thought out my mind that
the next time I step out, I could be bungled into a car,
and never to be seen again.'

'Come on, don't think like that. Look, if you're really
worried, let's go to the police on Monday, and see
what they say, huh?' Alana turned a vulnerable look to her,
sniffing and nodding. 'Yeah, I'd feel a lot better if we did that.'
Katerina patted her shoulder blade, and folded the card and
replaced it in the envelope. 'Now, it's the eve of your birthday,
for goodness sakes! So cheer up, forget this weirdo for a couple
of hours, and let's spend!' Both of them giggled at her
enthusiasm, then raised themselves off the bench and proceeded
to the Broadway.

For a minute or two, they glanced round, with the speeding
wash of shoppers and commuters closing in on them, from the
shopping mall they now stood before, underneath the concrete
awning and the geometrically-arranged display panes on either
side of the entrance, and dimly lit inside the wide clearing,
mirroring against the white vinyl floor tiles. Then they focused on
the more familiar one on the opposite pavement. Katerina then
glanced at her watch – it read twelve-thirty. *Mmm...it's a little
early. I can give her a choice to play down the suspicion...* 'So,
where do you want to go first?' Alana thought with a finger to her
lips.

'Umm...let's go into this one here. Then we can go into
that other one. I haven't seen up here for a while, so we'll
check out both.'

'Okay. Take my arm and let's go.' Alana interlinked her
arm with Katerina's, then butted past the perpendicular flow of
people to the entrance. 'Hey, this is great – just like old times
with those two,' Alana said joyfully.

'Hey, with any luck, this'll be better than old times!'
Katerina answered equally zealously, sneakily referring to her
plan for today in her mind.

Around half an hour later, Katerina and Alana breezed out
onto a corner patch of the pavement, holding one carrier bag in
each hand. They purposelessly scaled the upper and lower ends of

Uxbridge Road, with nothing but vehicles, vehicles and more vehicles sluggishly going both ways. 'Nice day for a traffic jam, eh?' Katerina commented mockingly, emitting a snort from Alana.

    'Yeah. Enjoy shopping in there?'

    'Sure! I'm glad to have got myself a couple of nightshirts. You know, that black satin one was the only one I personally liked. My parents really chose some horrible ones!'

    'Really? Well, I'm glad to get a nightshirt too. I've got enough clothes, which I haven't worn for weeks, probably months, but I've got to get rid of that horrid grey one – it's past it!' Both girls cackled aloud with their heads tilted back. While Alana was still laughing, Katerina stole a quick glimpse of her watch – it read quarter-past-one. *Oh God, it's nearly time*... 'Oh dear...anyway, how about the other mall now?'

    'Sure.' They began snaking through the stagnating traffic, smelling the air becoming equally foul and stagnant, reaching the other pavement quite quickly, and dashed into the sliding doors of the shopping mall. They were instantly hit by a fresh gust of air conditioning, and the subtle smell of perfume and continental food. Alana twisted her head around, refreshing the memory of her favourite place; nothing had changed at all. 'Aaah, this is nice – lot better than that other place. This is why I loved hanging out here so much.' They then halted, almost solitary in the centre of the clearing, between the escalator and the doors.

    'It is lovely. I actually liked here too – especially the Italian stuff on the upper floor,' Katerina commented positively.

    'Well, I've never eaten here before. The only place we ever ate was that other café – the one we passed with the French-style awning?'

    'Yeah, I do. Let's give it a go to recharge our batteries before doing any more shopping. Besides, it's too damn cold to think about eating outside.'

'Sure.' She then grumpily snorted, turning her head away from Katerina.

'What is it?'

'Huh! Well, I know *that* place only too well.' Alana pointed towards an all-too familiar shop – the tuxedo shop. Katerina sighed in realisation.

'Oh, is that the place that Blake met Freda, then?'

'Sadly, yeah. God, Kat, why didn't I go in with him while Leila bought her dress for the party, huh?' Alana moaned, almost breaking down. Katerina patted the top of her spine. 'It's okay, Al. Come on, let's go to the café. We'll all feel better in a while.' *I hope*, she thought anxiously.

'Okay.' Katerina led Alana up the escalator in the centre of the floor by supporting her falling weight by her shoulders. *Don't worry, I'm sure everything will be okay soon...*

'Hey, Blake, isn't this great? Us walking together arm-in-arm again without that bitch bustin' our chops?' Blake cracked into a throaty laugh at her ending, soon joined by Leila.

'I know, but there's one person missing on my other arm.' Soon both their laughter faded into near-sorrowful expressions. 'I know. Don't worry.' Her arm loosened from his grip, and went to stroke his shoulder blade compassionately. She saw his head cower slightly to hide his fallen face, at a loss of what to do herself. He then leaned over the steel barrier, shielded with frosted glass, and peered down an approximate distance of twenty feet. His eyes automatically rolled to the tuxedo shop in the corner from the sliding glass doors, then narrowed in bitterness as his brain felt as if it was combusting. 'What is it, Blake?' Leila asked, trying to focus through his eyes.

'That down there. Why didn't I get out of that shop while I had the chance, Lill? I could've gone somewhere else,' he asked, partly to himself and partly to Leila, in a watery, breaking voice, stroking his slightly itchy wounds on his cheek. She turned him around, and outstretched her arms and curled him in them. 'Stop blaming yourself, Blake.

You dated her out of naive flattery as well as what you told me –
I'm sure that's her way with soft-hearted guys like you.' His head
shot up to a relentless stare at her. 'Are you saying I'm soft?'

'No – what I'm saying is, she pinpointed you as an
easy target.'

'Humph. Funny thing is, I grew up with two girls for
friends, and a little sister, and yet I know absolutely
nothing about love or how to tell good from bad girls!'
Leila chuckled heartily again, then patted his shoulder. 'Blake,
that's not the reason you let Freda mess up your mind like that.
You've had lots of experience with females, of course, but only a
little romantically.'

'That's why I'm frightened I'll screw up with Al again,
because I'm soft; no nice girl has ever seen me as more
than just a friend. The horrid ones take advantage of me
as their slave, and if I attempt to further our relationship,
she'll… hate me as much as I hate myself for treating her
like that.'

'I understand totally, but it's also true that love is a
great teacher – if you got through with this, love will
teach you both to love each other. After all, she's only
ever had one relationship, which wasn't much, so she's
just as inexperienced as you. That's another reason she's
resorting to her fixation on Adrian McCraedie.'

'I suppose…'

'Look man, stop being paranoid. Looking back, I was
so man-mad, I scared them off. Both you and Al were
recluses compared to me! I wondered why until now –
it was only a matter of time till you discovered each
other. You really are soul mates, Blake – trust me on
this, and trust your feelings.' He couldn't help but break out
into a very wide grin of satisfaction, at himself and Leila's wise
words of advice. He reached an arm round her and locked in a
half-hug. 'Thanks Lill – you're the best.' 'No problem. Come on.
We'd better go now.' She linked her arm with his again, and
hauled him from the railing to stroll the main path behind them,
which was about seventy paces to a ninety-degree bend, at which

the social commotion in the diffuse lighting was situated. 'Did you know that's your first philosophy that's ever made sense?' She threw her head back in modesty and humour in reply. He smiled at his own joke and the reaction it provoked.

In a shadowy corner of the café, Katerina was smacking her lips after scoffing the last bit of a slice of cake, while Alana noisily vacuumed the last forkful of spaghetti into her mouth, splattering a few drops of the sauce on her face a bit. 'Uh! God, we're so alike in the way we eat, you know!'

'What, like pigs?' Katerina asked comically, dabbing the corners of her mouth.

'Exactly!' They laughed loudly and broadly grinned. 'Well, the food's great here – I can't believe I've ignored here for all the years I've been here,' Alana concluded. Raising their glasses of red wine, they clinked them together. 'Cheers Al, and have a great birthday tomorrow!' she rejoiced.

'Thank you!' They then simultaneously sipped at the glass, leaving slight coloured lip prints – pale pink from Katerina's mouth, a plum shade from Alana's. 'Anyway, when's your birthday, Kat?'

'Tenth of Feb seventy-seven.'

'Same year as me. So you're only a few weeks into twenty-two, then?'

'Yeah.' Silence as they supped up the remnants of their wine glasses. 'Hey, look, I'm sorry if my breakout downstairs disturbed you. It's just it makes me so angry when I think I could've stopped all this from happening,' she reasoned earnestly. 'It's not your fault.'

'Then why do I feel like it is?'

''Cause you don't know who to blame.'

'I suppose… yeah, exactly – who do I blame? Him for being so stupid and gutless, or that whore for obvious reasons? Or Leila for being such a cruel cow?'

'I don't know, but I do know it isn't your fault. I'm sure they're more sorry than you think.'

'Oh yeah? Then why aren't they here to put that into

words?' Silence. *Because they aren't here yet, Al...* 'Exactly – no answer. The more I try to forget them, the less I'll blame myself, so sod them.' Katerina nodded unable to utter anything. She raised her head to the entrance of the café – and saw two familiar figures, very prominent, although in decreasing dimness – they were Blake and Leila. *Right, time to activate my plan...*

'Look, they're over there!' Leila pointed to a distinctive diamond-bright blonde head and denim jacket right at the rear seating area.

'Oh yeah...holy Jesus, Lill, that *can't* be her...' Leila's mouth broke out into a smile in empathy to his joy.

'It *is* her, my dear Blake!' she replied in a teasing posh accent, slapping his shoulder blade to keep him from zoning out from reality. He felt his knees falter slightly at the sight of Alana in a blue jacket fastened by one button, a black roll-necked top and studied her blue-jean covered legs under the table. His eyes moved up to her brown hair, the same length as he remembered it, but shone as auburn in the light. Then he was whisked back to the time when he dreamt about asking her to marry him on that desert island. 'Blimey – the last time I saw that face, she had tears in her eyes...I don't deserve her, Lill...' he gasped in awe, almost tearful himself. Leila punched his shoulder, almost bruising it. He recoiled from his hallucination in pain.

'Oh come on, don't be stupid! She's there – it's going to hurt, but she can't be in your dreams for the rest of your life when she's right over there.' He sucked in a breath, brushed a tear away with his knuckle, and tugged down his coral silk shirt through his leather coat.

'Yeah, you're right. Let's go.' Blake stomped forward with determination in his steps, with Leila trailing behind him...

'Well, that filled the gap. Another glass of wine, or on to shopping?' Katerina breathed out, leaning against the padded back of the seat, patting her stomach.

'Umm...well, that glass of wine was a pre-birthday treat, but I don't trust myself to have another, even though

you're here, so we'll go shopping!' Katerina snorted out a
controlled laugh, followed by Alana. Katerina then raised her arm
to alert a waiter standing nearby. 'Can I have the cheque please?'

'Certainly, miss.' He urgently dashed over to the counter
opposite the wall of the dark blue hollow the two girls sat in. He
returned with a piece of paper and pen. She signed it and handed
him a ten pound note, which also covered the tip. 'Okay, all paid
for – let's go.' *Oh no, too soon – they're still looking for
us...think, Kat, think quick...* They raised themselves, slightly
restricted by stiffness. Alana slung her handbag on her shoulder.
As Katerina swung her black satchel over her shoulder, its
contents sprinkled onto and around her feet. 'Oh shit, all my
things fell out. Hold on...' she hissed, then crouched down to
pick up bits of paper, make-up items, and so on. Alana's eyes
rolled down curiously. 'You want some help?'

'No, I'm okay. Damn, I hate these zips...' She couldn't help
but chortle at her little mishap. But she composed herself, and
stepped out the cavity between the curved seating area and the
table, intending to wait on the opposing side of the table. It only
took a foot forward to slam her full front painfully into some
guy's solid one. 'Christ, can't you look where you're...' she
ordered, which slurred as the face came into focus. Her eyes
rolled up to meet the guy's blues, and up to his scalp to his mid-
blond hair in messy tufts. 'Oh my God...' she whispered through
a dry throat.

'Oh my God...' he repeated, almost lachrymosely. Both
people felt their eyes gradually slipping out of their sockets as
they studied each other.

'Blake?' she murmured.

'Al?'

'Al?' a girl's familiar voice emerged from the background.
The face of that voice finally showed itself in the form of...

'Leila?' she shrilled. Music, conversation and clinking of
glasses and plates were simply engulfed by each other's sights.

'Hey, I've managed to pick up all the stuff...' Katerina
bolted up from under the table, and slowed her speech on speedily
browsing her eyes over the still, staring figures of Alana, Blake

and Leila through an expectant frown, unsure of and dreading
what reaction was to follow…

Chapter 19.

'Wha…what…what *are* you doing here?' Alana wheezed through a tightened chest, her eyes widened and her pupils dilated to the brink of popping. She felt every sensory organ and limb seize up. 'Al?' Katerina asked in enacted concern.

'What the hell are you doing here? How did you find me?' Alana snapped with a furrowed brow. Now it was Blake's and Leila's turn to widen their eyes.

'I…we came here…to see you…' He just about managed to stutter out.

'Don't give me that bullshit! What did you come here for?'

'Al, don't be mad. We hadn't forgotten about you, you know,' Leila reasoned gently, still rather taken aback by her reaction.

'Well, for a minute, no wait, the past *twenty months*, I thought you did! And you – why aren't you with your bitch?' His surprised eyes lowered remorsefully.

'Please Al, listen – me and Freda…we split up. You were right all along about her. She beat me up, gave me these scratches on my face, so I had to leave,' he sighed in a negative tone.

'Well, don't say I didn't warn you, Blake Turpin! Now, what was it you said? Oh yes! "Surrounded by bigots left, right and centre, how can we make a relationship work?", and "Friendship love only goes a certain limit?" See! I haven't forgotten what you said. But you, being the stupid asshole you decided to be, went against the advice from the person who knew you best for that cow, whom you hardly knew at all!' Blake, Leila nor Katerina were all utterly dumbfounded by the bitterness, and the truth, behind her words.

'Please, Al, I know what I'm about to say is pitiful, but we're here to apologise for the pain we've caused you,' Leila pleaded, her eyes burning with disobedient tears, and a lump rising in her throat.

'No! It's gonna take more than an apology to ever make
up for the pain you caused me! If you ever cared about
me, don't you think you'd have called to see if I was
alive or dead? Or was this just a spur of the moment
thing? Do you know how much you are full of shit?'

'But Al...' Blake begged in a strained whisper, with a tear
leaking from each eye subsequently.

'No buts! Both of you are selfish fuckers! You blanked
me out when I needed you most, and when I tried to
warn you about that fucking bitch,' then she sided her eye
to Leila, still standing behind Blake. 'And you, instead of helping
me get over my drinking, you walked out on me and left me to do
it myself! And I had my mother to deal with, but instead of
sleeping over at your place or Blake's, like I normally would
during an argument, I had to stay in a shitty hotel and then a bed
sit that wasn't any better. I thought you understood me, out of all
the people in the world, after ten years, but I couldn't have been
more wrong, could I?!' she literally screamed, turning one or two
heads in the restaurant to that corner they stood.

'I don't know what to say to you. You have every right
to be angry. Even my family don't want to talk to me
anymore because of Freda. It was the biggest mistake
of my life. I hate myself so much for doing that to you –
probably more that you hate me, and so does Leila,' he
reasoned sombrely. With those words, Leila collapsed her head
into her palms, and broke into a full sob. He half-spun around in
response, and took her in an arm round her.

'Oh don't you start! Your tears are nothing compared to
the ones I've shed over you! And don't you flatter
yourself, Turpin! You're the reason for all my pain,
depression and drink! I've only just got my life together,
while you still left me in the lurch! What did you expect,
huh? For me to leap into your arms, make up and pretend
everything's going to be alright?' she yelled throatily,
waving hand gestures violently.

'No, but...' Blake tried to cut in with a whine.

'Both of you stay away from me! I've yet to prove that

I can make it on my own! Anyway, how did you know
I was here today?' Silence, as all held their heads down,
including Katerina. Alana span her head, examining each and
every face surrounding her. There was one face that was only too
evident with guilt though, which looked more so than Blake and
Leila. 'Kat, you didn't, *did you?*' Katerina shot her head up to her
hardened gaze, then lowered it again in repent.

'Kat, how could you? *How could you?!* How did you
get them here?' Alana insisted irately, gripping her
shoulders and shaking her up.

'I…asked Mr Sutton for their parents' phone numbers,
I called them, and they gave me Leila's and Blake's
numbers, I called them, and talked them into coming
here. They've been here since Saturday.' She gawked at
Katerina's unsteady eye contact to Alana. Then she suddenly felt
a relentless swipe of fingers against her pale skin, causing blood
to instantly rise to and sting the surface. Placing a comforting
palm over the emerging marks, Blake and Leila just stood
motionlessly, while mouths dropped open.

'You…so that's it! That's why you kept sneaking out,
and was using the course as an excuse! God, what a
bloody mug I've been! I should've known you were
up to something! Kat, I've told you what I thought
about those two, and yet you still had the craftiness and
the brass neck to bring us together today. Shit, you are
more stupid than I thought! Well, guess what? You are
not coming back with me to the bed sit today – you are
staying somewhere else! I don't care where, just as long
as you all get your sorry asses out of my sight! All of
you, you make me sick!' Alana hissed loudly and
mercilessly. She snatched her bag off the table, and shoved past
and interlinked Leila and Blake. Halfway to the dimly-lit exit, she
turned round for a last look at them, completely immobilized by
shock. Nearly everyone in the café halted their conversations and
from eating. Alana pointed a finger collectively at them.

'You know something, I've always thought the older
you get, the less something you say or do when you

233

were younger makes sense – and that applies to both
of you. Have a nice life.' Leila bawled into Blake's
shoulder so hard, she felt a throbbing inside her eardrums. 'It's
okay, Leila, it's okay,' he softly comforted, feeling every illusion
he had of her shatter. *It's like I told you, I don't deserve her…*

'We need to go after her,' Katerina puffed, still stroking her
cheek with her palm.

'Did she…hit you hard, Kat?' Leila attempted to utter
through her hyper-breathing and blubbers.

'No, it's okay. I deserved it.'

'Why? You tried your best. Anyway, let's follow her,'
Blake said sorrowfully, only just releasing Leila from his
embrace.

'Okay. Let's go. I already paid the bill.'

'Okay. Leila, are you ready to go?' he whispered
sympathetically. Leila sniffled, then nodded her head. With his
arm still round her shoulders, they ignored the imposing glares
from the staff and customers and dignifiedly perambulated out the
exit.

At the bed sit, Alana carelessly slammed the door and
slumped her back across the bed, now loosely stretched out. She
then slapped her fingertips across her eyes, aiding herself to blink
back tears. *God, why the hell did she do that for, when she knew I
never wanted to see them again?* Wounds she'd thought had
disappeared by giving up the booze and her crush on Adrian
McCraedie had been torn open once again. She felt somewhat
guilty for not letting them explain after telling Katerina that she
didn't hate them, but after being proven right in the long run, she
also felt that a what-for was long overdue. She was disturbed by
desperate pounding from outside. 'Al, come on, open the door – I
need to talk to you,' a muffled male voice yelled. *Oh fuck – don't
tell me he followed me back here…* 'Look, Blake, just go the hell
away!'

'No! Keep telling me to go, but I'm still not leaving, so
open the damn door!' *Oh, I give up…* Alana hurled herself
upright onto her feet, and twisted the doorknob aggressively.
Blake stood seriously, his hands in his coat pockets. His stance

reminded her of when he was about to tell her he was going away, making her wish even more he'd fade away from her sight. He retracted a little on seeing her blood-deprived face, which looked as if she'd been crying. 'Right, what the fuck do you want?' she screamed, squinting her eyes.

'We need to talk, and there's no need to be so coarse.' She turned her back against the door, leaving him to close it himself, and plonked herself on the edge of the bed and crossed her legs in a funk. 'Why not? You piss me off so much, I can't think of any other approach.' He wandered his head around after hearing that, taking in the still filthy surroundings. 'I can't believe you've been living here for the past two years. Look at this place.'

'Well, it was a roof over my head while the pair of you walked out on me, and it's cheap. Plus, where did you expect me to stay?'

'I don't know. Listen to me, please. Can I sit next to you?' she shrugged apathetically.

'Well, there's no where else to sit, is there?' He removed his hands from his pockets, and sat a reasonable distance away from her, not wanting to cause anymore trouble, even though it wasn't where he wanted to sit.

'Look, I admit I have been an asshole…'

'Oh, hallelujah!' she squealed, throwing her hands up.

'Are you listening or what?' he said impatiently.

'Yeah, sorry.'

'Okay, I admit I've been an asshole, and that I should've listened to you when you said Freda was trouble, I mean, God knows, my face and mind will be scarred to remind me not to make such a mistake again, but there's no need to hate me…' He pleaded, stroking the scabby skin his healing scratches left.

'I don't hate you, Blake – I pity your stubbornness, your gullibility, and your stupidity, but I'll *never* hate you. I'm angry, 'cause I don't hate you – I told Katerina that. But if we do become friends again, I'm afraid that I'll have to torture you for the rest of your life!' He sniggered under his breath.

'Good, cause I think I deserve it.'

'Well, bully for you!' she exclaimed cheerily. Both of them then laughed briefly. Then an uneasy, but short, silence followed as they broke eye contact and fiddled their fingers.

'So, uh…where are you staying?' Alana stumbled out.

'You know that little bed and breakfast up the road?'

'Yeah.'

'Well that's where Leila's staying. Kat said she'll get a room there till you cool down.'

'Oh. Good. Um…I…do you mind me asking about what happened between you and Freda?' she stammered, knowing what a delicate subject she was bringing up.

'No, I guess not. Last week, Thursday it was actually, I received a phone call from Kat, saying she knew you, and that you needed me there, but I didn't pay much attention to it till she told me you were in hospital. I tried telling her that I wanted to go and see you, but she wouldn't let me. Then later that day, when she wanted to go out but I didn't, because I was too upset to do so, she called me a lazy ass, I protested, then she knocked me onto the bed, then beat me and beat me and beat me, dug her nails into my cheek, hence these marks, then she…tied my wrists to the bed…and…' Blake's voice cracked as he was to approach the worst point, just when he thought he could sail through it.

'What? What did she do?' Alana asked frantically.

'…she…raped…raped me, Al.' He had to wipe a falling tear. 'So go on, poke fun at me, ask why couldn't I fight a woman, but I'm still haunted by it, and I don't know when I'll ever get over it. But I…felt I had to tell you, so you had a better outlook on why I'm here, trying to patch things up with you. It wasn't just some trivial tiff – it was serious. It wasn't the first time she'd beat me though. She slapped me a couple times, especially when the chores weren't done, and sometimes for no reason at all, but she'd never done anything that brutal to me before, ever.' He inhaled deeply, regaining some of his composure.

'And you fell for that? Jesus, Blake – I thought that at
nearly twenty-three years old, you'd have more sense
than that. Well, you've learnt your lesson.' His mouth
dropped open at her response, which wasn't one he was quite
expecting.

'Well, I'm actually amazed by your reaction to what the
hell I've been to and back – so cold, unsympathetic and
emotionless,' he said cynically.

'What the frig did you expect, huh? "Oh, I'm so sorry
to hear that?" If neither Leila or me suspected her from
the very beginning, then my reaction would be very
different. But we warned you, for Christ's sake! We
warned you over and over and *over*, ever since she made
you cry that day! And yet you still let her ruin not just
your life, but my life too! What does that say about you,
huh? That you're nothing but a weak, namby-pamby,
foolhardy wimp who couldn't get out while you had the
chance!'

'Thanks a lot! You know, you should be showing a
friend's sympathy to my problems, like we used to do.
But I should've known you wouldn't understand, that
you'd milk it for all it's worth, knowing I'm in repent
for my mistake.'

'You know what your problem is? You're still living in
the past, refusing to accept that we're grown up now –
that's a direct quote, in case you didn't remember! Well,
I'm not talking to you again till you grow up,' she replied
in toxic tone of irony. He sighed as he gritted his teeth in
annoyance.

'Right, that's it! If you're going to throw my quotes back
at me, then I'm going!' he snarled, leaping to his feet
instantaneously and stomping to the doorway.

'What? Can't handle the truth now?!' Before she heard or
saw any feedback, he slammed the door with a rifle-like bang.
You son-of-a-bitch... She collapsed her head into the pillows, and
lulled herself to sleep by her muffled cries and a blistering pain

inside her stomach, still half seated and half lying down with her arms round her pillow.

Chapter 20.

Blake pounded his fists lazily, but forcefully against a door almost immediately after his return to the hotel. He got a curious gawk from the owner as he ran up the stairs clumsily, like he was being chased by a wild animal. 'Come on, Lill, open the door now,' he pleaded breathlessly. After about a series of five clustered knocks, it opened to reveal Leila wearing a grey baggy t-shirt and faded blue jeans. Her face still looked tear-strewn from earlier. 'What is it, Blake? What happened?' she asked, concerned by his anxiety.

'Oh God, I've fucked up more than I originally thought, Lill, and it would've been worse if Kat came with me,' he groaned hopelessly.

'What d'you mean?'

'One minute we were on the route to making up, then the next we were arguing about Freda when I told her what she did to me,' he squeezed out in one unstable, lachrymose breath. Leila, with fresh tears welling out of her eyes, stretched an arm out to him, which he accepted to envelope him in a short hug. Cupping his jaw in her palms, she stared up her bloodshot eyes at his equally bloodshot ones. 'Okay, calm down – we've only just started, so come in, and tell me about it.'

'Nah – I appreciate it, but I'd rather go for a walk, and maybe have a drink at the pub in Shepherd's Bush.'

'Okay – don't get too pissed, though!'

'I'll try – I think Kat is down there, so I'll meet up with her.'

'Yeah, she asked me to join her, but I said I'd rather rest here with Tre.' She pointed a finger towards the bed, illustrating a flat-out asleep Tre, with a couple of hair locks over his forehead, and his head flopped to one side. Blake snorted in humour at his appearance. 'Shit, is he alive or what?' he jested through a niggling in his throat. Leila reflected his snort, smiling a little.

'Sure he is – he just isn't now! See you later.'

'See ya.' She shut the door gently as he turned his back to it. Blake whizzed back down the stairs, whoever that was downstairs missing him and vice versa, and before he knew it, he was on the virtually desolate pavement, a few paces from the bus stop. He looked at his watch – it was a little past four.

'Same again, please,' Blake ordered in an increasing drunkard's slurry voice. The landlady, whom he remembered being there the last time he was in that pub, rayed a frowned look of concern at the way he was halfway draped across the counter, and collected his whisky glass. 'Are you sure, boy?'

'Yeah. Fill 'em up,' he drunkenly drawled. His eyelids fought to keep open, but suddenly got a jump start when a finger tapped him on his shoulder. He whipped round in alarm. 'You? Kat? Only now you've arr-arrived?' He asked, tripping over his words unintentionally between breaths. 'Yeah, only now – are you drunk?' she reasoned despondently, pausing for a split second on inhaling the powerful stench of whisky reeking off his clothes and his breath as he spoke.

'What makes you say that, huh?' he drawled almost incoherently.

'Huh! Just as much – do you always slouch over the counter when you drink in a pub?' He laughs almost hysterically, raising a few heads around the bar.

'Come on, this is not funny, Blake – give in! Getting sloshed isn't going to solve anything,' she pleaded, attempting to haul him from the counter, but he was stuck like a piece of chewing gum on the pavement.

'Let go!' he growled, attempting to free himself from her.

'No! Come back with me, Blake.' He weakened his grip, and sighed. Then she observed a teardrop or two splashing on the glossy, mahogany-coloured marble surface on deciding to loosen her force. 'Hey, hey, what's wrong?'

'Al was more out of reach than I could have possibly imagined – and it's all my fucking fault. I wish there wasn't a law against killing, then I would…really do horrible, horrible things to that Freda! I would, I swear…

by this glass of whisky, I'd kill her!' he yelled to the point
of almost roaring the building down. Katerina, now very
disturbed by his behaviour, entwined her arms round his
shoulders through his armpits, and tugged him away with all his
might. 'Come on! Let's get out of here!'

'Hey! He hasn't paid for that drink yet!' The landlady
resonated, looking somewhat bemused by the state of him.

'S'okay, I'll pay – how much was it?'

'Two-eighty.' Katerina delved her hand into the breast
pocket of her denim jacket, and popped out the exact change.

'How many has he had?'

'About six.' her eyes burgeoned in disbelief.

'Jesus! Okay, Blake, time to go home,' she firmly ordered,
and slung a weighty arm round her shoulder, and guiding him out
the door to the dimly-lit pavement. His resistance stopped them
just outside the graffitied shutter of a shop.

'Oh please, no! Don't send me back to Freda...' he begged
croakily.

'No, I mean, to the hotel...'

'No, not there, Kat! I want to see Al again.' She unloaded
his arm off her; to her surprise, he stood up straight, if a little
wobbly. She then looked an obdurate stare at his droopy eyes.
'Are you sure?'

'Yeah. Please...take me there...' he sluggishly said between
short breaths.

'Okay. I don't trust you to go there on your own, so I'll take
you there, okay? Then I'll go back to the hotel.' He
shrugged his shoulders in unprompted acceptance.

'Yeah.' He protruded an elbow for her to link her arm with,
and they strolled at a pace that wasn't too demanding on Blake's
inebriated legs.

'You can take...my room. I'll...I'll give you the key...'

'Okay – thanks, Blake.' For half an hour, they said nothing,
and Katerina kept a very vigilant eye on his stability betwixt the
seemingly awkwardly-walking pedestrians along Uxbridge Road,
almost all speeding in the opposite direction, blinded by the night,

despite the street lamps. Before she knew it, they were facing the
doorway of the bed sit building.

'Here we are, Blake. Good luck with Al.'

'Thank…you. Oh, before I forget…' he reached a jerky
hand in the waist pocket of his coat till he heard a jingling sound.
'Here's the key to my room. Tell the owner I said you could have
that room.'

'Thanks. And here's the key to my bed sit. You know
which room it is?'

'Yeah. Went up there today.'

'Brilliant. Goodnight, Blake, and take care up the stairs.'

'I will. Goodnight, Kat,' he murmured. With that, she
proceeded her short journey to the suburban crack of the main
road – the bus stop, occasionally turning back to see if Blake got
in without falling flat on his face.

'Al?' he whispered in vain; despite his limbs still twitching
madly, he still made it up the two steep flights of brown-carpeted
stairs to her door. Searching for the correct key between two keys
seemed like searching amongst a thousand keys, especially as he
couldn't remember which key he found by trial and error to open
the front door. Finally finding it and slotting and twisting it
through the doorknob, he shoved the door open. He was still
drunk, but he sobered up in a flash at the sight before him – Alana
Higgins, wearing a stained grey t-shirt and crossed legs on the
edge of the bed coated in a black fabric trousers, her head tilted
back as she downed an entire bottle of…alcohol. 'Al?' His mere
whisper caused her to splutter the contents of her mouth all over
her chin, knees and carpet. 'Oh it's you…what the fuck are you
doing here? How did you get in?' she hissed in a similar drunk
tone as Blake. 'Kat gave me…the key here – told her I…need to
talk to you…is that vodka?'

'What's it to you, huh? When is that Kat going to stop
ruling my life? And when the hell are you going to get
out of mine?' she growled in increasing gradients. Startled
not by her words, but by the fact she was also drunk, he felt brave
enough to stumble his way to sit beside her. She just inched away
towards the pillows.

'Look, I didn't come her to fight with you – I came here
to make up.'
'I don't even know why I bother with people like you –
if everyone did things only when they felt like it, the
world would be in a right state, just like our relationship.'
He sighed again, feeling brief pessimism. He gawped at her
swigging from the vodka bottle again. Then he imagined her
lying in hospital, unconscious with tubes branching out form her.
'Stop it, Al! Why the hell are you drinking, huh? To dream of
Adrian McCraedie again?' he growled as he attempted to wrench
the bottle from her hands. She spitefully glared back at him, but
he kept wrestling, refusing to be scared by her anymore. 'How the
fuck did you know?' she roared through her teeth.
'Does it bloody well matter? Every time there's a crisis,
you turn to the damned bottle and Adrian!'
'Well, who or what else is there to turn to, huh?'
'Nothing if you carry on killing yourself like this!'
'And besides, you can talk, I must say! You're just as
sozzled as me, and you're calling me a drunk!'
'Give me the bottle!'
'No!' They grunted in frustration as neither usurped the
bottle. They tugged and tugged, till one of them lost grip, and its
contents pooled in the carpet fibres. Both stared at the floor for a
few seconds, then at each other. Alana's face dropped into her
palms, and made barely audible hiccupped sobs, except to Blake,
still comprehensive to a face and sound of sorrow he knew he
caused, despite being far off sober. He tried encasing her
shoulders, but she just shoved him away, and almost off the bed.
'Don't touch me!'
'Why? You'll always be unhappy if you keep drowning
yourself in drink to dream of Adrian-fucking-McCraedie!'
he snapped, retracting back upwards.
'It's all you fault! *All* your fault! You're the reason I'm
like this! You're the reason why I can't move on! Adrian's
a damn sight more reliable than your sorry ass!'
'But he's not real! What use is reliable if he's not real?'
'Oh, just fuck off and leave me the hell alone!'

'No! Can't you see you're killing yourself here?'
'Can't you see you're wasting your time? For nearly
two years, you never cared whether I lived or died,
and now you say you care?'
'I've always cared...'
'Oh bullshit! I warned you about that bitch, and all you
gave me was grief in return, which is still embedded in
me to this day! That shows how much you care about
me! So don't tell me it was a lapse in judgement, 'cause
you knew what you were getting into!' despite her searing
words, he still lovingly looked at her, even if she didn't return the
sentiment, feeling regret and internalised anger at himself.
'True. I made a horrible mistake. My punishment was
losing you. It stung the most obscure part of me, more
so when I heard you were in hospital. If Kat hadn't
caught you in time, you could've been out of my reach
forever. You think I'd be here if I didn't care?' He
discontinued his pleas as her cries stopped dead, and she raised
her bloodshot, drooping eyes to him, startling him with the
extreme colour contrasts of greens, whites and reds. 'I suppose...'
she whispered, gazing at him from the floor for a split second. He
chuckled slightly.
'Of course, you silly girl! Look,' she laughed briefly and
lowly, but made Blake feel bolder to approach her. He cupped her
jaw in his palms, and ran his thumbs along its outline. Alana
knew she couldn't get any drunker with the vodka spilt on the
floor, but she still felt forced to surrender her verbal shield to him.
'You nearly died, Al. I don't want you to kill yourself on that
stuff again,' he strained through a rising lump in his throat, his
fixed connection with her eyes falling softer the surer he felt
about her.
'Why do you care?'
'Because I'll never leave you again.' Then everything
blacked out...

Katerina snuck up the stairs, knowing it was nearly ten o'
clock at night. She then turned to the short corridor leading to

Blake's hotel room door. 'Hey, where the hell do you think you're going?' She whipped round at the thunder in her voice. 'Leila!'

'Kat! Sorry, I thought you were someone else. Why are you going to his room? And where the hell is Blake?'

'Well, Blake is at the bed sit, talking to Al – I'm not sure if he's having any success, or just too drunk to call my mobile!'

'What?!' she shrieked.

'Yeah, but I lead him to the bed sit, and took the bus back here. He's fine – made a slight fool of himself in the pub, but he's fine.'

'Shit, I told him not to get pissed! Well, that's the stubborn asshole he can be, as you probably know by now.' She disguised a snigger in vain.

'Sure I do. Anyway, he's staying there for the night in my bed, and he said I could stay in his room.'

'So, when are you going back?'

'I don't really know, Leila. Have you got her anything?'

'Not really. I still haven't thought of anything.'

'Never mind. So, where's Tre?'

'Still asleep – this city has tuckered him out! He's been asleep since about three this afternoon. Must have gotten fed up waiting for me.'

'Oh. Well, it's been a hell of a day, so I'm going to bed. Goodnight Leila.' Both of them glanced over their shoulders at each other as they entered their doors.

'Goodnight, Kat. And despite what happened today, thanks for everything you've done – on my and Blake's behalf, we appreciate it.' Katerina smiled and nodded, and entered the room. *I know she thanked me, but why do I feel guilty when I should be feeling good about myself?*

Good God – my head! she groaned in her mind as she torpidly raised herself upright from her bed, and began circling her fingertips firmly on her temples. *Sheesh – what a weird dream*... She began recollecting and piecing together her fragmented memory through her throbbing pain...

'Because I'll never leave you again.' Al felt her face encased in Blake's hands, being tugged gently towards him. 'Blake...' Before she could complete her sentence, she felt her lips being pressed against his, then massaged softly by them, no longer feeling angry or bitter at him, but just savouring the lovely sensation as much as he was. The last things she felt was a sharp pain in her loins, then shuddering bolt of pleasure through her body with Blake's face in focus as she lied on her back, then all light around her shut off, including Blake.

No, I couldn't have... she wondered, now feeling slightly, but strangely perturbed by her memory, because that's exactly how it seemed – a memory, not an illusion. She rolled to the edge of the bed, intending to boil the kettle, and felt a chill hit her entire body as she stood. She peered down, and gasped aloud, her eyes widened – she was totally nude. She sat back down, flinging a corner of the duvet around her chest, also covering half her thighs. *What the fuck is going on? I don't usually sleep na-*... Without meaning to, she cautiously looked behind her, and felt her heart and jaw drop as they solidified to stone. There was Blake, his head tilted to an arm behind it, his chin a little dark from stubble. *No...please God, tell me this didn't happen...no, no, no, no*... 'Noooooooooo!' she screamed, unable to contain the alarm in her thoughts. Blake shot up, blinking in disorientation, then shooting an equally disorientated stare at her. 'What the...what's going on?!' he wheezed out.

'Why don't you look down the duvet, huh?! That should tell you!' she screamed, her limbs trembling. 'Huh?!' He exclaimed then obliged, and bobbed his equally aching head back up with a glare and dropped jaw of panic. The throbs against his skull worsened on seeing himself naked too. 'Oh my...'

'Yeah! "Oh my..." That's all you can say, huh? You stupid, frigging bastard!'

'Don't yell at me, Al!'

'Why not? Look at the state we're both in, for Christ's sake!'

'Calm down, Al, calm down...'
'Don't tell me to calm down, you son-of-a-bitch! We
slept together, that's something to be real calm about,
isn't it?! Fine way of not leaving me!'
'Look, I didn't know, I don't...oh shit – I don't know...'
'Neither do I, so maybe you could shed some light here!'
'Okay, let's get dressed first, and we'll try and piece
together what happened.'

'Damned right we will!' Blake attempted to raise himself to
his feet and reach his clothes on the floor without his corner of
the duvet dropping off him, but was unsuccessful in preventing a
full view of his backside to Alana. She shot her eyes down to
cover her blushing reaction as she sat observing. 'Why are you
covering up for? There's nothing I haven't seen now!'

'Oh don't you start!'
'Start? *Start?* You know what I'd like to start? Beating
your ass up, that's what!' She yelled animally, scaring
herself for a second.' He fastened the last button of his shirt, and
marched round the bed to sit next to Alana, who was also now
fully dressed. She shifted away a little, still feeling uncomfortable
about sitting next to him.

'Look, I really don't know what's happening here, or
what the hell I was thinking last night, but...'
'Huh! Call the papers! Mister Morality here got drunk
last night, and had a one night stand with a girl who
used to be his friend! We had sex last night, for Christ's
sake! How difficult is that to understand?!'
'Shut up, Al! If you've got something personal against me,
just say it!'
'Oh nothing, except your hypocrisy and stupidity, of
course!'
'Thanks for the compliment! Look Al, can we just talk in
a calm, rational manner for a change, instead of screaming
like animals?'

'Gladly! Since *you* started it, *you* begin first!' she ordered
venomously; that tone caused his hairs to stand on end and a chill
spearing down his back.

'Alright, here goes…I know last night shouldn't have happened…'

'Damn right it shouldn't!'

'Damn it, Al! Stop interrupting!' She raised her brow silently, gesturing her answer.

'Thank you! I know it shouldn't have happened. I feel rotten for letting that happen and all I can say is…I'm sorry, and is there any way of forgetting it?'

'Unbelievable!'

'What? Here I am offering a truce, and you're evading me!'

'Of course I am! I can't even look at you in the face anymore! And after the way you treated me…how the hell can we ever call a truce? There's only one of two things we can do now,' she said solemnly, staring down at the floor, wanting to forget he was sitting there. 'What?'

'One – become a couple, which is highly unlikely, considering the way things are going, or two – get out of each other's lives.' Blake felt a tear or two sting his eyes, seeping into the healing crack of his wound, feeling it blister open again – mirroring the tears of his wounded heart. *Please God, no, Al, don't do this…* her words brought an ache to the rising lump in his throat. 'Don't do this, Al.'

'Blake, there's no other way. You've hurt my feelings very much, in fact, way too much for anything to be left of this relationship. And sleeping with me, even if it was just an accident, doesn't make everything alright – in fact, it doesn't make any difference at all,' she reasoned equally shakily, squinting her flooding eyes.

'But…there must be a way, somehow, to get it back the way it used to be…' he croaked unsteadily, his composure losing ground fast as the saltwater became too much for his eyes to contain.

'No – it's over, Blake. There's nothing left now.'

'God Al, why are you doing this?! Look how long we've been together, all we've been through, and you're throwing it away? For what? I can't live without

you, Al. I lost so much just to realise that, and now that
I have, you don't want me anymore?' he bawled, feeling
bitter and as hurt as he could imagine her feeling.

'It hurts too much to even look at you, 'cause every
time I do, everything you said comes flooding back.
I'm sorry, Blake…'

'Yeah, I'm sure you are. Look, it's obvious you don't
want me here anymore, so I'll leave. I'll be at the hotel
if you… need me. See you,' he managed to say, his voice
thickened by choked-back tears as he grabbed his coat from the
peg next to the door, and slammed the door violently, unable to
turn back. He respired a breath through his narrowed throat, and
brushed aside a teardrop. Every dream he had of her, and for the
two of them, seemed so barren now. He sniffed, then removed
something from his coat pocket – it was a tiny box with her
engagement ring that he'd bought the day before – a tiny box, but
contained every happiness on earth made just for him. A tear
splashed onto the gold band, another on the square-cut blue topaz
stone, and another on the alternating garnet stone before he shut it
and replaced it in his pocket. *I love you, Al… I still love you…
how am I going to get you to see that?*

Chapter 21.

Alana tapped the pad of the side of her chilly hand against an unfamiliar grey front door, but with familiar net curtains on either side of it. *Is this a good idea? Well, too late for that – I've already knocked...* she wondered, every limb trembling nervously. She decided to switch from the path she planned on strolling to this suburban road alongside the University. She couldn't bear being cooped up anymore, but she wasn't hoping for anyone to see or be of any relief to the bleeding self-inflicted wounds to her heart. So here she was, up three flat steps, standing under a small porch, protected from further inconsistent drizzle damping her hair and clothes. Finally, she heard the door unlatch. Both women's faces contorted in shock as they studied each other. 'Oh my God...'

'Oh my God!'

'Al?'

'Mum?' Their eyes flared in amazement for several seconds, neither knowing how to continue this re-introduction to each other after nearly two years.

'Uh, um, oh blimey...you've knocked me off track, sorry.' Both breathed out a brief giggle.

'Look, Mum...is Navin in?' Alana asked seriously.

'No, he's...gone to work. I'm off today. God – only just now I was thinking about your birthday today.' Alana lowered eyes to the concrete for a split second.

'Well, can I come in?'

'Of course, of course! Sorry love – you've completely... I can't believe you're here, that's all.' Tracie extended her hand to a path guiding her inside the house. It looked exactly how she remembered it – the furnishings, especially that orange sofa, the colour, everything right down to the last detail. *Here goes...*

'Mum, you're the last person I can turn to right now. Can we talk?'

'Sure – what happened?' Tracie asked in a serious tone, a switch from the airiness beginning the sentence.

'Lord, what a long story,' she sighed drearily as Tracie shut the door behind the two of them. For an hour or so, Tracie listened unwaveringly as Alana described her situation from their argument to meeting Katerina to now, crumb by crumb of her memory fuzzy from grief, but was comforted by the warm welcome the house emitted. Both of them blinked back their tears. '…So, I told him to get out my life, because I thought at the time that his shadow was making me unhappy while he was gone. I felt somewhat bad for making him cry like that, but another, more vengeful part of me felt he deserved it. But now, now I'm not so sure what's making me unhappy – Leila, Blake, myself – I just don't know…'

'For God's sakes, why the hell didn't you contact me earlier instead of letting things come to this? And what's with the drink, huh? You could've killed yourself without me ever knowing!'

'Well I didn't, did I? And besides, I wasn't sure if I wanted to see you again after what happened.'

'You were in hospital, for Christ's sake! Didn't they ask to speak to a parent?'

'Probably…oh, I don't know. Maybe Kat told them not to bother, because like I said, I told her about my story.'

'How many times have I told you that drink doesn't solve anything? I've seen women with cases about their partners being roaring drunk…'

'Look Mum, I came here because you're the last person who I thought will listen to me. But I guess nothing's changed, has it? If you're going to offer nothing but lectures, I'll leave now!' She prepared to storm out. But Tracie clasped her wrist, and bade her to sit back down next to her, which she obeyed with a scowl. 'Look Al, I'm sorry, okay? I didn't mean to be so insensitive. I freaked because, well… I was worried about you, and not knowing where you were drove me crazy. Come on, let's work this out, somehow,' she croakily begged, still tugging on her t-shirt sleeve. Alana nodded.

'Alright. You have one more chance – don't screw it up.'

'I won't. Look, I may have been a horrible parent when

it came to your most difficult times, but I've spent the
past year and a half rehearsing how to be there for you
if you ever came back. Now you're here, it's coming
out all wrong.'

'You can say that again!' she breathed out. They sniggered
slightly away from their eye contact. 'Okay, you're right – I'm
guilty of negligence, and I want to rectify my mistake.'

'That's nice to know! Go ahead – I'm listening,' Alana
retorted scornfully.

'So, what're you going to do about Blake and Leila now?'
her prelude was a pathetic breath.

'I don't know. Last night just seems so unreal…'

'That's what happens when you drink too much…'

'Hey, don't just blame me – he was drunk, too!' She
shrugged off her interruption, and pricked up her ears once again.

'Alright, alright, sorry. Carry on.'

'Thank you. I… don't know at all, Mum. When you
share something like that with someone who's like a
brother to you, it changes everything, for better or for
worse. Right now, I think it's changed our friendship
for the worse, because I can't look at him in the face
anymore. I've been keeping my virginity for the right
guy, and what happens? I lose it to my best friend –
right before my birthday!'

'Well, just to make sure, you'd better have yourself
checked out…' she trailed off, making incoherent hand
gestures over her stomach area. Alana raised her brow in
realisation.

'Oh, I see…in case I'm… you know…' she began
mimicking her hand gestures.

'Yeah.'

'Okay, I will.'

'You said he cried, right? Well, I'm sure it's because he
needs you after the way he was treated by Freda, and
you blew him out, and he thinks he's lost you forever.
He's definitely sorry.'

'He did. He *is* remorseful for what he did, but that

don't help nothing – he still hurt me by upping sticks
with that cow. And anyway, who are you to talk about
me being there for him, when you weren't there yourself
for me?'
'Al, let's stick to the point for now, please. I'm judging
your situation in terms of a solicitor and a mother to see
if it's worth resolving, okay?'
'Sorry.'
'Well, he's not the one making you unhappy, I can tell
you that. You're just discontented with your life, because
you feel betrayed. It doesn't seem like you hate him at all.'
'Right now, I neither love him nor hate him. But I still have
respect for him, even though he didn't exactly return that
respect. It's about as unrequited as if I had a crush on him.'
Oh shit, what did I just say? she shuddered at what was currently
a contemptible thought.
'You feel hate because you love him. You wouldn't hate
him if you didn't care, would you?'
'I suppose…'
'Yes, it is. But tell me something – do you love him more
than just a friend after what happened? Have your feelings
changed for him?' A dumbstruck Alana stared into space
for a few seconds. 'Um…oh gosh, what a question… I never…
why do you always ask the hard questions?' she stuttered with a
deadpan expression. Tracie half-smiled with a softened look.
'Because I'd answer them if I knew the easy answer.
More tea?'
'Um, sure, okay.' Tracie raised herself from the sofa with
the two teacups encased by a forefinger, and the teapot with the
other hand. *Cor, what a question…*she thought as she flashbacked
to when they first met in that secondary school canteen all those
years ago, rewinding and replaying that scene when she and Leila
were talking, and when he felt bold enough to join them. The first
look when he sat at their table and started talking to them. *Why
did he sit there, when there were a whole heap of other tables to
sit at? Was it because he liked the look of one of us? Me maybe?
But then he said when he got drunk and snogged me that New*

Year, that we would've been a couple a long time ago if he felt anything. Maybe he was lying? Maybe worried that I wouldn't like him anymore if he said anything...I've always felt closer to him than to Leila – I always thought it was because he was the brother I never had, as much as Leila was the sister I never had. If he didn't care, he wouldn't have come back; he would've stayed and suffered with Freda. Everything's a haze from last night, but...there was a tone in his voice I'd never heard before when he said, "I'll never leave you again, Al." And how come I never got over him leaving as easily as Leila? Because my whole life revolved around him – despite being an asshole towards the end, no guy has been that wonderful to me, and I don't think there'll be anyone quite like him. But...I don't know. He hurt me so much, my judgment about him is seriously warped... he sided with her when she was unnecessarily bitchy towards us...

'Well, what's your answer?' she suddenly heard shrill through her ears, booting her out of her thoughts. She lowered her head in confusion.

'I don't know, Mum. Everything in my head is such a mess – and no, it's not because I'm hung-over.' They chuckled again, as they simultaneously sipped from their refilled cups.

'You'll find out in time, dear. Try to forget about it for now, as I can imagine how much grief you're going through.'

'Okay.'

'Al, you were right about me being only a part-time mother, and God knows I feel rotten for that. I've always taught you to be ambitious, but what I forgot to teach was that if ambition meant butting your loved ones aside for money or whatever, it's not worth pursuing at all. I didn't teach that, because I hadn't experienced that. I've achieved my goal, so it's too late to undo it, but it didn't bring you back, did it? I was worried out of my mind about you out there – you're my only child. If anything happened to you, I'd go barmy. I still have a maternal instinct – it's just my selfishness suppressed it.'

'Well, you were wrong to hide Navin from me. And do
you know what it was like to see you slam the door at
the crack of dawn every day, and not return till God
knows when?'

'True, and I'm sorry. Look I'll make a pledge. I promise
…not to…be selfish…or keep secrets…from you…again!'
Her deliberately slurred promise elicited the first belly laugh from
Alana after goodness knew how long ago.

'Great! I'll make one too – I promise…not to…walk
out…when things…get rough…or be a slacker…or
get drunk…again!' Tracie cackled almost sinisterly.

'Thank you! Aw, come here.' Tracie sat her cup down on
the tea table, and reached for Alana in a warm, prolonged hug,
both of them shedding a tear or two on each other's shoulders. 'I
love you, sweetie!'

'I love you too, Mum.' They released and looked lovingly
into each other's eyes with a smile of contentment. 'Happy
birthday, baby!' Tracie squealed quietly, brushing away a tear
with a thumb. 'Thanks. I honestly thought you'd react in a nastier
way than you did.'

'No point in that, is there. What's done is done – can't
change that. That applies to your incident with Blake,
too. Look, Navin is going to be at work for a few more
hours – it's eleven now, so how about we went shopping?'
Alana supped up the last bit of tea.

'Okay. Can I clean myself up here, then go back to the
bedsit and get some clothes? That bedsit bathroom is
like shit!' They laughed slightly.

'Course you can. I'll tell him what happened and where
we're going. And Al, don't worry about your exam result –
I can help pay for you to retake the course, and I can help
you find a decent place to live, okay? I realise you only
chose the bedsit because it was cheap accommodation.'
Alana smiled in pleasant surprise on the way to the bathroom.

'That's true. Thanks a lot, Mum.'

'No problem.' Tracie was startled by the bell of the phone.

'It's okay – I'll get it.' She stretched an arm to the small antique-mahogany stand near the hallway for the receiver. 'Hello?'

By midday, Tracie had changed into a pink floral skirt and a black skinny t-shirt which clung around her fairly bony torso, and had let down her curly blonde bob from the pleat she normally wore it in at home. She smiled at her reflection in the bathroom mirror, still feeling somewhat floating on air at the thought that she was not just dressing up to go shopping, but dressing up to go shopping with her daughter on her birthday, a time she thought was about as extinct as the reign of dinosaurs. *This is my chance to give her a birthday she'll never forget…* She was then hauled out of her thoughts by the doorbell. 'Hang on!' She twisted the doorknob to see Alana standing with her freshly-washed hair in a smooth French pleat, and wearing her fitted brown suede shirt over blue jeans under her leisure coat. 'Hi Mum – thought I'd disappeared again, huh?' she said jocularly, compressing a chuckle with her throat. 'Nah, of course not. I know you wouldn't be so cruel! You look great.'

'Thanks - so do you, Mum. So, let's go, shall we?' she said sweetly, leading a path with her arm

'Certainly!' Tracie pulled the door in, and the two ladies graced the stairs arm-in-arm, and started their catching-up chat during the short stroll to Ealing Broadway.

For the next three hours, Tracie and Alana sauntered from shop to shop in both shopping malls, as Alana did the day before with Katerina, indecisive of what to buy. It was certainly liberating for Alana to not have any of her friends on her conscience, which she thanked her Mum for, and herself for deciding to start over with her. She wanted something simple that she could use or wear beyond being twenty years old, which Tracie knew and took into consideration. They chatted and caught up with events, such as Tracie's year and a half-long ownership of the firm now, and her relationship with Navin, which has faced some obstacles, such as her mood swings when Alana was absent. She also mentioned that she, Blake's parents and Leila's mum were still a strong circle, unlike Alana, Blake and Leila themselves. Alana congratulated her without the slightest bit of bitterness or jealousy. The women nattered like nothing ever happened, the clumsy crowd and the night of gearing-up rain clouds meaningless to them. During their exhausting search for a birthday gift, they had a cup of coffee and a slice of carrot cake at coincidentally, the same Italian café she and Katerina sat, but they sat at a table nearer to the exit. It was only the day before, but it seemed so muscled in the distant past by the disbelief that so much could happen in twenty-four hours. Alana mentioned this to Tracie, causing their euphoric moods to dip and rise briefly; it returned to normal on the way out as they joked and laughed. They carried two small bags, neither of them containing her gift yet. On their return to the ground floor back to the clothes shops, Alana pointed out the shop Blake and Freda met in the corner next to the exit, no longer shuddering in guilt at the sight of it, but Tracie looked at it sadly before proceeding to enter a large, bright shop, boldly bringing out the rows of cloth racks in the corner opposite the escalator. About half an hour later, they both emerged with one more bag in Alana's and Tracie's hands, each containing a dress for both of them. Alana looked at her watch – it was four-thirty. They had got what they wanted; now it was time to go home and plan their evening. They rested themselves on the empty bench under the shelter of the bus stop a few paces past the mall, exhaling with the effort of carrying their bags. 'We must sort ourselves out before seven, Al.'

'Why seven, Mum?'

'Because I'm taking you somewhere special in my new car.'

'Good grief – you've learned to drive?' she shrieked, slapping a palm over her mouth.

'Yup, finished last year. I'll show you which car is mine when we walk back. I didn't bring it shopping, 'cause as you know, it's hell to park a car round these parts.'

'True. So, where are we going?'

'It's…a surprise. Just wear that dress, I'll wear mine, and just follow my lead,' she insisted firmly.

'Oh, alright then. Here's the bus.' They rose amongst the cue of seven or eight standing people leading to the screech of the double-decker's folding doors. They took their seats near the door. They peered out of the window for a few seconds, turning to face each other realising there was nothing else to see as the bus pulled off briskly. 'So, is it a club or something?' she asked cheerfully, widening her eyes anticipatorily.

'Alana!' She threw her hands up in defeat.

'Okay, okay, just asking!' Silence throughout the rest of the journey…

Alana hurriedly fiddled the haltered spaghetti straps of her new black holographic dress, the single-layer flamenco-style skirt tickling her ankles slightly as she scurried to the bathroom door and swung it open. She inhaled deeply, making a mental plan of not drinking too much if it's a disco they're going to, because only this morning, after God knows how long she'd plagued herself with her habit, she discovered how bad it could really get. At the end of the hallway, she stopped dead in her tracks in marvel at her mum on the sofa – leaning over strenuously to her ankle to adjust the strap of her dusky-red sandal; her foot looked painfully arched upwards by the four or five-inch heel. She was wearing a ruby, long length and long sleeved dress with a modest criss-cross neckline, of which its lines disappeared behind her in a flared skirt. 'Mum?' Her head bolted up, and her eyes gawped at Alana in her new dress. Both began wondering when was the last time they saw each other dressed up as boldly as that evening. 'Good God, Al – you…you look absolutely great,' Tracie gasped. 'Aw, thank you – you are too kind!' Alana replied cockily with a bow and grin. 'I certainly feel a lot better from earlier on – in fact, I can't remember the last time I felt this great,' she resumed with a contented sigh, earlier events simply floating away from her head as time passed.

'There's nothing better than a bit of retail therapy,
especially on your birthday.'
'I can't believe I'm twenty-two – I still feel under
eighteen!'

'What? An ex-alcoholic under eighteen?' Tracie sprung upright on feeling a playful punch on her shoulder. After on final tug on the shoe strap, to her surprise was Alana seated next to her on the sofa. Tracie preceded Alana in leaning back in

'Yeah – funny things happen these days.'

'True. Maybe it's because you felt your life came to a standstill for nearly two years, so you still haven't adjusted to your new age. Am I right?'

'Yeah. You know, that's what I've always admired about you – that analysis thingy you do to me and everyone you meet!'

'That "analysis thingy", as you call it, helps me distinguish right from wrong, even though it isn't always right. Anyway, that's now second nature to me – I analyse anyone and anything I see. But I always thought it made you paranoid, because you thought I was prying into your personal thoughts.'

'As a matter of fact, no it doesn't. When you do that, I feel reassured that you're making an effort to understand me, so that's great.'

'Thanks. I really want this to work this time. No more arguments, no more differences in opinions or anything else. Let's just get along.' They reached their arms out and locked around each other in an affectionate squeeze. They let go after a minute or two, and dragged each other's thumbs under their eyes to wipe away their black eyeliner, spilled by happy tears. Sighing out a laugh, they proceeded to straighten the ruffled tufts of Tracie's curls and the top of Alana's simple pleat. Tracie glanced at the gold, narrow-strapped watch she kept for special occasions. 'Anyway, it's six-thirty. By seven we should arrive there.'

'Where the hell are we going, Mum?' she demanded as they raised from the sofa, and approached the coat stand, rapidly losing patience. After the surprise Katerina arranged, the last thing she wanted was another one a day later, especially as she was still shaken up by its outcome.

'For the last time, I'm not telling you. Like I said

earlier, just follow my lead, okay?' Tracie insisted, hunching on her black woollen trench coat. Unconsciously, Alana placed her hand on what was supposed to be the brown coat, but was her old favourite – the bottle-blue jacket with the one-button fastening. *Hello? – I don't remember leaving this here, and it's in great condition for something hanging up for one and a half years...* Frowning, she accepted her own reasoning that her mum probably hung it there for the day. It teamed up with the dress a great deal better than that scrappy brown coat could have done, so she wasn't complaining.

'Alright, alright.'

'Why? Don't you like surprises?' Tracie queried with a slight tease in her voice as she swung a small black leather handbag over her shoulder.

'Sure I do. Just as long as I know in advance.'

'God, do you know how much like a control freak you sound?'

'Sorry. Course I like surprises,' she finally concluded as enthusiastically as she could as she hooked her leather satchel. The jacket whisked her back for a split second to old, almost ancient times, with her, Leila and Blake, when they shopped together, especially that last, fateful shopping trip. Back to her present thoughts, she shuddered slightly at the thought of where she had just been. *Oh God, not again - not more memories, please...*

'Okay, then. Let's go.'

On the pavement, Tracie directed Alana to the car she mentioned and showed earlier a few yards towards the junction of the main road. Only moments after they stepped out their front door, their legs were already stiffened by the freezing evening winds seeping through all the wrong places, and were folding their arms. Alana gasped at the car she pointed at – it was a curvy, claret-coloured saloon, obviously not second hand, judging by the unscathed appearance, and bittersweet chemical smell which still lingered in the upholstery and plastics as she sunk in the front passenger seat. 'So, what do you think of my car? I didn't get round to asking earlier.'

'It's lovely, Mum. I saw the car coming back here, but
I didn't think it was yours. I never thought I'd see the
day you owned one of these.'
'Well, I got it about a month after I passed my driving
course. Navin has his own saloon, which is a blue, older
model of this. Hope you don't wait as long as I did to
drive.'
'Oh, I won't. I'll do a bit of checking around of lesson
fees while I retake my course.'
'Great. Saddle up, 'cause here we go!' she howled joyfully
in an embarrassingly bad cowboy accent, educing a slight laugh
of awkwardness from Alana. She flicked the headlight switch,
heaved back the gear stick, and steered out onto the neither active
nor dead, main road.

About half-an-hour later, they were about a quarter-mile
away from their destination through the M4 motorway, virtually
empty but jammed in the opposite direction, seemed scarily dark
for Alana, although dimly lit by cats' eyes and sharply by lamps
in the central division. She noticed the mileage clock had ten
miles added to it. Alana felt more and more uneasy as the routes
Tracie took opposed her conjectures. Then they screeched onto
the hard shoulder just a few hundred yards short from the third
junction for no apparent reason at all. 'Hey, what're you playing
at? There's nothing wrong here!' she shrilled in slight panic.

'Hey, hey, calm down. Nothing bad is going to happen.' A
brief silence as Alana galloped through her mind for a reply. 'But
you just stopped – for no reason!'
'Take it easy. I'm just going to do something to stop
you finding out your surprise too soon.'
'What's that?' Tracie delved her hand into her handbag, and
popped out a band of black material. 'What the…?!' Alana
gasped hoarsely. Before she ever managed to say anything else,
Tracie uncompromisingly drew and knotted the blindfold firmly
round her temples. 'Just relax, okay?' she reassured softly.
'Relax?! I can't bloody see where we're going!'
'We're coming up to our stopping-off point, and I don't
want you to see it before we arrive. Besides, I thought

you liked surprises?'

'I do… it's just that… oh, never mind. Let's just get
this over with, please?'

'Sure.' For the remainder of the journey, her sight was
completely blanked out. She was squirming in her seat, her
thumbs and forefingers tugging at the cloth in temptation to tear
the blackout from her eyes. The quiet burring of the engine and
the odd hoot of horns was all that could be heard, and the sharp
turns flipped her stomach a couple times. 'Oh God! – are we there
yet?' she snarled impatiently, diverting Tracie's attention to the
road slightly.

'Yep, just a minute or two more.'

'You're killing me here, Mum,' she whimpered in mercy,
finally clasping her hands on her lap.

'Steady on! I know it's cruel, but I'm sure you'll like this.'

'I certainly hope you're right.' One final swerve of the
steering wheel lead to a deceleration, then a halt. Alana turned her
head, sensing Tracie concentrating at nothing through the
windscreen. 'Are we here?'

'Yup,' she spluttered in diverted attention.

'Can I take the blindfold off now?'

'Nope.'

'God damn it!' she hissed through her teeth, whacking her
fists against her end of the dashboard, and her forehead with
them. Tracie frowned in concern, finally attending to her by
circling her palm on her nape. 'Calm down, okay? We're here
now. Just stay there – I'll guide you out the car before you have a
heart attack!'

'I don't like this anymore. At first, it was fine. Now I
really, really, HATE this!' she screamed with her face to
the roof, squinting a cold tear under the blindfold. She heard the
click and close of the driver door, another click of the passenger
door, then a fluster of frosty breeze shot up under her dress to her
alarm. 'Take my hand,' Tracie softly said, guiding her hand onto
hers, and raising her to her feet. With an arm round her shoulders
for her reassurance, Tracie kicked the door shut. Her hand still in
her clasp, they trod about thirty paces with care along a gravelled

surface, considering to the shoes they wore. She then hunched her by her armpit up two flat concrete stairs, then stopped. Tracie, releasing her grip on her hand, pushed the doorbell button. She returned the hand to the back of her head, to the knot of the blindfold, slipped a finger in and loosened it off her eyes, smiling at the knowledge that she'll be relieved by the return of her sight, and that she would stop whining at last. Alana sighed with her fingertips over her eyes, then rolled them around the rust-red and blue tiled arch of the doorway, the beige and black smaller tiles on the platform on the last stair, then the glass panelled black gloss front door, also arched. Her brain sparked, she half-glanced at Tracie, then the door again. 'Hey, this place looks familiar...' she said in enlightenment. Then the door opened. The girl with bobbed blonde hair, a pale grey roll-necked tank top and denim blue fabric trousers, hauled in a laboured breath at the sight before her. 'Oh my God, I don't believe it! Al?' Tracie smiled.

'I don't believe it either! Christine?'

'Yeah!' They blew out a prolonged laugh in amazement, then flung their arms round each other in a short embrace. 'Happy birthday, Al! Where the hell have you been?'

'Oh God, it's a long story. Have you done something to your hair?'

'Yeah! I got it cut a few months ago. You like?'

'I like!'

'Well, come in you two – it's bloody freezing out there! Let's reintroduce everyone again!' she bellowed joyfully, leading Alana then Tracie through the warm orange corridor to the large kitchen. Surveying the short walls, she suddenly felt a negative pang in the pit of her stomach. *Oh no – did she just say... everyone? Oh shit...* 'Mum, why here?' she asked as casually as she could.

'Well, remember the phone ringing while you were in the shower earlier?'

'Yeah?'

'This is what we were discussing...' She pointed in the direction of the doorway leading to the living room, the only room without lighting. Christine hopped over to the switch, flipped it on, and...

'SURPRISE!' shrieked the crowd in there, before proceeding the birthday song. Alana felt happy tears sting her eyes as she looked at Tracie, who wrapped her arms round her for a quick celebratory hug. Looking back at the tea table, her birthday cake was a simple rectangle with white icing and deep blue cursive lettering, which read 'Happy twenty-second birthday, Alana!'. Everyone was there – her mum, Lily, Eliot, Marlene, Christine… Leila? Katerina? And, God forbid – Blake? She felt a lump rise from her throat as her shock and elation died down in her – it just couldn't get any worse, but her instinct was not to raise a scene at her mother in front of everyone. She swallowed her bad feelings for them and proceeded to keep up her initial reaction. *How the hell am I going to survive the evening now?*

Chapter 22.

Blake, Katerina and Leila looked on hopelessly from the circular kitchen table they sat around, their heads looping round a can of lager each as they wallowed to themselves. Tre as well, but mainly because one lager too many made him feel queasy. Alana was accepting gifts and congratulatory kisses and hugs from the family members in the adjacent living room, and worsening their despair with scowls from the corner of her eye. Katerina unexpectedly shot her head up from her can, and spanned an unreturned glance to all of them. 'Great, another cold stare. What the hell do we do now? She's past listening to what any of us has to say, so what do we do?' Blake finally rose his head up, exhibiting drooping, slightly tipsy eyes. 'I don't know.'

'I don't know either,' Leila reinforced. 'If we try to muscle our way into this situation, we'll end up spoiling her birthday with an unpleasant scene. If we carry on floundering in our lager, we'll gain nothing except more horrid stares from her. I don't know what to do either.'

'Well, I suppose all we can do is wait and see what the evening brings, huh?' Katerina sighed, returning her also droopy eyes to her can of lager.

'Yeah. An opportunity might rise sometime,' Blake replied gloomily. Tre looked as if he was about to fall asleep with his forehead on the table, which answered why he never said anything – not that there was anything worthwhile to be said, anyway.

'Thanks so much for the gifts, everyone,' Alana squeaked as she topped the stack of about five gifts she received with a flat, rectangular box on the tea table, then retracted back to her seat in between Tracie and Christine, one of them being the compact disc player she wanted, and a couple discs. They snuggled up closely to her, which she welcomed. 'So, what's it like receiving all these gifts after being away so long, dear?' Marlene warmly asked, leaning to her from her armchair.

'It's terrific, especially the necklace and the Discman,' she said, pointing to the box again. 'You shouldn't have gone to so much trouble, though. That must've cost quite a bit.'

'No trouble at all – we missed you, you know. We thought this should be a welcome home do as well as a birthday one.'

'Thanks. But I've got one question, though, and this is to Mum.' Tracie attended to Alana. 'What is it, love?'

'Was this something to try and get me and those ones in the kitchen back together again?'

'No. It was to get everyone back together again, not just them. Partly, but not wholly.'

'Well, I just want to tell you that it's not going to happen.'

'Why not? From what they told me before you arrived, they do seem sorry for treating you the way they did. After all, Leila apologised to me, and Blake apologised to Marlene, Eliot and Christine, and we all forgave them,' Lily reasoned daintily.

'I know, but my situation is slightly different. When I fell out with Mum over Navin, I had no one to even listen to me, because it was the same day Leila left. Blake, well… no offence to your son and your brother, but he is the ultimate model of stupidity!' The whole room suddenly erupted into echoing laughter. Their light-hearted response to her rather serious jest surprised her.

'Ha ha! That's the funniest damn thing I've heard you say about Blake!'

'Well, he was! Me and Leila, the ones who knew him the best after you lot, warned him time and time again about that whore, and yet he still ran off with her – know what I mean?! Does that sound like common sense to you?'

'Not really!' Christine groaned comically through her laughs, sporting a grin that almost outgrew her face. 'And no, no offence taken at all!' Their laughter died down on hearing footsteps loudening from the kitchen to the living room, stopping within their sight. It was Blake, standing by the doorway to the

shady room, arms folded, a mean stare shooting from his eyes.
'Having fun, everyone?' he spat out in scornful irony. 'What?'
Christine shrieked, widening her eyes in slight confusion.

'Are you having fun?' and repeated even harshly.

'Yeah, we are – out of you,' Alana answered unfazed,
returning his initial glare.

'Thanks – I'm flattered!'

'What *is* your problem, Blake?'

'You at the moment!'

'Oh, why don't you go back to your beer and leave me
alone?'

'Fine – I will!' He stomped off back to the kitchen in a
funk, leaving his parents, Lily and Tracie a little bemused by the
brief commotion. 'What's his problem – can't take a joke?' Alana
asked, scowling behind his back as she sipped from her glass of
red wine.

'That wasn't very nice, Al. Shouldn't that attitude show
how sorry and hurt he really is?' Eliot said as
compassionately as possible, leaning towards her from the
armchair next to Marlene's. 'Okay, we've all been treated badly
by him, but we accept his apology and it'll be great if you could
too.'

'Yeah,' Lily squeaked in agreement. *If only you knew the
half of it...* Alana thought, glum with the thought that it was too
personal to disclose, although would change their perception of
the situation.

'You know, usually I'm quite a forgiving person,
assuming that the wrong someone has done doesn't
affect your life as much as the wrongs Leila and Blake
committed to me.'

'I suppose so... well, do you see yourself changing
your mind and forgiving them a few years down the road,
if not now or tomorrow?' Eliot questioned with a raised
eyebrow, still angled towards Alana. Tracie and Christine turned
their heads towards her, a pair of anticipatory eyes on either side
of her face.

'Perhaps... in the next life! Seriously, maybe. Maybe

I'll feel about it differently about it when I've experienced more things and have become a bit more worldly-wise, you know?'

'Mmm… that's a good answer. Putting it on hold for now, right?'

'Yeah. But don't get your hopes up too much, though.'

'We won't! But do you want to see them again?'

'I don't know. At one point, I couldn't imagine life without them. But now I have experienced a little of that life, which was the total hell they put me through, I just can't face them anymore. But maybe, in a few years time…' she trailed off, shrugging her shoulders in a disheartening, uncertain manner.

'Okay, honey. We're not forcing you to make up to them. You're an adult – whatever you choose, we accept, but at least what Katerina did gave you the chance to tie up those loose ends,' Tracie said, patting and rubbing the top of her spine.

'Yeah,' the rest of the room muttered in a cannon sequence, nodding their heads. Alana sighed and smiled, pleased that she finally shut them up about her so-called friends without telling them too much. 'Thanks, everyone.' They all picked up the half-full glasses of the red wine they toasted with earlier, and supped up contentedly. A violent, insistent thudding against the front door intruded their few seconds of peace. 'Who the hell is that?' Eliot said, raising himself to approach the short hallway about twenty paces beside the settees and armchairs they all sat in. He tugged down his olive-green sweater, then twisted the gold doorknob. He was butted aside before he could carry out any identification. Then light shone on the person once in the living room. 'What the…?' Christine involuntarily squeaked, flinging her head towards the visitor.

'Where's Blake? Where is he?' she snarled with boundlessly furious look.

'Freda?' Tracie managed to choke out.

'Get the fuck out of this house before I throw you out!' Alana hissed.

'Oh well, look at this – the friend comes to defend!'

'Get out, Freda! Get out, now!' Christine roared scarily, now on her feet pointing to the door.

'What's going on here?! What's all the shouting…' came a male shout from the kitchen doorway, which emerged into a steel-blue shirted, black trousered figure. 'Blake,' Alana uttered with a frown. Then his eyes widened at the sight before him, wondering – and hoping – the black leather clad person was just some drunken vision.

'…about?! Freda! Wha…why're you here?' he stuttered out in disbelief.

'Come on! You're coming home!'

'What?' Marlene rose to her feet defensibly, looked daggers at the bare brazenness in her face. 'How dare you burst in and order him like this? Get out!'

'Keep out of this, you!' she retorted.

'No, Mum, it's okay – Freda, don't insult my family,' he warned gently, still not fully geared up to react to her presence.

'Yeah!'

'Chris, please, let me handle this.' Christine threw her hands up in defeat, and slumped back to her seat. 'Okay, fair enough.' Blake faced Freda again, this time with a harsher stare defiantly into her neutral eyes. Some more muddled footsteps from the kitchen clarified, then stopped. 'What's going on?!' Katerina yelped. Before Blake was about to say his piece, they all whipped their attention round to face Tre, Leila and Katerina, standing awkwardly beside one another under the doorway. They looked towards the sofa, then to Blake and… Freda? 'Freda?!' Leila screeched, narrowing her eyes in disbelief.

'Yeah – Freda!' she replied sulkily.

'What the hell are you doing here? Sucking up to Blake to ensnare him again?'

'Hang on – is this Freda?' Katerina interrupted, pointing at them.

'Yeah – the bitch, live and in person!' Alana exploded from her flushed face.

'Al, I may not have been able to handle our friendship,

but I can handle this. So, please, butt out for a few
minutes – okay?'

'Right, sure, no problem,' she deliberately gasped
sarcastically, taking a seat between Lily and Eliot. 'But if you
want someone to throw this succubus out, I'll be very welcome!'
Everyone on the sofa and standing, including Blake himself,
gasped at her egotistical address. 'Language, Lill!' Lily scolded
blithely with a finger in her face.

'Sorry,' she said in an unforgiving tone. 'Girl, just say what
you have to say, and get out.'

'Gladly!' she snapped. Katerina's and Tre's eyes were fully
focused, both refusing to say anything about a situation they
knew little about, but just watch. Blake used his initial gaze, only
to see nothing had changed in her eyes either. 'Freda, why did
you come back? I think I said all I needed to say at the airport.
Plus, how did you know I was here?'

'Please, Blake, I'm sorry for the way I treated you.
I love you, and I want to make things work.'

'Sorry, wrong answer.'

'Then what do you want to hear?'

'Just answer my damn question!'

'I thought you be still begging forgiveness from your
family.'

'Well, that's great deductive reasoning there, Freda!'

'Oh come on! I've come a long way just to see you –
don't you feel anything towards me anymore?'

'And I've come a long way just to see *through* you,
Freda! I've got scars to prove it. And since you asked,
I've lost all feeling for you. Anyway, you're wasting
your time!'

'Why?'

'I've met someone else – someone a hell of a lot better
than you!'

'Oh really? That was quick dealing! Who is this bitch,
anyway?'

'No way am I telling you!'

'Right! You're coming back with me, if I have to drag

you there!'

'Let go of me! What're you going to do if I refuse? Beat
me up again?'

'If I have to! And red raw too!'

'Well, that's just your style isn't it? Anyway, I'm a man,
not an object or a dog – even if you did this to a dog, it's
unacceptable. Want me to show you who it is?'

'Yeah, who?'

'Whoever I kneel before in this room!' He delved his hand
in his hip pocket, and re-emerged it in a fist. He flowered his fist
open to reveal… a little black velvet ring box. She gasped with
her fingertips over her mouth, droplets of tears running down her
face. 'Wha…you're…marrying her?'

'Yeah, I'm marrying her. Just stay there!' Blake approached
the centre of the room, so that he was surrounded by his family
and friends, the fireplace, the bedroom corridor, a bookshelf and
Freda. Eliot's face fell to an uneasy one as he returned to the
armchair. Tre and Katerina's stances became more and more
shifty.

'Son, marriage isn't a game. You've got yourself into
trouble by rushing before, in case you didn't remember.'

'It's okay, Dad. You'll change your mind once you
know who it is.'

'Okay, Blake. Whoever it is, you have our permission –
don't we, Marl?'

'Um, yeah, I'll try,' Marlene forced herself to mutter under
her breath, her eyes bulging as the knot in her stomach tightened.

'Okay. Everyone, see this ring?' he began, raising the ring
well above his height and spanning his arm around his 'audience'.

'Course we do, Blake. We're not as blind as you.'

'Alana – shut up,' he retorted in a deadpan tone.

'Ooh, sorry,' she snarled, rolling her eyes sarcastically. He
sighed, preparing to continue. 'Okay. This ring is an engagement
ring, and the person I'm about to ask to marry me is a truly
wonderful woman. She has given me so many things, but because
I loved her so much, it scared me. That's why I ended up running

away with Freda, which I know now is the biggest mistake of my life.'

'Blake!' Freda screeched with a frown.

'Sorry, dear, but that's the truth. I was raised to be
honest, and I couldn't be more honest than I am now.'

'Honest? *Honest?* You couldn't even be honest to
yourself to face up to the fact you love this girl!' Leila
interrupted shrewdly, signalling an inconspicuous wink. The
room echoed slight giggles from all. He half-grinned, receiving
and understanding her signal.

'True. That's the good thing that's come out of being
with Freda.'

'What?'

'I was finally honest with myself as much as I am with
everyone else.'

'Okay – enough with the waffling! We know it's not
the Freda bitch, so who is she, Blake? Kat?' Alana
impatiently demanded, yanking at her hair with entangled fingers.
Katerina rolled her eyes away from them and crossed her arms in
a silly strop.

'Oh whatever! Blake, say who it is, please – I don't want
people getting the wrong idea about me!' The room
chuckled louder than before, enough for a definite reaction.

'So who is it, dear?' Marlene coerced gently, raising an
eyebrow as she leaned forward from her seat.

'Someone I've not known days, weeks, or months,
but years,' he began, feeling every pent-up emotion pour
out of his heart as he approached the sofa cramped with Alana,
his sister, mother and Leila. His softened eyes rested on Alana's
without her even knowing it. He then touched the knuckles of one
of her hands resting on her lap. His fingers eventually snaked
round her entire hand into a gentle clasp. As she looked up again,
she had no choice but to accept the fact that those eyes were on
her. Suddenly, her head spun cartwheels, which sped up almost
beyond her consciousness. Short-winded exhales from everyone
in the room could be heard as he kneeled before her, her hand still
delicately held. 'Al, you are my bestest pal in the whole world!'

he began comically in a little boy's dialect, emitting a small laugh from both of them. 'Let me tell you something, and this comes straight from the heart – you've done absolutely nothing to be treated the way I've treated you, so don't punish yourself for my mistake anymore. You could've died because of me, and that would've killed me too, because it took her over there to make me realise I live because of you. My mum gave birth to me, but you've given me my life. What happened last night was a mistake, but unlike the mistake I made by leaving with Freda, no mistake I've made has ever felt so right. It hurt like hell when you said we couldn't be together anymore. I take full responsibility for wronging you, but I want to make it up to you, even if it takes the rest of my life. I've loved you from the beginning, Al, but look what it took and how long till I found out.' His voice cracked at that point, never speaking with such emotion to anyone before, but gave him an opportunity to raise the ring to her eyes, of which tears also smudged her perception of it. Sniffs could be heard from the women in the room, and the men glared in total disbelief. The only man with tears was Blake himself. 'Marry me, Al,' was all he could say in a strangulated whisper. Alana's jaw dropped open as she took the box between her trembling thumb and forefinger, and attempted to study the jewels, flashing almost electrically through her blurry vision. She then raised her eyes to his again, and studied his almost irresistible beseeching look beneath the overflowing wells. He wiped away both its trails in a split second. Then there was no one in the room at all. 'Oh my God.'

'No! Get away from him, bitch! He's mine! I'll kill you, Higgins!' Freda all of a sudden screamed from nowhere. She sprinted from where she stood over to Blake, then in an almost crushing grasp, tried weakening his wrist by wringing it free from the box. 'Leave her alone, Blake! You're mine!' Everyone was still stunned by his revelation to react immediately. With all his might, he wrung himself free from her, and battled her continuing power over him. 'Back off, Freda! I'm not your property anymore!'

'Yes you are! Yes you are!'

'Somebody get her off me!' Leila dashed from her seat, and curled her arms under her armpits. She dragged her towards the door with more strength than she ever thought she had. She then used the arrow-head of her shoe to fling the door open, then applied a kick to the base of her spine, boosted by the shoe. She rolled down the stairs, but was still twitching at the bottom stair. 'How dare you!' she hissed as she pushed herself upright.

'Oh, get the fuck out before I call the police! Man-beaters always scare me!'

'He can't marry her! He can't! What about me?'

'Excuse me, but I thought "Goodbye" was the key-word here?'

'He'll regret it, I'm telling you!'

'The fuck he will!' With that, she slammed the door loudly enough to rattle the whole house. She was faced with a loud round of applause from everybody, which she accepted with a playfully cocky bow. 'Aw, thank you, thank you, but really, it was nothing! She wasn't as tough as she made out to be.'

'You'd think differently if she had your hands tied up on the bed head!'

'That's true. Never mind – she's history now. So, umm... what were you asking Alana before?'

'Oh yes!' he blurted out, then spun on his sore knee back to Alana's dilated green eyes. 'Please Al, marry me. I may not be able to do a lot of things, like turn back the clock, but what I can do is never make you cry again... except happy tears, of course!' She giggled bashfully, took the box again from his hand again, but never looked at it – only him instead. Everyone disappeared from around them again, leaving them on their own. 'Blake, there's one thing I need to ask.'

'Sure.'

'Are you sure you're not tipsy again?' Moderate laughter once again from everyone.

'Positive. Are you referring to that New Year's party?' She nodded briskly.

'Well, I suppose... I suppose I could do worse. Yes Blake – I will marry you!'

'You sure?'

'Positive!' she rejoiced in a screech. All his reply was his jaw dropping open, and more tears damping his cheeks. This time, he felt no pain at all when they seeped into Freda's wounds. She couldn't help but laugh aloud by his frozen posture. She decided to help him by removing the ring from the slit in the black sponge, and controlled his grasp of it by squeezing his thumb and forefinger around it, which worked in animating him again. He slipped the ring on her finger, stood and heaved her from the sofa by hooked fingers, and slung their arms round each other in an almost suffocating hug, laughing into each other's ears. 'I missed you, Blake.' He felt every wound he caused to himself heal with his arms round her, if not his physical wounds. He assumed Alana must feel the same kind of healing, and he was right. It was the only time they realised their family and friends were applauding around them, and were watching the whole thing. They released each other, with difficulty avoided kissing in front of them, and faced the ones on the sofa. They each hugged and accepted congratulations from their sobbing mothers, and Blake accepted a handshake and hug from Eliot. Then came the time to face Leila and Katerina. Alana paced up slowly to her, still standing before the front door. 'Lill, I'm sorry I called you a fucker yesterday.' She laughed casually. 'No apology, Al. I am a fucker, on the fault of my dad.'

'Your dad?' Alana shrieked, raising an eyebrow.

'Yeah. I never told you the real reason why my dad left. She divorced him, because he was an alcoholic. His behaviour scared me so much, I hid under the table helplessly while he beat my mum up. Seeing my mum cry and covered in bruises when you're six years old is quite terrifying. I promised myself never to get myself in such a mess when I grew up – friendships, marriage, whatever. I was scared you'd turn violent later on in your drinking, so I ran away.'

'Why didn't you tell me about your dad, Lill? I would've listened, you know.'

'It was too upsetting, however how close we were. But of

course, keeping it in backfired. I'm really, really sorry,
Al. You wouldn't believe how shitty I feel for turning
against you, especially when you and Blake fell apart.'
'It's okay, now I know what the reason is. Haven't you
heard the expression "A problem solved is a problem
halved"? That's what I'm here for, silly, and will continue
to be there for!' Alana extended her arms to her, then they
hugged and cradled each other for at least a minute or two. Leila
expressed a cold sob of relief on her shoulder. 'I missed you, Al.
So I'm forgiven, then?'

'Missed you too, Lill. Do I have a choice?' Both girls
sighed out a laugh as they examined the renewed sparkle in their
eyes. 'Now I'd like you to meet my fiancé over here…'

'Fiancé?' she shrieked with widened eyes as she pointed to
a dark, spiky-haired guy in a beige shirt and grey combat
trousers…

'Whoa, I can't believe it – my son is going to marry
your daughter!' Eliot almost screeched to Tracie, with joy
almost bursting his broad grin out of his face. 'This is the first
time he did something out of haste that was right!' She nearly
spluttered her third glass of red wine.

'Well, I knew it was going to happen someday, but
certainly not like this! There was some kind of affinity
between the two of them, which I guess they didn't find
out as love until… Freda, really.'
'Even as a little girl, I've thought Al was a good influence
on Blake. Anyway, despite the feud, he's well and truly
forgiven if he's bringing home Al as Mrs. Blake Turpin!'
She reacted with a giggle through a sunny smile.

Alana and Leila approached a lone Katerina whilst her back
was turned, sipping from another can of lager. Blake was now
talking to his, Leila's and Al's family members, and Tre. She
whipped round to face her solemn expression, which shook her a
bit. 'Hi, girls.'

'Hi, Kat. Um, I wanted to tell you something.'
'Sure – go on.'
'Look, I'm sorry for slapping you yesterday. It's only

now I realise it's thanks to you I have something to
shoot towards. Not quite what I planned, but it's
certainly something! If you hadn't found these two,
I would be just waiting to die. I'll never forget what
you did.'
'Aw, it's no problem at all. I hated seeing you like that.
God, I'm going to cry now!' Katerina collapsed onto
Alana's shoulder, which eventually turned into a group embrace
between them. Releasing each other, Leila geared up to say
something. 'I have to admit I wasn't all that sure about you to
begin with, but you've made us again. For that, you've earned our
friendship! How do we repay you?'
'It's like I said to Blake when he said I could be a
bridesmaid or a maid of honour, a simple drink at
the pub would be great!' she jested hoarsely through sniffs.
'Sneaky bastard! Okay, drink – sorted!' Alana retorted in
fake horror. The three of them simply roared in laughter till they
almost keeled over. For the rest of the evening, they discussed
their wedding plans, and the talk about the dual wedding Leila
and Blake had. Leila and Tre got the pick of a date, which all
promised to agree on – fancying a simple spring do, she chose
Alana's birthday a year to that day – Saturday the eleventh of
March two-thousand, enough time for Blake and Alana's life
ambitions before the interlinking of them, as she reasoned her
choice. They all nodded in agreement. Lily felt a little sliver of
sadness through her elation at something everyone else had to
accept – that they'd only visit every weekend from Cardiff.
Thanks to Blake's hint, Katerina didn't have to choose between a
bridesmaid or a maid of honour, but be both, and be alongside
Christine, also chosen to be a bridesmaid, and Tre to double up as
a best man as well as Leila's groom on the day. An outline was
finally drawn up, so a cheerful toast of wine was an excellent way
to round it off. All that was left was the minute details. They
proceeded to retire at about eleven o' clock, but felt too inebriated
to go home. Eliot and Marlene quickly reintroduced them to the
three spare rooms. Tracie and Lily agreed to go in the room with
two single beds, Leila and Tre, and Blake and Alana to the double

bed rooms. Alana wanted to accept that what happened the day before was a mistake in their drunkenness, and decided to refrain any further intimacy till their wedding night. He agreed slightly disappointedly, so dealt the compromise that they could just kiss and cuddle – she agreed, lightening his mood a bit. Leila and Tre, though, had ideas well opposite theirs. Already like nervous newlyweds, they took turns undressing to their underwear in the bathroom, Alana first, so she could cover with the quilt, then Blake. She snuggled up to the muscular curve of his shoulder, and giggled shyly, still at a loss to begin a conversation. Alana ran her fingers lightly over the brown, flaky wounds on his cheek. She kissed them, smiling when he didn't recoil. 'They're healing up, Blake.'

'Good. Then I'll get the last of Freda off me.'

'I know. Can't wait to see the last of him, too.'

'Who?'

'Oh, didn't I tell you? Some nut has been sending me weird poems and flowers, and generally scaring the shit out of me.' Blake looked his fallen eyes away from her to the ceiling. 'Blake, you alright?'

'Al, I don't know how to tell you this, but I didn't mean to scare you like that.'

'No, hang on, wait a minute… are you trying to say… you sent those things?' He nodded in shame, feeling a warm flush to his face. 'The "everyone has to go their own way" thing? The "silent intruder"?' He continued nodding away from her eyes, feeling like he'd blown it again. He raised his head when he heard a choked giggle from her.

'But… why?'

'I thought… I don't know. Just one of those stupid things I did without thinking, I suppose.'

'Hey, cheer up. I'm not mad with you. I admit, I was a bit scared. I did think you were some sex-crazed stalker, but I took comfort that you knew my favourite flowers, and the first line of the first poem. I had no idea you were into that kind of thing.'

'Me neither – it was Tre's idea.'

'Well, he's certainly brought the poet out of you!' She finally heard a laugh of relief from him as he returned his totally besotted eyes to hers again, and pecked her forehead. 'I thought I'd blown it again with you.'

'Nah! I suppose if you think about it, we were each other's secret admirers, even at nine and ten. But because we were so young, we didn't know what love was till... you know, made us see our relationship for what it was.'

'I'm sure we would've died before discovering each other if we hadn't opened our eyes. I would've been thrashed to death by Freda, and you would've drowned in vodka.'

'True. We've been out of reach for so long, whether together or not. Then I got hooked on Adrian McCraedie, someone out of reach to the point of invisibility, instead looking for you.'

'I loved you so much, it scared me – scared I'd ruin our friendship and you'd hate me if I told you. That's why I ran off with Freda, and hurt the feelings of everyone dear to me – you mostly, all because I pushed you out of reach in cowardice.'

'Blake, you should've told me – I could never hate you. I was mad at you this morning, but I didn't hate you. But if you look at it, it was all about being out of reach.'

'True, but it has brought rewards. I mean, we have two new friends, and you've enhanced this ring's beauty by wearing it.' They mooned briefly over the gems of her ring as he held her hand like porcelain. 'Out of all the gifts I've received, you and this ring have been the best ones. I love you to bits, Blake.'

'I love you to bits too, Al.' He leaned his face towards her, but she retracted to his puzzlement. 'Since we can't do anything till we're married, how *in* reach of each other could we get?' she teased, twisting the shorter, darker blond hairs on his nape. Tightening their arms round their necks, they slid each other's free arms round their waists, bringing their bodies into contact, and let their smiling lips drift towards each other.

'Hmm… I'd say… about this close…' He muttered, then they lost themselves as they softly kissed and playfully fumbled each other. It ended when they slipped into sleep, but continued beyond their mutual restraints in their dreams…

THE END.

Epilogue.

<u>Saturday 11 March 2000</u> –

Hello, to whoever reading this. My name is Alana Higgins, or should that be now, Alana *Turpin*. Yep, I've just got married today to the biggest ass on the planet, Blake. I also celebrated my twenty-third birthday today. It should be interesting how this marriage will turn out. This is why I've decided to write this diary of every day we're married, and to share this first entry with you to give an idea what I'm trying to do. I really don't know who's the bigger git between the two of us. I mean, I'm so soft and forgiving on a guy who drove me to drink and depression, because I tried warning him against a nasty piece of work like Freda Henley, his bitch, I mean his ex, and under her influence, spat it, along with our friendship, or sibship as it was, back in my face. I'm mad, me – send me to the loony bin, now. I'm even mad to say I love him more than I used to, without convincing myself. I'm a total git. Mind you, I arranged a doctor's appointment last April, and my drinking problem didn't do too much damage to my liver, thank God. I'm still a healthy bunny! And I had a pregnancy test the day after his proposal, because of the 'accident' between us, and it came out negative, praise the Lord (claps palms and sighs!).

Anyway, on to the big day. In the Higgins household, we woke up at seven for breakfast with my mum and Navin. I'd actually grown to like Navin – he's astute, spiritual, talks well and above all, treats Mum really well. She's the happiest she's been for years, and probably helped keep her sanity when I was gone, which is great. They're not married yet, and both being modern thinkers, highly doubt they will, but I certainly wouldn't mind him as a step-father if they did. After our fry-up, he agreed to sort out the transport while Mum and I went upstairs to my room to fit me into my wedding gown. When she took out of my wardrobe, and off the hanger, I had to pinch myself to wonder if this was just a phantom dress and a phantom wedding, but it wasn't. I actually felt the silky material when I grasped it. At about nine, and one-and-a-half hours or being done up, I looked in the full length mirror. I nearly died. I couldn't believe I was looking at myself. My hair was still down, but had light ringlets down my back, and was fitted with a headband with small burgundy roses and tiny protruding pearls – my substitute for the highly annoying veils I dealt with when I was trying on the other dresses at the dress place. My make-up was very subtle – pale browns and pinks merged on my eyelids, and pale pink lip colour. The dress (sigh)… what can I say about the dress? Fit for royalty – a very long, sleeveless dress with no train; a modestly scooped, unadorned neckline, and an equally unadorned, flared-out skirt without a hint of a meringue in sight. It was almost like an ivory ball gown. After saying I looked lovelier than I'd ever looked, we left my room for the last time. 'Are you sure you want to go through with this?' she asked in a soft tone. Even though it was a reasonable question for a mother to ask, I nearly laughed. I mean, the guy not only said sorry, even though it wasn't enough, he promised to make it up to me when he proposed, even if it took the rest of his life. Now that's not the sort of offer you get every day from one of your best lad-friends, is it? It showed that he really, honestly was willing to take responsibility for his own mistakes, and I really couldn't say no to that. After all, it would give me an opportunity to punish him for the rest of his life as I once promised! So I said, "Definitely sure!" She smiled. I put on my shoes, sat, fidgeted, chatted with Mum and waited for the chauffeur's hoot.

At around nine-thirty, I was sitting on the sofa, waiting for Mum to finish her half done-up self – she was only in her pink pencil skirt and single-breasted jacket at the time of making me over – and now had her hair, still in a bob, only smoothed and down. Her make-up also had pale pinks round her eyes and mouth. She really looked like a proud mother when I saw her march from the corridor. 'Ta-da!' she shrieked. I couldn't remember her looking that glam since that red dress on my last birthday. An hour later, the Rolls Royce arrived to escort myself, Mum and Navin to the

church we passed regularly without a second thought, about a
quarter mile from the shopping mall that was partly responsible
for the break-up of our friendship. We all waited in a little room
behind the church pews, where I met Leila, my other friend,
Christine, Blake's sister, and Katerina, whom I'd grown quite
close to after all we'd been through last year. Leila was supposed
to marry on the same day as me and Blake, but sadly, she felt she
couldn't go through with it, despite our promise to marry
together. It wasn't because she and Tre weren't together anymore
– it was because she felt it was too soon, and he agreed. We were
shocked, but we all understood, of course. So we reassessed each
other's roles – Leila was now a bridesmaid alongside Christine,
but Katerina still doubled up as bridesmaid and maid of honour.
Leila and Christine wore silver floral dresses with a similar skirt
to my dress, but with clinging bodices with spaghetti straps.
Katerina wore a gold one with the same design and floral motifs.
I had a bouquet of lilies, blue and burgundy roses like my
headband, only larger; the girls had bouquets of just lilies. I tried
chrysanthemums, but they looked too weird. Tre was still our best
man. We all gathered in a group hug, and Mum already had tears
in her eyes, and the ceremony hadn't even started yet, although I
could hear the rather soothing organ music echoing off the walls
entertaining everyone there, mostly made up of Blake's relatives
from Scotland, and Leila's and, believe it or not, Mr Sutton and
his wife, my journalism tutor who gladly suffered to re-tutor me
for the past ten months. Katerina's parents, Ian and Larissa, were
there too; she made up with them last Christmas. Nice people –
on meeting them, I realised how much she looked like her mum.
Katerina was finally allowed to have her own life without them
interfering, as long as it wasn't anything disreputable, which was
great.

After five minutes of reflection, I was facing the doors of the
church leading to Blake. Feeling very nervy, the girls were behind
me, rubbing my back, saying soothing things. Then it was time. I
strolled down the aisle of my dreams, one foot before the other,
and there he was – a very poised Blake, smiling at me beautifully.

He looked so cute in the tuxedo – then again, he looks cute
whatever he wears, even nothing(!). It was a darker grey than
Navin's, and had a grey shirt with a few buttons undone, and no
tie. He had Tre standing next to him, looking equally poised in
the same grey suit, but with a white shirt and no tie either. Then
my mind recollected to that time in New Year of ninety-seven,
when he was begging for forgiveness when he accidentally
snogged me, and what he pleaded through his hangover. "Why
would it take ten years to make a move on you? We would've
been boyfriend and girlfriend a long time ago…we were mates,
are mates and always will be mates, Al", or something like that.
Now I knew why. Now I fully understood this relationship, and
why he said and did the things he did, but I still think he's a
complete jerk to think I'd blow him out if he told me his feelings.
I also understand that this all happened for a reason – for both of
us to realise that not admitting what you feel can do more harm
than admitting them. Hopefully this new love between us and this
marriage will result in more openness towards each other. We
can't live without each other, but events have driven home the
fact that we never knew the meaning of those words. But if
anyone told me fourteen years ago that I'd be marrying this
nutter, I'd have laughed them into space! But here I was, united
with him on the top stair, and Katerina standing by my side as
Christine and Leila sat down in the front bench. We choked out a
"hi". There was a sparkle in his eyes that I'd never ever seen
before. *More sparkles like that, and we'll get along just fine,* I
thought comically with a smile as we faced the vicar. He said the
usual blah blah blahs, then the comforting, cherishing, honouring
and keeping vows. He said them with such emotion; he made
those vows his own. He took the ring from Tre, wiped a singular
tear, and slipped it on my finger. I took his ring from Katerina,
repeated the vows with equal sincerity, and on his finger it went. I
looked at his face as the vicar spoke again – he looked as if it still
hadn't sunk in that I'd just put a wedding band on his finger. A
couple of tears rolled down over what was a faint scar on his face
now, and inhaled to control further flow. I didn't even hear what
the vicar was saying, and neither was Blake from what I saw, till

he said "I now pronounce you husband and wife. You may kiss the bride." And so we did, quite a shallow snog, as we didn't like over-doing it in public, and of course, we had to save something for later! Blake shook Tre's hand, and I kissed Katerina on the cheek, then we faced everybody. We absorbed the applause, noticing the whole church was in tears, especially Mum and Marlene, his mum. Navin and Eliot, his dad, simply clapped proudly. Mr Sutton, or Glenn as I now call him, gave me a thumb up, which I returned. And so down back the aisle we walked with our arms interlinked, and everyone followed the bridesmaids to outside the church for the photos. We took them, and I tossed the bouquet. Guess who caught it? Katerina! Nice, especially as she was the only maiden there. Confetti was tossed over us as we returned to the cars back to Blake's house for a simple, private reception at about midday. I know it sounds like a cheapskate do, but which would you prefer – a loveless do glossed over with glitz, pomp and glamour, or a nice and simple one full of love, like ours? It's something to think about. Anyway, we drank, danced to songs, and did speeches just as if it were a hall. At around midnight, it was time to go to our new house a few streets away – a HOUSE, would you believe it? We scraped together the cash with minimal help from our parents, through his new job in advertising and my journalist's job at a national newspaper. We still have things in boxes, but here I am in the bedroom, sitting on the edge of the bed in a red satin dressing gown with sexy white undies on underneath, while Blake is freshening up in the bathroom next door. What a day, huh? But it was beautiful. Of course I'd seen Blake cry before, but not for the reason I saw today, which I thought was the most touching moment of the whole day. Oh, before I go, let me fill you in about Christine, Katerina, and Leila's careers. We're all getting along like sisters once again. Leila still lives in Cardiff with Trevor, and have set their date to early 2002, which is a hell of a lot better than another break-up. He still photographs and she still works at the diet club, and they visit every Saturday. Katerina passed her course with flying colours last July, has that behind-the-scenes television job – she helps to type the auto-cue for the regional news. It's nice to

see her name on the credits when I watch it. Christine is
modelling for catalogues, making use of those looks
photographers kill to exploit. We both wish she had a better job,
but she says its only temporary, but oh well…
Anyway, it's time to go. I just heard the door unlatch. Thanks for
reading my rambles. It's been a crazy three years, a crazy day
today, and judging by the fact that we waited till our wedding
night to… do *that* again, it's going to be a crazy night too!
Goodnight!